Austral...
family in the ...

Faye Avalon lives in southwest England with her super-ace husband and one beloved, ridiculously spoiled golden retriever. She worked as cabin crew, detoured into property development, public relations, court reporting and education, before finally finding her passion: writing steamy romantic fiction. Between writing, practising yoga, trying to remember the difference between a *plié* and a *relevé* in ballet class and keeping the keyboard free of dog hair, Faye can be found checking out Pinterest for hero inspiration. Visit her at fayeavalon.com.

HOTTER ON ICE

REBECCA HUNTER

SLOW HANDS

FAYE AVALON

MILLS & BOON

First Published in Great Britain 2020
by Mills & Boon, an imprint of HarperCollins*Publishers*
1 London Bridge Street, London, SE1 9GF

Hotter on Ice © 2020 Rebecca Hunter

Slow Hands © 2020 Faye Avalon

ISBN-13: 978-0-263-27752-4

MIX
Paper from
responsible sources
FSC™ C007454

This book is produced from independently certified FSC™ paper
to ensure responsible forest management.
For more information visit www.harpercollins.co.uk/green.

Printed and bound in Spain
by CPI, Barcelona

HOTTER ON ICE

REBECCA HUNTER

MILLS & BOON

To Mr Hunter,

who has entertained so many of my crazy ideas over the years,

including the one about staying in a hotel made of ice and snow in Northern Sweden.

I love this journey we're on together! xo

CHAPTER ONE

WHY THE HELL is he taking so long?

Alya Petrova had peeled herself out of bed at six thirty in the morning to be on time for this meeting. Now she found herself sitting at the Blackmore Inc. conference-room table alone, fifteen minutes after the hour, staring out blankly at Sydney Harbour, waiting for Henning Fischer to show up.

In the world of virtual communication, Henning was the most reliable person she knew. Apparently, those skills didn't translate into real-world punctuality.

Being nervous as hell wasn't helping. What would it feel like to meet the surveillance expert she'd talked with over the phone for the last three years? She knew almost nothing about Henning himself. His name had floated around in conversation for as long as she'd worked with the elite security service Blackmore Inc., and she had gathered scraps of information from her former bodyguard, Max Jensen. Surveillance specialist. Ex–Australian Federal Police officer. Who never, ever appeared in person.

So, of course, she'd turned to the internet, which was surprisingly stingy on Henning Fischer–related information. A couple track and field championships from years ago. An occasional statement by him in connection with police work. And only one clear photo, an official-looking portrait from his cadet days. Physically, he was striking, his dark brown eyes intense. Though the photo showed only to his shoulders, it was clear he was built. She had stared at that photo more than once, trying to connect it with the man whose voice rumbled through her phone. She couldn't make it fit.

This was the person who had watched over her through her front hall security camera, giving her a boost of support on her weakest days, those vulnerable times she'd worked so hard to move past. She hadn't wanted to lean on someone else—a man, no less—for comfort, but Henning had been a safe bet.

Now that distance between them was about to disappear. Soon he would walk through the door, a flesh-and-blood man, not just an idea. Okay, *maybe* she had developed a tiny bit of a crush on him. It had been a completely harmless escape when she thought she'd never meet him, a safe place to put all sorts of fantasies.

But her modeling shoot on the Great Barrier Reef had changed everything. When her former bodyguard devoted all his off hours on the island to her sister, Natasha, the two had fallen in love. Alya had definitely seen that one coming. Shortly after, Max stepped down from working one-on-one with all clients, including her. That one she hadn't seen coming, though, in the end, it was for the best. Alya had taken this change as an overdue nudge to reassess her security situation. A lot had changed in the three years since she had moved an ocean away from her stalker ex, and she didn't really need a bodyguard in most cases anymore. Surveillance of Nick, her ex, was enough.

This week was the exception: a fashion shoot on the other side of the world was a long way to travel without security. But with Max no longer working in that role, a new plan had been hatched: Henning would take Max's place.

The longer she waited in this quiet conference room, the more the anticipation buzzed through her. She had imagined many versions of him, but what would it feel like to be close to the real Henning all day long? Standing next to him, almost touching, his deep voice in her ear...

Alya stood up and started for the door, looking for a distraction. Maybe the receptionist would point her to the coffee machine?

She crossed the room, slowing as a familiar voice came through the closed door. Henning's. After three years of phone calls, she'd know it anywhere. Alya froze, her hand just shy of the door handle. Did she continue her search for coffee or return to her seat?

Then the door opened, and she was buried in his

chest. His hands closed around her arms, steadying her. His warm, musky scent… Relief hit her first, and then—*oh, God*—something powerful. Urgent. His breaths were sharp and erratic in her ear. He towered over her, his presence everywhere. *Oh my*, her harmless crush was sooo not harmless anymore.

"You okay?" His voice was a familiar rumble, and the sound of it in person turned the fluttering inside into molten lava.

Alya nodded against him, too stunned to speak. Her fingers, her arms, her breasts, her stomach— everything tingled with awareness. Was her body calling to him or answering his call? It felt like both. After things went so terribly wrong with Nick, she had had a growing suspicion that she was just too wary to feel this…captivated by a man. Wrong, so very wrong. Her reaction to Henning was bone-deep and intoxicating.

There was no good explanation for what she did next. Alya lifted her hands and touched him, pressed her palms against his stomach. Checking if he was real. Yes, he was definitely a solid, warm, very real man. Henning sucked in a harsh breath, and his muscles twitched, turning rock-hard under her touch. His hands tensed around her arms, and a low growl came from deep inside him.

Alya froze. Shit. She was feeling up Henning Fischer, uninvited. In the Blackmore Inc. conference room. What the hell was wrong with her? She stepped back.

"Sorry. That was totally out of li—" She met his gaze.

The first thing she saw was his eyes. Dark brown and even more serious than his picture had let on. Intense enough to steal her breath, and for a moment his gaze flared even hotter, darker. A rush of awareness ran through her, aching, burning.

Then she saw the scars.

Jagged, unnaturally smooth, down the left side of his face. Skin that had been stitched and patched together. Her eyes widened. The old, grainy photo online had shown him as good-looking in a clean-cut, impersonal sort of way. But he was so, so far from clean-cut now. Alya followed the longest scar that tugged at his left eye, distorting one side of his face, then disappearing into the collar of his shirt.

His big body, the scent of him, the rawness in his voice, his dark eyes, the scars—all of these pieces came together into one thought as she stood in the doorway gaping at him: this man knew trauma. He understood it. Her heart jumped and pulsed in her chest, expanding. She understood it, too.

Shit—how long had she been staring at his scars?

Too long. When her gaze flickered back up to his, all the burning intensity she'd seen seconds before had vanished. His face was shuttered closed, giving nothing away, and his expression was cool, impersonal. The only hint of emotion he showed was the rapid ticking of his pulse at the base of his neck.

Slick introduction, girl.

Time to start over, preferably in the way regular people introduced themselves.

"Sorry again. I'm Alya, in person," she said. "And doing a crap job at making a good first impression."

Henning blinked down at her, his gaze softening a little. "Henning Fischer, very much in person. As you clearly noticed."

"Clearly," she said dryly, trying to preserve the last of her dignity in this exchange. Was he teasing her about feeling him up or about staring at his scars? Probably both.

The tiniest hint of a smile tugged at the uninjured corner of his mouth. Heat was rising into her cheeks, as he studied her in the quiet room. She studied him right back.

"Max should be right in," he finally said, gesturing to the conference table. "You know how this works."

Yes, she did. She had sat across from Max at this table many times, going over her security details. But never once had she been so fully aware of each breath, each movement, the way she was right now with Henning.

Alya took a seat and flipped open the folder in front of her, skimming through the papers in it. Henning sat down facing her, silent, alert, an overwhelming physical presence. He radiated a protectiveness that wrapped around her, settling inside her. It was the same feeling she had gotten over the phone, somehow both calming and incredibly engaging. In person, it was magnified a thousand times.

She glanced up to find his gaze fixed on her, his dark eyes unreadable. The old Alya, the woman who had gotten herself tangled up with Nick Bancroft back in LA, would have looked away. That version of herself had given up her jobs and friends three years ago and fled the country when Nick wouldn't leave her alone, despite the restraining order. But she wasn't that woman anymore, so Alya stared back at him. He was a solid, motionless mountain of a man, with hulking shoulders and thick biceps that stretched the material of his shirt. His power and prowess were controlled but not at all concealed, as if his body was a well-honed tool, ready for use.

The current between them ran hotter, and with every breath, heat coiled inside her. But she couldn't mistake this strong, immediate pull between them for something more than it was—plain sexual interest. She had been down that road of powerful attraction before, and it led to disaster. She searched for something to say. "So…you ever been to Sweden before?"

"Nope."

"Me neither. Cold, dark and snowy this time of the year, I hear."

"Yep."

"Not my favorite conditions, but my agent thinks the photo shoot plus the *Behind the Runway* documentary filming, with its daily YouTube outtakes, is too good of an opportunity to pass up."

"Mmm."

She bit back a sigh. He wasn't giving her any help here but seemed perfectly content to just watch her talk. Thankfully, the click of the conference-room door ended this one-sided conversation.

"Sorry to keep you waiting, Alya," Max said, striding over to the table. "I trust you and Henning introduced yourselves."

That was certainly an understatement. Her former bodyguard seemed oblivious to the tension between Henning and her, but knowing Max, she couldn't be certain.

Wordlessly Henning opened the folder on the table in front of him. The muscles of his forearms rippled and flexed as he sifted through the stack of papers with large, blunt fingers. He pulled out a document and showed it to her.

"Here's the master schedule for the week," he said. "It includes flights, hotel contacts, dinners, photo sessions and interviews."

He walked her through the details of each day as Alya followed along on the pages. His voice was gravelly and deep, as if whatever had scarred his face had roughed up the inside of him too. He was a practical speaker, his sentences short and clipped, his answers no longer than absolutely necessary. Pretty much the exact opposite of Max.

"The chances of Nick Bancroft showing up are very low," said Henning, closing his folder. "It also helps that the Icehotel is in a remote corner of north-

ern Sweden. We have plenty of warning when anyone flies into the tiny Kiruna airport."

She didn't doubt that. What he didn't say was that
he had all sorts of connections from his Australian
Federal Police days that fed him information when
he needed it. And with the kind of details he found,
she was pretty sure the routes couldn't all be legal.
But she was starting to get the feeling that Henning
did things his own way.

"Blackmore Inc. has done an amazing job at keeping Nick out of my life. I'm not worried." She sat up
straighter in her chair. "I considered going on this
trip without security, but if he showed up and I had
to deal with him alone, he'd make sure to stir up public drama. Public displays of personal problems are
toxic in my industry, and Nick has already hijacked
my career once."

There were models whose lives played out in the
tabloids. Drugs, tantrums, drive-through marriages
and bitter custody battles—the world had an insatiable hunger for these kinds of stories. She had been
at the center of one of those stories three years ago
when, after Nick wouldn't leave her alone, despite the
restraining order, he'd publicly called her emotionally
unstable under the guise of worry. She had worked so
hard to keep their break-up quiet, but when he twisted
her own words into evidence that she was becoming
increasingly erratic, just like her mother, the press had
been all too ready to pick up that story. Each move to
distance herself from Nick became another example

of her "irrational" behavior, another incident he used against her in the court of public opinion. All because ultra-rich, ultra-privileged Nick Bancroft had decided he wanted something—her—and he always got what he wanted.

Never again would she let that happen.

Henning was watching her closely. "Nick won't get to you."

The hot intensity in his eyes flared for one, brief moment, and then it was gone. A flush crept up her neck. Five days with Henning next to her—two on a plane and three at the Icehotel in Sweden. Was his effect on her obvious? She glanced at Max to gauge his reaction, but he was looking at the paper in front of him.

"I understand what I'm getting into by taking this job," she said quietly. "Sasha Federov probably wouldn't have given me this chance to represent his brand if my mother didn't still hold her cult-like status in Russia. I'm sure he's expecting me to follow in her footsteps, not just as a model but as an attention magnet. But in my agent's words, I need to grab this chance and hold on to it. Even if it means being followed around by a documentary crew."

Max nodded. "Henning will be connected with the team here if there's anything you need to be aware of. You'll be in good hands." He lifted an eyebrow. "But I think you already know that."

Yeah, she absolutely did. But now that they were in the same room together, the idea of spending the next five days with this man was getting more... complicated.

"Have a safe trip," said Max, standing up.

Alya walked over and hugged him. "Thanks for everything."

He had been part of her support system for over three years, and now their professional relationship was over. But the fact that he was at her and Natasha's apartment almost daily meant this was far from goodbye. With one more nod at both of them, Max left.

Alya was alone again with Henning. He stood up and took a couple steps toward her. His gaze swept over her, dark and guarded. They were so close again, and the silence crackled with tension. Alya took a deep breath as the room seemed to heat up a couple degrees. It was too late to close herself to this connection, but she had no idea what to do with it. So she started with the obvious.

"I'm sorry for earlier. When I, um—" she bit her lip "—felt you up. I certainly wouldn't want a guy doing that to me when we met."

Henning's eyes widened a bit, and then he smiled, but the half of his face marred by scars moved only slightly. It was a broken smile, filled with dark humor, and yet his uninjured eye crinkled at the corner, a hint of lightness in him.

"I don't think it's the same, Alya," he said. "At least not for me. Truly, I'm okay with it."

Was there a hint of laughter in his voice? Good

to know. The meeting was over, but somehow, she didn't feel like their conversation had ended. He crossed his arms in front of him, his biceps flexing as he watched her, taking her in.

Finally, Henning spoke again. "We are going to be spending every minute together for the next five days. I want you to feel very comfortable with me."

Alya felt as if he were opening himself to her, just a little. His gaze said *you can trust me*, and she couldn't look away.

"I doubt we'll have any problems," he continued in that low, rumbling voice. "But there is always the possibility that I will need to protect you. Physically."

He paused, swallowing, his Adam's apple bobbing, as the last word sank in. It ran through her body, suggesting much different ways he could physically affect her. Damn, she needed to get this under control. Attraction was about nothing more than sexual interest…which her body was clearly expressing right now. She felt the barely concealed desire in his eyes, and she was almost sure he could see the same in hers. She felt the pain Henning's scars must have caused, and her mind was already at work, connecting that with the intense sense of…protectiveness… she had felt from him over the last three years. Everything else faded as this all fit together, like the final pieces of a puzzle, somewhere deep inside her. She was opening herself to this feeling, she didn't know how to stop it. Or if she wanted to.

"I understand," she said, her voice steady.

He gave her a little nod. Then he rubbed the scar on his neck absently. "I'm aware that with my size and my scars and what Max calls my aversion to conversation, I can come off as a little rough around the edges," he said, cracking a hint of a smile again. It faded quickly. "But I never, ever want to scare you."

Alya frowned. "You don't. Not it all."

She had a strong urge to clear up that misunderstanding, but elaborating would mean wandering into inappropriate territory. Her attraction was raw and very real. Any hints of wariness he had detected were about the intensity of her reaction to him, not fear.

Alya had to make him understand, and words didn't seem to be the right path. So, instead, she raised her hand and slowly reached for his forearm, crossed over his broad chest. She gave him plenty of time to back away, but he didn't, so she touched his skin. The electric spark between them surged once again, and she swallowed a gasp. His muscles twitched under her fingers, and his lips parted. Was he thinking about kissing, too?

"This isn't fear, Henning," she said, her voice steadier than she felt.

His chest rose and fell and she tried—and failed—to read his expression. Finally, he nodded. "You can touch me, do whatever you need during our trip. I don't want to go into this with any hesitancy on your part."

Alya's heart jumped at each image his words conjured. *Touch me. Whatever you need.* The physical memory of her hands on the hard ridges of his abs came back, mingling with things she had only imagined.

There were nights he had watched her through the security camera in her front hall, making sure she came home safely. But what about the night she had come home, half-drunk, with her date, and had sex against the door in full view of the camera? The idea that Henning might be watching was a turn-on at the time. Now her mind wandered further. If he had watched, had he gotten himself off to it, too? Damn, that would be hot…

Get your mind out of the gutter, girl. You're in his workplace.

She lowered her hand, breaking the connection. Then she smiled up at him. "Is the permission to touch standard in your Blackmore Inc. contract?"

The hint of a smile returned to Henning's lips, and he shrugged. "I have no idea. I'm just letting you know how I work."

"I'm sure you have plenty of satisfied clients," she said, laughing.

"There are no other in-person clients for me. Not now, and not in the future." Henning shook his head. "Only you."

His eyes were dark flames, flickering, captivating. She was getting used to the way he watched her, his gaze unwavering. As if every bit of his focus was on her, as if nothing else in the world existed.

What did it mean to be intensely attracted to her

bodyguard, right from the first moment she crashed into him? She had never felt this way about Max, so his appeal wasn't just the role of protector. Henning awoke a hunger she knew couldn't—shouldn't—be fed…should it?

Maybe this was the wrong approach. She was done running away from her fears. Maybe it was time to take control of the situation, to explore it, to figure out what she was looking for, not just what to avoid.

But Alya didn't know what was going on in Henning's mind. She was almost positive he felt the same intense attraction, but maybe he had reasons he couldn't or wouldn't act on it. Like the obvious ones. What were the Blackmore Inc. rules about personal involvement with clients? Maybe she could just find a way to ask him…somehow. Alya's face flushed as more of that current of sexual interest sizzled between them.

"I'll pick you up at your place tomorrow morning at six," he said.

"I'll be ready for you."

"Alya?" His voice had lowered to almost a whisper. "Please send me a message if you think of anything you need. Or want. Anything."

CHAPTER TWO

THE WORDS WERE out of his mouth before all the reasons not to say them registered. Henning's mind was still stuck on the moment when her slim, tight body brushed against his. When she pressed her hands against his stomach, exploring before either of them seemed to fully register what was happening. Alya was soft. Slim but not frail. So very alive. She smelled of honey and sunshine, and every dark desire Henning had ever had.

But the reason to bury all those thoughts came crashing in seconds later. Her expression when she saw his face. He couldn't forget that for a moment.

Henning took a step away, giving Alya a clear path to the conference-room door, giving himself a little distance from her intoxicating scent. Finally, her bright blue eyes flickered from his.

"I'll walk you to the elevator," he said, heading for the door before she had a chance to respond.

The reception area of the top floor was quiet and bright, the morning sun filtering through the frosted glass and reflecting off the polished wood surfaces.

They headed for the elevators in silence, Henning's body on high alert, fully tuned to her every move. She stopped in front of the heavy metal doors, but she didn't reach for the call button. Instead, she turned to face him again.

"I'm beyond thrilled that Max and my sister found each other. Natasha's happiness means everything to me," she said. "It meant I lost my bodyguard, too, but that's a small price."

Henning could see that this was hard for her to talk about, so he waited, letting her take her time.

"Hiring security is a crutch I've leaned on for a while." She swallowed, the movement sweeping down her long neck. "It used to be necessary all the time, but now it's more often for a peace of mind than actual protection. It's like a little bit of me believed his claims that I was turning into a train wreck, that I doubted myself. And I don't like that feeling of vulnerability."

Henning restrained his urge to react. His deep desire to comfort her, to protect her warred with what he heard in her words: she wanted to stand on her own. So he said nothing, just nodded, storing the information away for later inspection.

"You know a little about what happened with Nick, the way he wouldn't leave me alone and made me out to look unhinged, so I think you might understand why it's been hard to move on. It takes a long time for me to trust anyone. So I wouldn't want any other bodyguard," she added, reaching for the call button. "Only you."

The elevator doors slid open, and she walked in without looking back, vanishing as the cold metal doors closed. Henning took a deep breath, then another, slowing his heartbeat, forcing himself back to the starkness of reality, where she was just a client and this was just a job. Nothing more. He blew out one more long breath and headed for the hall to his office.

The receptionist gave him a neutral smile as he passed and busied herself with something at her desk. When Henning first came to Blackmore Inc., it had taken that woman a few weeks to hide her reaction every time she saw the jagged scars down his face. He remembered the widening of her eyes, the way her gaze drifted over him each time he passed. Not so different from Alya's reaction, really. She was a model, for fuck's sake, paid to live in a world where looks were everything. Of course she'd react to his injuries.

But it had hit him hard. Alya had given him a look that was far too close to the look Corinne had given him five years ago at the hospital, at the very lowest point of his life. Or at least he thought it was similar. Alya had said so convincingly that he didn't scare her, too. Maybe she was one of those women who got turned on by a man who looked more beast than human? That thought alone should have been sobering enough, but the electric current of desire didn't seem to be waning.

Why the hell was he still thinking about this? He had made peace with his scars years ago. He had escaped that disastrous drug bust alive, which was more than his right-hand man got. That one day changed everything, and usually he welcomed the visual reminder of the event he never wanted to forget. Now he was mulling over the way he looked? Damn.

As he headed down the hall to his office, Max caught up with him. His hands were shoved in his pockets, his expression relaxed, like nothing in the world bothered him.

"That went well," Max said lightly. Henning jerked his head in time to see a hint of a smile on his friend's face.

"I'm not sure this is a good idea," muttered Henning.

Max shook his head slowly. "You were the best in the Australian Federal Police force, so I know you're not talking about your ability to protect Alya."

Henning blew out a breath and shook his head. "Most obvious issue, I'm going to attract a lot of unwanted attention, which she doesn't need. It's a fucking fashion shoot, no place for a bloke with a face like this." He rubbed his left cheek, where one of the scars pulled his taut, injured skin tight. "And though I don't track fashion shit, I'm pretty sure this doesn't go with whatever the hell the season's look is."

Max gave a little snort of laughter, then raised an

eyebrow. "You saved a dozen officers from a meth-running gang. You will make sure Alya doesn't spend one minute of this trip worried something unexpected might happen." His mouth curved up into a full smile as he spoke. "Who the fuck cares what this season's look is?"

Henning's mouth twitched until he was smiling, too. Max clapped him on the shoulder. "Seriously, you've been surveilling Alya for over three years now. You know every single thing about her situation and where she might feel vulnerable."

Understatement of the year. But it also meant spending a few days in the cold, which wasn't ideal. The nightmares rarely came these days, and occasionally he took a winter trip to the Blue Mountains with his sister's family and faced the cold without too much trouble. Still…not ideal. But he'd make it work.

There was understanding in Max's easy smile. Had he picked up on the more personal aspects of the job Henning was struggling with? Yeah, that was his problem. Keeping his distance from Alya had been a Herculean effort in the past, but all those hours alone… Henning still wasn't sure how he was going to pull this off. A captivating woman, strong but in a vulnerable place, who needed his help—this scenario was a temptation too strong to resist.

Cameron Blackmore, the company CEO, had offered him dozens of opportunities to work directly with clients since he'd quit the AFP and come to

Blackmore Inc., and he had turned every single one of them down. Henning didn't usually care much about the looks of shock at the wreckage of his face, but it didn't make for the best guard-client relationships. Even before the scars, most people left him alone. Now working surveillance, he was pretty sure he scared most of the IT department shitless.

He and Max came to a stop in front of Henning's office. Henning reached for the handle, but before he turned it, Max quietly cleared his throat, getting his attention.

"I wouldn't have pushed you to do this if I didn't think it was a good option. For both of you."

Henning scowled. "For me? I highly doubt that." He blew out his breath in frustration. "You have no idea."

"Maybe I don't," said Max, his voice almost maddeningly easy and smooth. "Or maybe I can guess why you'd want to stay far away from her. And why you said yes to this job anyway. But I pushed because I think this assignment is different than any other one for you."

Henning grunted in response. That much was true. But it didn't mean he'd survive this week with his sanity intact. Before he could respond, his phone rang. His heart thumped in his chest. It couldn't be Alya, taking him up on his impulsive offer of *anything*…could it? Henning squashed that thought as he pulled out the phone and looked at the screen. *Suzanne*. He sighed.

"It's my sister," he said to Max. "I should take this."

Max nodded and clapped him on the shoulder again before walking away. Henning pressed the button on the screen to answer.

"Hi, Suz," he said, opening his office door. "What's up?"

"Kids melting down, work and an occasional conversation with Kenny," she said dryly. "The usual."

Henning smiled. His older sister's house was pure chaos, but she was happy. She and her husband Kenny had tried for years for a baby, first by themselves and then with some help. Suzanne was at the point of desperation when finally, little Molly came. And then Liam. Growing up, their parents weren't much for outward displays of emotion, and though Henning was close to his sister, neither of them were much for probing conversations. Suzanne had never said a lot about the whole experience with infertility, but just stepping into her house, he knew she was happy. Seeing that was still one of the best things in his life.

Henning headed across his office for his desk and sank into his chair.

"I was calling to see if you have plans this Saturday," said his sister. Dishes clattered in the background. "Molly has a dance recital. Princess themed, of course. And we'll go out to dinner afterward."

Henning took a breath and dropped the bomb as gently as possible. "Thanks, but I'm going out of town tomorrow."

"What?"

The shock in his sister's voice made him roll his eyes.

"You know, on an airplane," he deadpanned. "They even let *me* on those things."

She gave a huff of exasperation. "Stop it. You know I'm just in shock that you're actually going somewhere. Are you..." Her voice turned syrupy, exaggerating the incredulity in her question. "Are you *actually* going on vacation, Henning?"

"Nope," he said curtly. "It's for work."

"You sit in front of a computer for work these days," Suzanne said. "Explain."

"I need to be on the ground for this one."

She was silent for a bit, and the clattering of dishes died down. "You said you'd never do this kind of thing again," she said slowly.

Yeah, he did say that. But the last thing he wanted to do right now was discuss why Alya was the exception to that promise. Suzanne was quiet for a long time, so he leaned back in his chair and propped his feet on his desk, waiting her out.

"Where are you going?"

"Northern Sweden. The Icehotel. Danger level is very low."

More silence. Henning swiped a hand over his face. He knew exactly what his sister was thinking about now, but he didn't want to talk about it. He didn't love the location of the assignment, but he wasn't going to let it be an issue.

"It's cold there," she said quietly.

He frowned. "I've been in the cold since…" Fuck, he really didn't want to talk about this. "It's under control, Suzanne."

"Is there a woman involved?"

Henning choked in his next breath, then disguised it as a cough. "What?"

"You heard me," said Suzanne. "Is there a woman involved?"

He closed his eyes and massaged his temples. "Yes, the assignment involves a woman, but that question makes it sound like something it's not."

"I knew it," she whispered, but he heard it, loud and clear.

He huffed out a breath. "Whatever you're thinking, you're wrong."

"Okay, Henning." Her words had a hint of that syrupy tone again.

"Look up *Behind the Runway* on YouTube. You'll see what I mean."

"I've watched it. The behind-the-scenes show about modeling?" His sister paused, and he was pretty sure understanding was sinking in. He wasn't a fool. There were so many reasons that whatever connection he had felt with Alya in the conference room would die a quick death as soon as they entered that scene, and his scars were just one of them.

When Henning didn't respond, Suzanne finally said, "I see. Do you want me to water your plant while you're gone?"

"My pla—?" He caught himself. Right. The plant his sister's family had given him for Christmas. The dry, brown tangle of leaves in the corner of his living room.

"Don't worry about coming all the way into town," he said quickly. "I'll figure it out."

"You already killed that plant, didn't you?"

"Um, maybe?"

"Henning." She said his name slowly, adding a dramatic pause before continuing. "The kids picked it out for you."

He cringed. "I know. I'll get a new one before they come over here next time."

"That's not the point, and you know it."

He did.

"At least it wasn't a puppy," he grumbled.

A puppy was the kids' first idea, and thank God he had nipped that one in the bud. Judging from how plant ownership had gone, his sister was probably thinking the same thing. Suzanne meant well, but he was the last person a helpless little animal should be dependent on.

"I know you would have done better with a puppy," she said softly.

Henning wasn't sure about that, but he let the statement stand.

"Take care of yourself, Henning," Suzanne added. This time, there was a mix of worry and affection in her voice. "Please."

"I'll call when I get home." He swallowed back his own emotions and ended the call.

Henning set his phone on his desk and ran his hand through his hair, shaking his head. It had taken his sister only one short phone call to uncover all the conflicted feelings for Alya that he was trying to tamp down. Which meant he was going to have a hell of a time putting aside every reaction he had to her the moment he showed up at her door tomorrow morning.

But he'd do it. His job was to watch her every moment of the day. And every long hour of the night. Just the two of them, alone in the darkness, in a remote resort in northern Sweden.

Holy hell.

CHAPTER THREE

HENNING STEERED THE big black SUV over the packed snow that made up the desolate road to the Icehotel, keeping his gaze fixed straight in front of him. The pine forests, covered in white, stretched out along the road on both sides. Alya was looking out the window at the passing landscape, dotted with occasional houses painted bright red and topped with snow. He didn't need to look in her direction to know what she was doing.

He'd been tuned in to her every movement since he'd picked her up at her Sydney apartment. That was expected. What was unexpected was the sense that she was just as tuned in to him. He had kept himself awake half the night going over her response to him yesterday in the Blackmore Inc. conference room. Imagining all the other ways he wanted to end that meeting.

"It's cold here," said Alya, clutching her down jacket tighter around her. "I mean, of course it's cold, but I didn't know it would feel like this."

Henning knew exactly what she meant. When

they'd stepped out of the airport, the wind found its way through his jacket immediately. He had seen snow in person, but nothing like this endless blanket of white. It was fascinating to look at, or at least it should have been. Now, the fascination was tainted by the memory of the ice-cold concrete floor of the warehouse where he had lain, watching his team member die from the shards of glass that had hit them both in the explosion. But he could put that re-action aside for the next few days. Besides, he was Australian for fuck's sake—of course he reacted to the cold.

Henning checked to make sure the seat heater was on max and hiked up the temperature a couple notches. "I thought you were from Russia."

"We left when I was six," she said with a snort of laughter. "And I think my parents did a better job of dressing me for the weather."

Henning smiled. "I should probably call them for some tips."

He glanced over at her. Other than the parka and boots, Alya was dressed for late summer in Austra-lia. She'd walked onto the airplane in tight jeans, a silky top that showed skin, and sunglasses. The look-don't-touch vibe rolled off her. A good thing, as far as Henning was concerned, since the travel portions of the assignment were the most unpredictable—and the most critical for her to feel safe. While he accepted that he could never completely shut down his reaction to her, this cool, polished Alya was easier to separate himself from. But right now, after a day of traveling halfway across the world—hair mussed from fits of sleep, curled up in her puffy down coat with her feet tucked under her—keeping a professional distance was close to impossible. Had he caught her staring at his ass when they were getting off the plane? That didn't help. It triggered a vivid image of her that he'd conjured up in the shower the night before as he came: Alya up against the door, his cock deep inside her as he put his mouth on her soft, slim throat.

Heat flooded to his groin. Fuck. Enough of that.

No encounters with Nick. No scenes that called attention to her personal life. That was his job. Nothing else. Unless she said explicitly that she wanted more. It was this last thought that had kept him up way too late.

Alya yawned and reached into her bag, pulling out the master schedule, scanning the pages.

"Today you have a meeting when you arrive, and then there's drinks in the Icehotel, right?" he asked.

She nodded. "I was just checking to make sure we have time for a nap between those two."

"Can you nap in that igloo?" He had seen photos of the Icehotel rooms, glowing with the tint of ocean blue. They were works of art, really, elaborate beds, chairs and sculptures carved from enormous blocks of ice. Strikingly beautiful but not made for casual napping.

"I could probably nap anywhere at this point,

though I think the frozen portion of the hotel is more like a museum during the day," said Alya, stifling another yawn. "But we're not staying in the part of the hotel with ice rooms tonight. We're scheduled in the regular heated building, right next door, for the first night, so we can use the beds in our room anytime today."

Use the beds. Unfortunate phrasing. As the words left her lips, an image came of using a bed, naked, with Alya riding on top as he fucked her. Henning swallowed back a groan. How long had it been since he'd gotten laid? Too long, clearly.

There were places he could go to fuck, clubs where women got off on having a big, scarred man over them, holding them down, just the way they asked for it. And the women had no problem with his limits either—they had no interest in touching or kissing him anyway. Maybe he should have gone there last night, just to burn off some of this intense want.

But Henning had quit, cold turkey, when he found himself searching for tall, blonde women with endless legs. He had never had a preference before, and he knew exactly why this one was forming. Which was more than enough reason to cut that habit off immediately. What he felt for Alya was so many worlds away from what he wanted from those women. Henning couldn't bear to mix the two worlds.

So it had been a while. Maybe that was why he had thrown caution to the wind and offered Alya anything she needed. Or maybe, after watching those blue eyes come alive under his gaze, he couldn't resist.

During his undercover work with the AFP, he had built a career in part on reading people, looking past what they said and concentrating on what they did. Yesterday, he hadn't missed the way Alya had stepped closer instead of backing away from him, the way she'd licked her lips, the way her breath came faster when she'd touched him. In the days before the disastrous bust that marked the end of his AFP career, he had gotten more than his fair share of attention from women. And he understood his responsibility as a man bigger than most other people, the responsibility of making sure he understood exactly what a woman wanted from him before he touched her. His days of propositions in bars were long over, but he hadn't forgotten how it all worked. He had to be really fucking careful.

The GPS on the car told him they were nearing the place. He pulled off into a little parking lot in front of the unassuming wooden buildings. Tall pine trees rose up on both sides, and Henning assumed the actual Icehotel lay somewhere behind them. He found a parking spot at the far end of the lot, and turned off the car. Then he rested his hands on his legs, ready for whatever came next, but Alya made no move to gather her belongings and climb out. Instead, she turned to face him. He had the feeling she wanted to speak, so he watched her, waiting her out. After her chest rose and fell a few more times, she met his gaze.

"Yesterday, you said you had no other in-person clients," she said. "Why did you take this job?"

Henning swallowed, taking his time to consider his answer.

Because I couldn't say no to you. Because the chance to be next to you for five days was too much to resist.

No, he definitely couldn't go there. Instead, he went for an easier truth. "Because you deserve to feel safe."

She tilted her head to the side. "So does everyone."

"Of course," he said. "But after what happened in the AFP, I won't take an assignment unless I'm sure I understand all the threats and would do whatever it takes to keep that person safe. Anything."

As the words left his mouth, he knew he shouldn't have said them. They hinted at both the past that haunted him and the intensity of his feelings for her, neither of which had any place on this trip. Henning scrubbed his hands over his face. The bristles from his unshaven jaw pricked at his right hand, but under his left hand the scar that pulled at the side of his mouth was unnaturally smooth. A reminder of how wrong things could go.

Alya's expression was completely unreadable. "Henning, I'm going to ask you something I'll probably regret, but here it goes." She took a deep breath.

"If I kissed you right now, would that interfere with our bodyguard-client relationship?"

He stilled. He didn't even breathe, but his cock jolted to life. Did he hear her right? Fuck, he had thought about kissing her so many times it was hard to register this was really happening. In his head, he could imagine the kiss as his old self, before the attack, before the scars. Soft, beautiful before it turned hungry. Perfect.

But deep inside, his past was still an open wound. Lying on that cold warehouse floor, fighting his own pain while trying to save Sanjay, watching the bastard who caused the explosion get away, he had seen his actions for what they were. Selfish. He had been blinded by his own goal, taking a risk to grab the leader, a risk that ended Sanjay's life. *That* was reality, a cold, hard reality he would live with for the rest of his life. Never again would he let his own wants drive his actions. So how could he consider kissing Alya, knowing all this?

Henning blew out a breath. Shit. Why the hell was he thinking about all this right now?

His expression had no doubt grown darker because her smile had faded.

"Sorry," she said, her voice filled with false cheer. "Should have gone with my first instinct to keep my mouth shut. Let's just pretend I didn't say that. I'll find someone else to proposition."

Henning flinched. A storm hit him, a storm of

protectiveness and something else he didn't want to acknowledge, despite the ache of his cock.

"No." The word came out sharp and urgent before he could stop himself. Alya drew in a quick, startled breath, and he winced. But *fuck, no.* The idea of watching her flirt with another man was doing crazy things to his insides. It sent a surge through him, twisting into every long-dormant competitive urge to show her all the ways he could satisfy her better. It was the kind of drive he used to thrive on.

No. Just no. He had sworn to himself when he took this job that it had to be *all about her.* So what the hell was he supposed to do with this situation? Let her go off and find another man, someone who probably wouldn't give a shit about what she needed? If he said yes to this, gave her what she wanted, it would have to be with his sole focus on her, not selfishly chasing his own needs.

He reached for Alya, touching her cheek, coaxing her to look at him. She did, meeting his eyes, and he found traces of embarrassment. Did she think he was rejecting her? Hell, no. *Take it easy.* He swallowed.

"There's nothing in the world I want more than to kiss you right now," he whispered. "I don't want you to ever think otherwise, no matter what happens."

Her eyes widened, and they came alive with unguarded interest. So much better. He pushed on.

"And, to answer your question, no, it wouldn't interfere. Especially not if the doors are locked."

A slow smile spread over her face, a glow of happiness returning. Damn, it was breathtaking. Then she reached for the dashboard and pressed the lock button.

Henning's body jumped to attention, his cock all in, the eager fucker. *Slow the hell down.* He took a deep breath. This was for her. He had to get it right.

"But before we continue, I need to tell you something," he said, keeping his voice quiet. "I haven't kissed anyone since before the attack where I got these scars. It was five years ago."

Her eyes widened. "You've been celibate for five years?"

The uninjured corner of his mouth tugged up. "That's not quite what I said."

Understanding registered in her eyes. "Got it," said Alya, and a hint of amusement twinkled in her eyes. Thank fuck for that.

Henning pressed on. "I'm telling you because I don't even know if I can kiss you the way I want to right now. The way you deserve."

She quirked her eyebrow at him. "And what do I deserve?"

"A kiss promising you that you're the only thing in the world that matters."

She blinked, swallowed, as if his words were sinking in. Good. Because he wasn't fooling around here. Anything that happened with her would get his full attention. She was quiet for a while, and then she straightened up in her seat.

"You know what *I* think I need?" she said with

a little smile. "Something that's hot and fun with someone I can trust. And I'm pretty sure that's what I'll get."

Henning blew out a breath. He could do this as long as he kept his focus on her.

So he looked straight into the endless oceans of her eyes and shut everything else out. "Okay. We can try for that."

Holy shit. Alya took a couple steadying breaths, trying to slow down her runaway heartbeat and jumpstart her brain. Last night, alone in her apartment, this had all sounded way more reasonable. Somewhere around midnight, Alya had decided to simply ask for what she wanted: a few days of sexy fun. Except, the morning after, when Henning showed up at her doorstep, she still hadn't quite figured out what to say.

Are you interested in spending a few of your off-duty hours naked with me?

Maybe a little too direct. Alya had spent a good portion of the seemingly endless procession of flights to Sweden contemplating how to test Henning's interest. His aloofness during the travel had her second-guessing the idea, but once they got into the car, the intense attraction she had felt after yesterday's meeting was back. So, she went with it.

Then came the words she was sure she'd never forget: A *kiss promising you that you're the only thing in the world that matters*. She couldn't resist the intensity in his voice. How did he know this was her personal kryptonite, the thing he could say to send her body into flames? But these were dangerous words, too much like the lies that kept her going back to Nick Bancroft, long after she should have fled for good.

Except Nick was the past, and she wasn't that woman anymore. Just a few days of fun.

Still, the questions kept rolling through her mind. Did the scars around his mouth hurt him? Who had he had sex with for the past five years without kissing? And, most of all, how did she make sure not to get sucked in too deep?

Alya filed her questions away and took off her seat belt. She reached over and unlocked Henning's. He slipped it off his shoulder but made no move to touch her. His eyes were hot but guarded, burning into her. He seemed to be waiting for her, so she unzipped her down parka and shrugged it off.

He smiled a little. "Getting hot already? We haven't even started."

"I was up late thinking about this last night." She winked at him playfully. "Move your chair back a little."

"Anything you want," he said softly, amusement dancing in his eyes. The more they talked this way, close, intimate, the more she could read him. He unzipped his own coat and eased the seat back, tipping it at an angle, making enough room for her to climb on. So she did. The car was big, but so was Henning, so they shuffled and laughed and adjusted until she was facing him, knees tucked on both sides of his thick thighs. His body radiated heat, and God, it felt so good. *He* felt so good.

"Your hands are big," she said, fitting them against her own. His were so much thicker and longer.

"Does that turn you on?"

She laughed. "Maybe?"

Some of the lightness in his eyes faded. "Meaning you wish it didn't?"

She paused. "It's just complicated."

"We can stop anytime."

"I know." She could see he needed that reassurance that she would speak up if she wanted to stop, and he relaxed a little under her touch, his smile slowly returning. But stopping wasn't her worry at all. It was that she really, really liked this—his size, the way he was with her, everything—and she wasn't sure she wanted to know why. But that didn't have to figure into kissing him.

Henning slipped his hands around her waist and cupped her ass, bringing her up against him, closer, until she brushed against the enormous bulge in his pants. His eyes were heavy with humor and lust. Right now, Henning was worlds away from the hard, impassive bodyguard who had traveled next to her all day. For all his big body and muscles, he was... gentle with her. There was no other word for it.

...you're the only thing in the world that matters.

Alya swallowed. He was talking about the kiss, not making some larger declaration. This was sexy fun, just what she had wanted. And she wasn't going to taint it with her past hang-ups. So she pushed all of those ideas out of her mind, and focused on the stunning man in front of her. The man whose heavy cock was currently pressing against her.

"So you want this kind of kiss?" he asked, smiling.

She nodded and moved up and down against his erection, using it to stroke her clit. He flexed his hips and ground against her, sending more sparks of pleasure through her. He did it again, rubbing his cock in every sensitive place, making her moan and shudder.

"Yes," she said, a little breathless. "This is definitely the kind of kiss I want."

He flexed his hips again, and her eyes rolled back as another wave of pleasure coursed through her. *Oh, yes.*

Henning looked like he was enjoying this slow, hot grind just as much as she was, but after hearing about his five-year kissing dry spell, she couldn't help but wonder if he was also distracting her. If it was easier to give her his cock than his mouth.

"Henning?" she whispered.

"Mmm?"

"I want to kiss."

He stilled under her, his fingers tense. Then he nodded. "I do, too."

His gaze was dark, unreadable. She lifted her

hands to his face, and, gently, she cupped his jaw.
He closed his eyes as her fingers met his skin. Slowly
she ran her thumb over one of the ropy scars by his
mouth. A rumble came from deep inside him.

"How does this feel?"

He paused, his breath uneven. "Intense."

"Does it hurt?"

Henning gave a raspy laugh. "Hell, no. Very much
the opposite."

"Good." Alya smiled. "Ready?"

He nodded. Alya leaned forward, resting her
hands against his biceps. She waited there, looking
for hesitation. There was tension, so much tension,
as they waited there on the edge of this precipice.
But he gave her a little nod, willing to jump. So
she brushed her lips against his, testing. His cock
throbbed against her, and the muscles of his arms
hardened under her fingers. She tested again. His
lips felt…different. A good different. She stayed
there, not moving, breathing in his warm scent, getting used to this new tentative exploration. Letting
him get used to her. More breaths, each uneven rasp
stoking heat inside her. She pressed her mouth more
firmly against his, and this time he responded. He
parted his lips and tasted her. Every brush of his
lips, every swipe of his tongue was achingly slow.

Alya tilted her head, learning how their mouths fit
together, learning what made him groan. His hands
tightened around her, and she slid her fingers along

his jaw, the heaviness of each scar line weighing under her hand.

And then something flipped. It was as if he finally let the pent-up want from those five years loose. His kisses turned greedy, and a growl escaped from his chest as he nipped at her lips and sucked on her tongue. All the softness from before was fading, and God, how she loved this new, hungrier side. She moved, letting the stiff, thick ridge of his cock drag along her core, and he responded, tilting his hips, giving them both that exquisite friction. Sighs. Moans. Wordless pleas from her lips for more. Her body was on fire, the pressure building inside as his cock moved against her clit. She kissed the scarred corner of his mouth, his jaw, finding the rough lines, the smooth lines, the stubble. She wanted all of it.

"Fuck, you turn me on." His whisper rasped in her ear. "I want to make you feel good. Can you come like this?"

Alya hadn't thought that far, but now that he mentioned it… "I think so."

"Good." His teeth scraped her neck. "Hang on tight."

She rested her hands on his shoulders and closed her eyes. Damn, just the muscles of his shoulders were enough to send a jolt of pleasure through her. Then, he began lifting her up and down in a slow, steady rhythm that was…oh, God, it was exactly what she wanted.

"Like this?" he whispered. "Does this feel good?"

His voice was a rasp in her ear, a low, rough invitation.

"Yes, Henning," she moaned, her head dropping to his neck as the pleasure built.

The moment his name left her lips, a new rumble came from deep in his chest. Then another. Sounds of raw, insatiable hunger, of contrasts, pleasure and pain, want and fear. And need. So much need. His voice called to something buried inside her, uncovering it. New desires bubbled, still not fully formed. The aching sound grew louder, but it was her own moan that filled the car. She was right there on the edge of coming as he thrusted his hips harder. She searched for his mouth again. The kiss was rough, each aching stroke of his tongue matching the thrust of his cock against her.

Pleasure shot through her as she moved, drawing out the orgasm, losing herself in the heat of their bodies, in the scent of sex, in *him*. Her eyes fluttered closed, and she rested her cheek on his thick shoulder, breathing in his scent. Henning's heart thudded in her ear.

What had just happened? The connection between them was so powerful, almost as if—

Slow down. She wasn't going to mistake pleasure and affection for something else. The ecstasy-induced haze was clouding her brain. So, instead, she took one last, long inhale of turned-on male and put a little distance between them.

"Well, that was certainly a full-service kiss," she said, her voice languid with pleasure.

Henning chuckled, the sound echoing deep in his chest. "It exceeded expectations in every way."

She really should get up, do…something, but he was so warm, and she really didn't want to move. Henning's cock throbbed urgently against her. She peered into his dark brown eyes.

"You didn't come yet," she said with a little smile. "I can help you with that."

He shook his head. "It would be messy, and it's going to get cold in here soon. I'll take care of that later."

"You'll take care of it?" She tilted her head at him. "Alone?"

"I'm good at it," he said, laughter in his voice.

Alya raised her eyebrows. How much lightness and humor did this man have, buried inside him? "I'd like to see that."

His cock pulsed against her, and he groaned. Then a hint of a smile drew at the uninjured side of his mouth. "I bet you would."

CHAPTER FOUR

"Time to wake up," said Henning, a little louder.

Alya still didn't stir. As soon as her first meeting had ended, she'd crashed into bed and hadn't moved since. He had let her sleep as long as he could, watching her from the chair by the window of their hotel room. Her long, blond hair was a halo around her face, and her full lips were parted. In another life, he would have woken her up with his lips, but not in this one.

Still, she wasn't waking from his voice alone, so he stood up and crossed the room to her bed. Resting his hand on the bare, white wall, he bent down and brushed his fingers over her cheek.

"Sweetheart? We need to go."

Her eyelashes fluttered, and she drew in a sleepy breath. Henning braced himself against the warmth swelling inside him. For years he had watched her through someone else's lens, in magazines, on billboards, and through the Blackmore Inc. surveillance system. This was so different, so real, so raw. He had no words to understand what was happening inside him now that she had chosen him to be here. To protect her. To satisfy her. He'd devote himself to these tasks, keeping his past at bay, controlling this tightness in his chest, this swelling of *something*, something he wouldn't name.

Alya blinked a couple times, brushing off sleep. Then she met his gaze, parted her lips and…smiled. She fucking smiled, her eyes dancing with lightness as she looked up at him. Coming out of sleep, unguarded, vulnerable, she smiled like he was exactly who she wanted to see when she awoke. The swelling inside him was threatening to burst.

"The time change is disorienting," she said, seemingly unaware that his entire world was tilting. So he took a breath and let her warm voice pull him in. "I was hoping this wasn't a dream."

It was all happening so fast. When she parted her lips, his brain short-circuited. *Kiss her. Kiss her.* The temptation was so sharp and bare that it almost overwhelmed him. He closed his eyes and gritted his teeth. Not happening. This was for her, and *only* her. If they were going to spend the next couple days in close quarters, he needed to get this situation under control.

"Listen, about earlier," he said. "About what happened in the car…"

Her cheeks turned a pale pink, and she propped herself up on her elbow. Her mouth was so temptingly close. "I kinda jumped on you. I'm sorry if I put you in a bad position. Again."

"I didn't mind that particular position at all. I was very into it," he said with a laugh.

Alya smirked at his comment, then gave a sigh. "But we shouldn't? Is that what you're trying to say?"

He shook his head slowly. "I'm happy to do that as many times as you want. Or anything else you're interested in. That's up to you."

"I think I made it clear I'm interested." She blinked at him. "Still, I sense a *but* coming."

He blew out his breath. "The moment we walk out of the room, I'm your bodyguard."

She tilted her head to the side and smiled a little. "You're warning me that we won't be sneaking off to try out one of those ice beds?"

"That sounds really fucking cold."

"I understand." Her smile faded. "Because I'm interfering with your job?"

Henning frowned. To be with someone physically scarred like him would make her—and him—the center of attention. Henning had watched her life in the media enough to see exactly how it would play out: grainy photos of them on the front of all the tabloids. And then what? With Alya's more recent dates, the comments were pettier. But Henning was a big fucker with scars and little patience for people in general. After studying Nick Bancroft for three years, Henning knew how that bastard worked. He was almost sure the guy was a clinical narcissist. Nick still hadn't forgotten that Alya left him, and he might use this chance to make a fresh dig about her unstable mental health or make up some story about how she called him again, begging to take her back, and use it as a reason to show up. Just the idea of it made his blood boil, but how the hell did he talk about this with her?

Henning blew out a breath and tried his best. "Look, you hired me so there was no drama on this trip. And I don't want any…speculations on my watch."

"I spent three years shaping my life around avoiding Nick. I turned down jobs because they required traveling to Los Angeles. I've hired a bodyguard to go to events, even when you were checking to make sure Nick was still across the Pacific. I'm done with that," she said. "It's true that I don't want to attract too much attention to my personal life, but I'm not going to let that mean I can't have one. It just means we need to be careful."

He shook his head. What she was saying made sense. She wasn't making decisions based on fear, and she was willing to take some risks. But what was the point of this risk? So he could hold her hand in the Icebar? Nope, not worth it.

Alya opened her mouth, as if she was going to argue with him, but she hesitated. Then understanding registered in her eyes. "You meant speculations about you," she said softly.

He frowned. "I'm not concerned about that."

"I am." She blinked up at him, her sky-blue eyes clear and unwavering.

Then she bit her lip, and his eyes dropped to her mouth. *Focus*.

"But if you're not by my side, there will be other results, ones you might not like," she said.

Like a hard-on from watching her all day long? He had already reconciled himself with that reality. He gave her a little smirk. "I can handle it."

She raised an eyebrow. "We can talk about it after you see what I mean." She was looking at him, like she was assessing him. He leveled his gaze on her, letting her look her fill. Better if she saw him clearly from the beginning.

At last, she nodded. "Fine. But you're okay with a little fun when it's just the two of us?"

"Anything you want." He touched her cheek. Her skin was so unbearably soft under his fingers.

She covered his hand with hers. "What do *you* want?"

He looked down at her, so close to him on this bed. She was waiting for his answer.

Finally he sighed and told her the truth. "I want you, any way I can have you."

Her breath came out somewhere between a sigh and a moan, and the memory of the kiss in the car came crashing down on him. The memory of the sweet tenderness of her lips that so quickly burst into flames. Alya straddling him, her hands holding him so tight it felt like she'd never let go. And he wanted that again, fuck, how he wanted that. Badly. Just one moment of selfishness, one kiss because *he* wanted it. Henning put his knee on the bed next to her and leaned down, searching her expression. And, oh, that smile as he came close, more than an invitation, with a dizzying lightness that took his breath away.

He closed the last distance between them, his mouth on hers again, and she sighed—*she sighed*. This was too good to be real, but the ache inside was too strong for it to be otherwise. Henning licked the seam of her mouth, and she opened for him. She was here, solid under his hands, all soft lips and hungry explorations. The aching need, the gaping hole inside him opened right back up, and he couldn't contain it. He gave her soft strokes of his tongue, and she matched them with her own. Then she reached up, threading her fingers in his hair, and pulled him down on top of her. They landed on the bed, him over her, laughing, kissing. *God, yes.* He could kiss her all day. Wait. No. She needed to be somewhere right now.

"Your schedule," he murmured, his lips so close to hers. She nodded, her nose brushing against his. So intimate.

Mine. The thought was there before he could shove it back down, and he struggled to bury it, along with the surge of protectiveness that followed. Alya wasn't his. She couldn't be.

Time to turn it off. Time to be the person she needed. He closed his eyes and blew out a breath. *Remember the fucking limits, Henning.* If just kissing her was enough to loosen something inside, he needed to be really careful. Especially in a little hotel room. Where they'd be alone. Together. All. Night. Long.

His dick gave an unhelpful throb, so he pulled back, untangling himself from her arms.

"You're due at the kick-off party in the Icebar," he whispered, straightening up, adjusting himself. "I'll put on my winter gear."

That turned out to be a project. Getting dressed to sit around in freezing conditions took a lot of energy, as did walking around in the gear. The snowsuits the hotel loaned all the guests were warm as hell, which really wasn't working inside, but his discomfort was far outweighed by the knowledge that Alya wouldn't be cold when they sat in the Icebar. Still, by the time they made it out of the hotel room, Henning was burning up—and for once, Alya wasn't the reason.

"I can't wait to see this place," she said as they walked through the quiet hallway, seemingly unfazed by the heat. "Ready to be amazed?"

He shrugged and gave her a hint of a smile. "All I'm thinking right now is that this has *cold as fuck* written all over it."

Alya laughed. "Probably. But I think it'll be more than that."

The farther they walked from their room, the quieter the hallway seemed to get. Every step took them closer to the fashion world, where she was at home and he so clearly didn't belong. Henning frowned as he held open the door for Alya, and they both walked out into the snow.

The cold wind slapped his face, triggering memories that caught him off guard. Everything inside him seized up, and for one, terrible moment, he was back in that warehouse. Lying on the ice-cold concrete floor, with pain everywhere. The shards of glass from the explosion embedded in his skin. Knowing that fucker had triggered the explosion on purpose, just big enough for him to get away.

Shit.

Hell, no. Not going there. Henning swallowed. He had faced the cold a few times in the last five years, but with Alya, every sensation was intensified, including this. How the hell he was going to get through a night in a room made of ice was still a mystery, but he'd do it.

Breathe in, breathe out. Everything was under control. *She* was fine. The tightness in his chest eased a little as he took another deep breath. And he was ready as the next gust hit him. Just one foot in front of the other.

Alya looked up at him. "You okay?"

He gave her a stiff nod. "Thank fuck they loan out winter gear here. Back in Sydney, I couldn't have imagined just how cold a place like this could be. You okay?"

Her long legs and slim waist meant she had a lot less built-in protection. But she didn't seem uncomfortable. She stretched her arms out as the snow fell down on her, welcoming it. "I'm great. Even warm."

So he blew out a breath and concentrated on that.

It was still daytime according to the clock, but there were no traces of the sun. Instead, there was a hazy dusk-like glow near the tops of the trees, the sun having barely scraped the horizon hours ago before sinking out of sight again. Now, the only lights were electric, hung everywhere, sparkling on the blanket of snow that covered everything.

There was no mistaking where they were headed. The arched entrance to the frozen structure that made up the cold half of the Icehotel glowed a mysterious blue at the end of their path, and the enormous white mounds of the snow structure stretched out in all directions, disappearing into the darkness. Little wooden houses stood around the hotel, each with candles in the windows. They walked through the quiet stillness, side by side, together.

"Are those...reindeer parts?" asked Alya, her gaze latched on the doorway.

They came to a stop in front of the entrance to the Icehotel, and Henning studied it. She was right. The door was covered with what looked like reindeer pelts, and the handles were made of...antlers?

Henning chuckled. "I think this is a sign that the accommodations will be on the rustic side."

As he reached for the door handle, Alya sighed and closed her eyes. The snow was falling in large fluffy flakes, and they clung to her dark lashes.

"Still okay?" he asked.

Her eyes fluttered open, and she smiled at him.

"We only get one chance to see this place for the first time," she said. "I just want to make sure I'm paying attention."

Henning nodded slowly. He knew what she meant. Already today, he had felt it more than once: the wish to stop time, to somehow save that first sensation. But for him, that urge had come when he touched her. Kissed her. This wouldn't last forever, not the feeling, and not this intimacy, but the memory might last if he was careful with it.

He rested his heavy glove on the antler. "Here we go."

Henning held the door open for Alya and stepped in behind her. And stopped. The entire interior was ice and snow. Everything. Of course, he had seen it in photos, but to experience it was an entirely different thing. The structure itself was domed, made of snow, with blocks of ice everywhere, clear but with a hint of blue echoing throughout the space. It was nothing like the ice that came out of his freezer. Absolutely incredible. The packed snow of the ceiling and floor reflected the tiny lights set up to make the ice sculptures glow. There was a chandelier hanging in the entrance hall—ice, too, Henning suspected. In the middle of the foyer, there was an enormous ice sculpture of what looked like a Nordic god, bearded and armored, with sword in hand. The bluish cast to the place made him think of the ocean or even the sky.

Alya had come to a stop next to him. There was no one else in the entrance hall, just the two of them, dressed in snowsuits and hats and boots, staring at this miraculous place around them.

"It's breathtaking," she whispered.

"You were right," he said. "Definitely more than just cold."

And then he was inside one more of those moments, the kind he was trying so hard to hold on to. It wasn't just the Icehotel itself, but that they were both standing there, together.

Alya walked across the snowy floor to one of the pillars and pressed her gloved hand against it. "Where did they get all this ice? And how do we know it's not going to crash down on us?"

"I read that the skeleton of the structure is metal, covered with layers of an icier version of snow. The blocks of ice are carved out of the river just outside in the spring, when the ice is the thickest. They're stored in an enormous freezer building until the next winter comes around." Henning had done extensive research, off-hours, to answer all his safety questions. To make sure this place was well-engineered. He walked over to another pillar, running his finger along the seam of the ice blocks as he made his way toward her. "Seems pretty sturdy to me."

Alya looked up at the ceiling, then smiled at him. "Look who did his homework."

He shrugged. "I was a good student."

Her laugh echoed in the open room. The sound

was magical, and *he* was the one who had made her laugh. Fuck, that felt good.

"I bet you were," she said. "You seem very... focused."

Her eyes flickered hotter for a moment, so he took it as a compliment. Corinne had called him many things, long before the disastrous bust. Too intense. Too closed off. But the way Alya said this felt different. He moved closer to her until he was standing right next to her, looking down into her blue eyes, peeking out from under those dark lashes and fluffy hat. His gaze strayed down to her full red lips.

He wanted to kiss her right now, to make these first moments in this ice palace come alive in new ways. Just a kiss, to make this moment everything it could be. Anything intimate in public was supposed to be off the table, but right now, it was hard to remember why. Slowly, he tipped his head down toward hers, and Alya parted her lips. Just one little taste.

But before his mouth reached hers, the door to the Icehotel opened again, filling the room with voices and then people. Henning took a step back, blew out a breath and frowned. Fuck. What the hell was he thinking?

The group of models started through the entrance hall, their voices dying down as they passed. He caught some curious glances and a few nods in Alya's direction. They weren't afraid to stare, and he had almost given them something to stare at.

The group of women continued down the large ice hallway, but the magic was gone. It didn't stand a chance when the real world crashed in. Even putting media concerns aside, what did he think this was between them? Henning could protect and he could satisfy, and years ago in the hospital, Corinne had made it clear that those two things were his worth. He didn't have more to offer, and Corinne left when he couldn't give them anymore. The idea was hard enough to swallow as he lay on the hospital bed, his face a wreckage of stitches and angry red scars. He never, ever wanted evidence that Alya felt the same.

Henning frowned and nodded in the direction the models had headed. "Ready to continue?"

Alya nodded.

The hall glowed with dim lights, positioned behind the carved blocks of ice. Henning slowed as they passed other ice sculptures. Someone had made each Viking warrior, carved each link of the belt, each fold of the warrior's tunic. How many people had worked to imagine and build this monument of art?

Reindeer pelts hung from the doorways of the rooms. Alya lifted one to look inside, and Henning moved in, peering over her shoulder. The scent of her hair was muted by the sharp bite of reindeer fur. Yeah, they were definitely the real thing. The room had the same mystical blue glow as the hallway. In a twist of irony, the theme seemed to be a tropical island shipwreck. Ice statues of palm trees stood in both corners, and at the far end of the room, a grass hut was carved at the shore of a clear, glassy beach. The bed stood alone in the center of the room, the base of it an ice sculpture of a driftwood raft, floating in the sea of snow. Reindeer pelts were spread where the mattress should lie.

Alya sighed. "This is incredible."

Henning was so close to her, her fuzzy white hat tickling his nose. He leaned in for a breath of the sweet scent of her hair, and a rush of lust ran through his body. What would it be like to lie in this bed with her, just the two of them, all alone in this shipwreck? Cold, that's what it would be, unless they worked to keep each other warm. The image was there before he could think better of it: him on top of Alya, looking down into the blue depths of her eyes, heavy with the same want he had seen in the hotel room, his cock ready to sink into sweet, wet heaven.

Henning bit back a groan and frowned. That was a fantasy from another life, before he left the AFP, before the nightmares that meant he should never sleep in a bed with anyone. Fuck. They had two beds in their warm room, so they must have the option of two beds in these ice rooms, right?

"When we stay in one of these tomorrow…" he started.

In his pause, she finished his sentence. "It'll be incredible."

Henning opened his mouth to make it clear that they needed separate beds, but when he looked down, the awe in her expression stopped him. She only got to experience this for the first time once, and he couldn't drag his own shit into that. He could ask her later. This moment was for her, and he wanted it to be good.

So he pushed all those thoughts aside, and went with the next thing that came to mind. "You think there are bathrooms in this place, too?"

"You mean ice toilets? I hope not." Alya gave a little snort of laughter. "I think we passed them in the warm hotel, just before we went out the door. Thank God."

The sound of her laughter was magical, and it melted some of his tension. He could do this. The corners of his mouth tugged up. "Just checking."

Alya let go of the pelt in the doorway, and they continued down the hall. The muted din of voices grew louder. They were approaching the Icebar, and Henning steeled himself for the scene they'd face. He had to wipe his face of all traces of the emotions Alya stirred in him—want, lust, protectiveness and something more he didn't want to name. Something that felt way too close to—

"Henning?" Alya tugged on the sleeve of his coat. She had come to a full stop in the glowing hallway, and she was eying him with a stubborn look on her beautiful face.

So he stopped, turned to her and nodded his head in acknowledgment, waiting for her to tell him what she wanted. Whatever it was, he'd give it to her.

"Sasha Federov, the designer, is a force of nature, but anything you see is about his business, not me personally."

Henning swallowed. "You're letting me know it's going to be intimate between you."

"It's going to *look* intimate," she corrected.

"You're okay with that?"

"It's the way this business works."

Henning swallowed again and kept his expression neutral. Nodded. Put aside that mix of protectiveness and jealousy that crashed down on him. "No pissing contests. I promise."

"Stay with me," she said. "Stay right next to me all night."

Henning stilled. What was this about? He took off a glove and swiped a hand over his face. His skin was cold, and he had the urge to touch her, to see if she was cold. But he didn't.

"Is this in any way about your security?"

She shook her head slowly. "No."

Fuck. He wanted to stay with her for every self-ish reason. Because, in some alternate universe, he could see the scene so clearly, walking into the Ice-bar, touching her, kissing her. Making it clear to everyone that upsetting her in any way would have consequences. But he could never, ever mistake that imaginary universe with the one he lived in.

Henning studied her face, her cheeks pink. The idea of saying no to Alya was causing him physical pain. His hand ached with the need to touch her, but if he did, it would make this even harder. So he put his glove back on.

"I can't," he bit out.

She tilted her head to the side. "Can't or won't?"

"In this case, there's no difference. You don't need me right next to you, and it's not in your best interest."

She rolled her eyes. "Now you're patronizing me. *Why*, Henning?"

Henning looked up and down the empty hallway. She wanted to discuss this, right here? Fine. "Because you're here to spread your wings, not to have your hulking bodyguard next to you, glaring at every man who touches you." He blew out a breath. Shit. Did she hear the jealousy oozing out of that statement?

He could feel himself getting worked up, so the last thing he expected was for her to smile. But that's exactly what she did. It was a beautiful smile, so wide and full of…amusement? That tightness in his chest was easing.

"You're very intense," she said, laughter in her voice. "Anyone ever tell you that?"

"Once or twice," he said dryly.

She chuckled, shaking her head. "Fine. So you're going to brood in the corner while I mingle?"

"Pretty much." He was trying his hardest not to smile. It wasn't working.

"Are you going to be jealous?" Her voice was smoother now, seductive.

Damn. She must have heard it in his voice. He narrowed his eyes at her and frowned. "What I feel when I'm working is irrelevant."

"What about afterward, when we're back in the room?" she said, her voice so soft, tempting. "What if you still feel it then? Will you tell me?"

The question spilled from her red lips, bringing his cock to attention. He scanned the empty hall again, just to make sure they were alone. Then he took a step closer and gazed down at her, letting her see all the want he was keeping tightly leashed inside.

"You want to play with that, baby?" he whispered. "You want to see if that makes you hot?"

She didn't hesitate, despite the warning in his gaze. "I already know the answer. I'm asking if it makes you hot, too."

This could either go very wrong or very, very right. Alya was really hoping for the latter. That don't-fuck-with-her vibe he radiated when he was next to her was a huge turn-on, but she couldn't—wouldn't—use a man as a crutch, just because it felt better than standing on her own. That was her mother's path, and the result was a career and a life that crumbled each time the relationship fell apart. Back in Sydney, she had started to lean on Stewart, her most recent ex, until, finally, she wizened up and decided to take a break from relationships for a while. So Henning was right to turn down her offer, to take a step back when she didn't need him. But…they could play with this set-up a little. Knowing he was watching her across the room, imagining the way he ached for her—that was about desire, not fears.

As long as Henning understood what he was getting himself into. She hadn't missed the sharp flash of heat in his eyes as he sketched the image of a big, ripped bodyguard, there to protect her…and more. He had quickly covered it up with that stoic expression, but now, that sharp mix of heat and intensity shone in his eyes again as he stared down at her.

But he didn't answer. Instead, the uninjured corner of his mouth curved up a little more. It looked like his smile took effort, as if he had forgotten how to do it somewhere along the way. But when he did, his eyes lit up, too, filled with pure, untainted pleasure. It was addictive to watch, to figure out what made him react, and she wanted him to smile a thousand times while they were here. She had some ideas about how to do that.

Henning leaned in, his mouth brushing against her ear.

"You're late," he whispered. "Go in there and do your thing."

He straightened up, wiped the smile from his lips and the desire from his eyes, and nodded toward the Icebar. Game on.

She brushed passed Henning and headed in the direction of the voices. The arched hallway opened into a larger room, even more stunning than the entryway. The Icebar was a work of art. Glittering glassy ice surfaces were everywhere, the walls, the floors, the pillars, the arched ceilings of snow. It was a strange scene, filled with clusters of people, all dressed in the same outerwear. The documentary camera crew added to the vibe, like they were on the set of some futuristic film.

"I feel like we're at the canteen of the rebel base," she said over her shoulder to Henning. "What was that ice planet called?"

His voice was low and intimate. "You mean Hoth?"

"Exactly."

"Definitely an upscale version," he added.

True. Much like in the hallway, everything was ice—the bar, the small, round tables, the benches that lined the walls. Candles burned and torches lit with a flickering haunted beauty. The only other non-ice elements in sight were the pelts that lay on the seating.

Alya wrinkled her nose. "More reindeer? How many had to die to make this place?"

"All so we don't have cold asses," he said, patting the fur on a nearby bench. "Or slide off the bench onto the floor."

She laughed, but this time it was a little too unguarded, a little too free. A dozen heads turned their way. Gazes flicked from Henning to her and back to Henning. And damn, she could see the conclusions in the arches of carefully plucked eyebrows and the parting of pouty lips. She could read those looks.

And if she didn't walk away soon, the documentary camera crew would turn their attention to them, too.

"I'll hang back here," he said, sitting at a table in the corner. He glanced over at the crowd. Heads were still turned in their direction.

Her smile fell, and her heart twisted. *Fuck them all*, she wanted to say. *Come with me*.

But he seemed to know what she was thinking because he shook his head. "I'd rather watch you."

His eyes glittered with…playfulness? Henning? Oh, God, fuck them all indeed.

"You do that," she said, her smile coming back. "Just watch and brood from the corner."

Henning lifted his chin at her and then settled on top of one of those poor reindeer along the bench. He leaned against the snowy wall and crossed his arms, his deep brown eyes fixed on her, intense and guarded. She smiled a little and walked away from him, slowly making her way into the crowd. This was going to be interesting.

Long ago, Alya had come to terms with what it meant to be a model. For so much of this job, she wasn't a real person, just a form for designers to hang their clothes on. But if she really wanted to make it in this industry, she had to be more than that. She had to be the embodiment of other people's desires. These were desires that the magazines and ad campaigns fed into, the desire for happiness, the desire for a life of luxury, and the undercurrent of those desires was sex appeal.

But being this person was a strange thing. From a very young age, she had been told she was exceptionally beautiful, and her mother groomed her for a life with this at the center. She had grown up with an equal mix of both stares and glares because of it. Thank God her parents' marriage didn't explode until after they had their second kid; Alya might have withered up in loneliness without Natasha. Even today, her sister was one of only a few people in the world she was truly close with. Most women kept their distance, as if they assumed beauty somehow made her exempt from more banal desires like conversation and companionship.

The sex appeal part was the most complicated. On the pages of a magazine, she sold the allure of touch, of sex. She wasn't even undressed for these photos, at least not all the way. And yet, as a rule, a stranger off the street was much more likely to approach cute Natasha than they were her. It was as if Alya had some sort of bubble around her with a sign on it: *look, don't touch.* Plus, men's real-life tastes tended toward women with bigger breasts and bigger hips. She elicited a more impersonal kind of desire.

You know you want me. I have what you need.

This was her job, but having Henning here while she did it was…well, different.

She looked over her shoulder and smiled at Henning one more time, focusing her attention on the scene in front of her. Though she had worked in this industry for years, it was hard to call anyone here a

friend. Alya wasn't much of a partier, which ruled
out the easiest way to bond with a good chunk of this
crowd. There were others she might have been more
than just business acquaintances with, but between
her mother's antics and the mess with Nick, she could
imagine why those people had stayed away. Her
mother was known for her off-screen drama as much
as for her on-screen performances, and Alya and Natasha's younger years were filled with Ilana Petrova's
inappropriately young partners, public break-ups,
and accusations of infidelity. And then, just as her
mother finally settled down, Alya's break-up with
Nick turned ugly. For too many years, her life was a
closely followed train wreck, and anyone with good
business sense would have stayed far away. These
days, she kept to herself more out of habit. *Aloof* and
snobbish were much better, reputation-wise, than
train wreck.

A couple models known for partying were settled
up at the bar and clearly past their first drinks, with
a sort of *fuck caring about my image—I'm going to
have fun with this* air to them. Alya understood the
impulse, but it wasn't her path. One of the women
she had worked with before—Brianna?—flagged
her over.

"That guy in the corner," she whispered, *sotto
voce*. "Are you with him?"

Thank God her cheeks were probably already
pink from the cold because she was finding it harder
and harder to hide her attraction. She glanced over

at Henning. His gaze was cool, impassive, but it was fixed on her. Could they see through that hard mask he wore, beyond the scars, to the man who had stood over her in the hallway, whispering in her ear, turning her insides red-hot? That couldn't be it. This was just the usual curiosity.

Alya looked back at Brianna. "He's security."

"I'd hire him," she said, and her tone suggested exactly what services she'd be looking for.

Should Alya be offended for Henning? No, he probably wouldn't care. The fashion industry rested on others' perceptions, but Henning so clearly didn't. She got the feeling that he was a man who only did exactly what he chose to do.

Brianna's gaze drifted back to him, and she smiled. "Yes, I definitely wouldn't mind having him watch me."

Alya bit back a smile. Was she going to ask for Henning's business card next? Alya could see the scene, Brianna sizing Henning up with those bedroom eyes that she was known for. The clench in Alya's gut came out of nowhere, sudden and intense. And completely unexpected.

Oh, this was ripe. Of course other women saw Henning's sex appeal. But when she glanced at him, his eyes were still on her, his gaze unwavering, and his words from that first day in the Blackmore Inc. conference room came back. *There are no other clients for me. Not now, and not in the future.* A hot flame of lust licked through her body, setting it on fire. Oh, now she understood this game she had suggested back in the hallway in a whole new way.

Except she was here for work-related mingling.

"Enjoy the view," she said, smiling at Brianna, and turned to scan the crowd.

The hotel wasn't actually that big, and Sasha Federov's team and the *Behind the Runway* crew had reserved all the rooms in the place, warm and cold, for the next two nights, which meant that everyone here was associated with this campaign. Being at the center of Federov's collection could be a serious career boost, making up for all the time she spent rebuilding her career in a new country after Nick. If she played this right.

She spotted Federov and smiled at him, and he made his way over to her.

"Ahh...you're here," he said, his Russian accent strong and familiar. He kissed her on both cheeks and gestured at the crowd, smiling a little. "Lots of people are asking about you. I know Jean Pierre would love to spend a little time with you."

Right, Jean Pierre Rus. Notorious flirt. The man who would wrap his arms around her in the shoot tomorrow.

"He'll find me," she said.

Federov's eyes were on her, sharp and assessing. Some people would mistake the intensity of his stare for sexual, but she knew what it really was: surveying a part of his empire, an empire that reached beyond the thousand-dollar neckties and one-of-a-kind dresses he created. Everyone in that room was part of it, part of the inventory he handpicked, worshipped, then culled. And right now, he was looking at Alya the way he'd look at his favorite suit, set apart, making sure it was hanging right where he wanted it.

Alya had no illusions about Federov. She was the flavor of the day for a man known for his obsessions that surged and then fell just as quickly. But the artist-muse thing didn't seem to revolve around sex for him—no way she would have signed on to this job if there were hints otherwise. The fucking was optional, though he certainly was known for that, too. In the end, she had taken a good, hard look at this job for what it was: an amazing opportunity to stand on her own and carve out her own path.

"Let me know if you need anything during your stay," Federov said, then leaned in to kiss her cheek. "Though it looks like you have someone else to look after that."

He nodded over her shoulder, and Alya followed Federov's gaze. Henning's expression was stony, his eyes darting from Federov back to her.

"My bodyguard," she said, though her voice might have given away more.

"Interesting." Federov's expression hinted at mild amusement as his gaze flicked back to Henning. "Your mother had many admirers, too."

Her first instinct was to deny the connections he was making, between her and Henning, between her and her mother. But direct responses rarely were taken at face value.

Instead, she gave him a dry smile. "My mother would be the first to say that men were the downfall of her career."

Federov chuckled. "And yet she couldn't resist."

He kissed her again and turned to call Jean Pierre over. She had worked on projects with him before, and she had to admit she kind of liked him, despite his well-deserved reputation as a man-whore. Men like that either seemed to hate women or love them, and he was definitely in the latter category. He was good-natured and laid-back, basically a breath of fresh air in an industry with a few too many divas.

Jean Pierre was also an insufferable seducer, and, from the smile on his face, those efforts were going to be aimed her way. It was actually a good thing in small doses since, tomorrow morning, they would probably be spread out on a bed of smelly reindeer fur, looking into each other's eyes. It was a lot easier to do sultry with someone who actually liked her.

"Alya Petrova." He settled a hand on her back, though the intimacy of this gesture wasn't as effective through the thick coat. "Can I get you a drink? Their signature drinks are *in* ice here."

Alya had no idea what he meant, and she wasn't much of a drinker, but when in an ice bar... "Vodka martini, please."

Jean Pierre raised an eyebrow. "Not my first guess. I would have thought you'd order champagne."

He nodded to the group of models at the bar.

She gave him a little smile. "Family drink."

A preference for vodka was one of the few Russian traditions her mother had maintained after their move to California. One of the many things Illana Petrova, model-turned-actress, was known for.

Jean Pierre flagged down the bartender and ordered, then turned to her as the woman mixed their drinks. He was as good-looking in person as he was on camera, which wasn't a given, with tousled hair, deep blue eyes and a hint of a smirk in his smile that very few guys could pull off. He was assessing her, too, but Alya wasn't sure what his conclusions were, though she was almost sure sex was on the table if she gave any indication she wanted it.

"The last time I saw you, your boyfriend Nick Bancroft was breathing down your neck."

Trust Jean Pierre to get right to the point.

Alya rolled her eyes. "The whole world knows we're not together anymore. He made sure of that, along with implying I was crazy."

Jean Pierre's mouth turned down in a rare frown. "I'm sorry you went through that. That bastard really tried to drag you through the mud."

"Great taste in men, right?" She snorted. "I'm a lot more careful these days."

"And does that bodyguard go everywhere with you now?" asked Jean Pierre in a low voice.

Alya had answered versions of this question, full of insinuation, many times when Max was her bodyguard, and there had never been anything between them. So she answered it the exact same way for Henning.

"Everywhere."

"Huh." That was all Jean Pierre said, but he was definitely registering something.

He looked like he was about to make a comment, but the bartender brought them their drinks. Jean Pierre handed one to her. "Vodka martini in ice."

"Ahh, I see," she said, studying the "glass" made out of ice.

He raised his own ice glass to hers and winked. "To the sexiest winter collection ever."

Alya clinked her glass with his and took a sip of the vodka. It made a cool trail down her throat.

"Want to check out the Viking Room?" he asked. "That's where our first shoot starts tomorrow, no?"

The suggestion itself wasn't out of the ordinary, and the full-on snow gear didn't lend itself to sexy-times. Still, she was getting that vibe in spades.

Alya gave him a hint of a smile. "Not tonight."

"I should have guessed. Someone else has plans for you," he said, his voice filled with amusement.

She shook her head. "He's just doing his job," she said, though she knew Jean Pierre wouldn't believe a word of it.

"Looks like fun."

She followed Jean Pierre's gaze across the room, to Henning. Fun wasn't the first descriptor that came to mind. He definitely didn't belong in this world, and his scars weren't the biggest tell. He was too big, too intense, too guarded, too…everything. He had the presence of a person still in the rough. But what set him apart from this crowd most was that he sat, arms folded, resting against the wall, as if he didn't care how others saw him. Henning didn't seem to care that Jean Pierre was staring at him, assessing him right now, and he answered that stare with a *fuck off, asshole* glance of his own. Damn, she admired his attitude.

Alya took one last gulp of her drink and said good-night to Jean Pierre. Then she started across the room. Henning was watching her like there was nothing else around except her, so she held his gaze, coming to a stop right in front of him.

"Is all that reindeer fur keeping your ass warm?" she asked.

He ignored her question. "Who is that?"

Slowly he stood up until he towered over her, his jaw working, each tense movement, each moment of restraint sending hot bolts of lust through her, making her legs weak. His voice was cool and even, but his eyes blazed down on her. She could think of a handful of answers that were almost sure to stoke this fire hotter. This game was working a little too well for both of them. They were already walking a thin line right here, in front of everyone she worked with. If she taunted him with answers about Jean Pierre, one of them was going to step over the line, and judging from Henning's well-practiced restraint, it would probably be her.

"I'm ready to go back to the room," she said.

His eyes flared with heat, and he glanced once more in Jean Pierre's direction. "You're done with everything here?"

She nodded slowly. Finally he lifted his chin in ascension. "Lead the way."

She brushed by him and headed toward the front entrance. He was right behind her, radiating a hot desire, and his gaze burned into her back. She wanted to turn around, to get a read on what all this tightly reined tension meant, but she wouldn't let herself. Not until they were alone.

She walked out the front door and into the darkness of the night. Henning's boots crunched, so close, but he didn't touch her. Didn't say a word. When they came to the warm building, he held the door open for her, and they stepped in. The hallway was empty, and Alya was ready to continue their conversation right there, but she had enough of her wits about her to ditch that plan and look for a little more privacy. She found a door and pulled it open. An upscale locker room, but at this point she didn't care.

The door closed behind them, and the only sounds were their breaths, fast and ragged. Alya slowed to a stop, and so did Henning, still right behind her. She swallowed. Then slowly, she turned around. *Oh, God.* His eyes were alive and dark, and her entire body exploded with need.

He tugged off his gloves and hat, dropping them on the floor. Next he grabbed the zipper of his snowsuit with his big hand, and she watched, mesmerized, as he unzipped all the way, until the fly of his thermals showed. He adjusted himself so that his thick erection jutted into the V, straining at the material. His chest rose and fell quickly.

"Fuck," he muttered. Then he met her gaze.

When she didn't say anything, he reached for her zipper. He tugged it down, exposing her slowly. His scars twisted as he watched this slow reveal, turning his expression into something darker. Oh, God, this was the sexiest game, and she wanted to play it so very badly. She dropped her gloves on the floor and reached up to his face, touched it, the rough side and the smooth side both under her fingers. He took a ragged breath and stepped toward her, her breasts pressing against his chest. She shuffled back to keep her balance, but he stepped forward again. Step. Step. Slowly, he backed her up against the rough wooden wall. There was nowhere left to go.

Then he slipped his hands into her snowsuit, around her waist and down her ass, cupping it in his enormous hands. He bent down.

"You like to be watched, sweetheart?"

"Yes," she whispered.

"You like knowing that you're the only person I see in that room?" His voice was rougher. "You like knowing I'm hard as hell, wanting you, even while you talk to another man?"

"God, yes."

He had been watching her all day, but it was nothing compared to what she saw in those dark brown eyes right now. It was raw and dirty, twenty-four hours' worth of pent-up lust. Or more.

Then his mouth came down on hers, cutting off all other thoughts as her body burst into flames. They were a tangle of hands and hats and snowsuits, and it was impossible to get close enough. It was a storm, sudden, torrential, drenching everything with its hot, wet downpour. She was so achingly hungry. His teeth caught her lips, his tongue stroked hers with unleashed craving. Alya moaned and kissed him back, showing him what she liked. He was claiming her, not by force or demand but with pledges. The kiss was a string of erotic promises, of all the ways they could be together, of all the ways he wanted to take her. *You know you want to be mine.* His hands had found their way under her sweater, his fingers slipping up her back, pulling his body against hers. She moaned again, and he answered with a deep groan.

And then, as suddenly as it had started, he pulled back, dragging in a harsh breath.

"Holy fuck," he muttered, letting her go.

Alya inhaled deeply, her mind still reeling from kissing, touching, wanting so badly. "The room. Let's go back to the room."

Henning was silent for a moment, and then he nodded. He straightened her clothes and arranged her snowsuit over her shoulders, his touch almost gentle now. He zipped up his own snowsuit a bit, hiding his erection, and then picked up her gloves and the rest of his gear off the floor.

His eyes were filled with that guarded lust he had looked at her with for so much of today. She waited him out, watching him, wondering if he'd speak his thoughts aloud. He swallowed, working his jaw, and he ran his free hand through the short bristles of his hair.

Then he rested it on her face, cradling her cheek with his big palm. He took a ragged breath, and then his mouth was on hers again. His lips stroked hers with more finesse this time, but that edge of longing and need was still there.

"Whatever you want from me," he whispered. "Take it."

CHAPTER FIVE

FOR ONE, HOT KISS, Henning hadn't held back. In that quiet locker room, with Alya up against the wall, her body flush with his, he let himself react, let her feel how deep his want ran. Because the twist in his gut as he watched that man—a man who was everything Henning wasn't—touch her and smile at her? That was a real reminder that she would never really be his. That chasm had opened inside, exposing deep fissures, and all the buried want and need flooded out.

Neither of them had said a word since they left that little locker room. But now, as the door to their hotel room clicked shut and she came to a stop in front of him, they were on again, for real this time. He stepped up close and slid the top of her snowsuit off, guiding it down her body. He got on his knees, easing the material over her ass and down her legs, tracing her curves with his hands.

"Hold on to my shoulders," he said softly.

She held on, balancing herself as he lifted one foot to tug her boot off, then the snowsuit. He moved to the other side to pull off the other boot, her hands warm on his shoulders. God, it felt good to take care of her. He got to his feet and hung up her snowsuit on the hook next to him. Then he stilled as he took her in, dressed in thermals and a soft white sweater. With that searing kiss still licking flames through his body, everything else was fading except the need to give her what she wanted.

He was going to give her a place to let down her guard, to indulge in her own wants. Over the last three years, he had learned a lot about Alya and the way she quietly shouldered the weight of her family. The way she'd supported her sister financially at age eighteen, taking care of Natasha when her mother was too distracted by the drama of her own life. Alya had even sacrificed nursing school so that Natasha could go to college. This was a woman with an enormous heart, and Nick Bancroft had taken advantage of it.

Of all the reasons for Henning to drag himself out of his self-imposed years of seclusion, this was the strongest: he would give her whatever she needed for a few days. And if that meant his cock and his mouth, then hell, yes, he'd give it to her.

He shed his own outer layers and then stood behind her, closer. His thermal layer did nothing to hide his erection. He couldn't resist pressing it between her ass, the urge to have her growing stronger.

Henning brushed her hair to the side and pressed his lips on her neck. "You have the sweetest scent.

I could do this all day long." He caught her earlobe between his lips, and her breath hitched. He took a long inhale and groaned. "You want to know what I've been wondering?"

"Yes." She turned her head toward him, looking over her shoulder, and her blue eyes were electric, shining, alive.

Fuck, he was so hard right now, his cock pushing against the fly of his boxers, hard to ignore. Her voice was a siren's call, so he answered it. "I want to find out if you smell just as good between your legs."

Slowly, Alya turned around, her eyes hot and intense on him, and his body was on fire, overheating in all the layers of clothing. His blood pounded through him, an unrelenting chant. *Mine. Mine. Mine.* Henning swallowed. No matter what he felt, this was a game for her, and he wouldn't forget it.

"Are you at all cold right now?"

She shook her head. Good. He wanted to kiss her, but he held back, knowing how easy it would be to lose himself the moment it began. Not yet.

"You've been watching me all day. Now I want to undress for you," she said, her voice huskier. "And while I take my clothes off, I want you to stroke yourself. Pleasure yourself while you watch."

"Fuck, yes," he groaned as a shudder of pleasure rolled through him. Henning closed his eyes, pulling himself together. Then he slowed his breathing and looked at Alya again.

She smiled and took a step back. Another. Her

eyelids were heavy, her dark lashes falling over the endless blue of her eyes, and her smile transformed into something so clearly seductive.

"You ever look at photos of me?" she said, her voice luring him into this game.

Holy hell. His body was already fully there, but his conscience was pricking at him. They were veering into murky territory, territory he had spent three years trying to resist: his fantasies about her, fantasies he shouldn't have had about a client. So he had pushed them deep down, letting the frustration fuel his determination to protect her from afar. Until now.

She wanted them, and fuck, how he wanted to give her everything she asked for.

"Yeah, I looked," he whispered, testing her reaction. "You like that?"

Her eyes lit up. "A lot."

Oh, fuck, this was hot and dirty and so, so good, and *she* was asking for it. He reached his hand inside his thermals and his boxers and palmed his cock. Her eyes followed his movements, and her pulse ticked hard at the base of her neck.

Alya took the hem of her sweater and pulled it over her head, leaving her in a layer of tight, gray thermals. Her nipples poked out of the material, and she toyed with one. No bra. His cock was leaking, so he spread his precum on his palm and gave himself a stroke as he watched her pleasure herself.

"You ever get off thinking about me?" she whispered.

Shit. He shouldn't admit to it, but this game was too tempting. "I tried not to," he gritted out. "But, fuck, you get me so hard."

She played with the hem of her thermal shirt, then slowly lifted it over her head. Henning braced himself against the wall and stroked himself hard. He was caught in a sea of lust, drowning. Her breasts were small, and her nipples, a delicate pink. He looked down at his hand, rough and big, crassly jacking himself as he watched the most achingly beautiful woman in the world strip. Just for him. Beauty and the beast. The contrast sent a dark swirl of lust and depravity through him. Did it turn her on, too?

"You want this hand on you?" he rasped, pulling down the waistband of his boxers, letting her see each rough jerk of his hand. "The one I use to make myself come when I jack off to you?"

Her mouth fell open a little, and for one long second, he thought he had gone too far. But just as a jolt of fear entered his system, a fear that despite his caution, he had stepped over the line, she smiled. It was a real smile that broke through their game, wide-eyed and full of wonder. Fuck, it was glorious.

Her expression turned seductive. "I like it a little dirty."

The message echoed inside him, urging him on. Yes, she wanted this. She traced the curve of her body down, over her hips, her fingers inside her thermal bottoms. She lowered them, stepping out, and when she stood up, his cock jumped in his hand.

"Nude." The word fell out of his mouth as he stared between her legs.

Alya's real smile peeked through again. "Occupational hazard. Are you into that?"

Henning's chuckle was a gritty rumble. "I'm into *you*, Alya. Everything about you."

A hint of pink colored her cheeks, sending a stab of tenderness through him. It was almost as if she wasn't used to hearing someone tell her how amazing she was. How was that possible? He resolved to tell her as many times as he could.

But right now, he was going to show her. His cock was weeping, as he looked at this beautiful woman in front of him.

"You gonna let me put my dirty mouth on that beautiful pussy?" he whispered, his voice rough. "You gonna give me a taste?"

"Yes," she breathed. "Give me what I need."

Give her what she needs. Don't fuck it up.

Holy hell, that smile was going to bring him to his knees. It was soft, so private, a secret just for him. Now that he knew what it was like to have her all to himself, he could never go back to looking for her in a magazine. Not when he knew *this*.

"Christ, you're lovely," he whispered.

Her eyes fluttered closed, as if hearing these simple words had given her pleasure. Then she turned, glancing over her shoulder as she walked toward the bed. And, fuck, this woman knew how to walk for an audience. She knew how to make each slow sultry step a new promise. And this time, the promise was for him.

She climbed on the bed, her ass arched up to him. But she did this with a kind of effortless grace. It was nothing like the women he had fucked in the club, pretending to be someone else, just for that night. This was part of her. Alya lay down on her side, propping her head on her hand. "You coming?"

Henning nodded, but he didn't move. Not yet. First, he needed to take in every bit of this moment, storing it away in his memory, saving it. In the years to come, he wanted to remember how this felt. When once, for a few short days, he had her all to himself.

There was no hesitancy in the way she lay there looking at him. He loved this confident, hot-as-hell side of her. And after watching her bloom from that dark place Nick had driven her into, he wanted this confidence to fill her until she was bursting at the edges with it. He was going to make sure this was for her.

Henning followed the curves of her body, along her thighs, over her hips, down the dip of her waist and over the curve of her pert tits, up the slim column of her neck, and finally, to her smile. Alya waited, lounging on the bed, watching him, her expression full of lazy desire, like they had all the time in the world. But the flush in her cheeks hinted at other possibilities. That she was aching for him, too.

"You are stunning," said Henning, his voice a little hoarse. "It's *you*, Alya, not just the way you look. It's everything about you."

She blinked at him with a hint of surprise. Her cheeks flushed, and then she smiled. "Then why are you still across the room?"

"I want to enjoy this part. When you look at me like it's my mouth you want, no one else's." His voice dipped lower. "I want to savor it."

Another sharp jolt of urgent lust shot through him, and he palmed his cock and gave that impatient bastard another rough stroke.

It had been so long since he had gone down on a woman. Years, despite how much he got off on it. Since that first kiss with Alya, he had been thinking about it. What would she like best? What would she sound like? Now, finally, *finally*, he would find out. And oh, God, how he ached to know.

He took one slow step, then another, watching each reaction from her, the parting of her lips, the quickening of her pulse as he came closer, closer. Henning pulled off his top and bottoms, but he left his boxers on. Then he knelt on the bed, one knee on one side of her, one knee on the other. She rolled onto her back, and he lowered himself onto his forearms until he could feel the heat of her skin under him. Until her quick breaths warmed his cheeks. Because beneath all this beauty was so much emotion. She had been burned. Nick had used her emotions against her, trying to manipulate her, to drive her back to him. What Henning could give her right now, on this bed, was a safe place to let that guard down and simply feel. And fuck, he had so many plans for how to make her feel.

He bent his head and pressed his lips to her pale, slim neck, exposed just for him. Heaven. He kissed her jaw and then her lips.

"You smell so fucking good," he murmured, looking down at her.

"You do, too," she whispered.

Then she wove her fingers into his hair, tugging his head down, guiding his lips to hers. The onslaught of sensations took over, washing through him as her lips melted onto his. Hungry strokes and sucks and nips…he couldn't get enough. He was drowning again, lost in the drive to press his skin against hers, move his hard body against her soft curves, drive his cock into the heaven of her wet, tight pussy. To never let this end.

This last thought jolted him back to reality, and Henning pulled away.

"You're distracting me," he said with a heavy, low laugh. "I have other plans."

"Plans that don't involve kissing?" Her eyes were glassy, unfocused, and her voice, husky.

"Oh, baby." Henning groaned. "There will definitely be kissing. Everywhere."

He started with her collarbone. "Here," he whispered, his mouth on her salty-sweet skin. He kissed a line down her chest, up the rise of her breast. "And here." Her nipple was hard under his tongue, and she hissed out a breath as he took it between his lips. He cupped one breast with his hand and fit it in his mouth, sucking. His cock gave a kick, and he groaned and sucked harder. Oh, fuck, why did her perky little tits turn him on like they did? If he kept this up, he was going to come before she did. He ran his tongue over her nipple one more time and moved lower.

"You wet, baby?" he rasped, his lips on the soft skin of her belly.

"For you," she whispered, sending another jolt to his cock.

Those two words made his heart stutter. *For him.* The scent of sex was everywhere, pulling him down her body, over her naked mound until finally, finally he was there. How many times had he imagined this, never once thinking that it could really happen? His cock was begging for attention, the insistent fucker, used to getting its share when he played through this scenario, but there was no way he was focusing on that. Because this was so achingly real. So he took another deep inhale and tasted.

Oh, God, his mouth. He was covering her with his mouth, worshipping her with it. Swirls of his tongue, little scrapes of his teeth, all working some kind of magic spell on her. He was a man of few words, but he definitely knew how to use his mouth when he wanted to. Never had she felt a man so intensely focused on her experience. It was as if this was the ulti-

mate turn-on, the moment he had waited for, which…
couldn't be right, could it? But, ooooh, he certainly
seemed intent on proving her wrong. He licked and
groaned and licked again, like going down on her
was getting him just as worked up as she was. With
each grunt, coarse and guttural, he went in for more.

"You like my mouth?" he said, his lips, his breath
teasing her.

"I love it," she whimpered.

"You taste so fucking good."

He sucked on her clit, sending her dangerously
close to the edge. Her moans were loud, scraping
her throat as they poured out, and they seemed to
pour fuel on his fire.

"Christ," he muttered, and one hand left her hip
while the other slid between her legs.

She opened her eyes and looked down at him. One
of his enormous hands was inside his boxers, and his
eyes were closed, his teeth bared. Was he jacking
off while going down on her? Holy hell, she didn't
realize this could get any hotter, but it just did. She
shifted to get a better look at this quiet, restrained
man as he gave himself over to a moment of pleasure.

But when she moved, his eyes snapped open, and
a dark smile tugged at his mouth. "You like seeing
me like this? All strung out on the taste of you, on
the feel of you under my hands and my mouth?"

"God, yes." The answer slipped off her lips. For
once, she wasn't worried about why she loved this
or what it meant. She simply let go.

Then he pressed his mouth against her clit and slid two fingers inside her, taking over, filling her senses, erasing everything except the vision of him, pleasuring her like it was the only thing he had ever wanted.

Whatever you want from me. Take it.

His words came back as white streaks of heat exploded. Her orgasm rolled through her. It was too much. She was making sounds like a wounded animal, cries, whimpers as she came down. Henning growled, lapping at her, drawing out her pleasure. Just…bliss.

Finally Henning kissed her softly, almost tenderly. Then he rose up on his knees. His face was tight, strained, and his cock twitched in his boxers, leaving a wet circle where his tip pushed at the material. He heaved in breaths, the muscles on his chest rippling, his biceps tense. His hands flexed. And she knew exactly what he was holding himself back from doing.

"Do it," she whispered.

Henning groaned and reached inside his boxers, pulling out his hot, thick erection. *Whoa.* She had felt it against her, but seeing his enormous cock was still a shock. His smile was dark as he gave himself a rough tug. "See how hard you make me?"

The hottest words were coming out of his mouth, and she loved it. Her hand moved to her clit instinctively as she watched his hand sliding up and down his huge erection.

He took her in once more, head to toe, and then he roared. He thrust, pointing his cock at her and came, came, came. A second orgasm ripped through her, her slick body shuddering, as she watched the ecstasy take over his features, his hips pumping. The room was filled with sharp gasps as they both stared, openmouthed, at her stomach, slick with his come. Henning looked even more shocked than she felt.

Alya's mouth dropped open as ripples of pleasure still rolled through her. A burst of laughter bubbled up and came out, loud and sudden, and once it came, it didn't stop. She covered her mouth, but it didn't help. The laughter escaped in snorts. Henning's eyes widened, and he stared at her like she was bat-shit crazy.

"I can't believe that just happened," she said between giggles. "That we did that."

Henning's eyes moved from hers to the ribbons of come and back to hers. He lifted his hand to his face, touching his scars with his fingers absently. Then he frowned. "That got way out of hand."

"No. Don't say that." Alya shook her head quickly. "That was the most amazing thing I've ever done. So don't you dare look at me like you regret it."

He was still staring at her with a stunned look. "You're really okay with it? Because I said a lot of things…"

Alya fell back onto the bed, chuckling. "I loved every one of them." His forehead wrinkled, as if he couldn't quite believe it, so she added, "I trust you, Henning. You have to trust me, too. It goes both ways."

He stared at her some more, so she waited him out. Then, finally, his expression eased. "Okay. You're right. But let me help clean you up."

Something about his offering, the way he was looking at her, tugged at her heart. And she flashed to a scene of him following her into the shower, taking his time to clean her, to explore her body, all that intense focus—

No. Having him care for her like that would cross the line she had drawn for herself when they started. It would take them into more vulnerable territory, areas where she had failed spectacularly. Alya was so much stronger on her own, and with this newfound freedom, she'd traveled across the world for an amazing career opportunity and had just had the best sex of her life. There was no way she was going to tangle this up with her old baggage. She had watched her mother get sucked in by each new boyfriend or husband, and it never ended well. Alya had sworn to herself that she wouldn't be involved with another man until she was sure she could stand on her own. Only then could she find something healthy, something real.

Alya forced herself to smile, to wave his offer off. "I'll just take a shower."

His expression darkened, but she ignored another tug at her heart and climbed off the bed, heading for the bathroom. Once safely inside, she leaned against the door and closed her eyes. This was a game about attraction and wish-fulfillment, with clear boundaries around it. She couldn't let herself cross them, no matter what Henning made her feel.

CHAPTER SIX

WHEN ALYA'S ALARM went off the next day, Henning was already up, showered and working on his laptop. He had been in the same place when she fell into bed. Judging from the last two nights, Henning definitely didn't get enough hours of sleep. Was he always like that, or was it the job? She, on the other hand, had rambled, probably barely coherently, over the dinner he'd brought for her from the restaurant the evening before, and he seemed perfectly content just listening. Okay, she had been a little disappointed that he didn't crawl into the narrow twin bed with her, even if his huge body would have taken up most of it.

Alya rolled over, stretched and sat up. Henning looked up from his laptop. His eyes traveled over her silky nightshirt, his expression impossible to read.

"Sleep okay?" His voice had that gravelly quality to it, contrasts of rough and gentle.

"After the hottest sex of my life, followed by a warm shower and food delivered to the room?" Alya laughed. "Um, yeah. I slept well."

A hint of a smile teased at the right corner of his

mouth. His eyes traveled over her once more, slower this time, heat seeping into his gaze.

"We have less than an hour until your day officially starts," he said. "You want me to bring some breakfast to the room while you get dressed?"

"Mmm, thank you." God, this man was amazing, more than—

Yikes. *Don't make this complicated, girl.* She had hired him to support her…though he was giving her things that had nothing to do with the job. Alya rolled her eyes and told that little voice of doubt to shut up. Time to enjoy herself and the company of her supersexy, brooding bodyguard.

"Any preferences?" His voice was filled with all the ways he'd like to serve her, the seductive promise that he would do anything, *anything* to please her.

She stretched and then slid out of bed. His gaze raked over her from head to toe, pausing at the line where her shirt stopped, right at the tops of her thighs. She had slipped on only the shirt of the pajamas set last night, just to see if she could tempt him into bed, but he hadn't reacted. Now he seemed to have noticed.

His lips parted, and his eyes were heavy with lust. He was definitely watching her right now, but he didn't get up, just looked as she walked across the room and searched through her bag for some clothes, her shirt riding up, giving him a nice show of her ass. Good. He could take a bit of teasing.

Her back was to him, so she pulled off her pajama top and let it fall to the floor, leaving her in only panties. A sharp inhale came from behind her, but she didn't turn around. Just smiled as she slipped on a long-sleeved shirt, then a sweater.

"No bra?" His voice was low.

She looked over her shoulder and shook her head. "Not in a fashion shoot."

"You know I'll be thinking about that all day."

Alya laughed and picked up her favorite pair of leather pants. She made a show of sliding each leg into the soft material with an extra little wiggle of her ass. Henning's groan was quiet. She looked over her shoulder, and found one surly, turned-on man.

"My preferences? I'm willing to try lots of things. I think you'll know what I like." She smiled as his eyes narrowed. "I'm answering your breakfast question, of course."

Before he could react, she slipped into the bathroom and closed the door. Leaning back against the wood, Alya let out a whoosh of a breath. Well, that was a fun start to the day, but now it was time to get herself together.

The plan: have fun on this job without freezing her ass off, make it through the *Behind the Runway* interview without saying anything too revealing, have superhot sex with Henning, which hopefully included a chance to explore his pleasure this time, and then sleep in one of the ice rooms. Five-star day in the making, as long as she could tone down her angst.

By the time Alya came out of the bathroom, Henning had returned, and the little table in their room was set with full breakfast plates for both of them: yogurt, breads, hard-boiled eggs, cheeses, meats, fruits…and a large carafe of coffee, thank God. She poured herself a cup and took a long gulp.

"A delivery came for you, too," said Henning. He raised an eyebrow and pointed across the room, next to her bed.

The box was large and round, like an oversize hat box, sky blue with a card on top.

"Not shipped," she said. "Must be designer samples, swag."

Henning wrinkled his forehead. "Designers just give you stuff? Don't people pay ridiculous amounts of money for these things?"

"It's not out of the goodness of their hearts," she said, taking another sip. "They're hoping I'll wear their clothes, preferably on camera for the documentary filming. Free advertisement."

"Huh. Interesting."

Alya zeroed in on the hard-boiled egg. How long had it been since she'd eaten one of those for breakfast?

"You're not going to open it?"

She took her eyes off the egg and waggled her eyebrows at him. "You think there might be something in there that interests you?"

The corner of his mouth turned up in a slow smile. Even on the scarred side of his face, she saw a hint

of lightness. "If it's a lacy thong for you to try on,
I'd be into that."

"I bet you would."

Alya took another gulp of coffee and walked over
to the box. She pulled off the lid and peered inside.
Tissue paper covered the top, soft, light blue. She
pulled out the first layer and found a white, silk camisole. She held it up.

"Yeah, I'll wear this," she said. She turned around
and shucked her top, smiling over her shoulder at
Henning. His eyes were wide. He clearly wasn't used
to the unabashed undressing and dressing that took
place in her world. She slipped the camisole on and
faced him.

"You like it?"

His laugh was low and sensual. "I love it."

"Good," she said, bending down to look through
the box. More silky shirts and lacy undergarments.
Nice but not very practical for the Arctic Circle. Alya
took off the lid of a little box to find a…tiara? She
held it up, laughing.

"I can't believe this one," she said, looking at Henning. "Who wears these?"

Henning shrugged. "I know someone who wears
them."

"Um, the queen of England?"

"Yeah. And my niece," he said with a smile. "Just
about every time I see her, in fact."

Alya stared at him, trying to picture this jaded
man with a little girl in a tiara.

"Your niece?" she asked. "How old is she?"

Henning's broken smile was warm. "Five next weekend. She has a dance performance while we're here, and I'm almost positive she'll be wearing one of those."

She was still having trouble fitting this information into her understanding of Henning. At the dance recitals of his little princessy niece? She tried to picture the scene: Henning squatting down to five-year-old height as a little girl in a dress and tiara stood in front of him. She'd be explaining something to him, and he'd focus all his attention on the child. His size, the scars, the quiet intensity of him, everything that kept people at a distance—that he *used* to keep people at a distance—wouldn't matter to his niece.

"You missed her dance recital," she said slowly. "For this job. With me."

He shrugged, like he genuinely wasn't worried. "My sister and her family live over in the Manly Beach area, close to where I grew up. I see them all the time."

She knew so little about him, and she was gobbling up this little peek into his life. He was so much more than the version of himself he presented to the world.

Alya brought the box with the tiara over to the table and placed it in front of him as she sat down. "This is for your niece. If she'd like it."

His crooked smile was full of warmth and indulgence. "Thank you. I'm sure she'd love it."

His gaze stayed on her as his smile faded. All that was left was his intense gaze. The breakfast to her room, his anticipation of everything she needed, the orgasms… He was going to ruin her for the real-life version of boyfriends whenever she started dating again.

Alya swallowed and scanned the breakfast spread again. She picked up a little tube, turning it over in her hand. All the writing was in Swedish, of course. "What's this?"

"I think the server said it's caviar paste for the boiled egg." He gave her that little twitch of a smile. "Because you said you were up for anything."

She lifted an eyebrow at him. "I might actually like it. My mother used to eat stuff like this when I was a kid. I think it's a Russian thing, too."

She got to work peeling her egg, and the room was quiet again. Alya peeked up at him, that stoic expression back on his face. What was he thinking about? He wasn't regretting last night, was he?

"We're okay, right?"

He blinked at her, his gaze filled with…irritation? Confusion? She pressed on.

"I mean, after last night, I just want to make sure—"

"Of course we are," he said, his voice gruff.

Of course they were. Sex didn't have to be followed with the avalanche of drama that came with her mother's boyfriends or Nick or any of the other unhealthy relationships that had blanketed her life.

It could just be sex. She bit her lip and focused on her egg.

But before she got a bite into her mouth, Henning had stood up and was making his way around the table. He tapped the front of her chair, and she scooted it out to face him. Then he knelt in front of her, between her legs. He was a big man, big enough so that down on his knees, they were the same height. He settled his hands on her thighs. The gesture was warm and possessive and everything her mind needed to read too much into it.

"I'm not good at this, Alya," he said, gesturing between them. "Even before I…" He looked away, retreating. She lifted her hand to his left cheek, running her fingers down his scars, letting him know she understood, that he didn't need to say it if he didn't want to. He let out a long breath, swallowed, and looked back at her. "I'm sorry if I've done something that makes you feel anything less than incredible. Because that's what you deserve."

She blinked at him, stunned. For someone who didn't like talking, he really struck gold when he chose to speak. His statement was so direct, so opposite of what she had come to expect. Maybe it was that newly found space to simply think and feel for a bit, without distractions, or maybe it was all the orgasms, but when Alya found Henning's steady gaze on her, his dark eyes so clearly telling her he was there for her, all her worries just flowed out.

"The short interviews they're doing for the doc-

umentary—at some point, it's not going to be fun,"
she said. "I know the woman is going to ask me
about all the things Nick said about me, especially
about leaving Los Angeles because I was buckling
under pressure. Maybe she'll ask today, maybe tomorrow. And I have to decide how much to say
about it."

Henning's jaw clenched at the sound of her ex-
boyfriend's name, but he nodded and waited for her
to continue.

"I've worked so hard to get to this point, where
I'm not steering my life around him, even from
across the Pacific." She blew out a breath. "But if
I'm not careful, he can still get to me. With the film
crew here and the publicity this is getting, I start to
worry he'll do something to get attention. And he
may do that." She frowned. "But I have to learn how
to shift my own focus."

God, she never talked about this kind of thing
with anyone except Natasha. And these days, Natasha was too busy to talk much. But now that she
was saying this aloud, she could feel how much these
worries were weighing on her. But, ugh, this was not
the sexy fling he'd signed up for.

"Sorry for the overshare," she said, rolling her
eyes. "I'm just a little nervous."

"Don't apologize," he said, and he sounded almost
angry. But he winced as soon as the words left his
mouth, and grumbled something under his breath.
Henning's eyes were stormy, though she was almost

sure it had everything to do with Nick, not her. His voice was softer when he continued. "You're an incredible woman, so strong. But that doesn't mean you can't voice your worries. I'm listening."

He blew out a breath and looked down at his own fingers, now pressing into her thighs. He loosened them, stroking gently up and down. "So if that interviewer catches you off guard, you're worried you'll say something that will trigger harassment from Nick."

She smiled a little. "Yeah, basically. But in my head it doesn't sound nearly as reasonable."

He opened his mouth as if to speak, then shook his head. He started again. "You want me to come with you to the interview? Glare at the woman if she asks about your private life?"

He was joking, but Alya was trying to ignore how good that idea sounded. She shook her head. "I can handle it."

"I know you can handle it," he said, his voice serious. "I'm just asking if you want someone to share that burden, just for a little while."

She lifted her hand to his cheek. "I think that's just about the nicest offer any guy has given me."

"Sounds like you need to check your taste in men," he grumbled. "You should be hearing that every day."

She smiled a little and tilted her head, considering his words. "You must keep your girlfriends very happy."

"There are no girlfriends for me," he said flatly.

"Never?"

"Not anymore."

She wanted to kiss him so badly. Henning watched her lips as she spoke, like he, too was thinking about kissing. So she did it, leaning forward, brushing her lips over his. His hands moved up her thighs, around her hips to cup her ass. A smile tugged at the corners of her mouth, and the relief flowed through her. She kissed him again, and his lips were full of aching desire, like he was giving her a glimpse at just how happy he was making her right now.

CHAPTER SEVEN

"THE LOCATION IS going to make this shoot a little crazy," said Alya as they headed down the hall of the warm portion of the hotel to the lobby, where they'd meet the rest of the crew. "There's a lot of running between the warm and cold parts of the hotel to change, and the ice means that the lights can't be on for too long, so we don't melt the place down. Each shoot needs to happen quickly...you get the picture."

"And then there's keeping you warm," grumbled Henning. He sized her up. Hot, as usual, but the skintight pants and thin fluffy sweater barely looked warm enough for the heated portion of the hotel, let alone in the fancy igloo where they were headed. "How long are you supposed to lie on that bed without a coat?"

Alya shrugged. "They have saunas to warm us after we're done."

"You mean those hot rooms where a bunch of people sit around naked together?" he said, lifting an eyebrow.

She laughed. "Yeah, those. You interested?"

"Sitting in a room watching other people look at you naked?" He shook his head. "I'm pretty sure that would cross my limits."

This morning was already pushing up against the limits of his restraint. And as they walked down the hallway, watching men pass, their gazes lingering on her, he could see those limits were going to be further tested. Nothing about this scene had changed from yesterday; if anything, it should be easier to stomach these looks, knowing he had spent the previous night doing the kinds of things with her he hadn't even let himself dream of. He should be relaxed, especially given the way he had come more intensely than he ever had last night. But he wasn't anywhere near relaxed.

They had come to the lobby, and she slowed to a stop. Various models and staff wandered in and out of the area, speaking different languages, throwing glances at them, their eyes darting from Alya to him and back again to Alya.

To some degree, this was inevitable. He was a big motherfucker, and his scars upped the intimidation factor enough that people tended to give him a wide berth under any circumstance. But here, he stuck out even more. This was an industry designed to make people forget how brutal life could be. Henning was a snarling beast of a reminder that even for someone of his stature, life never turned out like one of the glossy magazine spreads.

Alya tilted her head, studying him, but she didn't

say anything. Maybe she did understand all of this better than he was giving her credit for.

"You ready?" he asked, nodding across the room, where a woman with blue hair and a tablet was waving her over.

"You can stay with me, you know. Watch me get ready." Her smile turned intimate, her voice soft. "You might enjoy it."

Henning gave a rough laugh. "I'm sure there are plenty of things to enjoy about it," he said, letting his gaze travel down her body.

But that would mean watching someone else touch her, dress her, brush her hair, knowing that there were hours before the next time he would be alone with. Hell no.

"I have some catching up to do." He held up his laptop. "I'll be out here waiting for you."

Her eyes stayed on him, clear, assessing, making everything else fade away. So he rested his hand on her lower back. Such a small thing, too subtle for anyone else to notice. Henning hadn't even fully thought it through before his hand was there. They were only a few paces away from the others, a short distance, but as they walked those steps, Henning let his guard down momentarily. He let himself imagine that this amazing woman could be his, really his. He let himself pretend that he wasn't too broken to be the kind of man who would make her feel safe and strong at the same time. Both independent and owned. Always cherished. Everything she deserved to feel. And he let himself forget that he had so much shit buried inside that would destroy this raw, new connection the moment he let her in for real.

None of these things he imagined were truly possible, so he simply let himself have those few steps. And when they ended, he didn't bother looking around. He didn't want to see the stares this time. He didn't welcome the reminder that he had lived and Sanjay had died, the way he usually did. This time, what he felt was the deep chasm between the person that Alya needed and the person that he was. And for the first time since he had been carried off the cold floor of the warehouse, he wanted those deep wounds to heal. But he had no idea how the hell to do that.

So, instead, he took one last whiff of her warm, honey scent, wiped the emotion off his face and walked away.

Alya came out of the makeshift dressing room laughing, all wrapped in a sweater and scarf, her hair artfully piled on her head, dramatic makeup drawing his gaze to the deep blue depths of her eyes.

Laughing. She was laughing, and that fucker she would be photographed with was the one who was making her laugh. Henning gritted his teeth. Hell no. He was *not* one of those jealous pricks who wanted to control his girl's every move.

P.S. This isn't your girl, so take it down a notch, asshole.

But then Alya turned to look at him, and all the

tension inside turned into something else. The look was there for only a moment, private, but it was personal. A warm, vulnerable hint of a smile. A reminder of all the holes in his defenses that he had spent the last hour trying to patch.

He refused to react. Henning closed his laptop and followed behind Alya, the male model and a few others, keeping his distance. Watching Alya was no hardship. When she walked out of that room, her makeup had surprised him, but seeing her from farther away as she turned her head to talk, he understood the effect. Her blue eyes sparkled, even from a distance, and her dark red lips were so fucking hot. His gaze was drawn back to them again and again. How many men would stare at those lips between the pages of a magazine, imagining what they would feel like around their cocks? Fuck, he wanted to protect her from that…which was the wrong line of thought. He took a couple deep breaths.

They walked outside into the cold winter morning. Snow sparkled in all directions, and the sky was clear and dim. Outside the cold part of the Icehotel, a couple generators hummed, their cords disappearing into the structure.

Henning had gone back to the room to gather the outerwear the hotel had lent them, but Alya wasn't wearing hers. Instead, she had on a sleek winter coat that looked way too thin for the temperature. He glared at the blue-haired woman's back for leaving her underprepared for the weather, though he knew

it probably wasn't her call. But, Christ, Alya must
be cold. He could have held his tongue about anything else, but not the cold. He caught up to them
and opened the door to the Icehotel.

"You warm enough right now?" His voice was
rough.

She nodded.

Still, he was dying to test her temperature himself, feel her hands. It was hard as hell to tamp down
the bone-deep urge to take care of her, but he forced
his hand to the side.

Just relax.

Jean Pierre and Alya followed the assistant down
the ice hallway, the model's hand now resting on
Alya's back. The way Henning's had been. But the
winter jacket meant his hand was nowhere near
her skin. Yet. That would change the moment they
started the shoot. Henning blew out a breath. He
was going to spend the day watching her from the
sidelines. How the fuck he was going to survive this
was unclear, but he was banking on the belief that he
could make it through just about anything as long as
Alya didn't get hurt.

The assistant led them past doorway after doorway, each room hidden behind a reindeer pelt. Henning had seen photos of a few rooms online, but they
were from past years. Each spring the entire structure melted, and each fall, it was built anew. The
walls and beds and sculptures he passed right now
were temporary; each room represented so many

hours of work that wouldn't last. There was probably some deeper meaning in all this, but since when did Henning look for meaning in a world where terrible things happened without reason? And why the fuck did he keep coming back to his past, letting it taint this burst of happiness that was his present? The Icehotel was still and peaceful, the opposite of the world his memories belonged to, so it was time to get his head on straight.

As far as Henning understood, the designer had the models in different rooms for the morning sessions, some in pairs and some in groups. Then, in the afternoon, there would be a larger session in the Icebar, and that damn documentary crew would be following them everywhere. There was a longer break in the middle of the day, when Alya would have a chance to warm up as the crews shifted locations. At least he wasn't the only one thinking about staying warm.

The assistant led them down the hallway, the stark beauty of the place cluttered with cords and people and collapsible tables full of God knows what. With all these real-world items, some of the magic of this place disappeared. The blue-haired woman stopped in front of the last doorway.

"The Viking Room," she said, moving the reindeer pelt to the side.

Alya and Jean Pierre walked in, but when Henning moved to follow them, the assistant narrowed her eyes at him.

"Security," he muttered to her, not waiting for her answer.

The first thing he saw was the bed. It was an enormous Viking ship carved of ice, with its curved hull and the stern in the shape of a serpent's tail, curled and flourished. At the bow was some sort of sea monster, facing outward, warding away other monsters that lurked under the sparkling depths of the icy sea. The entire boat glowed and sparkled from underneath, though he couldn't see any electricity hooked up to it. The actual bed was yet another cluster of reindeer pelts. There were lights positioned around the scene, some behind screens and some from below, though none of them were on.

Henning's eyes went to Alya. She was wandering around, taking in the snow waves and the mermaid ice sculpture along the opposite wall.

"Beautiful," she whispered.

In the middle of the night, long after Alya had fallen asleep, he had lain in the bed next to hers, trying to imagine today, trying to prepare himself for the worst. But his imagination had gone down an entirely different route, one undoubtedly influenced by scenes he had watched in the club, mixed with porn. He had pictured Jean Pierre and Alya and a lone, horny photographer watching them. The reality was a hell of a lot less sexy. For starters, there were a lot more people than he expected, and the conversation was on logistics. Henning suppressed a growl as he also noted that everyone else was dressed warmer than Alya.

"We'll turn on the lights for five minutes, then let them cool, so we don't melt this place down," the photographer was saying in a thick Russian accent. "We tested it earlier, so that's the last thing we'll do."

He sat down on the bed with a clipboard, and Alya and Jean Pierre joined him. "This is a rundown of what I'm thinking. I want to do as much as we can while you have your jackets on. We're going for sexy, not arctic frozen," he added dryly.

The photographer continued to give directions, and Alya and Jean Pierre asked questions and made comments about power dynamics and seduction like they were all talking about the weather. Henning found himself tuning in more closely as the three of them discussed ideas to so carefully play on people's emotions.

Henning's own line of work required him to suppress his emotions, to see through situations carefully and make decisions based on facts, details. It was a skill that surprisingly few were good at. Did Alya suppress her emotions, too, in order to give the photographer what he wanted, or did she know how to find them, on demand? Would he be able to tell the difference?

There were more directions and positioning, and then it was time to begin. A man came up to mess with Alya's hair, though Henning couldn't see anything that needed fixing. She looked fucking perfect because she was Alya, and anyone who thought otherwise was an idiot. Then again, that had nothing to do with fashion.

Soon it was time for her to take her coat off. Henning shivered as she tugged on the zipper, pulling it down, exposing her body covered in a skintight sweater and pants. He clenched his jaw and reminded himself to settle the fuck down. Alya shrugged off the jacket, oblivious to his reaction, and she looked around for a place to set it...but everything was ice. Henning crossed the room.

"I can hold that for you," he muttered.

When she smiled up at him, a little of the tightness inside loosened. Henning retreated to the corner, leaving some woman to finish fussing with Alya's clothing. He unzipped his own jacket and tucked her coat inside, keeping it warm against his body for when she needed it again.

Then the lights went on and the photo shoot began.

It wasn't quiet or private at all, the way the photos made it look. The photographer gave directions, and Alya and Jean Pierre climbed onto the bed, setting up a wintry seduction scene. He had seen countless photos of her, on sofas or beds, with men or alone, all for background research, of course. He had tried not to step over the line, but sometimes it was so hard. Once he even bought *Tropical Bliss* magazine because there was a photo of her alone, walking out of the water in a tiny bathing suit. He'd jerked off to it. Not one of his finer moments, but that was back

when he didn't think he'd ever come face-to-face
with her.

There was a series of shots taken standing up,
with the bed, covered in the reindeer pelts, in the
background. Then, during a quick warm-up break,
while he covered her with the coat he had warmed
against his body, a red satin sheet was fitted over
the mattress that lay on the bed of ice. First Alya
was alone, dressed in all white, her hair carefully
positioned by the same guy who had messed with
it earlier, and then, at her side, Jean Pierre eased
down next to her. It was all an act, choreographed
by the photographer in his running commentary, and
yet, seeing it twisted something deep in Henning's
gut. He was watching this other man, a man with
the kind of easygoing lightness Henning had never
had, looking down at her like he wanted to eat her
up. And fuck if he didn't want to shove that asshole
right out of the bed and onto the icy floor. That man
was the one who lay next to her, even though Henning was the one who had made her come last night.
He should be the one lying next to her right now. He
was getting hard just thinking about all the things
he wanted to do.

Henning took off his glove and swiped a hand
over his face. It was going to be a long day.

Alya was shivering by the time Henning opened his
coat and pulled hers out again. He was trying not to
react, but when she looked up at him, he got the feel-

ing she saw something anyway. Henning wrapped the coat around her shoulders, giving him an excuse to look away. She wouldn't ask questions there, in the middle of the bustle of equipment-hauling and cleanup crews around them.

But he was close enough for one, intoxicating breath of her scent, and it took only that one breath for the sharp ache of want to flare up again. Henning forced it back down. But then Jean Pierre was approaching; he could see him out of the corner of his eye, heading in their direction.

"Feels longer in the cold, doesn't it?" Jean Pierre came up next to Alya, getting all in her space in a way that crawled under Henning's skin. "Heading to lunch?"

Alya shook her head. "I'm having lunch in my room."

Henning frowned. They headed out through the snowy cold, but when they were finally in the warm part of the hotel and alone, Henning stopped, right in the middle of the hallway. He was trying to figure out how to say this without being an asshole. Finally he blew out a breath and gave up. "I hope you're staying back from lunch has nothing to do with me."

"You mean you want me to ignore the way you were glowering at me for the last two hours while Jean Pierre and I lay on the bed?" she asked, leveling him with her gaze. "You want to spend more time watching us together?"

Henning closed his eyes and massaged his temples.

"Or you didn't mean to stare at me like you were thinking of everything you wanted to do with me on that bed?" she said, her voice husky. "Am I mistaken?"

"I didn't mean to—"

Alya burst out laughing, cutting off his grumble.

"Yes, you did," she said, still laughing. The sound was beautiful, soft and musical, and finally, reluctantly, he smiled too. "But I also need a little time to relax." She raised her eyebrows at him. "You want to go back to the room and relax with me?"

She tugged on his arm a little, and he blew out a breath and followed her. He probably would have followed her anywhere if she asked. They walked in silence, into the warm building and down the hallway, the tension from the day building with every step closer to the room. Two models passed, their glances bouncing from Alya to him in open curiosity, and Henning scowled at them. Yeah, it was obvious what was going on, but at this point, he didn't care. All he could think about was Alya in white, lying on that red satin bed, looking at him.

Henning entered the room first, giving it a quick sweep because he would never, ever forget that he was here first and foremost for her protection. But the room was silent, the beds made and the breakfast dishes gone. It was simple, impersonal, so much like a setting from a magazine he'd see her in, and, yet, this was real. And of all the men in the world, she was looking at him right now. No one else. What a lucky bastard he was. For a few short days.

He turned to her and fingered the zipper of her coat.

"Are you warm enough?"

She blinked at him. "You have something about the cold, don't you? You don't like it."

Henning swallowed. "We can talk about that later."

She shrugged. "I'm fine. My jacket was warm when you gave it back."

He stroked her hair, but he wasn't convinced.

"Besides, when I lay there on that bed, I found a way to keep myself warm." Her voice was soft and silky. "Want to know how?"

He tugged on the zipper of her coat, drawing out this moment, drawing out this time before the wave of want and need came crashing in. Slowly, he revealed the elaborate wrap of her sweater, soft and white. It twisted around her body, and he reached in to find the ties that held it together. Her stomach was warm under his hands. "Tell me."

Alya licked her lips. "When I lay on that Viking bed, I was thinking about you last night. Kneeling with your cock in your hand. And what you'd say if you were next to me."

Henning chuckled and took a step back from her. "I'd say let's get the hell out of this ice prison and get you warm."

CHAPTER EIGHT

STEAM CLOUDED THE bathroom mirror as Alya peeled off her pants and camisole. She slipped her fingers under the waistband of her panties but paused when she caught sight of the peach, lacy material.

She wiped a patch of the fog off the mirror and studied her arms, her stomach, her hips. In a world where women bonded over dieting wins and failures, she had gotten this body. Tall, slim but a little curvy, with small, rounded breasts and very little sun damage—that last part thanks to her mother's own aversion to the sun, ensuring that not only her mother but also that she and Natasha were camera-ready. It was a body that brands designed for, before they translated those styles into real-world sizes. If she believed everything the fashion industry had taught her, this body was for show, not for real-world practicalities. But Alya didn't care what the rest of the world thought. Today, she cared about what Henning thought.

Did he see her through the lens of the magazine descriptions? *Ethereal* was one of the words that surfaced, again and again, with its companions, *otherworldly* and *untouchable*. That last one she particularly hated. What kind of person didn't want to be touched? Not her, that was for sure.

God, she hoped Henning didn't see her that way. The electric tension between them yesterday had been very much grounded in the physical world.

She stepped out of her panties and into the hot shower. She stood under the showerhead, letting the warm water seep in as she replayed the morning. Henning on his knees in front of her at breakfast. On the Viking bed, with Jean Pierre stretched along her side as Henning's gaze burned into her. Henning keeping her jacket warm against him.

How many times had other men touched her? Her job required close contact with other models, and not once had any one of those intimate poses awoken feelings this intense. But all it took was Henning's gaze to send bolts of heat through her, fighting the cold.

The way he towered over her left her breathless. And the sound of his breath stuttering as she pressed her hand against his stomach. The strokes of his tongue between her legs. Now she was standing under the falling water, naked and burning up inside that memory. A flush crept up her neck, her body alive, craving more.

Alya climbed out of the shower, towel-dried her hair and then wrapped another towel around her body.

When she finally opened the door again, Henning was sitting on the bed, his forearms resting on his knees, his head hung. A T-shirt stretched over his hard, muscular chest, his biceps ripped and cut from years of physical training. Slowly, he sat up, and heat spread through her body in new waves as she took him in. Any traces of smoothness to him were long gone, if he ever had them. Just barely visible on one side were the ropy scars that lined his neck and disappeared under his shirt, healed but far from gone. Henning Fischer was the most incredible man she had ever seen. He had wanted to give her pleasure yesterday. Now she wanted her turn.

When her gaze finally reached his face again, Henning's eyes were on her. His expression was dark and hot, and the tension between them crackled. He couldn't know about the way she had imagined them together, but it was as if he was thinking about those exact same things.

Alya swallowed. Then, slowly, she walked toward him. His legs were parted, and she continued until she was standing between his knees. Liquid heat rolled from his gaze, turning her insides red-hot. The pull between them sparked, alive, electric. His hands moved to her thighs, touching them, but it felt more like an assessment than seduction.

"You warm now?" he asked softly.

"Yes, thanks." She smiled. "You realize the temperature in our ice room will be zero tonight, right?"

His jaw tightened. "Yeah. I'll deal with it."

Henning wrapped his arms around her legs and urged her to sit on top of him, so she was straddling him much like she had in the car. But this time if felt different. More intimate. She rested her hands on his bare arms and explored the heat, the solid muscle, as her towel loosened from around her chest. Henning leaned in closer, dropping a trail of kisses down her neck. "How do you want to relax? Tell me what you'd like."

Alya pulled back a little and raised a skeptical eyebrow. "What about what you'd like?"

"I'd like anything with you, Alya," he said, his face solemn. "Anything."

She had never met a man who had so seriously professed his interest without asking for something in return, and it still threw her off a little. Nick had been so closed off when they were alone, which was partly why the intensity of his pursuit had surprised her after she broke up with him. And the restraining order she took out only seemed to make him more determined. But now wasn't the time to think about Nick.

She focused on Henning, so close. "How about for everything I tell you I like, I get to take off one piece of your clothing."

Henning laughed. "If that's what you want." He gave her a sexy wink. "I'm willing to get naked in exchange for a peek into your mind." His hands moved up and down her back and slow caresses. He kissed her neck again and then her collarbone. "You first."

"I really like this position right here," she said, running her hands up his biceps and over his shoulders. "You're here right in front of me. I can touch you and explore you and look at you."

"And that's what you want?" His voice was getting a little deeper.

"Yes." She fingered the edge of his T-shirt. "This first."

He chuckled. "Not my socks? You don't have a thing for my feet?"

She shrugged. "Maybe I do."

"Do you?" His dark eyes sparkled.

She shook her finger at him. "Not your turn to ask questions."

Henning's smile was full of warmth and humor. "Fine. Undress me."

Alya took her time, moving her hands over his wide, rounded shoulders, over the broad flat planes of his chest and down his stomach. He was muscle all over, hard, ripped muscles that flexed under her touch. His breath quickened as she moved lower. She lifted the hem of his T-shirt and found the top of his jeans. Slowly, she ran her fingers underneath the material. He drew in a sharp hiss, then gave a harsh bark of a laugh. "Does this all count as undressing?"

"It's the best part," she whispered.

Instead of pulling up his shirt, she placed her hands on his waist and slid them up, exploring, inching the material up.

"Holy fuck," he muttered. "Is this how you plan to take off everything I'm wearing?"

"Hell, yes." Alya laughed.

He shook his head slowly. "You better have some good answers to my questions."

Her hands traveled higher, and when she reached his arms, he lifted them for her to ease off his shirt. She pulled it over his head and dropped it on the floor, then leaned back to take him in.

God, was he magnificent. He seemed to be made of an entirely different substance than she was, his muscles carved and rock-solid even in their resting state. He had very little hair on his chest, just a dusting around his nipples and a dark trail down the center of his abs that disappeared into his jeans. So intimate. So sensual. Slivers of light shimmered from between the curtains, dancing up and down the sculpted muscles of Henning's chest. Damn, this man was ripped. The level of fitness that a body like that required spoke to his determination and persistence, especially considering his job was now entirely behind a desk in the IT department. Yet he kept his body in such incredible condition that Alya couldn't help but wonder if he was still preparing for a night that ended long ago.

Either way he was hot. And real. The tufts of hair under his arms and down his stomach looked soft and inviting, but this was a body meant for action. Alya smiled. And no doubt he used his body for action of all kinds.

Her gaze traveled up to his face, and she found him smiling back at her.

"You like what you see, baby?"

Baby. She had never liked that term of endearment before, but it sounded just right out of his mouth.

"Yes," she whispered, continuing her explorations back up his chest. His scars weren't visible from the front, just a hint of them on his left shoulder was all she could see. Slowly, she moved her hands higher. Closer. She reached his shoulder and let her fingers glide to his neck, tracing his scar down.

That's when she felt more of them. The rise of scars along one side of his back, some long, some shorter. When she looked up at his face again, his smile had faded, and his eyes were dark.

"When glass explodes, it's like a spray of bullets everywhere," said Henning quietly. "We were in a warehouse, where these crazy fuckers were cooking ice on a large scale. One of my team members and I went in first, just to take a look, to see what we were dealing with, to try to contain the danger. Thank God I held back the rest of my team because the gang leader set it off on purpose. He even killed some of his own crew, just so he could escape. I got lucky, no burns, but Sanjay, my team member, he got a piece of glass right in an artery. I stayed with him instead of following the leader, but he bled out before help came. I have these scars to remember him by."

A heaviness squeezed at her chest. He carried this with him every day. "I'm sorry," she whispered. She knew her comment was like putting a Band-Aid on a severed limb, but she said it anyway.

"It was a long time ago," he said, softer, stroking her hair.

"Where is the guy who did this?"

"Prison. I was off the force by the time they caught him. Probably better that way."

She lifted her hand and pressed it against one of the scars. He sucked in a deep breath and stiffened, as if she was causing him pain, so she pulled her hand away. But the moment she did that, the pain in his expression seemed to get worse.

"Don't stop," he said, his voice heavy. "It's just been a long time since anyone has touched me this way."

He took her hand and laid it over his scars again. She had so many questions, but she could see it was a painful subject for him. And this was about making him feel good. She'd ask later...whenever that was.

His hands were back on her legs, slowly caressing, moving higher with each stroke. The pull between them was growing stronger, bringing her attention back to where this was headed.

"Your turn again," he said. "What makes you hot, Alya?"

"The way you're saying my name right now is making me hot."

Henning's crooked smile broadened, but he shook his head. "Doesn't count. I need something to work with."

She wrinkled her nose, searching for a good answer. "Big," she finally said. When Henning chuckled, she added, "I'm not talking about what's between your legs. Regular size gets the job done nicely, too."

He raised his eyebrows. "Lots of things get the job done. We're setting the bar higher than that."

"Gladly," she said. "But I meant this."

She found his hand and lifted it up, matching it with hers so they mirrored each other. But it wasn't a mirror at all. Henning's hand outsized hers in every way. His long fingers stretched above hers, and his hand showed on both sides, so much broader.

"It turns me on. To feel the size of your hand when you touch me. The way you touch me is…" *Protective.* She paused, not sure how far she wanted to go on this topic. But he had taken a risk when he talked about his scars. It was her turn. She laced her fingers with his and continued. "I've been wary of this appeal since Nick. It also makes me feel vulnerable." She took another breath and let the rest come out. "I broke up with him in a restaurant, in public. I guess somewhere inside, I knew he could be dangerous. But when we got in the car afterward, he wouldn't let me out. He just kept driving, and when we finally got to his house in the mountains, he wouldn't take me back. He told me that I didn't get to break up with him. I was scared, but before things took a turn for the worse, I snuck out. And I ran, straight to the police."

He nodded slowly. "But he wouldn't leave you alone."

"Exactly. He came to my work, showed up at our door." That part was common knowledge at Blackmore Inc.

He was quiet for a while. "You're worried that because you're turned on by someone with physical power, something like that could happen again?"

"At first I was really worried about that," she said quietly, "but I know what happened with Nick wasn't my fault. And I would never be with someone who intimidated me again. Now it's more of a wariness about myself. I don't have the best relationship track record. Is my attraction to big, powerful guys part of the problem?"

He wrapped his hands around her waist and pulled away a little, staring at her, as if he was taking in what she had just said. Weighing it. Finally he took a deep breath.

"I was really hot for you the day we finally met," he said. "But I will never, ever make you feel like this is a risk. Protecting you will always come first for me, but I can see why that could make you feel wary. The moment you feel like this isn't working, I'll walk away. It's your call."

His eyes were intense, and she could feel how much he meant it.

"I wouldn't have told you all this if I didn't believe that, too," she said. She moved her hands over the thick muscles of his biceps. "So I'm just going with it for now."

"I'm glad you are," he said. "I'm still getting my head around the fact that this is really happening. All these things I've wished I was doing with you."

Wished. He had been thinking about this for a while…when it was his job to watch her. The question she had asked herself the day before came back to her, when he mentioned getting off to photos of her. He had had all-access permission to her feed, but when she and Stewart, her ex, had messed around in sight, it had been off-hours.

She licked her lips. "Did you ever watch?"

She didn't have to say more than that. The flare of lust in his intense gaze told her he knew exactly what she was talking about.

"Yes."

"Did you get yourself off when you watched?"

His breath was sharp, harsh.

"Right afterward." His answer was half words, half groan. "I thought about all the ways I'd make it better for you." He paused again. "I'm being honest with you because you should know this. And if it doesn't feel good, we should stop."

She shook her head. "I thought about it, too. I wondered if you were watching."

"And you didn't stop?"

She leaned forward and whispered, "It turned me on. I wanted you to watch."

"Fuck," he muttered. "You thought about me while you were fucking your boyfriend?"

"Yes."

His cock was throbbing in his jeans, moving against her clit.

She scooted back on his legs until her feet reached the floor. She took a couple steps back and then fingered the towel wrapped around her. His gaze was fixed on her hands, so she took her time as she opened it, letting one side fall. Henning's lips parted, and he muttered something under his breath.

"You owe me a piece of clothing." She smiled a little. "Stand up."

Slowly, he rose. Her heart thumped in her chest, and her breath caught in her throat. Damn, he really was a big man. Alya laid the towel in front of her and knelt down on the floor, the bulge in his pants at eye level now. He was so close, and tension radiated from him, but he stood absolutely still.

She reached up to find the button of his jeans and unfastened it. His breath was a harsh gasp.

"Did you ever see me suck him off?" she whispered. A rough noise escaped from his mouth as she pulled down his zipper. "Did you think about what it would feel like to have your cock in my mouth?" A string of curses came next, and, damn, it was hot. "You want to find out?"

"Yes," he groaned. "Fuck, yes."

Alya's heart jumped in her chest. Her body was on high alert, in tune with his every movement. This was the ultimate high, the moment when she knew this guarded, dark man let himself want. And he wanted *her*. Henning was staring down at her with rawness that made her come alive.

His jeans hung on his hips, open, his cock pushing at the material of his boxers. She was so close she could smell the heavy scent of sex from him. God, this man turned her on, and she wasn't going to worry about all the reasons why right now. She looked up at him, into this stormy darkness of his eyes, and all she could think about was the ways to make that storm ride higher.

"I think the next piece of clothing I'll take off is your boxers," she said.

"I see." His eyes narrowed, and his smile was dark. "You like to play dirty? I'll remember that."

Alya laughed. "I'm sure you will."

His smile faded as she slid her fingers under the top of his boxers. His cock was moving, straining against the material, but he made no effort to adjust it. What would he taste like? The cut muscles of his stomach tensed and moved every time her fingers brushed over his skin. She traced the trail of hair down his abs, to his boxers. Then, slowly, she lowered them, taking his jeans, too. Lower. His hands flexed and balled by his side, but he didn't move to help or speed it up, just waited for her, letting her take her time.

His boxers came lower, stretching over the enormous erection buried in his jeans, until finally it came free. His cock bobbed up, close to her mouth. She exhaled, and his whole body shuddered.

"Okay, I'll admit it," she said, smiling. "I like how big your cock is."

His laugh was short, and he brushed his hand over her cheek. "I'll use it to make it good for you. Really good."

God, she wanted to taste him right now, but this man was all about restraint. She wanted so badly to test the boundaries of that restraint. So instead she concentrated on his boxers, easing them down his legs until they were in a pile on the floor with his jeans. She nudged his feet, and he stepped out. Then Alya sat back on her heels and sized him up.

His skin was golden bronze, a little darker on his chest and lower legs from the sun, but also around his cock. Lord, that cock. It was thick and long and hard to the point that it looked painful. He had both the disposition and the body of a warrior—stoic, ready, with those thick, well-honed muscles. It was easy to understand why the police force had its appeal, and she wondered where he channeled all that energy now. Another query for another time. If there was one.

She pressed her hands on his legs, tracing the edges of his thigh muscles, exploring the insides with her thumbs, moving higher, getting a feel for him.

"I've never taken my time with the undressing part," she said. "Usually I just jump right in."

Henning let out a bark of laughter. "Yeah, we're certainly taking our time today."

Alya suppressed her smile of satisfaction. His voice was full of growly frustration, but still he didn't rush her. Her hands came higher, higher, until she reached the juncture of his legs.

"I have to ask," she said, looking up at him. "Have you been tested recently?"

He nodded. "I'm clean. You?"

"Me, too. And I'm on birth control."

He reached out and caressed her cheek with so much tenderness. "We can still use condoms." His voice was so low it was barely there.

She shook her head slowly. "No condoms. I want to taste you."

His hand tensed as she said that, but he let it fall away immediately. "Just tell me at any time if you want to do things differently."

"You, too."

His laugh was a sexy rumble. "I'm pretty sure I'm not going to change my mind about your mouth around my bare cock."

His crass comment together with the undercurrent of tenderness each time he touched her was doing crazy things to her insides. Alya leaned forward and pressed her lips against one of his balls. A string of curses toppled from his mouth, so she kissed the other, using her tongue.

"Your mouth is heaven," he rasped. He smoothed her hair back for a better view.

"You like watching me like this?"

"You know I do."

She moved a little higher, pressing her lips against the base of his cock. A shudder ran through him as she moved higher, licking the smooth skin. Drops of precum gathered at his tip, and she flattened her tongue and licked them. He answered with a heavy groan. His taste, his scent, the softness of his tip, his sounds of arousal—each element of this experience made her hotter.

"Did you ever get yourself off, imagining this?"

"Fuck, yeah. Too many times to count," he whispered. "But the real thing is so much better."

She licked him again from base to tip. Then she wrapped her hands around his base and took him into her mouth. He was big, really big. She tilted her head up. His expression was twisted in a silent balance between agony and pleasure, but he made no sound.

Alya took him in again, slowly sucking his thick cock deeper into her mouth and pulling out. She could see his hands fisted, the veins popping out of his forearms, but he didn't touch her. Did he want to? She definitely wouldn't mind if he showed her what he liked most. Was he gentle, or did he like it rougher? She was pretty sure she could get behind just about anything with this man. Well, almost anything. But for right now, he seemed to be leaving her to explore on her own.

She sat back, aching from the kneeling, though she hadn't noticed just a moment ago. She was so into this. Into him. "I want to learn more about what you like. But right now, I want you to make it good for me."

He helped her up, his hands gentle on her, stroking up and down her arms slowly as she stood in front of him.

"Fuck, Alya, I want you," he whispered, moving his hands up her shoulders, stroking her jaw. "Can you feel how much I want you?"

She nodded. "You're very direct," she said with a little smile.

His intense gaze burned into her, telling her just how badly he ached for her. He bowed his head, resting his forehead on hers. His fingers traced the line of her jaw, then moved down. His hand settled at the base of her neck, callused and possessive, though he didn't pull her closer, just looked at her with his dark brown eyes. This was Henning, naked and wanting her, and finally, she would have him. She touched his face, too, his lips, his scars, the creases in his brow. She parted her lips, wanting him, aching for him.

Alya lifted her hands and wove them into his hair, tugging his mouth to meet hers. His kiss started soft, surprised, but it quickly turned hungry. She pressed herself against him, skin to skin, and his fingers tightened around her neck as he took the kiss deeper. She sucked on his bottom lip and then bit down gently. His tongue stroked in and out of her mouth as he let out a deep rumble from his chest. He pulled back, a dazed look in his eyes.

"Holy fuck," he muttered with a laugh.

He took a step back and sank down on the bed, and she climbed on his lap. They had sat this way before, her straddling him, but they hadn't been naked. Now, she pressed her body against him, feeling the way her skin met his, the way his hard muscles felt as they moved against her. And the heat—there was so much heat coming off him. He settled his hands on her hips, gently stroking her, moving his palms down, over her ass and then back up again.

"You're incredible," he whispered, his voice reverent.

His cock throbbed impatiently, so she scooted closer until his erection pressed up against her. She grabbed on to his shoulders and moved herself up, using him to stroke her clit. She was so wet as she slid against his cock. His fingers tightened around her ass, and he flexed his hips as she moved back down. The sounds of raw pleasure came from both of them as they shifted and moved against each other. When she slid down again, he ground his hips against hers, whispering how badly he wanted her, how hot she made him. Still, he wasn't speeding this up, just stroking her. Like he was waiting for her to make the next move.

She lifted herself up again, but this time, she reached between them and positioned his cock right at her entrance. Then she raised her gaze to meet his. He was staring at her as if she were the only thing in the world that mattered. And in that moment, it felt like so much more than sex, so much that it took her breath away. But she had promised herself to enjoy this feeling, not worry about it, so, slowly, she lowered herself. Her body needed time to adjust, so she eased down just a little bit, then pushed up again.

Henning's hands dug into her hips, but he didn't move, just coaxed her on.

"That's it," he whispered. "Just like that, baby. You like that? Do you want to ride my cock?"

It was the kind of talk she had ached for. His words were making her even hotter, reminding her all the time that he was the one fucking her. Like he didn't want her to forget. She sank lower and lower until finally he was deep inside her. They sat that way, looking at each other. She had never done a lot of talking in bed, but Henning was being so open about how he felt that she just said what was going through her mind.

"Rougher." The word slipped out, and she didn't want to take it back.

Henning let out a desperate groan and thrust his hips up, deep. He let her set the pace, his hands over her, his hips flexing when he was deepest. He grunted but didn't say anything, just let her slide up and down his thick cock as the pleasure built. Over and over, he pressed deeper inside her, lighting up her whole body each time, until she was dizzy. His breaths were coming fast and hot, and a sheen of sweat built on his forehead. She knew he wouldn't let himself come until she did, but he sure as hell felt ready. He was waiting for her.

"You want me to touch you?" His voice was a gravely whisper. "You want me to make you come?"

He said the words like making her come was the hottest thing he could imagine. She nodded, too breathless to speak, and Henning reached between their bodies and stroked her clit. The orgasm crashed through her as she slid down his cock again. He grabbed on to her hips and kept up her pace, as pleasure rolled through her. Then a ragged groan tore through him, and he buried his face into her shoulder as his hips bucked under hers, setting off another wave of ecstasy.

Gasps. Pants. Henning fell back onto the bed, taking her with him. His breath was in her ear, and she closed her eyes and let this be her world. The kind where all this pleasure and happiness was so easy. Where the past fell away, and she and Henning could simply exist like this.

"That was intense," she said after a while.

His chest rose and fell under her. "The good kind of intense, I hope."

She smiled. "The amazing kind."

The kind that will disappear after we leave this place. God, she really didn't want it to disappear. That last thought was clear and strong, and she struggled to tamp it back down.

Unless…could this be more? Or was that the op-

144 HOTTER ON ICE

posite of standing on her own? Alya swallowed. Later. She could think about that later.

He lifted his head and pressed his lips into her hair. She took in the warmth of his body, the brush of his hair against her stomach, his scent that swirled around her, paying attention to every detail, memorizing this moment.

CHAPTER NINE

"REINDEER? SMOKED MOOSE?" Alya wrinkled her nose as she scanned the cold buffet. "Not sure about this."

She took some caviar and lox instead.

Henning eyed her. "Your mother didn't feed you this stuff, too?"

She shook her head. He served himself a taste of both along with two kinds of pickled herring.

"You're really going to eat that?"

"When in Sweden…" The right corner of Henning's mouth twitched up as he gestured to the various dishes and breads and cheeses beautifully laid out on the tables. "Besides, if no one eats the reindeer, then these animals died for nothing."

His tone was low and intimate, for her ears only, but by the time she opened her mouth to make another comment, the humor in his expression was gone. It was the first hint of lightness she had seen in him since they had watched members of the film crew walk into the restaurant, cameras in hand. And it disappeared so quickly.

The rest of the day had been full, with a second

photo session in the Icebar and a relatively painless interview. Dinner with the photo shoot crew didn't sound very appealing, but after eating in their room for the last few meals, Alya decided they should venture out for dinner, not just for her job but for Henning and her. To take the little cocoon of intimacy they had found out into the world, just to see what happened. But the cool, distant expression on Henning's face when they headed out of the room and through the snow had her second-guessing this idea. The moment they left the hotel building, crossing through the cold darkness of the Swedish night to the little restaurant, he was back to being the man who sat next to her on the plane, the impassive bodyguard who was there to protect her with his life. Exactly what he was hired for. Except now, she was watching him, too.

It was clear that he hated the fashion scene. Though his expression was flat, hard, she read every one of his tells: the working of his jaw as industry snark hummed from the tables, the flexing of his large hands at every stray gaze that lingered on her, the narrowing of his eyes when gazes lingered on him instead. Was his aversion to this scene worse now than when they arrived, or was she just more able to read it? Yes, it had all led to some amazing sex, but watching him right now was driving home the point that all of this had a cost for him.

Still, she was also sure he walked into this job with no illusions, so why was his reaction bothering her? What had she expected? That a few incredibly intense encounters would somehow change the world they lived in? She shouldn't even care since this was all over as soon as they left the place, and yet she did.

"You okay?" Henning's rough voice cut into her thoughts.

"Of course." She gave him a real smile, and his expression softened.

He gestured to an empty table in the corner. "I'll be in the back if you need anything."

Alya opened her mouth to protest, then closed it. She didn't *need* Henning. But watching him choose to walk away, to sit in the corner instead of next to her made her insides sink.

Alya frowned. She was here for work, not fooling around with her hot, surprisingly tender bodyguard. This was probably what her mother sounded like, right before she followed husband number two to another country, dragging young Alya and Natasha behind her, letting it all play out in public. Alya hadn't expected the public drama Nick tried to stir up after she broke up with him. With the intensity of the last couple days, she couldn't help but wonder if she was getting on yet another emotional rollercoaster that would somehow end badly. That despite all her efforts to avoid her mother's path, she still kept stumbling back onto those tracks.

But she and Henning were just having a few days of fun, nothing more. She could worry about all these complications later, after she was done with this job.

They still had tonight alone in the Icehotel, plus a little time tomorrow before they got back on the plane.

So she straightened up and made her way to an empty chair at the table with Jean Pierre and two of the other models. She sat down and nodded to them, searching her brain for their names... Audrey and Katherine.

"Saw your interview this afternoon," said Audrey, glancing over at the film crew, just a few tables away. "Nice job dodging the question about Nick Bancroft's statements about you."

Alya rolled her eyes. "Thanks. I knew it was coming, and truthfully, I thought she'd press harder. I'm just hoping that being professional and open with the interviewer will be the best answer to anything Nick said about my *instability.*" She put air quotes around that last word. "But I'll probably get another form of that question tomorrow."

"You didn't respond when she asked about someone new in your life. And she suspected it was me." Jean Pierre laughed. "Which, of course, I didn't confirm or deny."

"Of course not."

Audrey and Katherine laughed, and Jean Pierre shrugged. "It's what they were looking for. Why not?"

"It could have been worse," said Alya. Like if they had instead turned their eyes to Henning, who was doing his best to stay as far away from the camera as possible. He had left the room entirely when she sat down for the interview.

"Change of subject. I heard from the hotel staff that Daxon Miles is coming tomorrow," said Katherine. "He was on some endurance ski trek in Sweden, and now he's heading here."

Alya wrinkled her brow. "Who's that?"

"The hot guy from that YouTube show, Pure Adrenaline, where he cliff-dives and scales mountains—that kind of thing." Katherine smiled. "Hot, single, with *that* kind of reputation."

Audrey laughed. "In other words, Katherine's staying an extra night here."

"Sounds entertaining," said Alya, taking a bite of smoked fish. "You're probably not the only one staying on."

"I can't believe you've never heard of him." Jean Pierre chuckled. "That bodyguard of yours keeping you occupied?"

Katherine looked over her shoulder at Henning, then back at Alya. "I can see the appeal. That brooding, tortured vibe he has going on can make things interesting in bed."

Alya resisted the urge to look back at Henning. She resisted the urge to contradict this one-dimensional view of him, that his scars were about sex appeal, not him. But saying any of those things was as good as admitting the truth: not only were they sleeping together, but she was starting to want more. So instead, she waved off the comment, like it was just another half-serious insinuation. Like he didn't matter to her, one way or another. And it felt like shit to do that.

Alya stopped in front of the doors to the Icehotel and turned around, looking at him with those beautiful blue eyes. The snow was falling in tiny, shimmering flakes all around her. She was so lovely it hurt, but Henning couldn't look away. Her eyes glittered, and her cheeks were flushed from sex after dinner. It had happened, urgent and wordless, as they changed into thermals before putting on their snowsuits. Alya still hadn't spoken more than a handful of words since they left the restaurant, which was fine in his book, but now, as she looked up at him, he could feel that something was on her mind.

"You sure you're okay with sleeping in this place?"

Oh, that. Henning's half-smile tugged at his lips. "I'm feeling pretty relaxed right now."

"Me, too. But that's not what I meant."

"I know." He did. Looking down at her, he drank in the warmth of her expression. "I'm fine."

Surprisingly, he really did feel fine. The shudder of dread that had run through his body the first time the cold wind hit his face was gone. Maybe it was the sex, all that intimacy that was loosening something inside him, or maybe the sharpest edges of those memories of the explosion were finally dulling, but he felt so much better than fine…as long as he kept his mind on this moment. Not the past, and not the future.

Alya's gaze stayed on him for an extra beat, and then she nodded. So he reached for the reindeer antler handle and opened the door to the frozen palace in front of them.

All the cords and equipment from the shoot were gone, and the hallway was silent. Inside, away from the gusts of wind, the only sounds were the crunches of their footsteps on the snowy floor. The tiny lights behind the sculptures shone through the blocks of ice, but otherwise, there were no other hints of civilization except this marvelous creation of ice and snow that surrounded them. There were others from the shoot staying the night in the Icehotel, but even they felt far away. He and Alya were alone.

"You know where we're staying, I assume," he said. Henning had been a little distracted on that first day, when the receptionist gave her the details.

She looked up at him. "Um, I changed our room."

He nodded, waiting for whatever was making her hesitate.

"I had originally reserved a room with separate beds, so I changed it."

"I see." Henning swallowed.

She frowned. "Judging from the look on your face, I should have asked first. But I just thought…" Her voice trailed off, and she sighed. "Sorry."

He gritted his teeth. Time to put aside his own

baggage and be what Alya needed for one more night. He could give her that.

"Don't be sorry," he said softly. "There's nothing I'd love more than to spend the night next to you."

She blinked up at him, searching, but if she was looking for hesitation in that statement, she wouldn't find any. He had spoken the truth, full stop, and if she wanted him close one more time, he was going to give that to her. Besides, he rarely had nightmares anymore. And with Alya next to him, her body against his, the scent of her surrounding him—these sensations had slowly carved a little opening of light into the cave where he had buried himself for years. It would be enough to get him through tonight.

She must have found an answer because she smiled. "Good. Because I switched us to the Viking Room."

Henning tipped his head back and laughed. All morning in that room, he had watched as another man touched her. Even lay with her. All for the camera. But tonight, he would be the one to lie with her for real in that bed. Hell, this woman understood how his mind worked.

"I thought you'd like that," she said, chuckling. "I want to be here with you."

She grabbed his hand, glove in glove, and started down the hallway toward the Viking Room. They stopped in front of the reindeer pelt that covered the doorway.

"Not a lot of privacy in this place," he said, holding the fur curtain aside for her to enter. When she passed by, he leaned in to press his mouth against her neck. "You're not very quiet, you know. That's not at all a complaint, by the way, just an observation."

She laughed. "You're not either. Between that and the layers of clothes we'll need to keep on, I think we're going right to sleep tonight."

Yeah, right. No books or TV or anything else to distract him. And just the idea of her body next to his on the Viking bed was making his cock hard. How the hell was he going to fall asleep?

The room felt bare without the people and the equipment that had filled it earlier. The bed itself stood out in the center, its rounded hull and sea dragon bow rising up out of the snow, as if it were floating. Henning walked over to inspect the setup. The pelts had been replaced with two puffy sleeping bags, zipped together, and when he lifted them he found a mattress on top of a short platform. He breathed out a sigh. Thank fuck they weren't sleeping directly on the ice.

Alya followed him over to the bed and started to unzip her snowsuit.

His eyes widened. "What are you doing?"

"We're supposed to stuff everything except our boots at the bottom of the sleeping bag, right?"

"But that sleeping bag is about zero degrees right now. You're going to need some body heat to warm it up," he grumbled. "Let me go first."

Henning shucked his boots and climbed onto the

ice ship, slipping into the sleeping bag. Once he was
inside, he shoved his gloves to the bottom and then
unzipped his snowsuit, wriggling out of it until it
was at his feet.

"Fuck, it's cold," he said, shivering.

The cold was everywhere, and for a moment, his
muscles tightened, and his breath stopped. A vision
of Sanjay on the floor next to him came without
warning, blood gushing out of his neck, dying right
in front of him. *Hell, no.* Henning was not going to
let this happen tonight. If he just focused on Alya,
warm and safe next to him, he could get through
this. Just breathe in and out. The warmth of his body
began to spread, and his breath came back. *Focus on
this moment, nothing else.*

Henning took off his extra fleece and made it into
a pillow for them both. Then he rolled onto his side
and looked up at her. That flash of dread apparently
hadn't shown on his face, or at least she hadn't seen
it, so he waggled his eyebrows at her. "Okay, baby.
Time to climb in and strip."

Alya pulled off her boots and then slipped into
the sleeping bag. It was a tight fit, good for keeping
the warmth in but not ideal for undressing. Henning
pulled down her zipper, and they moved and shifted
until her snowsuit and gloves were at the bottom of
the sleeping bag, too. Then, finally, they were facing each other.

"You better hope I don't need to use the bathroom anytime soon," she said, smiling up at him. "It's going to be a project."

Henning chuckled and slipped his arms around her, pulling her close, against the warmth of his body.

"Mmm." She sighed, snuggling in. "Very nice."

It was all so good, her soft body, the sound of her satisfaction, the peace of having her all to himself like this, so, of course, his cocked stirred again.

"Ignore that," he grumbled.

"I'll try, but it's what I'm thinking about, too. We need a distraction." She moved against him, and he groaned. "Let's talk."

"I'm not much of a talker under regular circumstances," he said. "And with the most amazing woman lying next to me? I've got nothing."

Her eyes widened, as if his words had taken her by surprise. Then she brushed her lips against his.

"Let's have an AMA session," she said. "Anything is game, and you have to answer truthfully."

"I can ask you anything?"

"Anything."

Well, that was one way to distract him. There were things he'd rather not talk about, but in exchange for being able to ask her anything? Yeah, he could do this.

"I'll go first," he said. "Tell me about when you moved to Los Angeles."

"I was ten and Natasha was eight," she said. "We still spoke Russian together, so we didn't make a lot of friends. My mother's acting career was taking off, and she was caught up in that. All I had was Natasha for a long time. Probably why we're still so close."

He nodded.

"My turn," she said. "Tell me about your last girl-friend."

"Really?" He raised his eyebrows. "Because I don't want to hear anything about other men you've had sex with."

She rolled her eyes. "I just want a better picture of you."

He shook his head. "I've never been good boy-friend material, not then and not now."

"You sure? You've got that big, protective vibe written all over you," she said, stroking his bicep with her hand. "But no diverting the conversation. Tell me."

"Her name was Corinne, and, looking back, I can see I was a shit boyfriend to her. I worked all the time when I was on the AFP, always canceling dinners because something came up. Even when I wasn't working, that's what I thought about. After a while, the only place we got along was in the bedroom." He glanced over at her, gauging her reaction. Her expression was solemn, like she knew what came next. She nodded for him to continue, but this part was the hardest. Henning took a deep breath. "Then, the explosion happened, and I was in the hospital for a bit. She broke up with me. It sounds harsh, but I can't really blame her. The only thing we had at that point was sex, and that wasn't happening while

I was recovering. Plus, I looked like a monster with my stitched-up scars. Romantic, right?"

"Honest," she said. Worry lines creased her forehead, and she opened her mouth like she wanted to say more, but she didn't. Instead, she reached for his injured cheek to stroke it. Henning blew out a long breath, sinking into the comfort of her hand on his skin, just for a moment. But the room was so cold. He moved her hand to his shoulder, under the covers, as he thought through his next question.

"If you weren't modeling, what would you do instead?"

"That's easy. I'd finish my nursing degree." She brushed her hair out of her face. "I'd like to work in the emergency room, I think. There's a lot that happens there, a lot on the line at those moments."

"Why didn't you finish?"

"It cost a lot, and modeling paid instead of cost. And at the time, Natasha and I needed to support ourselves."

She said all of this so matter-of-factly, without a trace of bitterness at being sidetracked from something she had wanted then and still wanted now.

"Do you have any plans to go back at this point?"

"Someday. Modeling isn't really a forever career." She sighed. "Plus I think nursing school will be better when I'm older. There were comments that made me think people didn't take me seriously, just because of the way I looked. They didn't trust me. And then there were doctors who…"

He must have reacted visibly because she narrowed her eyes at him. "Wait—you just asked more than one question, and now you're scowling." She smiled a little. "New subject. I want to know about five years with no kissing but not celibate."

He frowned. "I'm pretty sure you can guess what that means. You sure you want to know more?"

"I do."

He stroked her shoulder and then rested his hand on her neck, warming it from the cold.

"Fine. For a while I went to this…club. And I met some women there. It was just for sex, nothing more. No kissing, no touching." Henning silently begged her not to ask for more details.

Alya's cheeks were flushed, but she kept her gaze steady on him. "And that's generally your preference? Sex with no kissing or touching?"

"That's not my general preference. But under those circumstances, yes, it was."

She lifted an eyebrow. "Those circumstances meaning at sex clubs?"

He hesitated. But he had promised the truth. "Those circumstances meaning after I left the AFP."

"I see," she said. "But you don't go to that club anymore?"

He shook his head.

"Why not?"

"I realized I wanted something else."

"Did you get it?" Her voice was quiet now.

He had promised her the truth, but every version of the truth left something out. Did she already know that she was what he wanted? Maybe it didn't matter anymore.

Henning kissed her on the forehead and held her closer. "Yes. More than what I had hoped for. So much more." She looked up and stared at him, a little stunned, so he kissed her again. "You've gone way over your question limit. Let's go to sleep."

She nodded, her cheek brushing against his chest, her fluffy hat tickling his nose. He shifted onto his back so she could rest her head on his chest. Alya adjusted and then propped herself on her elbow. The sleeping bag fell off her shoulder, revealing the only layer now between her skin and the cold.

"Careful," he whispered, pulling the fluffy down cover up over her, holding it in place. "I don't want you cold."

"You're like a furnace. You'll keep me warm," she said, running her hand over his chest.

Then she brushed her lips over his. She ran her fingers over the scarred side of his face and kissed him again. The familiar desire was still there, but in the warmth of her mouth he found something more, something he wasn't ready to process.

The memory of the kiss lingered as she lay her head on his chest, and he brought his arm around her, holding her and closing his eyes. Even breaths of icy air didn't matter when Alya was warm, pressed up against him. Safe.

As he drifted off, somewhere in the space between awake and asleep, the last of his defenses fell. But for once, it wasn't visions of death that came. It wasn't the gaping hole inside him that he felt, the piece of him that he had left behind on that warehouse floor. It wasn't even lust for the woman who was nestled against him.

It was hope, dangling its sparkling lure, a tempting escape from the dark pool of the half life he had made for himself these last years. He knew what that shiny lure was attached to, knew its promises weren't what they seemed, but right now, it looked better than the waters he was in.

So, for the first time in years, Henning let himself hope.

CHAPTER TEN

ALYA STARTLED OUT of her sleep. Something had awoken her, and her body was on high alert. She was cold, she realized with a shiver. Somehow, the sleeping bag had moved down, exposing her to the arctic temperatures. She lay sprawled across Henning's body, tense underneath hers. One of his hands held her head against his chest, and the other was clamped around her shoulder.

She took a couple deep breaths as relief rushed through her. She was here, in the Viking Room of the Icehotel with Henning. The room was dark and silent, so what had jolted her out of her sleep? She tugged up the sleeping bag and lifted her head to see him.

He was lying on his back. The shadows hid most of the scars along his cheek, but she could see hints of the taut, smooth skin by his mouth. At some point she had read about scars in nursing school, how they could pull and stretch at the skin. Were his painful?

Alya studied him, his face so serious, even in sleep. She tried to picture Henning as a boyfriend, sitting down for a quiet breakfast, reading the news-paper. Not a chance. Had he ever imagined himself on the path the led to a wife, two kids and a picket fence? She just couldn't see that either. Sex? Definitely, but more than that just didn't seem to fit with him.

As she watched, his face drew up into a tight grimace. She sucked in a gasp as a strangled cry of anger and pain filled the room. It was the same sound that had awoken her—she was sure of it—and it came from deep inside Henning's chest. Her body tensed, as his pain echoed through her.

"Henning?" Nothing. She tried again. "Henning?"

His mouth twisted, like she was making it worse. She had to do something. Alya reached out her hand, touching his cheek. He flinched.

"Henning? It's me." She moved her hand along his jaw, down his neck, over his shoulder to his enormous bicep. Then she shook him a little, trying to wake him up.

It all happened so quickly that she didn't remember how he managed it, but in the next moment she was flat on her back. Henning was on top of her, his forearms holding her arms by her sides, her legs trapped between his heavy thighs. The traces of light from the hallway brought his scars into painful relief. He blinked down at her, his eyes unfocused. He squeezed them shut, and then looked down at her again. His eyes widened in surprise.

"What the fuck?" he whispered, more to himself than to her, it seemed.

It took a moment for her to get her voice back.

"You were dreaming, Henning," she said. "I… I had to wake you up."

He was still staring down at her as if he was trying to fit all the pieces of this moment together.

"Alya?" His voice was thick with sleep and confusion.

"Yes. It's me." If she had her hands free, she would have reached up, stroked his face, reminding him of where they were. Reminding him of *them*. But he was holding her down. She tugged her arms, but he didn't move, just stared down at her. Finally he shifted, loosening her arms.

"Alya." Her name was an answer this time, and he said it as if it were the one answer to everything. "You're not hurt. Thank God."

She leaned up to brush her lips against his, and he shuddered, the hard line of his mouth softening. Between her legs his cock grew fast, pressing against her. Heat rushed to her cheeks and a deep groan rose from Henning's chest. She looked up into his intense brown eyes and found a bottomless well of aching hunger.

Her hands were free now, so she brought them to his shoulders, pressing them against the fabric of his shirt. He hissed out a breath, and his cock throbbed against her, but he didn't move. He just looked down at her with a gaze somewhere between wonder and fear.

"I'm fine, Henning," she said, stroking the thick muscles of his shoulders, so tense and hard under her fingers. The air was cold and his body was hot, even through the material of his shirt.

"It was just so cold in my dream. You were so cold. And…" He closed his eyes, and his breaths were long and deep as he touched her bare skin, tracing the planes of her face, as if he was reminding himself of her. As if he needed to remember she was real. His touch wasn't sexual, at least not in the way she expected. He just seemed to want to touch and breathe, to hold on to this moment.

The cold. He had talked about the warehouse, lying on the cold floor, while he watched another man on his team die after the explosion. She was almost sure that's where his mind had gone, even if he didn't say it. That memory was there between them right now.

His eyes were still closed, the fear in his expression just starting to fade. She lifted her head and pressed her lips to his. He didn't move or even kiss her back, but his lips were soft against hers. She did it again.

"Let me comfort you," she whispered.

He shook his head and lifted himself, like he was going to move off her.

She frowned. "You don't want that?"

Traces of hurt came through in her voice, and Henning froze.

"Oh, baby," he whispered, lowering himself over her again. He brought his hands to her face, cupping her jaw as he looked down at her. "I want you so fucking badly right now."

She shifted so her her legs were around his, his throbbing erection against her. "Then have me," she whispered.

"Oh, hell," he muttered, and he drove his hips against hers. She met his thrusts with a tilt of her hips so his cock slid right along her core. Oh, God, he felt so good, his big, hard body over hers.

He stopped, staring down at her, his eyes blazing with intensity. She moved her hands up and down over his biceps, feeling them as they flexed under his weight. She took in this connection, this man who was so many things to her, and tried to put it into words. "Right now, when you look down at me, it makes me feel like you'd do anything for me."

"I would," he said quietly.

"The way you made me feel when you called to check in with me for the last three years—I know it was part of your job, but I can't tell you how important it's been. I had never met you, and the only time you could see me was when I was in my apartment. But it was enough. That was the support I needed for a while." She slipped her hand under his thermal shirt, the warmth of him filling her. "Tonight, please let me give you that feeling you gave me. I want to be what you need right now."

He was still under her hands, as if he was just taking in what she said, so she moved her hand over his shoulder, tracing his scars, then kissed him again. "Let me."

Some people talked while they were thinking, but he wasn't one of those people, she was almost sure. Words were not what he needed. Henning's cock pressed against her, and she tilted her hips, letting him know exactly how she wanted to help him right now.

He rested his forehead on hers. And despite all that she had said, despite all the evidence that he wanted her, she still had the feeling that he was going to turn her down.

"It will be good for both of us," she whispered. "Let me want you, too. Even now."

His erection jolted against her. A heavy breath. Another.

"Jesus," he finally whispered. "God, yes."

The sleeping bag didn't give them much room, but after some shimmying, they were both naked from the waist down. He didn't seem to be in any hurry, and she got the sense that he needed a little time to wrap his mind around this, so she threaded her hands into his hair and let him explore. He traced her body, first over her clothes, and then inside. His rough hand skimmed over her skin, sending shivers through her.

"Fuck, you're so soft," he rasped.

Lower, teasing lower until finally, finally he reached between her legs. Henning groaned.

"You're so wet," he whispered, his voice was full of awe and wonder. "Even right now, you want me."

She closed the distance between their mouths and kissed him. "I want you, just like this."

As those last words left her lips, he guided his cock inside her in a long slow thrust. *Oh, God.* It was pleasure and grief, longing and relief, all in one push as he sank so deep inside her. Their gasps filled the room, but he didn't move, and neither did she. Then Henning positioned his hands under her shoulders, holding her to him, and he pulled out.

Her voice. It had broken through his half-waking nightmare, slow and sultry, changing all the buried memories and fears into something much, much different. Henning gritted his teeth, resisting the urge to fuck away every last vision of the warehouse and the blood and Sanjay's body on the floor, the body that, for one terrible moment, his dream had transformed into hers.

He needed to get that image out of his mind, and fucking was a way to get his world back under control, to clear the slate. But this wasn't some woman from that club, using him as much as he was using her. This was Alya. And he never, ever wanted to use her like that.

"Oh, fuck," he muttered, and he drove his hips against hers, unable to resist. She met his thrusts with a tilt of her hips so his cock slid right along her core. Oh, God, she felt so sweet, her soft, slim body under his.

Her hands moved inside his shirt, slipping down over his bare skin, leaving a scorching trail of heat. She moved her hands around his ass, and he couldn't resist. He thrust his cock against her, and her moan of pleasure was almost unbearably erotic.

He closed his eyes and gritted his teeth to ease the tension building inside him again. If he didn't stop now, he was going to use her. He was no longer moving, and when he opened his eyes, Alya was looking up at him, glaring.

"I decide what I want, not you," she said, like she knew exactly what was going through his mind right now.

He had endless reasons why they shouldn't continue, but she had just given him the one argument that won over all of his. This was going to happen.

"I want to fuck, Alya," he warned. "That's what this will be."

If she was afraid of him, she didn't give any sign of it. Instead, she brought her hand to his face again, and her face lit up with want. "And I want to be the woman you want to fuck."

Henning closed his eyes, trying to contain the last hold on his self-control. "You're so much more. Don't you know that?"

Her nails dug into his skin, and his self-control snapped. In one, hard thrust, he entered her. His mouth crashed down on hers, and he unleashed all his wants and fears in a kiss. Lips, tongue, teeth, anything to have more of her. More. Her hips met each of his strokes, over and over.

"Do I make you wet?" he growled.

"Yes," she cried. "Yes, yes." Her voice was a mix of lust and frustration.

She closed her eyes and moaned.

Over and over, he thrust in and out, and she whispered, *yes*, again and again.

"Is it my cock you want?" He bit out the question.

"I want y—"

He couldn't bear to hear the answer, not right now. So before she could finish, he pushed in hard. The sound that came from her mouth was so beautiful, so full of desire and satisfaction, and it was for him. Christ, yes, it was for him.

"That's fine, baby," he said, holding on, trying not to break. "I'll give it to you whenever you want." He swallowed, the urge to let go warring with the urge to take it slowly, to be careful with her. No, it was better that this happened now, that she understood this other side of him. So he leaned down, taking a breath of her intoxicating scent and whispered in her ear. "But tonight, you're mine."

Her lips brushed the rim of his ear, sending a shudder of pleasure through him.

"Yes, Henning," she said, her voice a heavy rasp. "I'm yours. And you're mine, too."

He turned his head, and she looked at him, her

long, dark lashes low over her eyes. This was all just for him. So he let go. The urge to be rough and selfish was strong, to show her just how broken he was. And he was sure he wore it on his face, a face more beast than human, and the unleashing of this part of him brought the most primal satisfaction. Her cry filled the room, and her nails dug into his skin.

"Henning."

He closed his eyes, drowning in the clusterfuck of emotions that wouldn't stop coming.

"Oh, fuck," he muttered, and she came around his cock, his hips pumping over and over, deep inside her.

CHAPTER ELEVEN

ALYA SAT DOWN on the couch of the hotel's lobby, smiling at the *Behind the Runway* crew, trying to get her head on straight. One guy tested the lighting, and another swept her hair over one shoulder then the other. All she could think about was last night. It had been intense and so incredibly raw. Alya had seen a part of Henning that she had felt, lurking beneath his restraint this whole time. It was a side he tried to bury.

The sex itself had been out of this world, in a category all by itself. That connection, the desperation with which he clung to her, the way he finally let her give when he needed to take, holding her against him so tightly—it made her heart ache. They didn't speak after it was over, but Henning held her against him as he rolled over on his side, his cock still buried deep inside her until she finally nodded off to sleep.

How long did he stay awake? There were no more nightmares, at least none that she was aware of, but when she woke up, she could feel the shift between them. They had crossed a line that they couldn't uncross. Did he regret it? He was gentle with her, so gentle, and he barely spoke. The connection between them hadn't disappeared, but all traces of the playfulness that had bloomed since they had arrived at the Icehotel had withered. She could feel he was letting her go.

All these ideas swirled around in her head as she smiled up at the *Behind the Runway* crew, waiting for this interview. She should be nervous by now. She always was when *she* was in the spotlight, not just a designer's clothing, especially these last few years. But the stomachache that usually plagued her before anything where she was supposed to "just be herself" was absent. In fact, in her interview yesterday, it hadn't been there either.

Alya thought back to Brianna, getting drunk in the Icebar, laughing so freely, daring anyone to judge her. The all-night partying wasn't Alya's path, but maybe another part of it was. She had been groomed for this role for her whole life, her mother's comments laced with warnings about men, backed up by her mother's own real-life cautionary tales. So Alya had carefully constructed her life, her career, her image, knowing that it had to work for both her and Natasha.

But somewhere along the way, their situation had changed. The move to Australia had been a relief, a chance to start over, and it wasn't just Nick she had needed some distance from. Here in Sydney, no one seemed to care who her mother was, and she and Natasha both had found that refreshing.

But still, that fear she dragged around from Los Angeles had clung to her, the fear that she was one public relations disaster away from becoming her mother. She hadn't really understood how much it had guided everything she did.

Before last night, Henning had let Alya lead in the bedroom, so careful around her. Then, last night, the roles had flipped. He hadn't held back, but it didn't just set him free. She felt freedom in it, too, a totally new kind of satisfaction, beyond the pleasure itself. That's what it meant to let go of the past: the space to see Henning more clearly, to understand him, to give to him and to find more in what they could be together. It was the space where all the risks lay, but it was also the space where they could find endless rewards.

Their connection was so strong, right from the moment she'd bumped into him in the Blackmore Inc. office. Was she falling in love with Henning, after just a few days together? Could he love her back? It seemed crazy to ask herself these questions, but she let herself anyway. She glanced at him, across the lobby, his brow furrowed as he jabbed at his laptop. He looked up at her, and his expression softened, but he didn't smile.

The interviewer from *Behind the Runway* signaled her, and the cameras moved in, so Alya turned her focus to them. If there was anything she could say about the documentary crew, they certainly knew how to make her feel comfortable. And talkative. She had no idea how much time passed as the woman led her through topics: the best locations to work, craziest thing someone had said on set and the strangest working conditions. She even talked a little about her childhood, navigating her mother's career as well as her own.

"I was on the path to being a nurse. But…" She hesitated. "There was a lot going on, and it wasn't going to work for both my sister and me to go to college at the same time."

Her mother's career had taken a dive by then. They weren't going hungry by any stretch, but money was tight, even with both Natasha and her working part-time.

"So you took up modeling?"

"I had had some offers before, so I got in touch with an agency."

"You left nursing school behind and quickly became one of the most sought-after models in the industry." The woman added a dramatic pause. "Especially after you got involved with Nick Bancroft."

Alya hated this insinuation the most—the idea, floating out in the press, that her success was somehow hooked to Nick. The insinuation that the relationship could have been a strategic move. Countering that idea was part of the reason she had stayed in that relationship longer than she should have.

She realized she hadn't said anything in a while

because the woman added, "But I'm sure no one wants a rehash of a long-gone relationship here."

The woman sounded like she was hoping otherwise, but Alya just rolled her eyes. "I think that topic has been sufficiently covered in the media."

"You look a lot happier now than in those photos."

She snorted. "That's an understatement. I'm living on my own, traveling again. It's freeing, really."

"And what's next?"

"There are a lot of places I've wanted to visit. I'll be at fashion week this spring, both in New York and in Milan, so I think I'll start there."

As she spoke these words, something loosened inside, something that had been clenched for so long she had forgotten that feeling was there. The worries hadn't disappeared altogether, but she didn't have to let them dictate her life. There were so many things she wanted to do, and she could *do* all of them. She could enjoy all the travel modeling gave her while it still lasted, instead of worry about Nick or how it might affect her career or whatever went through her mind.

And maybe, just maybe, Henning might want to be a part of that life. But if he didn't, she'd still go. That's how she knew she was strong enough to ask him. But first, she had to finish the interview.

Henning had only said a handful of sentences to Alya today, and that was probably for the best. Especially since he had gone from melancholy to mad. Now, he had no idea what he was feeling.

But what the fuck was she thinking in that interview? Laying out her itinerary for anyone to have—including Nick? And then, after Alya had done it, she'd turned to him and smiled the most heartbreakingly beautiful smile, so he shoved all those feelings back down. He had no say in how she conducted her life. He was hired to be her bodyguard, nothing more, and that's what he had to focus on.

Henning had learned to point his laser-like focus at a goal as soon as he grew old enough to understand how things worked for a big man in the world. His body was a tool, whether he wanted it to be or not, and carefully managed, this kind of focus was used for good. But the moment he used it for his own wants and needs, he crossed a line. He had to get through this day without letting out this fierce wave of protectiveness that was threatening to pull him under. He was supposed to be letting her go, and all he could think about was pulling her closer. Especially after last night.

It happened every time he looked at her. Like right now, for example, as she sat in the snow, her cheeks pink from fiddling with her skis. His chest clenched. It hurt just to look at her, knowing this was almost over, so he looked down, fitting his cross-country ski boot into the binding. Then he straightened up, using his poles to balance.

"Need some help?" he asked, glancing in Alya's direction.

She shook her head. "I think I've got it."

"Good. Because I'm not seeing a way to move sideways in these things." He looked down at the long, slim skis attached to his boots. He had surfed and waterskied in his teens, so how hard could cross-country skiing be? It was all on water, more or less.

Alya stood up, lifting her feet, testing the bindings. Then she turned to him and smiled. "I have a feeling this will be a short excursion."

Oh, that smile, tentative but warm, despite how selfish he had been last night.

"I'll follow you," he said, and she started toward the frozen river, leaving him with his increasingly frustrating thoughts.

Somehow, while he slept, she had slipped her hand under his thermal shirt without his notice, and he awoke to find it resting over his heart. It hurt to have it there, hurt that she still reached for him the night before, after the way he had taken, taken from her. But the drive to give her what she wanted was even stronger than the hurt, and so he left it there. Let her wake up like that, let her kiss him wordlessly, all the while knowing that this was the very last time he would lie with her.

Tonight, they'd climb onto one airplane, then another, then another, each taking them farther away from this impossible world, this hotel made of ice— ice, of all things—that had him hoping beyond reason, if only for a night, that a broken man could patch himself together for someone who mattered.

Slowly she reached the enormous river, thick layers of ice covered with snow, and found a set of cross-country ski trails that ran along the near bank, cutting lines through the deep snow. There were four total, probably a set for each direction, but there was no one else in sight for miles, so she made her way onto one set and motioned for Henning to take the other. He fit his skis onto the parallel tracks and came to a stop next to her. His eyes still held heat and intensity when he looked at her—that hadn't changed. But she had seen an edge in that look a few times today, almost as if he was angry at her. And he was really quiet. Even for him.

Henning gestured to the flat, open expanse of snow that covered the enormous river. It was empty and still, and it ran for as far as she could see in either direction. "I don't know about this. We're standing on ice, and I can't stop thinking about what happens if it breaks."

She wrinkled her nose. "Think about how thick the blocks of ice in the hotel were. You said they cut them out of this river. We'll be fine."

His nod was more acknowledgment than agreement. "How far do you want to go?"

"I barely made it here, and it was downhill," she said, gesturing to the river bank. "I'd say I'll last ten minutes on this trail, tops."

Finally, a hint of a smile from him. "Remind me why we're doing this again?"

"Because I wanted to see all this," she said, sweeping her pole out along the broad, white landscape. The move threw her off balance, and she tottered on one ski for a moment before recovering. "At the time, it seemed like the best way to do it, though I'm having doubts."

Henning was definitely smiling now. "Okay. Lead on."

The sky was an ocean of thick, gray clouds, rolling and changing. The heavy darkness of the long winter night had eased into a dim twilight, but the sun was nowhere in sight. Instead, it was the snow that lit this vast world, shimmering and still. The only sound was the wind.

Alya had watched the Olympic version of this sport. The athletes wore some sort of thin bodysuits and raced through the forest. She, on the other hand, was bundled in a bulky snowsuit and moving at walking speed…at best. And she was already panting. She glanced over at Henning, who looked hot as usual and not at all winded, though he looked like he was having as much trouble getting into a rhythm as she was.

Alya stopped, one foot in front of the other, which, of course, threw her off balance again. She clutched her pole, trying to steady herself, but she toppled over into the deep snow between the two sets of tracks.

"You okay?" Henning asked.

"I'm fine," she said, looking up at the sky. "Actually, it's kind of nice down here."

Henning eased himself into the snow right behind her. She looked over her shoulder and found him so close. His gaze dipped to her lips, then back to her eyes, but there was more than just heat in that gaze. So much more.

"We could do this, Henning," she whispered. "For real."

He blinked at her, his brow wrinkling, but then he gave her a wry smile. "I doubt it. I'm a lousy skier, and I'm okay with that."

She shook her head. "I mean us. We could try it."

His eyes widened in surprise, and his smile faded. Then he frowned. She probably should have taken that as a warning, but she didn't. If she just laid it out for him, he'd be able to see how easy it would be to just try. "We'd just do the regular stuff people do when they're dating. We could go out to dinner, go to the beach. I'm going to one of Max's fund-raising events next weekend, and you could come with me, as my date. It would be—"

"No. Stop."

She pulled back and blinked at him. "Why?"

He closed his eyes but said nothing.

"No." Alya gritted her teeth. "You don't get to stay silent. After everything that's happened these last few days, if you don't even want to try, you need to explain. I want you to say it."

"We're both going to regret this conversation." He pulled off his glove and traced her cheek with his warm fingers. Then he swiped a hand over his face, and when he looked down at her, his expression was dark. "This is dangerous, Alya. You saw me last night."

Alya struggled to turn around and face him, but her skis were planted in the snow. She huffed out a breath and pushed herself to something that approximated a sitting position.

"Last night, I wanted you, too. I made that clear."

He waved off her comment, as if it wasn't relevant.

"You want to know what I was feeling when I watched your interview today?" His expression was hard. "I was furious, listening to you list off all the places you'd be next so anyone knows exactly where to find you. All that protectiveness I feel knowing how many men are watching you—maybe I could get used to that. But not you putting yourself at risk. I'm not in any condition to watch you do that."

Goddamn him. They lay there in the snow, dressed in bulky snowsuits in the middle of the frozen river, so they couldn't soften or deflect the conversation with sex. Which was probably better. She had sensed that things were off after the interview, and the more she thought about his reasoning, the more frustrated she was getting.

"You're mad that I wasn't sufficiently scared of Nick to hold back where I'll be traveling this year?"

He hesitated, like he knew this question was a trap but didn't quite see why. "Yes?"

"That conversation was a revelation to me. I've never felt freer," she said. The more she talked about this, the sharper her voice was getting. "But you wanted me to hesitate? To go back to how I felt before? You'd rather I cower?"

"You have to be more careful," he said, anger spilling out.

"So I don't have to worry? Or so you don't?"

Henning's jaw worked, his mouth in a grim line, his scars stark, white against the ruddiness of his skin. "Look how crazy this is making me, after just a couple days. How far will this need to protect you go? Until I smother everything that's good between us?"

God, he had been right. She really regretted starting this conversation. And now she couldn't let it go. "You're already planning out some terrible end for us?"

"It's my job to consider all aspects of a problem, Alya. One of us has to." It was such a low blow, to take her newfound lightness and turn it against her.

"Good news. This problem is about to disappear for you," she snapped back. "I'm officially done with having a bodyguard around."

His face twisted in pain as she said that, and her gut clenched. Shit. She was sinking to new lows, too. What hurt the most was knowing that no matter what came out of her mouth, no matter how terrible it was, he would still protect her with his life.

After that last comment, all the anger seeped out of his expression. He was staring at her with that same, intense gaze, but this time it made her even more frustrated.

"What the hell does that look mean?" she snapped.

At first she thought he wasn't going to answer, but then he whispered, "I'm just looking at you. So I remember."

Alya closed her eyes, pushing away the urge to cry. Because it wouldn't do a thing. So instead, she turned away and tried to get up. Unfortunately, her feet were stuck under her, and she tumbled back into the snow with an undignified plop. Why was she having this conversation with these damn skis on? She rolled around, her skis in the air, until they were pointing in the right direction. Then, using her poles, she managed to get herself upright and standing. Henning was watching the whole time, of course.

"I'll still be there to protect you. That will never change." His voice was soft. "If you change your mind. If you need a bodyguard at that event next weekend. I can…" He paused. "I can come home with you, too, if you want me there."

God, this was torture. He was offering to go back to the way they'd begun this trip. This was his compromise?

"I don't want you as a bodyguard or as a fuck buddy, Henning," she said, looking up at the gray sky. "What makes me angry is that at some point, I

know I'll actually be tempted. But I'm making myself hold out for something better. For someone who
thinks it's worth the risk to fall in love with me for
real."

CHAPTER TWELVE

YOU DESERVE TO be free.

Alya had found the note lying on top of her clothes when she unzipped her suitcase back in her Sydney apartment. Just these five words, written in Henning's blocky script. She had spent an embarrassing amount of time staring down at them for the second day in a row. The painful twist of her gut each time she looked had dulled, leaving room for other emotions churning in her stomach. Warmth. Longing. Desire. But frustration and anger overshadowed all of those.

Why the hell did he write these words to her? Henning Fischer wasn't an impulsive man, so he would have carefully planned these five words, planned the method of delivery, so she wouldn't discover them until after they had parted. She could picture that intense look on his face as he deliberated how to convey what he felt while minimizing his risk. He must have slipped the paper into her baggage when he took it out to the rental car, back at the Icehotel. She could see him, taking off his gloves, exposing them to the cold air he hated so much, just to avoid saying the words to her face.

She had opened the Pandora's box of her heart, and his response was to try to help her shove it all back in. Try to go back to the way she used to be. To the way they used to be. Hell, no. She had had enough of backtracking.

A knock at her bedroom door startled her out of her thoughts.

"It's me," said her sister from the hallway. "Can I come in?"

"Of course." Alya smoothed her hair and checked to see if her cheeks were flushed.

Her sister opened the door, and her eyes went instantly to the paper in Alya's hand. Too late to hide it. "Sulking again?"

Alya sighed. "Maybe."

"I suspected as much. So I brought you the solution to all problems," said Natasha, nodding toward the hall, her eyes sparkling. "Ice cream. Join me?"

Alya's mouth twitched up. "You're making it hard to maintain my sulky frown."

She followed her sister into the kitchen and took a seat at the countertop bar. Natasha took two bowls from the cabinet and headed for the freezer.

"Are you sure you want to go to the fund-raiser alone tonight?" Natasha asked, setting the chocolate ice cream on the countertop between them. "I wish we could all go together, but Max and I have to be there early. One of the many adventures of dating a famous Jensen family member."

Alya narrowed her eyes at her sister. "Did Max get you to ask me about going alone?"

"What?" Natasha frowned. "No. It's just that the event is so public. And after those *Behind the Runway* clips got so much attention…well, you'll be in the spotlight, I'm sure. I know that's not your favorite thing." She pulled out spoons from the drawer and started scooping.

"A week ago, I would have cared." Alya leaned her elbows on the counter and sighed. "Now I'm tired of making my decisions that way, based on my past. I thought it was just about Nick, but it's more than that."

Natasha took a bite off her spoon and nodded. "Explain."

"When we came to Australia, I put my life on hold for three years, shaped it around avoiding Nick." She paused for a mouthful of ice cream. "Staying out of the media, even when it would have benefitted my career, setting up a security camera in our apartment—which, by the way, I took down this morning."

A flush rushed to her cheeks as she thought about the other reason she had taken it down. Knowing that Henning could be watching her—watching but still staying away—was torture.

"Yeah, Max called me about it," said Natasha,

scooping out another bite. "I figured that's what happened."

"And then I let my relationship with Stewart drag out for months, just so I wasn't alone," she said.

Her ex-boyfriend was a male model, not the thin, androgynous type, but bigger, bulkier, with tattoos and scruff. Yes, he was hot, but long before their breakup, Alya had tired of Stewart's endless chatter about protein shakes and bench press maxes. But the lack of connection, the lack of drama had actually been a relief after Nick.

"Well, Henning definitely isn't Stewart."

Alya rolled her eyes. "That's for sure. But I want a different life. One that's not carefully constructed so I can avoid my fears. One where I'm actually living my life."

Natasha smiled. "I approve."

"Aww, thanks," Alya said dryly.

"For the record, I'm in favor of the idea of going alone, as long as you really want that," said Natasha, her spoon clattering in her bowl.

"Me, too," she said. "But the truth is, I miss Henning. A lot. Enough to consider some bad ideas."

"Like what?"

The heat pulsed to Alya's cheeks again. "Last night, I missed him so much that I was actually entertaining the idea of calling him, late at night, for a little pick-me-up. Grabbing at the scraps he offered."

Natasha laughed. "That idea has some pros, you know."

"Yeah, I'm well aware of the benefits." She shook her head. "But I'd be letting him into my life under his conditions. That's been my problem all along. I've been willing to compromise far too much. No. I deserve more than he wants to give. I'm not compromising, just for amazing sex."

Natasha raised her eyebrows, and Alya sighed.

"It was really, really, really good."

Henning stood in front of his sister's door and swiped a hand over his face. Uncles don't miss their nieces' birthdays. If it had been anything else, he would have said no, but he couldn't say no to Molly. Still, Henning stood at the front door of Suzanne and Kenny's quaint suburban home in the sweltering morning heat, unable to get himself together for a five-year-old's birthday party.

Tonight was the fund-raiser, and he wasn't going. He hadn't spoken to Alya since he left her at her doorstep, hadn't even seen her through the security feed. Max was the one who confirmed she had taken down the camera.

The last few days had been hell, alone in his office, sitting at his computer. At Alya's request, he had dismantled other parts of the system he had set in place for her safety over the last three years. He knew it was coming, but he just hadn't expected the camera from her apartment to go away so soon. It was supposed to be the way he could still check in on her, make sure she was okay even if she was keeping her distance.

He thought he would be relieved to get out of the cold, back to the summer heat of Sydney, but he was wrong. Nothing about this week felt like relief.

But nieces still had birthdays, even when the last remnants of his twisted heart were bleeding out. Fuck, he was turning into a sappy bastard. It was time to put himself aside and eat cake and paint his fingernails, or whatever Molly had planned for him.

Henning straightened up and knocked on the front door. Molly opened it immediately.

"Uncle Henning!" The pint-size ball of energy made a running jump into his arms, and he picked her up and swung her around in a circle.

"It's the birthday girl," he said, but his voice came out like it was full of gravel. Christ, how long had it been since he had spoken aloud?

"I saw you standing there in the window," she said. "Mummy said not to disturb you. What were you doing?"

Henning winced. "I was just thinking about…the place I got your birthday present."

It was as close as he could come to the truth.

She was hanging on around his neck, and she pulled back in his arms, her eyes wide. "Can I open it?"

"Of course. It's your day," he said, kissing her on the cheek. He set her down and handed over the present.

"Wait for everyone to see it, Molly." His sister's voice came from somewhere in the house. "Let Uncle Henning come in."

Molly grabbed his hand and tugged him inside. "We're having hotdogs and chips and carrot sticks and marshmallows and apple juice," she said, leading him into the kitchen.

Suzanne was standing at the stove, pulling the hotdogs out of the boiling water. Henning walked over and kissed her on the cheek. "Hotdogs and hot chips. My favorite brunch menu."

"Me, too," said Suzanne, rolling her eyes.

"Me, too," Molly echoed with a little squeal of joy. "I'm going to go tell Daddy and Liam to come downstairs. And then I can open my present, right, Mummy?"

She ran out before the answer came. Suzanne turned around, giving him the older sister assessment. "You okay?"

"Fine," he grumbled, knowing she could see he was so obviously not fine.

Henning sat down at the kitchen table, but Suzanne was still watching him like a hawk. Finally she sighed. "I watched the show."

Henning gritted his teeth. The YouTube snippets from the Icehotel. The footage he had resisted watching all week, knowing there would be glimpses of Alya. Those few days together were captured on film, suspended in time for him to relive, over and over, if he let himself.

"It's Alya Petrova, isn't it?" his sister said softly. "The reason why you went. She's the only one from Sydney, the only one it could be."

Henning pinched the bridge of his nose.

"If that woman did anything to hurt you…"

Henning gave a short bark of laughter. "You'll what? Meet her in the middle of Main Street at high noon?"

Apparently, the role of older sister didn't expire, even into adulthood, because she didn't smile. "She hurt you. I can see it." Suzanne crossed the kitchen and sat in the chair next to him. "I can't believe she did that, not when—"

"Enough," he grumbled. "Not that it's any of your business, but I was the one who messed it all up. Not Alya."

"What?" Suzanne pulled back and stared at him like he was crazy. "What the hell, Henning? You barely leave your apartment for five years, and then you travel across the world just for a woman—and not just any woman but Alya Petrova—and you mess it up?"

So much for the protective sister thing. "Thanks, Suzanne. Great summary of my life."

She shook her head, slowly, her forehead wrinkled. "But why? If you simply weren't into her, then fine, I'd accept that, but I can see that's not the problem."

"*You'd* accept that? Thanks again," he said dryly. "Can we not talk about this, please?"

Thank God Molly ran back in, cutting off their conversation. Kenny followed on her heels, with Liam asleep in his arms. Molly climbed up on Henning's lap and kissed him on the cheek, on his scars. It didn't usually bother him, not from her at least, but the last person to touch him there was Alya.

"Now can I open my presents?"

"You better ask your mum, sweetheart."

The moment Suzanne nodded, Molly grabbed the present, her chubby little fingers tearing at the wrapping paper. She opened the little box and pulled out the tiara. "A princess crown," she whispered, her eyes wide in amazement. "A real one. Mummy, he got me a real princess crown."

Molly put it on her head and scrambled onto her feet, wandering around the kitchen. She turned around and curtsied for her audience. "Did you get it from a castle?"

Henning smiled at her. "No, sweetheart. It's actually from a friend."

"The friend you were with? Mummy showed me on YouTube."

Even his niece knew about Alya? Henning swallowed back a fist-size lump in his throat. "How do you know about YouTube?" he asked, his voice wavering.

"I can do it myself," she said, her eyes shining. "I'll show you."

I can do it myself. Molly's favorite line. He started to protest, but she had already run off. Henning rubbed his temples. Shit. He really did not want to see this video, but how did he explain that to Molly without disappointing her on her birthday? He looked up at Suzanne in a silent plea, but she was giving him a strange look. No, his sister was definitely not going to help him out with this.

Molly returned a moment later with a little tablet, which she laid on the table. She climbed onto his knee and bent over the device, scrolling until she pulled up the video. Damn, the girl could barely read, but she knew how to find videos on YouTube.

"Do you really know how to do that by yourself?" he asked softly.

She smiled brightly, bursting with pride.

And then it was on, and he was back there at the Icehotel. The clip was from inside one of the cold rooms—the beds, the sculptures and even the damn reindeer pelts were all in view. He could see everything, feel everything. He could feel her.

"Mummy and me looked for you, but we didn't see you," she said. "Why not?"

Henning searched for an answer that a five-year-old could understand, but he was coming up with nothing.

Molly had already turned back to the screen. "Here she is, here she is. Mummy said she thought this was your friend."

And then Alya was there. On the screen. It was the day of the photo shoot, and the Viking bed was in the background. The clip started with her laughing at something that was said off camera. God, she was lovely. After spending all those days with her, it shouldn't have caught him off guard, but seeing her took his breath away.

The sound of her laughter hit him hard. The weight of the last few days without her crashed down on him, and his body felt so heavy, too heavy to even move. He was in love with Alya, and he couldn't have found a less suitable match if he had chosen deliberately. This amazing woman was everything he wasn't. Everything he didn't deserve, especially after that last day together.

Molly was expertly skimming through the video until she found a little snippet from an interview. It was from the last day, and he had waited in the lobby instead of following her into where they had set up a makeshift studio. Alya was answering a question about Federov's style, but Henning barely heard a word of what she said. All he saw were those big, blue eyes, those lips, her skin—so soft, he could still feel it under his fingers. He would never stop aching for this woman.

"Is she really a princess?" asked Molly, interrupting this downhill train of thought. "Is she magical?"

Henning felt the uninjured corner of his mouth tug up, despite everything. "Are princesses magical?"

Molly nodded eagerly, her eyes wide.

"Disney," Suzanne muttered, rolling her eyes.

"Is she?" Molly asked again.

Henning nodded solemnly at his niece. "She's not a princess, but I guess you could say she's magical."

"Can I meet her the next time you see her?"

He swallowed another lump in his throat and gave Molly a kiss on the top of her head. "I don't think there is a next time, sweetheart." The words were so painful to say, and he braced himself as the heaviness came back. "But if there is, you can definitely meet her."

Suzanne was staring at him, her lips parted, her eyes wide in shock. Shit, he had to pull himself together. Alya's interview was still playing, and Henning couldn't bring himself to tell Molly to turn it off.

"It must be difficult to have a private life in such a high-profile role," said the interviewer.

"Yes, though my 'private' life hasn't been that private, right?" said Alya with a little chuckle. Damn, she was amazing. She looked so confident, even as the interviewer asked about one of the hardest times of her life. "It's my experience that we don't choose who we fall in love with."

"So how do you manage that balance, the personal and the public?"

She shook her head, smiling. "I don't have any good advice in this department. I tend to fall in love with the wrong person, and it's never a secret for long. But each time, I still hope that we'll get it right."

Suzanne's voice broke into the interview. "Molly, put that tablet back upstairs, please. Uncle Henning has seen enough of that."

His niece frowned in confusion, and she looked like she was going to protest, but Suzanne added, "Now. Please."

As soon as Molly left the room, Suzanne put her hands on her hips. "That woman is in love, and now I'm almost sure it's with you. I saw it. You've got that look on your face like you're going to lose it soon. Explain to me what the hell is going on?"

"It's complicated," he muttered. "It's for the best. Really."

Except it didn't feel that way at all. It didn't even feel complicated anymore. It just felt like shit.

It felt like shit as he ate his hotdog and his pink cupcake and as he played Molly's favorite princess card game, and he felt even worse as he sat in his black Audi on the drive back to his empty apartment. Suzanne and her family were the most important people in his life, and he was spreading his brooding misery to them, too. At least Molly hadn't seemed to notice.

But Henning just couldn't let go of it. Somehow, in this unfair world full of death and sadness, the most beautiful, most amazing woman in the world had wanted him. And he had shoved the invitation to stand by her side tonight at the fund-raiser back in her face out of fear for her. He'd overreacted outside the Icehotel out of fear. Henning sat in his car long after he had turned off the engine, gripping the steering wheel, trying like hell to figure out why he had sabotaged the most beautiful week of his life. Why was he clinging to this fear, even after the threat had faded, still letting it guide him? For the first time in five years, he let himself examine the part of him he had tried so hard to bury.

He hadn't felt fear when he walked into that warehouse with Sanjay; it was one of the reasons he had quit the AFP. Instead, he had calculated the risk of going in early, just the two of them, and assessed it as the best option. If he had held them back, acted out of fear, would that have saved his teammate? Maybe, or maybe the explosion would have happened when the whole team came into the building. Maybe even more of his team would have died. Still, lying in the hospital bed in the days after the explosion, he had wondered if that absence of fear meant something was wrong with him, if years of seeing the very worst of people had turned off something fundamentally human about him.

But at Blackmore Inc. he had felt fear for Alya. It was the reason he had been so drawn to her, long before their days at the Icehotel, and the reason he had gone so far beyond the parameters of his job. It wasn't just about making her feel safe. His fear for her had let in a sliver of hope that his years on the AFP hadn't permanently damaged him, that there was a chance he could be whole again.

Which made him feel even more messed up about his blow-up at her about giving away her schedule. Had his reaction been so fucking selfish? He didn't truly want her to cower, just so he could get another hit of that deep-seeded need to protect her, to remind himself that he was not just a cold strategist in a man's body. And, yet, out on that frozen river, that's exactly what he did. He had dumped all her fears back on her.

As Henning closed the door to his apartment, he couldn't shake the sound of Alya's voice. He leaned back against the door as whispers of her fingers played across his skin, over and over, setting him on fire. His willpower was slipping at the memory of how she looked at him when she touched him, her breaths teasing him.

That memory led to others, taking him down the road he was trying so hard to resist. Now that it was here, he didn't stop it. Just once more. Just one moment of weakness, so he could remember what it felt like. The sounds she made as he thrust deep inside her, his cock unbearably hard and aching, holding on until she came.

Fuck. It was too much. This was why he shouldn't even see her, despite the way Suzanne had stared at him like he had his head up his ass. Because as soon as she came close, he wouldn't want to let her go again. And he shouldn't take another step into her life unless he was sure he could give her what she deserved: love, not fear.

Still, she was alone tonight, and he needed to know if she was all right. Maybe Max would be willing to send him an update. Just to make sure.

Henning swiped a hand over his face, picked up his phone and dialed Max's number.

CHAPTER THIRTEEN

"WE'RE HERE, MA'AM," said the driver, peering at Alya through the rearview mirror.

She swallowed. "Just give me a minute."

He nodded. "Of course."

Alya took a few yoga breaths, her usual preparation for stepping out of the car before an event, preparing to face looks or judgments or whatever came her way.

But just like at the Icehotel, when she waited for the interview, the usual twist-in-the-gut feeling was conspicuously absent. In fact, that little flutter of nerves in her stomach was surprisingly invigorating. It was refreshing to step out knowing that whatever went through the minds of everyone who was watching, it didn't change anything, not really. All along she had thought that not worrying about what others said about her meant the kind of recklessness that really had never been her style. But for her, it was something else. It was putting aside all her fears and looking forward. Not backward, not to the side.

Anything involving Max Jensen and his family—

who were like royalty here—attracted the Australian press, and this fund-raiser was no exception, which made it a great place to test her resolution to just relax and look forward. She was ready to enjoy the night with her sister and Max and the rest of the Blackmore Inc. group, off duty. Alya took out her compact mirror and checked her lipstick once more. Cherry red, as Natasha had called it, to match her dress.

Her lipstick was in place. Her hair was woven into an intricate knot on her head, exposing her neck. The pearl earrings and necklace gave the whole outfit a classy look, and all the red said sexy. It was the kind of look designers might dress her up in, but she never picked it out herself. Until today. Let the fun begin.

"I'm ready," she said to the driver. He climbed out and walked around the car to open the door for her.

Sydney's hot summer air poured into the car, along with a cacophony of voices and music. Bulbs flashed and the crowd moved as she stepped out into the late-afternoon sun and onto the red carpet. Alya hesitated, even looked back for a moment, instinctually searching for someone's hand to grab, someone who would make her feel less exposed. No. She was doing this on her own. The first times would tug on her vulnerabilities, but she'd learn. There was no way to move forward without risk. She had condemned Henning for not being willing to take risks, so it was time for her to step up her own game, too.

Alya held her head high and walked forward, ignoring the questions that were coming from all sides.

"Everyone has been talking about your *Behind the Runway* interview. Can you comment on who is the source of your thoughts on falling in love?"

"Who are you hoping to get it right with?" called another voice.

"You were seen talking intimately to Jean Pierre Rus. Can you comment?"

"Nick Bancroft posted about the flowers he sent you on social media. Are you two back together?"

She almost rolled her eyes at that last one. Of course Nick was going to find a way to make this about him. She took long strides to the circular part of the carpet, pausing there, turning for the cameras.

"No matter what I say, you'll probably come to your own conclusions," she said, smiling mischievously. "So, no comment."

Was it really so easy? Of course, she had answered questions with *no comment* for years, but still, the insinuations had lingered, each a new bite of insecurity that tore at her, deep inside. All this time, she had cared what they thought. But today? It was…fine. The speculations were so far from the truth, and if she told anyone the real story of her and Henning they wouldn't believe her. She had taken a risk for a man, he had offered her less and she had decided she wouldn't settle. So simple, and yet it was everything.

Alya smiled at the cameras one more time, and then walked into the entryway. The first portion of the event was an open-aired affair, on an enormous patio right on the harbour, lined with colorful flowers. Giant sails sheltered portions of the patio from the sun, and the guests gathered around standing tables under them. A passing server offered her a glass of champagne, and she took it, scanning the place for familiar faces. Max and Natasha were here somewhere, maybe talking with donors. The rest of the Blackmore Inc. team, whom Alya had met over the years, would show up with their partners at some point, but at the moment, Alya didn't see any of them.

She did see the society columnist for *Luxury*, one of the many magazines where Alya's private life occasionally had entertained the readership, despite all her efforts to avoid it. Nathaniel Woods. Over the past three years, she and Natasha had come up with coordinated plans to avoid him at events like this, but tonight, she walked straight up to him.

His eyes showed a hint of surprise, but he kissed her cheek and smiled. "Alya Petrova. You're voluntarily talking to me?"

Alya laughed. "I know. Can you believe it?"

"You look lovely," he said, and his smile was warm. He asked about the Icehotel, Federov's collection and her plans for the spring, and they chatted about other Sydney events. The more they talked, the more she felt her confidence growing. Whatever he ended up writing, she could handle it.

But just as he was leaning in to kiss her on the cheek again, Nathaniel froze.

"Just FYI…" He cleared his throat. "There's a

very…distinct-looking man staring at you intensely. He's quite large."

Alya's heart jumped. No. It couldn't be. Probably another one of the Blackmore Inc. guys. Henning had probably checked in with someone in the office to make sure they'd be there, just to make sure she was safe.

Still, she hoped. Damn, Alya had spent the week hoping. Wasn't she done with it? If she turned around now and it wasn't Henning, that was probably the one thing she couldn't handle in front of a crowd.

"Aaaaand he's coming this way," added Nathaniel. "I don't suppose you know who this is."

"I might."

Okay, she could do this. Just hold it all in. She had years of practice controlling her feelings, and it was time to put that experience to use. Her heart pounded harder in her chest, and she took another yoga breath, this one completely useless. Then, slowly, she turned.

"Henning?" She whispered his name as he stalked across the patio. She blinked, taking him in. He'd gotten a haircut, and he was wearing…a suit? In fact, he looked a lot closer to the cadet photo she'd found of him online, the one before the attack.

"I'm getting the *time-to-leave-us-the-fuck-alone* vibe from him," said Nathaniel quietly. "Strongly."

"That's about right."

Was this real? Henning took a few last steps and stopped in front of her. Alya's heart was pounding so hard she was sure everyone around them could hear it. She reached out to touch him but pulled her hand back as her mind kicked into gear. This was the man who had shot her down, and now he just showed up? Did he expect her to welcome him, just because he changed his mind?

She swallowed a lump in her throat and straightened up. "What are you doing here?"

"I'm here to say I'm sorry," he said softly, his voice was raw, vulnerable.

Her heart stuttered. Oh, damn. She was so in love with this man. And he had the power to hurt her. She looked around, and sure enough, no one was hiding their curiosity.

She gestured to Nathaniel. "Henning, meet Nathaniel Woods, columnist for *Luxury* magazine."

Henning tipped his chin in Nathaniel's direction. "I'll be reading your column for the next six months to make sure this moment doesn't end up there."

Alya raised an eyebrow. "Unless that's what I want."

"Unless that's what she wants," echoed Henning in a low grumble.

Nathaniel smiled a little. "Well, I think that's my cue to duck out of this conversation."

He kissed Alya on the cheek and walked away.

For a moment that impenetrable mask was back on Henning's face, but then he took a deep breath, relaxing, letting her see the longing in his eyes. It was painful to see. He looked like he'd been just as miserable as she had been since they returned from

Sweden. His fingers flexed. Did he want to touch her as much as she wanted to touch him? If so, he held back.

"I messed up," he said, his voice rough, "and I don't know how to make it right. I have no experience with this. But I promise I'll figure it out."

Alya scanned the patio, taking in the other guests who surrounded them. The closest were in listening distance, and she caught a few more furtive glances their way.

She looked back at Henning and frowned. "You want to do this right here, in front of everyone?"

His jaw was clenched, and he looked like he was in the middle of some sort of internal debate. Then he closed his eyes and swallowed. "I don't. I'll leave if you ask me to."

Alya blew out a frustrated sigh. She was still so mad at him, but, Lord, she had missed him. Tearing out the security cameras had felt like tearing out a whole piece of her, the last connection between them, forged during the most difficult years of her life. He had been there all along for her, and she had gotten over her fear slowly, so slowly, with so many missteps. Yes, he was allowed to have missteps, too, but this one seemed to scrape against her rawest wound. She knew all of these things, and yet Alya wasn't ready to ask him to leave. At least not yet.

The longer she mulled this over, the more that look of intense determination settled into Henning's expression. He opened his mouth to speak again, but she held up her hand. "Wait. Let's go somewhere else."

He nodded, looking a little brighter. Had he expected her to turn him away today? And he still came?

She scanned the area, looking for someplace with a little more privacy. There weren't a lot of options completely out of sight, but the guests were mostly clustered in the shade of the enormous sails, so she nodded over to the sunniest corner, where at least they would be out of ear range at the far end of the patio. It was lined with a white pillared railing that looked out onto Sydney Harbour, decorated with a few large plants in terra-cotta pots. Alya headed for the shade of a planted palm. Henning's hand brushed the small of her back as she walked, and for a moment, it felt as if they had rewound a week. They were so close. But his hand dropped almost immediately. They weren't at the Icehotel anymore.

Alya found a little nook behind the fronds of the tree. She hadn't spotted her sister yet, but if Natasha was watching, she was probably trying to get a better view. Max, too, and maybe even the whole Blackmore Inc. group. But right now, she needed a little space from the world.

She turned around to face Henning. He had wedged himself between the plant and the railing, and one leafy frond batted at his head. He brushed it away and looked down at her, the dark intensity of his eyes heavy. No one in the world looked at her like this, like he would get down on his knees for her, give her anything. The ache of their separation echoed between them, back and forth, turning her insides molten-hot, but she resisted reaching for him. Instead, she crossed her arms.

"I still haven't decided whether you should stay or go," she said. "You have five minutes to explain to me why letting you stay would lead to anything else besides heartbreak. For both of us."

He nodded, then drew in a deep breath. "I hurt you, and I'm so sorry. I've spent the last week thinking about it. You pulled security, taking me out of your life. And it's been hell."

She could hear this was painful for him, too, and she had to resist the strong urge to comfort him.

"It wasn't about you, Henning." Well, that wasn't quite true. She swallowed, pushing herself to continue. "Okay, maybe it was a little about you, but mostly it was about letting go of a past that I have to put behind me. All the way."

He didn't speak, but she could feel he was completely tuned in to everything she said, each movement of her lips.

"I need more than a protector, Henning. I need someone who will support me as I change my life to something that I want. Something that I love."

"You deserve that, Alya," he said roughly. "You deserve everything."

His words quaked through her, filled with emotion. He brought his hand to her cheek and traced her lips.

"I've spent the last five years with Sanjay's death

hanging over me," he continued. "What would happen if I lost you? Just that thought makes me want to hold you so tight, to make sure nothing ever happens to you." He closed his eyes and let out a long breath. "There's a part of me that's always going to want to protect you. But I need to deal with it in another way. This is my shit that I need to address, and I'm willing to do it. And if you need to wait for that change before we see each other again, then I respect that. I just wanted you to know that I'm choosing love over fear, starting right now."

Oh, God, this man. Just seeing him again felt so good, so right. He was promising her he'd work on this.

"I don't want to wait, Henning," she said quietly.

The intensity of his expression didn't waver. "There are parts of me that are broken, that might never get fixed."

She lifted her hand to trace the jagged scars down the left side of his face.

"That's what I thought about myself for so long," she whispered.

Henning smiled, really smiled with all the warmth and tenderness she had missed. His scars pulled on the left side of his mouth, making the smile all that more vulnerable.

"Can we please figure this out together?" he whispered.

God, she wanted that. Alya took a deep breath and nodded. His arms came around her, and he held her close as she slipped her hands under his jacket, against the hard muscles of his back. She wanted to stay here, just like this, resting her cheek against his chest, and she probably always would. But they needed to finish this conversation.

"Staying here with me means we'll both be in the spotlight, starting now," she said, pulling back a little. "Everyone watched us walk over here, and if you hold me like this and look at me like this, people will take photos and write about us and make all sorts of speculations about why we're together. They'll dig up the story of your scars and lay it out for everyone to comment on. If you stay, we're saying yes to all of that. Even if we go our separate ways in the future, you won't be able to take that back. Are you willing to do that?"

His broken smile was full of hope. "You're worth that risk. You're worth everything. I'm willing to show you that, again and again. Tonight or any other night." Then he raised an eyebrow. "And if I have my say in this, we're definitely not going our separate ways. You're the only one I've wanted for so long now, and that's not going to change."

She closed her eyes and let the words sink in. He was here. This was real. She looked up into his deep brown eyes, and she had the strong urge to kiss him, to remember all the things she had learned about him back at the Icehotel. Was he right, that what they had between them wouldn't change? God, she hoped this would last forever.

She threaded her fingers into his hair and tugged a little, urging his mouth down to hers. It was a soft, slow kiss, making her insides melt and her heart skitter in her chest. There was nothing hesitant about it. She put aside the cameras and the whispers and everything else, and she kissed him again and again. It was so freeing to simply kiss this man she was in love with, right here, for the world to see.

"I don't think the palm is hiding much," she said with a little laugh. "By the way, how did you get into this event?"

Henning smiled. "It started with a call to Max. I asked if he'd check in on you and to get back to me. But he told me no, straight up. If I wanted to know, I had to come myself. So I told him you didn't want security, and he said, 'looks like you've got a problem on your hands.' Next thing I knew, a courier delivered a ticket to my house."

She could picture his expression as he opened that envelope, struggling with what to do. "How long did you sulk at home before you decided to come?"

"Only five hours or so," he said with a grin. "Half that time was spent going through scenarios if you had brought a date, figuring out how to deal with that."

"What did you come up with?"

"Nothing you want to hear about."

She laughed. "Lucky for you, I came alone."

"Lucky for me," he echoed.

Alya found Henning's hand and laced her fingers with his. "You ready to get out from behind this tree?"

"I'm willing to try just about anything, as long as it's with you." His voice was soft, that gruff, gentle rumble she had missed so much this week, so she squeezed his hand, and together, they walked into the crowd.

Henning looked down at the loveliest, most amazing woman in the world. Somehow, he was the one holding her hand right now. Love, not fear. It was the answer to everything, really. "Where are we going?"

"To find Max and Natasha. And I think the rest of the Blackmore Inc. crew is here, too," she added with a mischievous smile.

Henning raised his eyebrows, and then started to laugh. He just let himself go, laughing and shaking his head. "Is this a test? Right in front of all the guys I work with."

"No backing out, right?" She kissed his hand. "But no, it's not a test. I told Natasha I'd come find her right away when I arrived. She's been a little worried about me this week."

Her sister had been worried about her. His smiled faded. "It was a hard week?"

She nodded, and, fuck, it was painful to see it all over her face.

"I hurt you," he whispered. "I'm so sorry."

She bit her lip and nodded.

He slowed to a stop and lifted his hand to her face,

resting it on her cheek. "It was an awful week for me, too, if that's any consolation."

"Maybe a little bit." Her lips twitched in a hint of a smile. "But I guessed it would be. I just didn't think you'd do anything about it."

He slipped his hand to the base of her neck and pressed his lips against hers. "But I did."

He wanted to stay like that, holding her, kissing her, but there would be time for that later. So he let her go, and they walked across the patio, decorated with flowers, toward the French doors that led inside. There was plenty of open staring at him as he and Alya wove their way through the crowd hand in hand. He could feel the gazes that traced his scars, then dropped to his hand that covered hers. It would probably always be like this, but as long as it didn't hurt Alya, he didn't care.

They were about to go inside when Natasha walked out alone. Her mouth fell open the moment she caught sight of them.

"I can't believe it," she said, her brow wrinkled.

Henning cringed. Shit. Alya told her sister everything, which probably meant Natasha hated him at this point. The last thing he wanted was to upset either one of them again. But Alya squeezed his hand, reminding him that he wasn't alone, that they were in this together.

Then Natasha broke into a smile. "I've got to go tell Max I lost the bet." Natasha wrapped her arms around her sister's waist and kissed her cheek. "But you look so much happier than you did all week, so I guess I'll get over losing it."

A little relief flooded in, and Henning let out his breath. It was going to be okay.

Natasha gave him an assessing look. "Henning Fischer?"

He nodded, kissing Alya's sister on the cheek.

She smiled. "Come on. We're all inside, out of the sun."

Natasha led the way across the open room, to a lounge area on the far side. But Alya slowed to a stop at the entrance, letting Natasha go ahead. The voices of the other Blackmore Inc. men echoed in the room. Henning squeezed Alya's hand.

"You okay?" he whispered.

But when Alya turned around, her face was lit with a smile of pure happiness. "I'm so much better than okay." Her blue eyes sparkled and danced as she looked at him.

"Only you, Alya," he whispered, brushing his lips over hers. "That's all that matters."

She stood on her toes and kissed him back, her mouth soft and warm. After days apart, the fire between them sparked and sizzled, almost irresistible. But this was so much more than attraction. This moment was a dream he had never allowed himself to hope for.

"Thank you for coming, Henning," she said, her voice serious.

"I'll always come for you."

Always. A word he hadn't believed in for so long. Until Alya.

Then, slowly, they entered the lounge. All the Blackmore Inc. principals were seated around a low glass table. Derek Latu and his wife, Laurie, were on one side of a long sofa. Derek and he grew up together, and he was the reason Henning had come to Blackmore, Inc. after he left the AFP. Right now, his friend's gaze moved between Alya and him, and his smile was wide. Jackson McAllister leaned against Cameron Blackmore's chest on the other side of the sofa. When Henning started at Blackmore Inc., if anyone had told him the CEO would fall head-over-heels in love, enough to chase a woman halfway around the world, he would have laughed. Then again, the same could probably be said about Henning. But seeing Cameron and Jackson gave him another surge of happiness. Cameron had made mistakes, and they were still together. Marianna Ruiz and Simon Rodriguez were there, too, squashed together on an oversize chair, Simon's arm draped over his fiancé's shoulder, holding her close. Their story began years ago, back in Miami, and it was another testament to the resiliency of love.

"I told you he'd step up," Max said from the far sofa, tugging Natasha onto the cushion next to him.

"You bet on my relationship with Alya?" grumbled Henning, but he couldn't hold back his smile.

Max smirked. "Hey, I bet *for* you. Natasha was the one who bet that Alya would turn you down."

Natasha turned around and swatted at him. Then she turned back to Henning. "I was just looking out for her. Nothing personal."

"I appreciate that," he said. "I messed up."

"See why I bet on him?" said Max. Natasha rolled her eyes as she shifted closer to him.

"Come sit down for a bit," said Simon, gesturing to the open spots on the far sofa. "You two need a drink?"

Alya looked up at him, and he shook his head. They had just found each other again, and he wasn't quite ready to share her. But if that's what she wanted...

"Not yet," she said. "I think I want to go down to the beach for a bit before dinner."

She winked at him, and Henning slipped his arm around Alya, breathing in the scent he had ached for all week long. Alya chatted with the others for a few more minutes, but he wasn't following the conversation anymore. The air was warm, and the breeze blew gently through the open windows. And Alya was there, so close. It was a heaven Henning had never believed in, but tonight, for the first time, he knew it existed for real. This was all he needed.

* * * * *

SLOW HANDS

FAYE AVALON

MILLS & BOON

For Dad: my very first hero

CHAPTER ONE

'You'll DEFINITELY BE needing a lawyer.'

April Sinclair's initial relief at having finally confessed her predicament to her best friend turned sour as Lizzie's mouth twitched.

'For pity's sake. It isn't funny.' April glanced around the crowded café, thankful that their conversation had seemingly failed to attract the attention of other patrons. 'I'm starting to think I'm the only one taking this seriously.'

Lizzie battled to keep her face straight. 'It is pretty funny.'

'Sadly, most of the lawyers I've approached share your view. They either fall off their chair laughing or look at me as if I'm running a bordello.' April drummed her fingers against her coffee cup. 'Maybe I'd see the joke if my business wasn't on the line.'

'You should tell the woman to piss off and stop bothering you with her idiot claims. Stupid cow. She'd be better off asking herself why the only way she can get her prurient needs met is via a piece of plastic.'

'Shh!' April looked around again before lowering her voice. 'Veronica won't back down. I've tried reasoning with her, but she won't budge. Why would she when she's been waiting years to get back at me? I played right into her bloody hands.'

'She won't go through with it. She's winding you up. Making you sweat.'

'Well, mission accomplished, then.'

April knew that Veronica Lebeck was not only capable of going through with her threats, but that she'd absolutely relish making April squirm. Back in her modelling days April had experienced Veronica's spiteful ways first-hand. Catwalk rivalry, the spreading of vicious rumours, garment tampering... And, of course, there had been the whole Richard thing. The woman was relentless when it came to her own interests, and she courted publicity as if it was going out of fashion.

'Don't lose sleep over it,' Lizzie advised as she picked up her coffee. 'Even if she does carry out her threat, your insurance will cover any costs.'

With a hard swallow, April looked her friend square in the eye. Showtime.

'Well, see...that's the thing. I don't have any insurance. The policy hasn't been renewed.'

Frothy latte midway to her lips, Lizzie froze. '*Please* tell me you're joking.'

Why the hell had she chosen to confess all to Lizzie in the middle of a crowded Covent Garden café? Her friend wasn't known for her shy and re-tiring ways.

'It got overlooked while I was dealing with my dad's estate. And, before you say it, I know it was stupid and I'm an idiot.'

Eyes fierce, Lizzie put down her cup. 'You're nei-ther. But I thought Rotten Richard was dealing with your business paperwork while you were up to your ears in funeral arrangements and sorting your dad's affairs? Don't tell me he screwed that up on top of everything else?'

April shrugged. She wasn't planning on revisiting that time. She'd put her ex into a box and shoved him, and the whole pitiable episode, into the cobwebbed recesses of her mind. At least she'd thought so until Veronica's threatened claim had required that she check out her insurance policy.

'Bloody hell.'

Lizzie stared across the table at her, and the con-cern in her friend's eyes made April's stomach spin. When Lizzie was worried there really was something to be alarmed about.

'You're definitely going to need legal advice.' She picked up her bag and dug for her mobile. 'And I might just know where you can get it. Miles men-tioned this guy who handled their CEO's divorce case. A real hard-ass, by all accounts. High-profile. High success rate.'

That sounded like music to April's ears, but since Lizzie's current squeeze worked for an international pharmaceutical company, April couldn't imagine a lawyer of such standing would be at all interested in giving advice about her predicament.

'I've already contacted just about every lawyer in the book,' she said as, undeterred, Lizzie tapped the keypad. 'I really can't see this one chomping at the bit to take me on.'

Lizzie waved that away as she brought the phone to her ear. 'He gave Miles his card after he did him a favour. Let's see if Miles can work his magic and get you an appointment.' She turned her attention to the phone at her ear. 'Oh, hi, sweetie. You know that lawyer you helped out…?'

Walking into the foyer of the eight-storey office building located on London's Chancery Lane, April reminded herself that she was out of options. She'd checked out Logan Fitzpatrick on the internet and he was most definitely going to laugh her out of his office. Lizzie had said he was high-profile, but she'd failed to mention that he'd handled prestigious cases involving politicians and celebrities, his successes ensuring that he was now pretty much a celebrity himself.

Ignoring the nauseous roll of her stomach, April went through the security booth and over to Reception. She gave her name and was directed to the sixth floor. Stepping into the elevator, she pushed the relevant button and seconds later exited into a long hallway with polished black and white floor tiles and monochrome prints decorating the walls. The only colour came from the scattering of plants and potted palms strategically placed along the space.

A woman with spiky brown hair emphasising a pretty heart-shaped face came to meet her. She smiled and reached for April's hand. 'Ms Sinclair? Come this way.'

April followed her to the end of the hallway and into a huge waiting room containing two massive white leather sofas.

'Mr Fitzpatrick is running a few minutes late. Can I offer you coffee while you wait?'

Hell, no. She was hyper enough already. 'I'm fine. Thanks.'

'Take a seat, then. I'm sure he won't keep you waiting long.'

When the woman had left, April took the opportunity to look around. It was all very smart and sophisticated. Minimalist, almost. She shifted a couple of deep orange cushions and sank into the sumptuous leather. Absently, she selected a magazine from the glass coffee table and flicked through it. Seconds later she popped it back on the table. It was fruitless trying to concentrate when she felt so wired.

How had things gotten to this? When was the moment she'd screwed up so badly? She'd thought she had it all worked out. Leaving London to care for her father, creating an online business so she could work from home and be there if he needed her, building that business into something she was proud of...

The strange thing was that although she'd chosen it as a stopgap, until she could return to London and resume her modelling career, she'd soon realised that she loved her online venture. Since returning to London several months ago she'd worked hard to rebuild her business after Richard had almost destroyed it, and now it was going from strength to strength. She'd been able to diversify, had garnered some prestigious link-ups with fellow entrepreneurs, and was slowly building trust and recognition amongst her growing list of customers.

Now all that was in jeopardy because of one bloody oversight. Thanks to Richard. Not that she could blame him entirely. It was her own fault for allowing him control—and not just of her business, but of her, too. She'd trusted him, handed the reins of her life to him.

Maybe she could console herself that she'd had reason to do so at the time, but that was really no excuse. Not that it would ever happen again. She'd learned a huge and valuable lesson from the whole debacle.

The woman returned and held out a glass. 'You look like you could use this,' she said as April accepted the water. 'Try not to worry. I'm sure he'll help if he can.'

If he can.

That was the crucial question.

Since she hadn't been required to divulge the nature of her business, beyond the fact that she was seeking advice on a potential litigation matter, April knew the woman wasn't aware of the reason for her appointment. That was unless Veronica had decided to go ahead with her threat, had procured herself a lawyer, and word had got around. Like most professions, law was probably an intimate world, and lawyers' dinner tables undoubtedly rife with humorous stories of client predicaments.

She could only imagine what kind of reaction her story would get were it shared amongst the legal profession. Not that she had anything to be embarrassed about. She ran a legitimate successful business. And she would do everything in her power to make sure that continued.

When a buzzer sounded, April was treated to another encouraging smile. 'He's free now. I'll show you in.'

The woman took April's glass and tapped lightly on the door. Without waiting for a response, she pushed it open and stepped back so April could enter a large corner office overlooking London's impressive skyline.

One glance at the man leaning against the front of the battered walnut desk and April was tempted to grab for the water again. There was no mistaking this was the man she'd come to see. He owned the space, filled it, swamped it. Confidence seemed to ooze from every pore. Okay, she'd seen photos of him while doing an online search, but in the flesh

Logan Fitzpatrick was formidable, and absolutely not what she'd been expecting.

Ruffled dark brown hair flirted with the open collar of a crisp white shirt—and the latter was the only lawyerly thing about his appearance. Dark jeans, a wide leather belt with a buckle that looked like some sort of Celtic knot, and battered leather boots. What looked like a full day's worth of stubble barely disguised an impressively square jaw, and beneath the slash of thick dark eyebrows shrewd blue eyes appraised her as she stood in the doorway.

His gaze didn't shift from hers as he thanked the woman, who popped April's glass on his desk. April stared back, and would have swallowed, but her mouth was currently doing an impression of the Gobi Desert.

While he looked nothing like her idea of a lawyer, he was most definitely a man to lust over while indulging in some very inappropriate daydreams.

'When you've finished looking your fill, maybe you'd like to come in all the way.'

Her instinct was to deny she'd been checking him out, and to challenge his undeniable ego, but there was no point annoying him from the get-go. If she could persuade him to help her, that very ego and formidable manner was exactly what she needed on her side.

With sensually masculine ease, he pushed away from the desk and held out his hand. It was big and rough, and a large gold watch circled his solid wrist.

Heat curled in her belly as she stepped forward to accept his handshake. His palm connected with hers, warm and solid, and his fingers curled firmly around her hand.

Little tingles joined the heat—probably because the sleeves of his white shirt were rolled to just below his elbows, displaying tanned and muscled forearms with a light covering of dark hair. She was a sucker for muscular arms—all that strength and power—especially when one of them displayed an intriguing tattoo similar in design to the buckle on his belt.

Before she could start musing on the possible importance the symbol held for him, she released his hand.

'You're Mr Fitzpatrick?'

'That's what it says on the door.'

The velvet cadence of his deep voice should have softened his edges, but all it did was add to the already dangerous air about him.

'Why don't you sit down and hit me with the reason for your visit?'

'Yes. Right.' She felt she owed him an explanation for her staring. 'You're not like the photographs on your company website.'

He glanced down at himself, then met her gaze again, treating her to a sexy glint from those blue eyes. 'Yeah, well. It's dress-down Friday.'

'No offence, it's just the photos show you in a snappy suit.'

'If it's a fashion plate you're after, try Models Inc.

a few floors down. If it's legal representation, take a seat. And no offence taken.'

No. He was too damned sure of himself for that. She really admired that kind of confidence, loved the self-assurance that came with knowing you were the best. And he was the best. Top of his game, able to take his pick of clients.

Before she could dwell on the implications of that, he walked around the desk, sat, and scooted forward. 'Now we've established I'm who you came to see, give me the details.'

April felt a smidgen of relief that he was safely back behind his desk, but she wished he'd roll those bloody shirtsleeves down so she could stop staring at his forearms. And how was she supposed to explain her current predicament with those steely blue eyes fixed firmly on her?

Because you've got no choice.

Best to blurt it out, then. 'I'm under threat of being sued. I need legal advice.'

'Then you've come to the right place. Who's suing you?'

'An ex-colleague during my modelling days. Veronica Lebeck.'

He raised dark eyebrows. The mention of Veronica's name tended to have that reaction, especially since she'd gained notoriety after appearing topless on a reality TV show.

'What grounds?'

'She's claiming negligence. That a product she

purchased from my company was unfit for purpose and caused her physical injury.'

'Was the product faulty?'

'I've sold hundreds before and it gets excellent reviews.'

'Reviews don't mean shit.'

Her instinct was to counter the patronising tone, but the words died on her lips. She could imagine him telling her where the door was and that she was most welcome to use it.

'What's the product?'

She angled her chin into the air. 'A vibrator.'

His expression didn't waver, but a glimmer of heat shot into his eyes. 'A vibrator?'

Deliberately, she presented him with what Lizzie called her pissy business face. 'I run an online store selling adult toys.'

His gaze stayed firm on hers, but his nostrils flared a little and she thought his lips twitched.

'Ever had anything like this happen before?'

'Never.' She pulled her chin higher. She was a professional businesswoman selling bona fide merchandise. Damned if she'd apologise or be embarrassed about it. 'Vibrators are my top-selling product.'

For the first time since she'd entered the office he released her from that intense gaze and scooted his chair nearer the desk and his laptop.

'What's your URL?'

She told him and he tapped it in.

In silence, April watched him peruse the site, his

gaze skimming over the screen. His eyes moved fast, but she knew he didn't miss a thing. The only sound in the room was the click of the mouse as he flipped through the pages, and an occasional tap at the keyboard. His long fingers adeptly negotiated each click, those muscles in his forearm flexing with the movement.

She was about to slide into a lusty daydream, imagining the kind of lethal damage he could do to a woman with that muscled strength, those supple fingers, when he pushed the laptop away and sat back in his chair.

'Your disclaimer could do with some fleshing out. Liability insurance? Who are your underwriters?'

She inhaled deeply, breathed out slowly. 'I currently don't have any—insurance or underwriters.'

That unnerving gaze was back on her, his eyes slightly narrowed with a *what-sort-of-idiot-woman-is-this?* glint.

'Why the hell not?'

April refused to react to his implication that she was lacking in the intelligence department. Now wasn't the time to allow those particular demons to surface.

'The policy renewal got overlooked. I've tried to take out insurance to start from now, but since I felt compelled to disclose the threat of potential litigation, nobody will accept me with that hanging over my head.'

He gave a slow, thoughtful nod. 'Has Lebeck mentioned a figure?'

'Yes.' April's stomach heaved. 'One million.'

Logan Fitzpatrick's face remained impassive for a moment, then he tipped his head back and laughed. A full-out laugh, crinkling his blue eyes and displaying teeth that were a perfect match for the white of his shirt.

Oh, but he was an attractive specimen of manhood—in a roguish sort of way. She might have put her love-life on hold after the whole Rotten Richard debacle, might have made a promise to herself to focus on building her business instead, but there was absolutely no harm in looking, was there?

'What sort of damage did this thing do?'

April thought the question was rhetorical until he raised his eyebrows, waiting. 'Some bruising, apparently. She said it gave her a kind of shock.'

He reached across his desk towards an ashtray which held a fat cigar. When he stuffed the cigar, unlit, between his teeth, April had the disconcerting impression that he'd done it to stop himself from laughing again.

Days of worry and pent-up irritation pushed to the fore. 'Look, I just want to know. Does she have a case?'

'Hard to say,' he said around the cigar. 'You said you once worked together. What kind of relationship did you have?'

April considered her response carefully. There

was no point telling him anything that didn't relate to the case. 'Let's just say we weren't the best of friends. Some minor work-related disagreements, but nothing like this.'

Hot colour flooded into her cheeks—probably because of the way his teeth clenched around that bloody cigar. It was ridiculously sexy. Which was absurd. She had more to think about than some sexy lawyer who, like all the others she'd approached, obviously had no intention of taking her seriously, let alone helping her.

He took the cigar from his mouth and placed it back in the ashtray. As he leaned forward the movement highlighted the width of his shoulders, the size of his biceps as they strained against the crisp cotton of his shirt. It made her want to rip that shirt right off his shoulders and check out the view for real.

'Tell me about your set up.'

Her face, which had lost a little of the heat, started to burn again under his intense scrutiny. She had the disconcerting feeling that this man didn't miss anything. That he listened, absorbed, dissected, and then either accepted what you said or spit it right out. Straight down the line. No middle way.

She took a covert deep breath. 'Like I said, I run an online shop. It's mostly mail order, but I also party-plan.'

'Party-plan? How does that work?'

The glint in his eye indicated he already had a

pretty good handle on how it worked, but she hiked a shoulder.

'Women get together with a bunch of friends, they order what they want, and I arrange to have their purchases delivered.'

'How do they make their choices?'

Oh, here we go, she thought. *Nudge, nudge. Wink, wink.* She'd handled this sort of smutty inference so many times before, and she'd handle it now.

Except this time it wasn't so easy—not with his eyes taking a long, slow perusal of her and making her womanly parts do a happy dance. She squeezed her knees together as the gleam in his eye shot across the desk like an electrical current and arrowed straight to her clit. Heat rose in her body, thick and potent, making her limbs feel heavy, her core muscles tight.

This reaction to him was ridiculous—especially since he was likely just having his fun before showing her the door.

She thought about leaving. Simply gathering up her bag, thanking him for his time and leaving with her head held high. Problem was, he was basically her last resort.

She met his gaze full-on. 'Website, catalogue and theoretical product demonstration.'

He nodded, then went back to perusing the screen.

While he hadn't been openly derogatory, April didn't much like his attitude. Although, she had to admit that at least he was listening to her. So far this appointment had lasted longer than any of the others, and the fact he was still checking out her website was surely a good sign. Unless he was just a pervert and was enjoying the models displaying the latest in sexy underwear. They *were* some of her most visited pages.

'What model of vibrator?' he asked suddenly, his eyes not leaving the screen. 'There are dozens listed here.'

'It's no longer listed. I took it down right after this happened, although I kept a sample.'

His eyes met hers, held there. 'I'll need to see it, check out how it works. Theoretically.'

She couldn't tell if he was being deliberately suggestive or if she was just being too sensitive, but he needed to realise that, like him, she wasn't about to take any crap. 'I run an online adult store. A legitimate business. If you can't help me, just say so. But please don't insult me or my business.'

His eyebrows rose in sardonic fashion. 'There's no insult—to you or your business. I merely need to be in possession of all the facts. If my request to see the vibrator offends your delicate sensibilities, maybe you're in the wrong business.'

Arrogant prick.

But he was right, of course. He did need all the facts. She could have kicked herself for not bringing a sample of the vibrator along, but in her defence she'd thought this would be a quickie appointment that would have her leaving with the sound of his laughter ringing in her ears.

He unsettled her. Not just his cool and commanding manner, but the fact she hadn't felt quite so attracted to a man in a long time, and certainly hadn't indulged in fantasies of the screwing variety for even longer. It was insane.

Shouldn't it take more than sinfully handsome features all wrapped up in one sexy and self-assured package to make a woman react the way she was reacting? Shouldn't it be about trust and respect? But then, in her experience, both of those qualities were in very short supply, so maybe there was something to be said for simple lust.

'I'd be happy to let you have a sample,' April said, yanking her focus back to the matter in hand. 'I can get it couriered over to you. Discreet packaging, of course. Wouldn't want to offend any of *your* delicate sensibilities.'

CHAPTER TWO

TOUCHÉ, LOGAN THOUGHT as she batted his comment back to him.

He was enjoying himself. There was something about her edgy manner, in the way she sat upright and determined in her functional grey jacket and black skirt, that made him want to push, see how far she'd push back.

Heat lay beneath the businesslike demeanour. Strength in the warm brown gaze. She was elegant, feminine and classy, but with a *fuck you* tilt to her pretty chin when she didn't like the flavour of his questioning.

Every now and again he caught a flash of thigh as she crossed and uncrossed her legs. A glimpse of cleavage every time she folded her arms. And, while her body was a definite cause for celebration, there was no real hardship in meeting her eyes. They were brown, with an intriguing mix of steel and satin glowing in their depths. Like the warmest cognac… soothing and yet with a punch that could momentarily steal a man's breath away.

He'd had sex on the brain from the moment April Sinclair had waltzed into his office, which wasn't really surprising. Self-imposed celibacy could do that to a man. But he'd sailed too close to the wind with his last lover, had allowed their casual liaison to slide dangerously into relationship territory. Her parting words still rang in his ears:

'What are you going to do, Logan? Fuck and then leave every woman you meet because you don't have the balls for anything bordering on a serious relationship?'

Yeah, that was pretty much it. Safer that way. Then he wouldn't have to hear the door slam as they left him. Wouldn't be forced to watch as they walked out of his life.

Since April was watching him with an air of expectation, he took a breath and stroked his chin. 'Never been accused of having "delicate" *anything* before. Certainly not to the point of worrying about people knowing the contents of my mail.'

Even her frown was sexy.

'I have to say I don't think you're particularly professional in your approach.'

Logan had to admit she was right. But she was testing his focus. 'Which shouldn't bother you any more than it bothers me.'

'It bothers me that you don't seem to be taking my problem seriously.'

'I take every problem that lands on my desk seriously.'

She stuck that chin in the air. It was slightly pointed, like a sexy fairy, and went with the rest of her. Sharp cheekbones, pert nose, mouth—and what a mouth it was. All her features came together to form one hell of a package.

'I'll have it delivered to your office.'

Logan blinked. He'd lost the gist of the conversation. Too busy deliberating on the very delicious prospect of stripping her out of those conservative clothes and discovering what lay beneath. Sexy underwear? Like the kind he'd seen on her website? Wouldn't that be a sight? He'd strip her out of that, too. Slowly. Until she was naked, willing and ready for him...

'After you've inspected it, can we discuss things further?'

No, let's discuss something entirely more gratifying.

Using what he considered heroic effort, Logan dragged himself back to the business at hand. He really wasn't behaving much like a professional. Time to rein it all back before he got himself some unwelcome tabloid attention when April Sinclair reported him for being a sleazebag.

He sucked in a breath. 'I'll be straight with you. I'm not your best bet for this.'

How could he be when Veronica Lebeck was the current lover of the man who was the closest thing to a father Logan had ever had? Okay, Haydon collected women—young ones—like the proverbial sugar daddy, and chances were that Haydon had already moved on to new pastures. But Logan owed the property tycoon. Big-time.

'Not my best bet?' Panic shot into her eyes. 'You're saying you can't advise me?'

Without Haydon's link to Veronica, Logan wondered if he might have represented April. It would have been interesting to see how far he could get with this leggy blonde with her throaty voice and tight-assed attitude. But, taking everything into account, and since he was involved in a case that would require a fair amount of overseas travel and a great deal of media coverage, he couldn't indulge.

Briefly, he considered telling her about his conflict of interest, but that panic in her eyes stopped him, pulling at something deep inside him that always sought to protect the vulnerable.

Not that it applied to her. He sensed a backbone there, and an integrity he had to admire. She hadn't technically been required to alert potential insurers of a lawsuit that might never happen, especially since it was outside their culpability as a future provider, but he liked that she'd been upfront about it.

'I'm saying I specialise in family law. You need a civil litigator. I can put you in touch with someone.'

She leaned forward and fixed him with a solid stare, and another fascinating glimpse of cleavage that did something interesting in the vicinity of his loins.

'Look, I just want to know what I might be fac-

ing. I'm tired of being dismissed and shoved out the
door. I don't want to have to explain all this to someone else, only to have them pass me on yet again.'

Her frustration shimmered in the air, and Logan
found himself sympathising. He knew what it was to
be pushed from pillar to post, to feel as if nobody listened or cared. He'd experienced plenty of that when
life had forced him to grow up and take charge. Feeling powerless was no fun, and he'd learned quickly
to take control, to protect his brothers and sister and
keep them safe after his parents walked out on them.
His siblings had trusted him to act in their best interests. They still did. As did his clients.

'Okay.' The least he could do for April was gather
all the facts, then she'd be spared having to explain
it all over again when he passed her along to someone else. 'Where do you get your stock?'

'Mostly I use drop shipping,' April said. 'Do you
know what that is?'

He did, but he shook his head as he folded his
arms. 'Explain it to me.'

The fact was, he liked listening to her. Enjoyed
the throaty timbre of her voice. Even more, he liked
watching the way her mouth moved around words.
The way that narrow upper lip and the fuller lower
lip curved around the syllables and sounds. A mouth
like that could do sensational damage to a man…

'And, since I have several regular repeat orders,'
she went on, unaware of the fire throbbing in his
cock, 'I rarely have a problem with supply.'

Logan tried to convince himself that she could be explaining the ordering procedure for tinned peas, but his mind kept straying to the items of her trade, how much he'd like to experiment, how much he'd enjoy using them on her, and his damn cock wouldn't let up.

To add insult to injury, blood pounded in his veins, shooting his imagination into overdrive. He pictured her mouth clamped around his erection, her blonde hair flowing over his thighs, her naked body stretched out while he explored every inch of her. Slowly. He'd use his hands, his mouth, his teeth, and he'd have her screaming and begging before he...

'Does all that make sense?' She sat back, her eyes wide. 'I'm sure you've got questions.'

Questions? He needed to think of some bloody questions. While she'd been busy outlining her ordering procedure, he'd been busy mind-fucking her. He was a real prince. What the hell had happened to his legendary professionalism? The professionalism that had heads of industry, eminent politicians and A-list celebrities knocking at his door, begging to be his clients.

He sucked in a breath. 'Yeah. The vibrator in question,' he improvised. 'It was supplied by one of these drop shippers?'

She frowned. 'No. Like I explained, they were on special offer from a source I'd never used before.' She reached into her bag, pulled out a wad of papers and handed them to him. 'When this blew up, I emailed the company to check if the stock was faulty. They haven't replied yet.'

Unlikely they'd reply at all, Logan thought as he flicked through the wad. Bogus companies sprang up all the time, especially online, and at the first sign of trouble they were the devil's own job to trace.

Since April seemed like a savvy cookie, he didn't understand why she'd taken a chance on an unknown and untested source. Nor why she'd allowed her insurance to lapse. There had to be more to it. Was she telling him everything?

He watched her closely, felt the stir in his blood as she levelled her gaze back at him. 'If you want my advice, you need to understand that I won't tolerate any fudging around the facts.'

She nodded, her shoulders visibly relaxing. 'No fudging. I've given you the facts.'

He maintained eye contact, pleased when she didn't flinch. But there was more here—more to her than she was letting on. The woman intrigued him more with every passing minute.

'Let me take a look at this,' Logan said, flicking through the file she'd given him. 'I'll get back to you.'

'Can you give me your initial thoughts now? Is there a case to answer?'

Not from what he'd gleaned so far. And from what he knew of Lebeck, she was an opportunist. Likely she'd yield to the prospect of some freebies, or cave to an out-of-court settlement with a token compensation claim. But he couldn't discount the possibility that she'd go to the press, and they'd have a frigging field day.

Until he checked out the current status of Veronica's connection with Haydon he wasn't going to risk upsetting his mentor and friend by helping April. But in the meantime, there was no harm in gathering those facts, so she wouldn't need to explain it all over again when he passed her on.

'Like I said, I'll get back to you.'

She hesitated, obviously wanting to press him for an answer, then closed her bag and stood. Logan followed her to the door, determined not to check out her ass in the process. He failed. Miserably. She had an exceptional ass.

At the door, she faced him, making his pulse hammer. He was tempted to hike her into his arms, bring that tempting mouth right up against his and kiss the life out of her. See if she tasted as potent as he imagined she would.

'I know for you this seems small fry and unimportant,' April said, cutting into his thoughts. 'But—'

'I never consider the threat of being sued unimportant.'

Her eyelids fluttered closed over those stunning eyes before he could once again be caught in their cognac depths. He'd need a freaking life jacket if he stared into them too long.

'Thanks for saying that. This thing has me tied up in knots.'

How he'd *love* to tie her up in knots. Watch those eyes turn languid and sultry...hear her moan his name as he drove her to the heights of sexual desire.

He had a sudden desire to take on her case himself. Whether to sate the intense sexual attraction that fired in his veins or just to make sure the likes of Veronica Lebeck didn't get away with screwing people using cockamamie stories about rabid vibrators.

Maybe both.

'I'm going away tomorrow, but I'll take a closer look at your file tonight.'

She drew a breath, the movement highlighting the curve of her breasts beneath the conservative jacket. 'I can't tell you how much I appreciate that. Thanks for fitting me in.'

Logan went to his desk, grabbed one of his business cards and scribbled on the back, all the while imagining how April could fit *him* in just fine. All the way. Hard. Fast. Deep.

With that particular thought thrumming through his head, he walked back to the door. He timed it perfectly, his hand connecting with hers as they both reached for the door handle. There was heat in her eyes, a definite pink tinge across her cheekbones.

'You like Italian?'

Suspicion layered over the heat. 'Why?'

With his free hand he held out his card, keeping hold of it for a moment too long when she tried to take it. 'I'm inviting you to supper.'

And hopefully more, Logan thought as her gaze

held his. He wanted her in his bed, but he also wanted her to look at him without wariness clouding her brown eyes. That might make him a fool, but he was a well-prepared one. Forewarned was forearmed, or so the saying went. What was wrong with a casual and mutually agreeable hook-up with a woman who intrigued him almost as much as she attracted him?

'Do you feed all your clients, Mr Fitzpatrick?'

He shrugged as her question pulled him from his thoughts. 'Two birds. One stone. And, since I'll need that sample, you can bring it with you.'

He caught another glimmer of suspicion, right before she looked down at the card. It made him smile. And push. 'And, since we both know we're heading way past formalities, let's make it Logan.'

She tapped the card a few times before her gaze met his. 'Isn't there some kind of code that says we should stick to formalities? A kind of client-and-lawyer thing?'

He liked it that she didn't pretend to misunderstand his meaning. 'You're not technically my client. I'm just giving you advice.'

A slight smile turned up the corners of her sensual mouth. 'I assume you're billing me for your time? That makes it official lawyer/client territory.'

He leaned closer, pleased when she stood her ground. 'Even so, there's no problem, since there's no code.'

Still she didn't move, but she looked at him with a measure of heat that shot straight to his loins. Fuck,

but he wanted her more than he'd wanted a woman
in a long time.

Hot nights. Hot sex. No strings.

'Maybe I'm not looking for a man, just a lawyer.'

'Who says you can't have both?'

She tilted her head as if she was weighing him
up. 'I've got too much at stake to muddy the waters.'

That suited him just fine. 'Then we'll make sure
to keep those waters nice and clear.' He waited a
beat. 'My private address is on the back of the card.'

She tapped the card to her chin, considering, then
she turned to the door.

Logan opened it.

'Seven o'clock.'

Unable to resist he leaned down as she passed
him, his mouth close to her ear.

'Don't forget the vibrator.'

CHAPTER THREE

APRIL ARRIVED BACK at the small apartment she shared
with Lizzie, her body still throbbing from the inter-
action with Logan. All kinds of lewd things had shot
through her brain when he'd told her in that deep,
gravelly voice to remember to bring the vibrator, his
breath warm and sensual against her ear. His intoxicating scent had wrapped around her and accompanied her all the way home.

He'd done it on purpose, of course, anticipating
a reaction. And that was after he'd basically propo-
sitioned her.

Had he expected she'd get all flustered, skittish
and embarrassed?

Dream on.

She was used to insinuations, and she was used
to propositions. In her line of work it came with the
territory. Most men made some smutty comment
when they found out she ran an adult toy business,
insinuating she might give them a personal demonstration of her products. A minority actually asked
her flat-out if she'd have sex with them.

Although irritated, she generally fielded those comments with a sardonic response or simply ignored them. Logan's smoky allusion had shot a reaction between her legs that had taken her by surprise. Well, kind of… The truth was she hadn't been able to steady her hormones since setting eyes on the man, ensuring she'd been thinking about vibrator-play with a certain sexy lawyer all the way home on the tube.

She'd told him she wanted a lawyer, not a man. He'd said she could have both.

Could she?

Wouldn't that make things complicated?

What if they had hot, steamy sex and then the attraction fizzled out?

But what if they had hot, steamy sex and it didn't fizzle out?

Hell, she could imagine Logan would be amazing in bed. She'd bet he didn't shy away from adventure, either. Not like Richard.

She blew out a breath, picked up her mail and took it with her down the hall, tossing her jacket on a chair as she went. The cosy apartment wrapped around her, settling her a little after the tumult of the day. In the galley kitchen, she switched on the coffee machine and gave only a cursory thought to the wisdom of adding caffeine to her edgy mood. She'd been jittery since leaving Logan's office—actually, she'd been that way since walking into his office. He'd pulled all kinds of weird things from her.

It was just sex, of course. Pure and simple. He made her think about sex. Made her *want* sex. All that hot and steamy sex.

Maybe part of the attraction was his directness, the way he'd warned her he wouldn't tolerate any fudging around the facts. After what she'd been through with Richard, dealing with someone honest and upfront was refreshing to say the least.

Sex with someone like Logan could be all kinds of interesting, and she was due, wasn't she?

It had been a while since Richard. Not that sex with him had been great. Richard had liked it vanilla, blatantly disregarding her occasional attempts to try something new and exciting using the perks afforded by the products of her trade.

It was only recently that she'd realised he'd controlled her in the bedroom, too, and while she wasn't entirely averse to that she would have liked to take the lead on occasion. To have made their sex life exciting, adventurous…electrifying. With Richard it never had been. Any time she'd tried to take things to another level he'd made her feel dirty and sluttish. Bad enough, he'd said, that she ran the kind of business she did. Didn't she know that men would see her as an easy target?

Worse than any of that was the fact that he'd kicked her when she was at her lowest point. She might have learned to live with their lack-lustre sexlife, and his pointed remarks about the nature of her business, but the way he'd controlled, manipulated and ultimately betrayed her was unforgivable. He'd fed on her fears, shattered her confidence, made her doubt herself and her abilities.

It wouldn't happen again. Ever. No way would she be that vulnerable, that naïve. Never again. Lessons had been learned and digested. Now she was in control. She was the one who knew what was best for her and her business. And if she wanted sex she'd have it. On her own terms.

She would keep control. She would call the shots. And, by God, this time she'd keep her wits about her. No man was ever going to screw with her again.

Before she could slide further down memory lane, her phone buzzed.

'How did it go?' Lizzie asked, without preamble. She was currently on a modelling assignment in Copenhagen. 'Did he give you any idea of how things stand?'

'Not really. When I first told him why I was there he could barely keep his face straight. Kept sticking an unlit cigar in his mouth.'

And damned if she wasn't remembering the way that cigar had sat between his impossibly perfect white teeth as he'd smiled wickedly around it. Her core muscles clenched hard, but she made herself focus.

'I'll wager you soon put him right?'

'I told him to treat me with the same respect he'd give anyone seeking his advice. He's looking through the paperwork tonight.' She waited, for effect. 'He invited me to supper.'

'Hmm…'

'What does that mean?'

But April knew only too well what it meant. Lizzie had been encouraging her to get out there and have some fun since she'd moved back to London.

'He wants me to bring a sample vibrator. And he told me to call him Logan.'

'Hmm… Are you interested?'

She could have lied, but what was the point? 'Very, as it happens. But I'm not sure it's a good idea. It has "complicated" written all over it.'

'Don't see why. Where does he live?'

'Chelsea. Farnsworth Place.'

'Swanky. Now, go convince him to take you on.' It was Lizzie's turn to wait a beat. 'And don't you dare refuse dessert. It could prove mighty appetising…'

As she walked up the immaculate stone steps to Logan's house April tried not to think about dessert. It was so bloody tempting, though—until she remembered that the man stirring all her juices was hopefully going to help save her business. That was what she should be focusing on right now, not hot, raunchy and undoubtedly fabulous sex.

April sucked in a steadying breath. Lizzie had been right about Farnsworth Place. Swanky. The house was one in a row of majestic three-storey

houses with cream-coloured wood cladding offset
with glossy black railed balconies.

Yet again, he'd thrown her off balance. It didn't
suit him, somehow. Too conventional, too…civilised.

Ignoring the flutter in her stomach, she pressed
the doorbell. While she waited, she pulled the strap
of her tote bag higher onto her shoulder and the box
inside bumped her hip, reminding her why she was
here.

A guy opened the door, holding a beer. 'You must
be April Sinclair. Come in.'

Thrown by someone other than Logan greeting
her, April teetered on the top step until the man ush-
ered her into the airy hallway. Her first impression
was of space and not one iota of clutter. Several large
abstract paintings hung along the ivory walls, pro-
viding a splash of bold and dramatic colour. The
tiled floors were cool and functional, with just a
few pieces of walnut furniture scattered along the
length of the hall, leading the eye towards the back
of the house.

'Let me take your coat. He's through there.'

April shrugged out of her coat, feeling out of place
in her black knee-length skirt and pale blue tee shirt.
She followed the man down the hall and into the living area. Terrace doors, stretching the full width of
the room, showcased Chelsea Harbour and the glittering waters of the River Thames.

Logan stood looking beyond the terrace doors,
speaking on his mobile phone. He turned to her and

she felt the punch of his heated appraisal right down to her toes.

The man was impossibly gorgeous.

He wore his dark shirt open at the collar, which seemed to emphasise the width of his shoulders—or maybe it was the way he stood. Tall, upright and confident, one hand holding his phone, the other slipped into the pocket of his jeans.

Master of his universe. King of his domain.

She tried not to react to the slide of lust that flashed in her belly and burned through her blood as, with his gaze on hers, he finished his call and walked towards her. The pull of attraction radiated between them, hard to ignore and definitely hard to deny. She wasn't at all sure about the intensity of this reaction he pulled from her. Despite the whole wanting to jump into bed with him thing, he made her feel strangely vulnerable. And that wouldn't do. Hadn't she vowed never again to let anyone hold power over her, over her life?

'I see you've met my brother, Connor.' Logan slapped the man playfully on the shoulder. 'He's just leaving.'

Connor turned and arched a sardonic eyebrow at his brother. 'I am?'

'You are,' Logan confirmed with a quick smile as he took Connor's beer. 'Keep working on that status report for me, okay? We'll catch up later.' He turned his brother towards the hall with a little shove, receiving a fulminating look in return.

'Drink?' Logan asked as Connor left, the front door closing behind him with a hefty thud. 'What's your poison?'

'Just coffee, please.' April followed him into a huge kitchen, which afforded another fabulous view of the harbour and with the most delicious smell coming from the double oven. 'I didn't know you had a brother.'

'Three,' he said switching on the coffee machine. 'Plus a sister. All younger than me, and each one a royal pain in the ass.'

Since he said it with a smile in his voice, April recognised the affection there. It was interesting to see this side of Logan, a glimpse of softness in the blatantly powerful and sexy lawyer. It tugged at something inside her. A little wistfully, she thought about how she'd always yearned for siblings. A big, loving family. Instead she'd been an only child, born late and unexpectedly to parents who had taken little interest in her except to manage and direct every aspect of her life.

'Do they all live close?'

She enjoyed watching the easy way he moved around the space. His tight ass in those exquisitely cut jeans, his broad shoulders, strong arms... Sadly, his forearms were covered by shirtsleeves tonight, although the cuffs were turned back, displaying firm wrists and sturdy hands.

'Connor lives in the city. The others are scattered all over, doing their thing.'

'Which is…?' April asked the question almost automatically, fascinated by the warmth that slipped into his tone as he spoke of his siblings, and mesmerised by his masculine appeal as he performed the simple domestic task of placing coffee cups, milk and sugar on a tray.

'Aiden and Ty are both in the forces. Colleen is at uni in Edinburgh.'

She leaned back against a unit. 'Do you see them much?'

'I make sure to. Gotta keep them on the straight and narrow.' He turned, mirroring her as he leaned back. 'How about you?'

'No siblings. No parents now. My mother died several years ago, and my father more recently.'

Logan frowned. 'That's rough.'

'I've got great friends.'

He nodded, then his eyes turned heated. 'A man?'

'Like I said, I'm not in the market for complications.'

The corner of his mouth hiked into that cocky grin. 'Doesn't have to be complicated.'

'Not at the start, but that's how it usually ends.'

'Not if everyone plays by the rules.'

The gleam in his blue eyes shone across the space between them and made the air positively sizzle. She'd told Lizzie she was interested in Logan. What she had failed to admit was that she was tempted beyond words to throw caution to the wind and jump him. Every moment she spent with the man made it harder to resist him.

And why the hell should she? She was long overdue some fun—the dirtier the better—and she knew
Logan was exactly the man to provide it.

Could it be that simple?

'What sort of rules?'

His nostrils flared. 'That's open to discussion.'

She remained silent, contemplating him and his
words while her thighs trembled. If she gave in to
temptation, wouldn't that negate the progress she'd
made in getting a lawyer who actually seemed to be
taking her seriously? Wasn't she better off focusing
on the reason she was here and resisting the temptation of his admittedly considerable sexual appeal?

'I think I'd rather discuss the threat to my business,' she said, hoping that her eyes conveyed that
she hadn't completely drawn a solid line through the
other discussion.

He studied her for several long moments, his blue
gaze penetrating and panty-melting, and she was on
the verge of telling him to scratch what she'd said
when he nodded, then placed the coffee pot on the
tray.

'Okay. Let's go and move things on.'

Considering the gist of the conversation they'd
just shared, April wondered what exactly they were
about to move on with. Business? Or pleasure? Both?

She followed him down the hall to the front of
the building and into a sumptuous study. Book-filled
shelves on every wall and a welcoming log-filled fireplace made the imposing space cosy and convivial.

Logan indicated the large leather sofa by the fireplace, then poured them both coffee before taking his seat on the matching sofa opposite. He'd switched to business mode, which gave her the answer to the *moving things on* question.

Settling back, he hooked his ankle across the opposite knee and started to flick through the folder she'd given him earlier. She found herself ogling his wide chest, the brawny shoulders. Since his forearms were covered by shirtsleeves, she let her attention slide leisurely downward. She almost smiled when she got to his shiny Italian leather shoes, wondering if it was true what they said about men with large feet.

'Did you bring it?'

'What?'

It was impossible to mistake the gleam in his eye. The man knew that she'd been checking him out.

'The vibrator.'

'Of course, that's why I'm here.'

'Then let's take a look.'

April reached into her bag and pulled out the oblong box showing a busty half-naked blonde touching the pink vibrator to her red pouting lips.

Bloody hell. It would have been bad enough handing the box over to any lawyer, but to a man who seemed to fan her sexual flame just by breathing? It was impossible not to imagine him taking it out of the box and using it on her. They'd both be naked, and she'd be spread out beneath him while he treated her to that cocky grin as his big capable hands slid the vibrator between her legs...

Her core was wet and throbbing, but she held Logan's gaze as she handed the item across to him. 'This is from the same batch,' she explained, her voice thready with lust. 'The only difference is the colour.'

He took it, perused the box as if it held something mildly interesting. 'These things come in different colours?'

April nodded. Her pulse hammered when he opened the box and held the vibrator up to study it. Her eyes zeroed in on his fingers as they slowly stroked and glided over the smooth plastic before moving to the ridged areas of the toy. More heat shot between her legs. She wanted to clamp her knees together, squirm in the seat to get some relief, but he was looking at her with that steady blue gaze.

Saying nothing, he flicked the switch with his thumb and raised his eyebrows when nothing happened.

'New stock,' April explained, annoyed that she'd forgotten to ready the toy. 'It needs batteries.'

'Right.' A flicker of something deliciously wicked came into his eyes as he handed over the toy. 'Maybe *you* should handle that.'

She wondered if he was imagining exactly what she was picturing. How his hands would subject her to the same slow and steady torture with which he'd made his acquaintance with the vibrator. Strong, leisurely strokes that would incite an aching need everywhere he touched…making her crave, making her burn…

Every cell of her body fired with the intensity of her thoughts as she slipped the batteries out of the box and pushed them into the toy.

She was so primed, so aware of him, that the sudden whir of the vibrator as it sprang into action made her start. The pink giant oscillated and pulsed, adding to the sensual heat April was trying her hardest to ignore. When Logan held his hand out for the toy she basically threw it at him. No bloody way was she going to make any kind of physical contact with the man while she was in this state of heightened arousal.

He smiled, and she knew he was aware of every thought and reaction she'd had.

'It's got three speeds,' he said, holding the toy in one hand, while reading from the box. 'And it can be used in the shower.'

Logan flicked the switch again and the vibrator went into top-speed mode. It started undulating. *Oh, for pity's sake.* She couldn't take much more of this.

Her intimate muscles contracted so hard she feared she might climax just from the sight of his adept fingers manipulating the thing as it continued to tilt and roll. Bloody hell, but she suspected Logan's hands were a damn sight better suited to manipulating more interesting things than a piece of plastic.

'And you've sold hundreds of these?'

Of what?

April gave herself a fierce mental shake. 'This kind of toy is one of my top sellers, but this is the first time I've used this particular supplier for them. They were offering a limited time deal and I sold them as a special offer. They turned a decent profit.'

Thankfully he switched off the vibrator, but he continued to hold and study it.

'Did Veronica Lebeck purchase the product through your website?'

'No. Party-plan. Most of her friends bought one. I pretty much offloaded all the stock I had with me that night.'

'When was that?'

'About six weeks ago.'

'Anyone else complain of problems with their purchase?'

'No.'

April had an image of him in full legal wig and gown, interrogating some poor sap on the witness stand. She imagined he'd look pretty spectacular.

'How's business right now?'

'It's good.'

'No need to cut corners? Take below-standard stock in the hope of offloading it fast?'

'No.' Her annoyance levels rose rapidly. 'I would never deliberately sell sub-standard stock. I've got a good reputation…a huge percentage of returning clients. If you want to see testimonials, I can provide those easily enough.'

'Testimonials?'

'Satisfied customers.'

His grin flashed quick and sexy. 'Excuse the pun?'

Still annoyed by his questioning of her standards, April glared at him. 'I'm glad you're finding this funny. I'm afraid I can't share the sentiment.'

'What's the deal with your insurance?'

'I forgot to renew it. Believe me, I've had sleepless nights about it, but I was distracted at the time. Personal matters. It was a foolish mistake.'

Logan studied the toy again, turning it this way and that. He placed it down next to the box on the table beside him, then walked over to his desk and picked up a sheaf of papers. 'You might as well complete these while I take a closer look at the terms and conditions on your website.' He handed them to her. 'Something wrong?'

'You need me to complete forms? Just to get your advice?'

He shrugged. 'You'll need to do them at some stage—might as well be now. Whoever handles your case will need the information, so go ahead and fill in the paperwork.'

Firm and non-negotiable, April thought as he went back to perusing his laptop. Did anyone ever get the better of Logan Fitzpatrick? Unlikely. Which only heightened her disappointment that he couldn't be her lawyer. Probably just as well, though, since April suspected she'd be paying off his fee like a second mortgage for the next fifty years. Lawyers of his calibre didn't do discounts or mate's rates.

Looking on the bright side, there was nothing stopping her from letting him be something else. Nothing in the way of her acting on her undeniable attraction for the man. She was single, unattached, and desperately in lust. It would just be sex. Where was the problem?

Somehow she managed to drag her thoughts away from carnal possibilities long enough to complete the paperwork.

'Done?' Logan asked as she put down her pen.

She nodded.

'Good. Now I get to feed you.'

The way he said it made her stomach do crazy, stupid things, but it might have been the copious amounts of caffeine she'd swigged down while completing the forms.

She was still on edge from that display with the vibrator, and her gaze flashed to where it sat on the side table.

Logan followed the direction of her look as he walked around his desk. 'I'll hang on to that. Unless you need it?'

Since her hormones were enjoying their own private disco, and her stomach had yet to settle from its vibrator-induced rollercoaster ride, April knew that she'd definitely be needing something. It looked as if her sample stock drawer would be raided the moment she got home.

This rampant flare of sexual attraction wasn't going to diminish any time soon. If anything, the more time she spent in Logan's company, the more she bloody wanted him.

'Keep it,' she said. 'You might want to do more research.'

'Yeah, I might.'

He held out his hand, his fevered gaze inviting her to take it…and much more. Shivers of awareness rippled down her spine as his fingers wrapped around hers, and heat burned between her legs and made her knees wobble.

'I'm starting to develop a fascination,' he said.

'With vibrators?'

His gaze dropped to her mouth, and he made a long and seductive perusal of her lips. Those shivers shot from her spine straight to her core. She was wet, and aching, and so turned on it was ridiculous.

'Not just vibrators,' he said, his fingers tightening even more as the compelling blue of his eyes caught her in their devilish depths. 'Although I'd like to know more about how they work.'

Oh, and how I'd like to show you.

'You've just had a practical demonstration.'

'Of the basics. Not the logistics. Can those things actually make a woman come?'

Oh, God.

'Of course.' How the hell did she sound so composed when her whole body was firing on all cylinders? 'Women don't always get their needs met by a man.'

He waited a beat. 'Then that man isn't doing his job properly.'

April pulled her inner muscles up hard. Anything to stop the constant throbbing and intense need. It was getting unbearable.

'I suppose you're going to tell me you've never had any complaints.'

Why had she said that? Did she have some hidden propensity for torturing herself? For baiting him?

'Not one.' He moved a little closer. 'Which is why *my* women prefer the real thing.'

Bloody hell.

'That's what they tell you.'

He caught her other hand in his, moving ever closer. 'They tell me with a satisfied smile on their face. That's if they've got the energy left.'

Unable to resist, and not wanting him to have all the fun, April stepped closer this time. She touched her breasts to his chest, enjoying the way he sucked in a breath.

'We women are good are bolstering men's egos. How do you know that as soon as you've fallen asleep your women don't go and seek out Mr Sparkly?'

His throat contracted, then his eyebrows rose. 'Mr Sparkly?'

Had she said that aloud? Who cared? 'It's one of the games we play. At parties.'

She was on a roll now, feeling bold and daring. If

this thing between them was going anywhere, then it made sense to let him know that he wasn't the one who'd be in the driving seat.

'Sex toy parties?'

He tilted his hips and his erection nudged her stomach. This time they both sucked in air.

'I prefer the term "adult toys".'

His hands settled on her hips, fingers digging in. 'How does it work? The game?'

'There's an instruction sheet inside the box. I put one in with all my vibrator products.'

His impressive bulge pushed harder against her. 'I'm not much for instruction sheets. Prefer working things out for myself.'

'Typical man.'

'There's not much *typical* about me.'

She shimmied against him. 'So I've noticed.'

His hands moved to her ass, tugging up her skirt and coaxing her legs apart to guide that impressive bulge between them. She was ridiculously wet.

He brought his mouth to within a whisper of hers, held there as they both breathed hard. Tilting her chin, she raised her lips to his. It was the lightest of touches, barely skimming, but the reaction pushed deep into her being and made everything come alive. Her heart hammered, her senses spun.

The kiss deepened until it was hard and hot. She dragged her hands up his masculine chest, felt his heart beating fast against her palms.

'I really, really want you,' she managed between kisses.

He groaned low in his throat, his hands gripping her hips and hiking her up so she could wrap her legs around his waist.

'And I damn well want you,' he said, his voice rough and edgy. 'It's time to eat… And I don't mean pasta.'

CHAPTER FOUR

APRIL DIDN'T KNOW which way was up right then. Her head spun wildly and all her senses were sharply focused on the feel of Logan pressed hard against her pulsing core.

Drugged by his kisses, she was only vaguely aware of him moving them across the room, and she could do nothing else but return those drugging kisses. It was only when he turned and levered her onto the corner of his desk that even the tiniest thought slid beneath the sensual haze.

The hard surface against her ass must have jolted something in her brain and brought her reasoning powers back from where they'd been languishing in erotic pleasure.

Logan stepped between her legs, the movement pushing her skirt up to her thighs. He swept a hand behind her, clearing the way to ease her back against the polished walnut surface.

'Wait,' she said, pressing a hand to his chest.

The feel of his heartbeat throbbing against her palm and his chest widening with each inhalation didn't help her focus. She had to suck in a couple of steadying breaths.

'Let me think, just a minute.'

She forced herself to do exactly that, ignoring Logan's frown and the brush of his fingers up and down her arms.

'What we're about to do doesn't usually need much in the way of thought,' he said, his voice rough and low.

'I know how sex works, thanks.' She took a huge breath in and let it out on a sigh. 'But I've got a whole lot at stake right now, and I'm not about to jeopardise it by enjoying a quick roll in the hay.'

His grin took for ever to get where it was going. 'I don't see any hay. Just a big old desk that's crying out for some action.'

'This isn't funny.' Strange, but she couldn't seem to take her hand away from his chest. 'If this all goes belly up, I'll be right back at square one.'

He stepped back just a tad. 'Regardless of what happens tonight, or any other night, I'll make sure you're not back at square one.'

'How?' April dropped her hands to her thighs and tried to pull down her skirt, but Logan was still between her legs and she couldn't get very far. 'Why would you even be interested in helping me if you're not the one handling the case?'

He placed his hands over hers and leaned in closer. 'For starters, someone has called in a favour. They asked me to meet with you, give you my advice. Then there's the fact your problem interests me—added to which it'll likely be a quick and easy fix. And I bloody love those.'

He dropped a kiss on her mouth.

'If you need any further explanation, let's just say I'm intrigued by you as much as your predicament, and that I like the idea of riding in on my white charger and coming to your rescue. Finally, there's the fact I'd like to fuck you senseless and watch that suspicion fade from your eyes.'

April's mouth had gone dry. 'I don't need rescuing by someone on a white charger. I just need a lawyer. And I'm not suspicious.' She needed to get those things out of the way before she zoomed in on his other comment. 'Do you really think it'll be a quick and easy fix?'

'Can't see it being a drawn-out affair—especially when the evidence seems thin.' His palms pressed down on her hands, angling her so that he pushed her thighs open wider. 'But as for fucking you…? I plan on that being a slow and extremely pleasurable process, which I intend to draw out as long as possible.'

Her stomach muscles clenched, the movement shooting right to her core. But still she couldn't quite let her mind relax around what was at stake if she gave in to this almost overwhelming attraction and need burning inside her and things went south.

'The timing seems off.'

He tapped the spot between her eyebrows. 'Because you're overthinking. We've already established that this doesn't have to be complicated. It doesn't have to be anything other than mutually satisfying sex.'

April shook her head. 'Maybe I am overthinking, but if the shit hits the fan I could lose my business.'

He took a breath and moved back, resting his hands on her knees. 'If you're not sure, then this isn't going to happen. If you want to call a halt—'

She reached up and placed a finger over his lips, certain that if she did call a halt he wouldn't press her further. 'I don't want that.' With a shake of her head, she ordered herself to go with the flow and stop looking for the worst-case scenario. 'I just need you to understand where I'm coming from.'

She laid her hands over his on her knee, then looked him square in the eye so that he could have no doubt of her agreement…and her intention.

'What I want is hot, uncomplicated sex.'

Heat burned in his dark blue eyes. 'I can get behind that.'

He leaned in, taking her mouth in a steamy kiss that made her lose all coherent thought and shot her into pure feeling. She slid her palms up his chest, wrapped her arms around his neck, pulling him closer to her so that she could press her breasts to the solid expanse of his chest.

She matched his kiss with a brutality of her own, demanding he give her every inch of his mouth, every inch of his tongue. There was nothing tentative between them, no easing in, no push and retreat, no chance of shifting perspectives, or doubts or qualms.

April wanted him, and she sensed that the lust sizzling between them wasn't the kind that would burn out easily. And even if it did, she knew that being with Logan was something she would never regret.

Maybe she really was an idiot, she thought vaguely as his hands settled on her hips and he pulled her closer to the edge of his desk, but she wanted this. She wanted him.

He kept up the assault on her mouth as he encouraged her back onto her elbows, leaning over her so that his strength enveloped her body. He seemed to be everywhere, his powerful presence sliding over every inch of her, his scent permeating all the available air in the room. She felt hot, cold. Sweaty and shivery. She felt…*everything*.

He eased away from her, drawing his hands down her hips, her legs, and then reaching beneath her skirt. April trembled, her body intensely alive from just the touch of his hands. How the hell would she survive anything else?

He reached up, curling his fingers around the edge of her panties. She jerked, and a needy sound rumbled deep in her throat as he tugged at the wispy lace.

Although he'd pushed her skirt up her thighs, it still covered the necessities as he yanked her panties down to her knees.

'Fuck,' he grated, his fingers tightening around the lace. 'You're a freaking wet dream.'

'The latest addition to my catalogue,' she said huskily, watching him as he continued to peruse her underwear. 'It's important to take every chance to advertise my wares.'

His gaze met hers, the gleam unmistakable and that cocky grin in evidence. 'Amen to that. I'm thinking I'd like to bulk-buy.'

'Women's panties?'

With his eyes on hers, he tugged the underwear over her knees and down her legs. 'Only the kind you wear.' Tossing the panties to the floor, he placed his hands on her knees. 'But right now I'm more interested in what they're designed to cover.'

Her stomach did a very pleasurable roll as his fingers dug into her flesh and he eased her legs wider. Her skirt stretched across her upper thighs and air whispered over her panty-less state, making her muscles clench in heady anticipation.

He pulled her even closer to the edge of the desk, before pushing her skirt up over her hips.

April revelled in the slight flare of his nostrils as he looked at her, in the way his chest expanded and a muscle flickered in his jaw. She tried to sit up, intending to reach for his zipper. She wanted him—wanted him right at the place where heat raged between her legs. But he stepped back, his hands sliding to her thighs.

She'd expected him to reach into his pocket for a condom, but instead he brought his hands up and pressed his thumbs to her folds, opening her up to his gaze.

Instinct had her trying to close her legs, but the heat from his eyes burned into her sensitive flesh, making her want too much. She wanted this, wanted him. She wanted adventurous sex, wanted to experience sex in its rawest and most explosive form.

But was she ready for it?

What about keeping control?

What about making sure she held all the cards?

Would she get that with Logan?

With someone as powerful and sexually adept as him? With someone used to calling all the shots, used to being in charge?

Damned right she would.

She widened her legs even more, offering herself to him and challenging him to take her body in whatever way he wanted. She was due. And then she intended to take *him*. To make him shiver and burn in exactly the same way he was doing to her.

Wanting to even up the scales, she tried to reach for his zipper again, but he batted her hand away.

'I told you. I need to eat,' he said, in a deep, husky tone that was barely a rumble. 'And right now I'm bloody starving.'

Anticipating what he was about to do, April bit down hard on her lower lip, preparing herself for the feel of his hot mouth, his exploratory tongue. But when he leaned down, instead of tasting her, he pursed his lips and blew a stream of warm air along her slit.

Her intimate muscles tightened and trembled as he continued to subject her to the same delicious torture. Her breasts tightened, nipples hardening to almost painful buds, and an arrow of reaction shot from her nipples to her core.

She wriggled her hips, trying to ease the almost painful pleasure that ricocheted through her feminine centre, but still Logan didn't let up.

'Bloody hell… Will you…just…?'

He touched a fingertip to her heat, just the briefest, lightest touch, but she rocked her hips so violently that she arched off the desk.

'Just what?' he said, giving her that cocky grin again and touching her lightly once more.

'You said you…needed to…'

'Eat you? Yeah, well. I always enjoy an aperitif before the main course.'

He touched her again, and this time he slid his finger along her wet length.

April arched again, pushing herself up against his subtle touch, wanting to make him increase the pressure. Needing him to give her more.

'What *is* this?' she grumbled, even as she continued to arch and buck beneath that barely there touch. 'Are you all talk…is that it?'

His low laugh echoed around the room. 'Baiting me won't help your cause.'

'What *is* my cause, exactly?'

Another laugh, this time accompanied by him pressing his finger a little way inside her. 'You want my mouth on you,' he said easily. 'You want my fingers deep inside you.'

'And you're waiting for what? An invitation?'

This time his laugh was downright lewd. 'You're lying there with your legs wide open, your nipples poking through your tee shirt, your pretty little pussy wet and throbbing for me. I'd say the invitation has well and truly been issued.'

'Then why don't you RSVP, for pity's sake?'

'Suspicious and impatient? That's quite a combination.'

'I've already told you. I'm not—'

She didn't finish the thought, or the sentence, because Logan tilted the angle of his finger and pushed deep.

'Yes...' Greedily, April clamped around him. 'More...'

He obliged, pushing in another finger, and started to work her.

Oh, hell, but he took his time. It was as if she felt every centimetre of her inner flesh, every part of her that he touched as he slid those adept fingers in and out of her heat.

Slow, she thought dazedly. So exquisitely slow. She'd always longed for slow, always wanted a man to take his time with her. To experience sex as a languid, drugging adventure that didn't need to go fast. She'd wanted the whole journey, not just the end product.

And Logan took it slow.

He brought her to the peak, then eased off just enough to bring her down a notch. She wanted to come, and yet she wanted this to last. She wanted to remember it all. To have a barometer against which to judge every future sexual encounter.

Funny, but from the moment she'd clapped eyes on Logan she'd known he would be her barometer.

She sucked in a breath as he took her up again, using the easy slide of his skilled fingers to work her into a frenzied state where her entire reality was pinpointed on the spot where he focused.

This time he didn't retreat, didn't ease off. He just watched her with those now slightly hooded dark and dangerous eyes. Watched her arch, wriggle, moan. Watched her as she came.

April wanted to close her eyes, as if doing so would pull the switch on the intensity of all that gleaming cobalt blue as his gaze bored into hers. But everything was heightened, sensation shuddering through her body like the aftermath of an earthquake.

Still he stroked her, playing her body like a bloody master. Soon she was rising up again, the orgasm gathering with each slow and masterful stroke of his fingers.

Leaning down, he pressed his mouth to the spot just above where his fingers penetrated, and April sucked in a breath. The tip of his tongue touched her lightly, pressing and retreating in the exact same rhythm as his fingers did inside her.

The dual assault sent her ever upward and she arched her neck, letting her head fall back. 'That's... that's incredible... Just don't...'

She hardly recognised the half-plea, half-moan that came from her throat.

In answer, Logan withdrew his fingers and pressed his mouth hard against her, sliding his tongue deep into her heat before retreating, then pressing down hard again.

The room began to spin and April grabbed at the desk, her fingers curling into the wood as she tried for purchase. Something, anything, that would keep her grounded. Finding nothing, all she could do was let herself go, enjoy the heady pull of that expert tongue as it played with her most sensitive flesh and pushed her ever higher.

She came again. A delicious roll of sensation that seemed to go on and on, shooting her into sensual orbit. She spun there, in a vast expanse of pure sensation, until her body went into lusty spasm and everything froze in space.

She sucked in a breath, her hips collapsing down against the desk as her whole body gave out in the aftermath of yet another intense orgasm.

Logan kept his mouth clamped over her until she found her breath, and then he slowly withdrew his tongue and, after a final press of his lips to her flesh, raised his head. His mouth was wet with her, his lips glistening with her desire.

April didn't know what to make of it. Richard had rarely gone down on her, and on the odd occasion he did, he didn't stay long enough to get her ridiculously wet.

But Logan had. Hell, the man had got her wet long before he'd even got her horizontal.

Logan stood, moved between her legs and slid his hands beneath her backside. With his eyes on hers, he drew his tongue across his lower lip, then grinned.

'I suppose you're going to say that wasn't bad for a starter course?' April managed, when she was sure she could string enough words together to form a coherent sentence.

'Complaining?'

Not about his ability to provide the most amazing oral sex.

'How could I? You made me come twice.'

'I can do better.'

Any better and she wasn't sure she'd be in a fit state to get herself home any time soon.

Now that she was coming down from those incredible orgasms she felt kind of disorientated. Unbalanced. Off-centre. He'd shaken her up, she realised. In more ways than one.

She'd anticipated a quick-fire release for both of them, something urgent, passionate, and mutually satisfying. What she hadn't expected was his steely determination to take his time, to ensure her needs were met, her pleasure achieved, before even considering his own.

She'd never felt that level of someone's focus before. Had never been looked at the way he looked at her. As if, in that moment, he wanted everything she had. He wanted her thoughts, wanted her secrets.

No, he didn't just want them. He demanded them.

It felt like he'd stripped away an essential part of her, and she didn't like it.

Time to level that playing field.

April hiked herself onto her elbows and sat. 'You've got impressive moves. I'll give you that. Now it's time to show you mine.'

She reached for his trousers, but again he batted her hand away.

'I haven't finished yet.'

April frowned, then glanced down at the very obvious bulge in his pants—the one she'd been unsuccessfully trying to get her hands on.

'This doesn't seem particularly fair.'

'What? Me giving you orgasms?'

'Me not giving *you* them.'

He still stood between her legs, his hands sliding up and down her thighs. But he was watching her as if he was trying to figure something out.

'What?'

'Just wondering why you're looking at me as if I'm some kind of snake charmer. The kind you can't take your eyes off for fear that he'll release his snake and make it bite you.'

April huffed, and glanced down at his bulge. 'That's exactly what I've been trying to do. Release your snake.'

'Ha!' He drew a few strands of hair back from her forehead. 'We'll be having sex, April. Have no doubt of that. But I'd prefer that you didn't have your eyes clamped open the whole time, as if I'm about to dupe you in some way.'

'You're being ridiculous.'

But it unsettled her that he'd clicked in to one of her biggest fears. Had she been that transparent? Had she been so intent on keeping control of the situation that she'd subconsciously sent out warnings that she didn't entirely trust the situation? That she didn't entirely trust him?

'Ridiculous? Maybe. My cock would agree with you, seeing as it's hard and throbbing right now, and I want nothing more than to be inside you. But not at any price. You're suspicious of me. You think our having sex will complicate things. You still don't entirely trust that I'll act in your best interests once I've gotten between your legs.'

'You have already gotten between my legs.'

He wrapped his hands around her waist and brought her off the desk to stand in front of him. 'And I'll let you think on that. On how it felt to have me go down on you. We'll call it a prelude of things to come.'

'I get to think on that, do I?' April said smoothing down her skirt. 'And what do *you* get to think on? You never even let me touch you. If I'm suspicious of anything, it's that. I mean, what kind of man passes up the opportunity of a hand-job?'

'This kind. Especially when I get the feeling the woman is keeping score.'

Logan half expected steam to come out of her ears. He knew April was up for some hot and steamy sex as much as he was, but he didn't like the way she looked at him, with distrust in her gaze. He wanted more from her. More *with* her.

Despite her impatience, her demands for him to get on with it, he sensed she'd held back. So he'd pushed her, coaxing her to let go, really let go. Which probably made him a bloody moron, looking a freaking gift horse in the mouth like this. Especially when he had a hard-on throbbing in his pants that definitely wasn't going anywhere any time soon.

He should be celebrating a woman who didn't seem likely to make demands, who didn't want anything other than casual, no-strings sex.

Yet here he was wanting more. He wanted to snap that fierce control, have her lay herself open to him. He wanted to know what locked her down tight and kept her one step removed from just letting go.

April had his juices flowing from the start, and he'd known the feeling was mutual. Beneath her suspicion he'd seen desire, need. But she didn't trust him. Which meant that if he wanted her—and he did—he needed to prove his assertion that sex could coexist perfectly well alongside his ability to act professionally.

That meant getting Veronica Lebeck to back off.

Since he'd be away for the next few days, he'd asked his brother to get the low-down on Haydon's current relationship with the woman. Logan needed to tread carefully, because there was no way he planned on upsetting his relationship with the man. If it wasn't for him, Logan would likely still be trying to piece his family back together, might still be trying to reunite his siblings after they'd been separated, scattered to the winds, all those years ago.

Even if Haydon was still seeing Veronica, Logan doubted she'd have any solid evidence with which to pursue her claim against April, so he just needed to make her accept the futility of threatening legal action. That would hopefully appease Haydon and take the weight off April's mind and leave her free to concentrate on other things.

Namely, heating up the sheets with him.

He wanted her. Shit, but he really did.

For one night? For several? He didn't rightly know. He liked the way she challenged him, the way she pressed for answers. How she wanted to know exactly where she stood. Add that to the apprehension, the doubt he glimpsed in her, and she presented an enigma.

Was that part of the attraction?

All he knew was that he wanted her to trust him. In and out of the bedroom.

'What do you mean, keeping score?' April said fiercely. 'What do you think I am? Some *femme fatale*, totting up my conquests for my little black book? I don't even know why you're making a big deal about this. You claimed it didn't have to be complicated and now you're the one making it exactly that. It's just sex.'

'Exactly. But when we fuck I want you completely at ease in my bed.' He placed his hands on either side of her face and held her steady. 'And, while there doesn't have to be complications between the sheets, something tells me you're a complicated woman. The kind who needs to work it all out in that head of yours, make sure all your ducks are in a row. You say you don't want the waters muddied, that you need to focus on your priorities. That's entirely understandable, and I get it.'

'But you thought you'd go ahead and muddy the waters anyway? Just to make sure you kept the upper hand?'

'What the hell does *that* mean?'

She stepped away, smoothed down her skirt again as she searched for her panties. 'You want the power here, don't you? To keep me dangling while you assess whether or not you're going to help me. Treat me to oral sex without letting me return the favour. I bet that feels great, doesn't it? You have all the control and I have absolutely none.'

'I still don't know what you're talking about. In what way do I have control, exactly? I've got a throbbing, aching cock, while you've had two orgasms.'

'And just to make doubly sure I'm aware that you're in the driving seat,' she said, as if he hadn't spoken, 'you're now graciously allowing me to ponder on those orgasms and accept them as a prelude. And where is my underwear?'

It took Logan a moment to get his head in gear, but then he looked down and saw the pillarbox-red panties at the side of his desk.

She'd pissed him off, accusing him of taking 'control' of a situation as if it was a dirty word. As if taking control was wrong.

Fuck that.

In his experience, someone had to do it. There were too many people in this world who thought they could renege on their responsibilities. Too many people who simply walked away when the going got tough, and to hell with who was left to pick up the damn pieces.

What was so wrong with wanting to be in control?

Because she'd annoyed him, Logan walked to his desk and snapped up the underwear. Okay, so if he was such a control freak, then he'd damn well give her something more to complain about.

She reached out her hand, cocking her hip when he simply held on to the scrappy lace.

'I'll keep these,' he said, shoving the panties into

his trouser pocket. 'Might as well live up to the label you've pinned on me. Or should I say labels? What have we got so far? Controlling, unprofessional, power-crazy…anything you'd like to add before I call the printers?' When she just glared at him, he shrugged. 'So, yeah, I'll keep these. We'll call it a little memento of our evening.'

Her fiery brown eyes narrowed and that sexy hip cocked even more. 'You've already got a memento, haven't you?'

Yeah, well, he couldn't argue with that. The taste of her lingered on his lips, her scent was heady in his nostrils. The touch of her hot, wet flesh was still making his fingers burn from where they'd sunk deep inside her.

'The vibrator's not enough? You need my under-wear, too? What? Have you got some kind of fetish? Maybe I should get a label for that as well.'

Shit. He'd all but forgotten about the vibrator. 'As far as I know, that hasn't been near you.' He tapped his pocket. 'I want something that smells of you.'

The patch of colour that swept over her cheek-bones soothed some of the irritation gnawing inside and made him grin.

She screwed up her mouth, then shook her head. 'Keep them. I've got plenty more. I'll just grab an-other pair from my stock.'

He had a mental image of her in some of the lin-gerie he'd seen when he'd tapped through her web-site earlier in his office. Picturing her in crotchless panties, a nipple-revealing bra, G-strings that would leave her ass on erotic display.

His cock throbbed and his blood heated. Why the hell was he torturing himself?

There was not one iota of suspicion in her eyes now—only challenge. That was more like it. But before he could reach for her she grabbed her bag and started towards the door.

'Thanks for your time. I trust I'll hear from you soon?'

Her haughty tone did nothing to ease the ache in his groin, but it made him want to provoke and push a little more.

'Want to share some dried-up pasta before you go?'

If either of them should be pissed off right now, it should be him. Not only because of those labels she'd pinned on him, but because he was sporting a hard-on that he didn't think would ease any time soon.

'I'm no longer hungry.'

Her eyes, still blistering with challenge, met his and held there. He wondered if she was expecting him to utter some flippant remark, such as he wasn't especially hungry either—not since he'd had his head between her legs.

However, since he liked to think he was a wise man on occasion, he kept his mouth shut.

'Let me know if there's anything else you need from me,' she said, with a snooty tilt of her chin. 'I'll have it couriered over to your office.'

Okay, a man could only take so much before he retaliated, and he'd just passed his red line.

'There's plenty I need,' he said, and moved to her. He slid his hands slowly down her arms, enjoying the way she shivered. 'But none of it can be sent by courier.' He brought her up close, his mouth an inch from hers. 'I'll be in New York for a couple of days. When I get back I'm coming for you, April Sinclair, and I'll be wanting the whole deal next time.' He gave her a feral grin. 'You'd better be ready.'

CHAPTER FIVE

APRIL HAD TAKEN to thinking about the encounter as *The Kiss*. It seemed more innocuous, somehow, relegating it to an everyday kind of occurrence rather than mind-numbing, hormone-tingling oral sex.

Cross-legged, April sat on her living room floor and finished boxing up her latest batch of orders. She tried once more to push the idiot man from her mind.

How hard could it be? She was a grown woman, wasn't she? She could choose what she focused on and decide what she'd allow to dwell between her ears. And between her legs, come to that.

Yet there he was again. Squeezing into the slightest little crack in her concentration, making her hot and decidedly uncomfortable.

Be careful what you wish for, she thought for the umpteenth time.

Hadn't she wished for adventure between the sheets? For a man who'd use his skills to make her tremble and moan? To take her on a sexually charged journey that would make her marvel at the reaction of her own body, her own sexuality?

Well, it certainly looked like she'd gotten that, and a whole lot more into the bargain.

She'd known from her first glimpse of Logan Fitzpatrick that he was dangerous. Known that he was a man beyond capable of giving her every single one of her desires.

One touch of his mouth to hers. One slide of those slow, lethal hands over her willing flesh. One press of his tongue and push of his fingers inside her and it had gone beyond wishing and dreaming.

He'd taken control, which was something she'd sworn never to allow to happen to her again. Except with Logan it was the kind of control that didn't strip away her own power.

She'd been at his mercy, but she sensed he'd been at hers, too.

His warning that next time he'd be wanting the whole deal had been issued with a question mark attached to it. As if he'd placed the ball squarely in her court. With him she knew she could say no and while he wouldn't necessarily like it, he'd accept it.

She wondered if that made him even more dangerous than the pull she felt to his raw masculinity.

One encounter with Logan had pushed her off-centre. Unbalanced her. Made her have to continually shove thoughts of him aside so that she could focus and concentrate on her business.

Which was what she had to do right now.

Despite Veronica's threat hanging over her, she was busier than ever. Orders were coming from every direction. Business was booming. She had copious website orders to fulfil, back-to-back parties to book, and a popular magazine wanting to run a story on her success. It was a prestigious publication, with a worldwide readership, and the publicity would be incredibly good for business.

Since the last thing she needed was Veronica getting wind of it, and making life even more difficult, April had reluctantly asked for a rain-check. While the people at the magazine had agreed, they'd stressed that they did need the article to coincide with an international event featuring entrepreneurial women that was taking place later that summer.

April prayed that this legal nightmare would be over well before then.

She hadn't heard a peep from Logan while he'd been in New York—except via the TV news. He'd been handling a divorce case for an American TV mogul whose young wife had been having an affair with an actor closer to her own age. Despite the lack of a pre-nup, it was reported that the wife's divorce settlement would now be a pittance, and nothing like the figure she'd demanded. No doubt due to Logan's skill and ability.

She'd taken to reading about his cases, and couldn't help but admire his drive, his passion and his tenacity to fight like hell for his clients. She only wished she could be one of them… But in the absence of that possibility she would at least be grateful if he'd contact her with his views on how things stood for her.

It was so frustrating. Patience wasn't one of her virtues. She needed something to happen—and soon. She wanted this thing dealt with once and for all, and the very next time she spoke to him she would press him for answers. At least professionally. As far as personally went he'd made his intentions perfectly clear when he'd issued his threat that night at his home.

She still bristled over the way he'd told her that he wanted the real deal next time, and that he'd be coming for her as soon as he got back from New York.

Despite her frustration over that, and the whole he'd-been-in-the-driving-seat thing, she couldn't stop thinking about having him touch her again. With those long, skilful fingers, those powerful hands, that adept mouth…

April closed her eyes, allowing herself a few minutes to enjoy a lusty daydream involving her snatching back some control of the situation and making Logan beg. As blood fired hot in her veins and her breathing became shaky she opened her eyes and waved her hand in front of her face, hoping to lessen the heat generated by the fantasy.

Heroically, she pulled her attention back to matters at hand and checked out the next item on her list. She'd received a bumper order from a regular customer who liked to organise her own parties for an army of adventurous friends. April always sent the woman a thank-you gift along with her twenty percent commission. As with all orders, she stuck a discreet and innocuous return address label on the package. Nobody would ever guess the parcel contained the latest in clit-stimulators.

She wondered what Logan would make of it. What he would *do* with it. Huh… He'd probably make some smart remark along the lines of *his* women not needing such things when they had him to administer to their every desire.

The jump in her belly, the heat that shot from her breasts to her core, confirmed that, whatever else happened, she was damn well going to find out if the reality lived up to his cocky predictions. Was he really *that* good? All the signs said that he was—especially if what she'd experienced so far was indicative of his sexual prowess and his ability to please a woman.

Before she could start fantasising about Logan again, a sound from the doorway made her jump.

'Thinking of giving one of those a test run before mailing them off?' Lizzie asked, tilting her head. 'Been having a little solo time, have we?'

'For God's sake!' Guiltily, April pulled the hem of her tee shirt firmly over her jeans. 'I've got too much to do to even *think* about sex right now.'

Lizzie picked up the nearest box and gave it a healthy shake. 'Seems you conveniently forgot to tell me that a certain lawyer is smoking hot and very eligible.'

'Because *you've* already got yourself a hot guy. What would Miles say if I set you up with Logan Fitzpatrick?'

'Ha! I wasn't thinking of me. And the fact your face is bright red right now tells me you weren't either.'

'Still not thinking about sex,' April said. 'Potential litigation, remember?'

'Wouldn't hurt to get your hair done, or something. Look the part for when the smoking hot lawyer gets back to town.' She shook the box again. 'Maybe you should get a Brazilian?'

'Maybe *you* should make yourself useful and help me tape up these boxes? Then you can take them to the post office for me.'

Lizzie shrugged and dropped down next to April. 'No problem. It's on my way anyway.' She picked up the tape dispenser. 'I'm meeting Miles from work. We're catching a movie and then having supper. I'll probably stay over.'

'Enjoy,' April said as she labelled the last package. 'I'm planning to unpack some new supplies and then get started on promo for them.'

While she and Lizzie taped up the rest of the boxes, April's thoughts turned to *The Kiss* again, but she ruthlessly shoved them away.

Bigger fish and all that…

When the doorbell rang, April thought that Lizzie had returned, having forgotten to take her key. Not an unusual occurrence. She headed to the door, brushing down her jeans, which were covered in glitter thanks to a vibrator which had split and emptied its contents all over her and the carpet.

Logan stood leaning against the doorframe, hands in the pockets of tailored black jeans. His gaze made a long, slow perusal, then came back to meet her own.

'Nice hair.'

Ignoring her suddenly tremulous stomach, and the pulse of reaction deep in her core, she reached up to the band holding back her shoulder-length hair. When she pulled her hand away it bore traces of lime-green glitter.

'I wasn't expecting company.'

'Since I was in the neighbourhood, I thought I'd pop by and touch base.'

All thoughts of her glittering hair vanished as she let her gaze roam greedily over him. She had the inclination to yank him over the threshold, get his kit off, and have her way with him before he knew what had hit him. Poetic justice for the way he'd gone down on her and hadn't allowed her to return the compliment.

Instead he'd offered her dried-up pasta before packing her off home like some naughty child who was being denied her pudding.

'Going to leave me here on your doorstep?' he asked, one of those thick and desperately sexy eyebrows rising towards his equally sexy hairline.

Hell, she found every single thing about him sexy.

'I'm in the middle of something, as it happens. Shouldn't I just make an appointment now that you're back in London?'

That slow and easy grin sent sparks flying through her veins. Damn the man. He knew she was deliberately playing it cool.

'I'm saving you a trip. How about a coffee, since I'm here anyway?'

She wanted a damn sight more than coffee, and if she invited him in, it would be only a question of time before she had that chest-hugging navy sweater off his back and those exquisitely cut jeans off his butt.

Acknowledging that, accepting that, she stepped back and let him in. 'So, not only do you invite clients to supper, you make house calls too?'

'Only when I'm in the neighbourhood.'

The kitchen wasn't the roomiest place in the house, but it felt positively claustrophobic with his big frame filling the doorway.

'Black, no sugar,' he requested, watching her fill the machine. 'Nice place.'

Seeing as he lived in some sort of fantasy home for the rich, she thought he was being facetious. Yet there was no sign of that when she glanced up. He was eyeing her with what could only be described as flat-out lust. She imagined it was like looking in a mirror.

She reached into the cupboard for mugs, and side-stepped when Logan came up next to her. He selected a mug from the shelf—one that she'd decided not to use.

'From your stock?'

Amusement tinged his tone, and April shrugged. 'A gift. From Lizzie, my flatmate. She thought it was funny. She has a bizarre sense of humour.'

Latex lovers do it covered

While she poured filter coffee into two mugs, she was aware of him beside her. Too close. Her pulse hammered and she shoved the coffee at him, thankful that it didn't spill all over his sweater. Then he'd have to take off that sweater…take off his shirt… wipe down his chest…and then he'd…

'Let's put these down a minute,' he said, taking the mugs from her and placing them on the worktop. 'There's something I need to do.'

She didn't need a degree in body language to interpret his intention, and if she wasn't careful he'd be running the show again.

'I don't think so. You don't get to call the shots this time.'

'You're not still smarting over me going down on you?' His nostrils flared slightly. 'Most women would be celebrating.'

April huffed. 'It wasn't *that* good.'

His laugh did ridiculous things to her female parts, leaving them trembling in anticipation.

'Well, now you've gone and thrown down the gauntlet. I can't possibly let that comment go un-challenged.'

April tried to move back, to get some distance before he took complete charge and she turned to putty in his sinful hands.

'Just stating the facts. You seem to have a high opinion of your skills.'

He moved in tighter. 'You know, maybe it's some-thing to do with the way you tilt your chin at me,' he said, his hands curving around her hips, 'or it could be that glittery look you've got going, but I'm find-ing it impossible to keep my hands off you.'

She looked at his mouth, at the curve of his strong jaw. Reaction simmered deep in her belly and made her knees go weak. Her response was to place her hands on his arms, feeling all that solid, warm mus-cle beneath her fingers.

'As long as you know my hands have some de-mands of their own. This isn't going to be another one-sided deal.'

'Fair enough.'

Then his lips touched hers, with all the incendiary potential of a live wire. Electricity sizzled along her flesh, intensifying the kiss and taking it from smooth to downright lewd in mere seconds. Crazy sensa-tions ripped through her, stealing the breath from her lungs as his arms banded around her, crushing her breasts against the solid wall of his chest.

It was only the determined press of his erection

between her legs, the erotic groan that came from deep in his throat, that stopped April from sliding into pure sensation and going with whatever Logan wanted.

She pressed against his shoulders and eased him away, gratified by the heat in his eyes, the ragged rise and fall of his chest. It seemed she wasn't the only one suffering from desperate lust and sensual need.

She could unsettle him as much as he unsettled her, and she intended to take full advantage of the situation.

'What?' His tone was husky and dark.

April slid her fingers along his shoulders, down his biceps. 'I told you... I'm not letting you have it all your way. I've got plans of my own this time.'

Before he could respond, she turned them so their positions were reversed and he was the one with his back to the counter. She nuzzled against him, letting her breasts stroke his chest, her hips roll against his. When he inhaled sharply, she smiled, enjoying the sensation of feminine power. It was an amazing aphrodisiac. Or maybe that was just Logan?

Right then she didn't care enough to reason it out. All she wanted was him.

His hands came to her hips and her instinct was to bat them away, but since they felt so good she let them remain there.

She moved in closer, shimmied her heat against his erection, loving the way he inhaled again, his jaw tightening. His fingers dug into her hips, encouraging her pelvis closer to his hard length.

'Do you remember what I told you?' he asked in that gravelled tone. 'That when I returned you'd better be ready for me?'

'I remember.' She ground herself against him, slow and easy. 'But the real question is, are you ready for *me*?'

Taking advantage of his quick jolt of surprise, she kept her eyes on his and slid down his body to kneel on the floor. Still watching him, she grabbed the buckle of his belt and loosened it.

'What's with the knot symbol?' she asked, unhooking the catch of his waistband.

He took another deep inhalation as she slid the zipper slowly down. 'Can't rightly remember at this precise moment.'

April grinned. She knew that feeling. It was the same way she felt every time he touched her.

With the zip down, she reached into his fly, past his boxers, and wrapped her fingers around his erection. He jerked in her hand, his stomach muscles contracting, his breath leaving his lungs in a grunt.

Her thoughts trickled back to that moment in his study when she'd been checking him out. Maybe it really was true about the relationship between the size of a man's feet and his appendage. He was certainly impressive.

Lucky her.

'Fuck… April…'

'Not just yet,' she said, squeezing her fingers lightly around him. 'I've got plans, remember?'

'Hard to forget when you've got your hand around my cock.'

With her free hand she eased his jeans and boxers down until his erection sprang free. He was wide and long. Impressive in both length and girth. Her belly gave a delicious shiver, her core muscles tightening as she imagined him filling her.

His flesh felt hot beneath her hand and she drew her thumb slowly across his tip. He jerked again, but she ignored it, bringing her other hand up to stroke slowly along the length of him, before touching her fingertips lightly to his balls. She caressed him leisurely, enjoying his reaction. The way his eyelids grew heavy, the low rasps of his breath, the tightening of his jaw…

He watched her as she watched him. 'Is this payback?'

All feigned innocence, she fluttered her lashes. 'Payback? Whatever for?'

'Don't be cute.' He sucked in a breath as she slid her thumb across his tip again. 'Not that I'm complaining.'

'Good. Because I'm just getting started.'

She could feel the tension in his big, masculine body. Could see it in his expression. He'd hit it straight on the nose about it being payback. She intended to re-establish the power base, to go down on him, make him beg. Just the way he'd made her beg.

But the base had shifted again—because she was in thrall to him. To the way he stood there, letting her do as she wanted, letting her take charge of his body, have control over it. And somehow she didn't get the impression that he felt powerless—far from it.

Unlike her, he seemed to revel in it.

It didn't seem fair.

Reflexively, her fingers squeezed around him and he tensed, hissing in a breath.

'Sorry.'

He huffed a laugh. 'Don't apologise. Just keep on doing what you're doing.'

Oh, she very much intended to do exactly that. And she also intended to stop thinking, stop worrying about balancing scales, and simply go with her instincts.

This was just sex, wasn't it? And going down on him would put them on equal sides of the same coin. Mission accomplished. Which meant she could just enjoy what this was between them without worrying about anything but their mutual enjoyment.

She let herself be ruled by pure sensation, increasing the pressure of her hands around him, loving his heat, his strength, his verbal encouragement. Then she bent forward, using the tip of her tongue to lick across the head of his erection, mimicking the way he'd done the same between her legs. Achingly slow and torturously light.

Logan's hips jerked forward, encouraging her to take more of him into her mouth, but she wasn't about to make things easy for him. She stroked her tongue around his engorged flesh, felt his salty taste on her lips, then slid her tongue along his entire length before returning to the tip.

Opening her mouth, she took him in barely an inch, withdrawing before taking him a little deeper. She stroked him with her tongue, loving the way he grunted and groaned and swore.

His fingers arrowed into her hair, the pressure against her scalp intensifying each time she took him halfway into her mouth before withdrawing, until finally she gave in to his tortured, 'For fuck's sake, April!' and took him as deep as she could get.

His hands were pressing against her scalp as she worked him. He hit the back of her throat and she focused on taking deep breaths in and out of her nose as his hips pumped and his cock pulsed.

Sensing he was close, April kept up the pressure. He grew thicker, and her lips stretched against his fullness as his taste sharpened in her mouth.

'April…'

His fingers tightened as he attempted to draw her head away, but April wasn't finished yet. Not until he was. There was no way she was stopping now. Not when she had him at her complete mercy.

'Shit… April…'

He came, muttering expletives, his salty taste filling her mouth and sliding down her throat.

April couldn't remember going down on a man

and feeling as if it was as much a pleasure for her as it was for him, but with Logan it felt exactly that.

His body sagged, but his hands remained in her hair as he pulled out of her mouth.

Tilting her head, April looked up. She felt victorious, triumphant. Having a man as strong and masterful as Logan at her mercy was…*empowering*.

After he'd sucked in a few more deep breaths he reached down and pulled her up against him. He grinned. 'Feel better now?'

Blinking, April placed her hands on his chest. 'I think that's my line.'

He reached his arms around her and squeezed her ass. 'So now we're even.'

'Looks like.' She couldn't resist smiling back at him as she placed her hands around his neck.

He kissed her, long and hard and hot. When they separated he cocked his head to the side, frowning as if trying to figure something out.

'What?' she asked, aware that her hair probably looked an absolute mess. What with being drawn back in a band all day, and with the added decorative effect of green glitter. 'Have I suddenly grown horns, or something?'

'Just giving a final check that it's gone.'

'And has it? Whatever "it" is?'

He looked some more, then pursed his lips and nodded slowly. 'Yeah. Can't see a trace of it now.'

'Excellent. Now we can all sleep better.'

She knew he was referring to her look of circumspection the last time they'd been together, but she wasn't going to admit to it.

He raised his eyebrows. 'I'm guessing you don't even realise you're doing it. How hard you work to make sure that everything between us remains on equal footing. Tit for tat, so to speak. I go down on you—you give me a blow job.'

Okay, he was spot-on, but his perception was unexpected and it hit too close to home for her to be flippant about it. Besides, it was best he knew the score if they were going to continue having sex.

'What's wrong with that? Where does it say that a relationship between a man and woman *shouldn't* be on a level playing field?'

'In no book I've ever read,' he conceded. 'Anyway, your turn.'

'My turn?'

A wicked gleam shone in his eyes as he yanked his jeans up over his hips, but left the zipper open. 'Where's your bedroom?'

'On the left. Why?'

It was fun, enjoying this teasing banter. She was starting to think sex *could* be fun. She hadn't had much experience of that before. The couple of lovers she'd had before Richard hadn't exactly been memorable, and sex with Richard had always been sober and over too quickly.

And why the devil was she thinking of that moron when she had her hands on Logan?

'I'd like a tour of your apartment—starting with

your bedroom, which has very much featured in my imagination these past couple of nights.'

'Don't get your hopes up. It isn't much larger than the kitchen.'

'Does it have a double bed?'

'Yes.'

'Then it's large enough for what I have in mind. Which is to fuck you, April. To do every single one of those things that have featured in my fevered imagination. And neither one of us is going to be keeping score.'

CHAPTER SIX

No, APRIL THOUGHT as Logan landed them both on the bed and the breath whooshed out of her. She definitely wasn't going to be keeping score. At least, not tonight. She wanted his hands on her, all over her. Those wonderfully accomplished, skilful and slow hands. She wanted everything he could give her.

He kissed her—wild powerful kisses that stole any breath she managed to grab and left her on fire. She fumbled to reach the edge of his sweater and pulled it up between them, desperate to get her hands on his flesh. The heat of him seeped into her, mingling wildly with her own, joining them together in a kind of scorching insanity that she wanted to explore until it burnt out beneath their frenzied clamour for each other.

Logan ripped at her tee and she heard something tear, but couldn't give a damn what it was. He yanked her hands above her head and slid the tee shirt off, his mouth feasting on her neck, his hands sliding over her collarbone and down to cup her breasts. April sucked in a breath as he reached into her bra cups and released each breast from its confines.

He looked up, his eyes gleaming, his teeth bared, his hair mussed from where her hands had been busy. He looked so masculine…primitive…wild…and it made every single one of her hormones sit up and beg for more….*so* much more.

She grabbed his sweater, tore it over his head. His hands were back on her breasts, his thumbs toying with her hard nipples, making them tighten to painful proportions. Lowering his head, he took one nipple into his mouth, circling his tongue around the rosy bud while his thumb continued to play with the other.

April arched from the bed, pushing her breasts up for more of Logan's attention. With adept skill he released her breast and his hand moved down to the catch of her jeans. The rasp of her zipper being pulled down was devilishly erotic, and she shivered even as her flesh burned.

She wanted to grumble when Logan sat back, and the cool air on her heated breasts where his mouth had been made them tingle and ache. He yanked down her jeans, taking her panties with them. When he'd tossed them away he eased her legs wide, so he could kneel between them. Then he reached for the fastening of her bra and dealt with that in the same way he had her jeans.

She lay naked, enjoying how he feasted his hot gaze on her. Her core muscles clenched, arrowing sensation up to her sensitive nipples and right back down again. The erotic sizzle seemed to radiate out to the rest of her body. Reaching up, she grabbed Logan's waistband and tried to get his jeans off his hips. But he was already leaning over her, his hands on her knees, pushing them up towards her waist.

The same cool air slid over her slit as she lay there, open to him, enjoying his heated gaze and the wicked look in his gorgeous eyes. Reaching out, she wrapped her fingers around his arms, sliding one hand down to trace the tattoo on his forearm. She wanted to ask him what it meant, what significance the Celtic cross held for him, when he'd gotten it, but she didn't want to waste time asking questions, especially when his head was lowering and his mouth was inches away from the fire of her core.

He didn't touch her lightly this time. Didn't caress her with the tip of his tongue, the tip of his finger. This time he pushed inside her with one swoop, his tongue sliding deep and hot. Her cry filled the room, but he didn't take pity. He moved his tongue in a motion that took her moments from climax. How could that happen so fast?

His hands pushed down harder on her knees, anchoring her so that she couldn't move even if she wanted to. She didn't. So she let herself go, let him take her where he intended. Two more swoops of his tongue and she came. So hard that the room actually spun. So hard that she stopped breathing.

'Logan…'

While she panted her way back from the oblivion
of an excruciatingly excellent climax Logan sat back.
His mouth was slick with her juices, his chest—such
a wonderfully wide and muscled chest—heaved.
Raw and savage, she thought dazedly as he reached
into his trouser pocket, that was how he looked right
then. It thrilled her beyond belief, and already she
was throbbing for more. More of him. Much more
of him.

She watched in a kind of stupor as he took a
packet from his pocket and handed it to her.

'Keep hold of this,' he said. and got off the bed.

He pulled off his shoes and socks, shucked out of
his jeans and boxers. April drank in the sight of him.
Powerfully male, incredibly built. She trembled a
little, but it was from raw need and impatience. She
wanted him inside her. Wanted to feel him driving
into her. Taking her. Pleasuring her.

And she wanted to pleasure him. So much more
than she'd ever wanted to pleasure anyone before.

He was a generous lover, attentive and astute, and
he pulled something from deep inside her. A need for
connection that existed on a primal level and which
she hadn't realised was there. She wondered if the
same need existed in Logan. If it did, she wanted to
be the woman to bring it to the surface.

Which was a dangerous thought to have, and she
pushed it away as Logan knelt between her legs again
and held out his hand for the packet. April kept her

eyes on his as she brought the packet to her lips, placed it between her teeth, and ripped it open.

Logan sucked in a breath, his stomach muscles jerking with the movement.

April took the condom out, tossed the packet away, then hiked herself up onto her elbows. Since she was lying with her knees bent, and Logan was between them, keeping her legs open wide, it was an awkward angle from which to slide the condom on for him, but she managed to get it over his tip.

He grinned knowingly. 'Maybe you'll let me do it next time.'

It took her a moment, hovering in a kind of sensual haze, before she caught his meaning. Was she still trying to keep a balance? Trying to control things in the bedroom? Even subconsciously?

She didn't want her fears and concerns to slide into her personal life to the extent that she ruined what was already becoming meaningful to her. She wanted to enjoy what they shared, for as long as they shared it. Despite her earlier thoughts about some kind of deeper connection, she wanted this to be fun. To be easy.

Slackening her grip on the condom, she let Logan finish rolling it on.

Fun, she thought. *Easy.*

'Maybe I could have managed if you weren't quite so big.' Grinning, she dropped back onto her elbows. 'Not that I should be bolstering your ego—especially considering the size of it.'

Having finished the job of suiting himself, Logan gave a grin that was feral. 'Big dick. Big ego. You certainly know how to compliment a guy.'

'While the ego part is assured, my compliment regarding your dick is only based on visual evidence at the moment. I might have to reassess after a practical demonstration. Say, give you marks out of ten.'

He leaned down over her, placing his hands on either side of her head so that she had to drop onto her back. 'Oh, I'll be a perfect ten.'

She laughed as he positioned himself at her entrance, the tip of his erection prodding her welcoming flesh. Reaching up, she wrapped her fingers around his wrists, wanting something to hold as he started pushing inside her.

Considering the rapid pattern of his breath, the urgency in his expression, it surprised her that he took his time. With each push he waited, watching her as if making sure she was okay. It was incredibly sweet, but right then April didn't want sweet. She wanted hot, heavy, lusty, debauched.

'Logan…take me…*hard*.'

He looked at her again, his mouth open, teeth bared, as if he was holding tight to something tenuous. Then he tilted his hips and pushed deep. He held steady again, waiting until April tightened her grip around his wrists and clenched her intimate muscles around him. Then he started to move.

Soon she was writhing beneath him, her hips matching the rhythm he set. Slow at first, then increasing in speed and intensity as he pumped hard, complying with her frantic demands.

Reaching between them, he flicked her clit with his thumb. Their gazes clashed, and in his eyes April saw the question. Right now, in this moment, she knew she could answer it. There was no need for caution, no need for suspicion or doubt. He wanted what she did. Hot, casual, uncomplicated sex that didn't have to mean anything other than mutual enjoyment and satisfaction.

So with one pointed look into his dark blue gaze she closed her eyes.

Lights flashed, shapes spun…and the orgasm rocked her over and over, leaving her dazzled and shaken. And when Logan shattered too, spilling into the condom with a harsh grunt, it ripped through April like a sharp, unexpected summer storm.

'Fuck…fuck…' She opened her eyes to see Logan piercing her with his heavy-lidded gaze. Still with his hands anchored on either side of her head, his chest heaved as he pulled air into his lungs. 'Okay?'

April swallowed, drew in a shaky breath. 'More than okay. You?'

'Way beyond.'

He kept looking at her with what seemed like reproach, but made no move to pull out.

'What?' she asked, sliding her hands up and down his arms. 'I closed my eyes, in case you hadn't noticed.'

'I noticed.'

'It's just sex.'

His gaze travelled over her face before meeting hers again. 'Yeah. Glad you pointed that out.'

For some reason April had thought she had to make that clear. But she wasn't sure whether it was for her own benefit or for his. It was probably just that she still felt shaken, dazed by the whole thing. Because the sex had been pretty explosive—something she hadn't experienced before.

Logan bent to kiss her, a light and easy kiss that served to remind her that this was all about having fun. Good—that was *good*. Because that was all she wanted it to be.

'Bathroom?' he asked, getting off the bed.

'Out and to your left.'

Taking a moment to enjoy the view, April watched him disappear from the bedroom. His back view was very much on a par with his front view. An exceptionally fine ass, muscular legs and wide shoulders.

Satisfied, April stretched, every single one of her muscles seeming to give a very happy sigh. They hadn't been worked that hard and pleasurably since… well, since *never*. Logan was the best workout they'd ever had.

The man was passionate, sensual, considerate, with a nice chunk of demanding mixed in. In the context of sex, she kind of liked that. Despite her vow to hold tight to the reins of her life going forward, after enjoying sex with Logan she wondered if she could make a tiny exception to that rule when it came to sexy bedroom fun.

Her answer came when Logan returned to the bedroom, a gleam in his eye and holding something behind his back.

Despite having just had him inside her, she wanted him again.

He moved to stand beside the bed. 'How much do these sell for?' he asked, and held out a glittering green vibrator. 'I think I'd like to buy one.'

April's inner muscles trembled, her core aching with anticipation. 'I haven't priced them yet. New stock.'

'I'll be your first customer.'

He plonked the vibrator on the bedside table and lay down beside her, hiking himself onto his elbow and looking down at her. He started a slow, easy stroke around one nipple.

'I'm wondering if I should actually sell them,' April said, trying not to be distracted by the slow, easy stroking. 'Considering one of them was damaged and leaked lime-green glitter all over me.'

He glanced up at her hair. 'I think green glitter can be quite a turn-on. Certainly was for me.'

'Oh, it was the glitter, was it?'

'Not entirely.' He leaned down, kissed her. 'You're serious about not selling them?'

April drew in a breath, still trying not to get distracted by the hypnotic slide of his finger around her rapidly hardening nipple.

'I don't want anything else rearing up and biting me on the backside. Not when this Veronica thing is hanging over me, and certainly not while I'm trading without insurance.'

'You're not.'

Her stomach jumped. 'What?'

'You're not trading without insurance.'

Despite the exquisite torture he was inflicting on her breast, she levered herself up on her elbows.

Logan dropped onto his back. 'I arranged cover for you. Through a friend.'

Dual emotions swept through her. Relief that one of the most pressing of her concerns had been dealt with. Annoyance that he hadn't even told her he was doing it.

'You've arranged public liability cover for my business, even though there's a potential claim against me?'

'Yeah. All you need to do is sign the form.' He reached up and tapped her nose. 'You don't look ecstatic.'

April sat right up, taking a moment to process what that meant. Then relief layered over the annoyance, and she drew in a breath as she turned to look over her shoulder at him, a jumble of emotions battling for dominance. 'I want to thank you.'

Logan wrapped his fingers around her arm and drew her down beside him. 'You can thank me by reaching over and grabbing my new purchase.'

April was still processing her feelings about his

setting up insurance without telling her. She was grateful, of course, but being left out of the loop didn't sit well with her. Did he think he could make decisions on her behalf and she'd simply accept it? Maybe it was time they got a few things clear.

'You haven't said what you think my chances are if Veronica goes ahead with her threat to sue me. Nor have you told me what your fee is for our consultation. I'd like to have your invoice so I can settle it.'

He cupped his palm around her breast. 'My fee? That's about the same price as your new glitter vibrators. So let's call it even.'

No way. That would put her well and truly beholden to him.

'We're keeping business and sex separate, remember? And I'd really like to know where I stand regarding the former.'

His thumb, busy stroking her nipple, ceased its exploration. 'You want to talk business? Right now?'

'Why not? You started this conversation.'

His eyes narrowed. 'You're pissed off at me.'

She was, even though she knew it was probably irrational, but she really needed him to understand that he wasn't in charge of her *or* her business.

'You should have told me about the insurance cover.'

'I just did.'

'How hard would it have been to shoot me an email or a text telling me what you were arranging?'

'I didn't realise it would be a problem. You need insurance to keep trading and I've sorted it.'

'Exactly. *You've* sorted it. It's *my* business, Logan. You should give me the courtesy of keeping me informed when you act on my behalf.'

'It's just insurance cover. What the hell's the problem?'

Since he didn't look in the least as if he believed it *was* a problem, but just continued to lie there looking mussed and sexy, and so damn masculine that she wanted to jump him again and to hell with principles and power struggles and keeping control of everything, April swung her legs over the side of the bed and stood.

She felt uneasy, out of sync, disorientated. As if she'd taken her eye off something fundamental and in doing so had slipped back into the murky shadows of the past.

She found her discarded tee and, despite the tear Logan had caused when he'd yanked it off, pulled it over her head. 'It's not unreasonable to insist I be kept informed of what affects my business before it becomes a fait accompli.'

Logan hiked himself up against the headboard, folded his arms and crossed his ankles. 'It's not unreasonable to act in someone's best interests when the opportunity arises, either.'

'It is when it's not your place to make decisions that directly affect the day-to-day running of my business.'

'I don't have a freaking clue what we're arguing about.'

April tossed him his jeans. 'We're not arguing.
I'm simply stating that *I'm* the one who runs my
business—not you, and not anyone else.'

Logan tossed his jeans to the other side of the
bed. 'I'm not running your business. I'm just trying
to help you out. You want to risk more trouble?' He
glanced at the vibrator, lying redundant on the bed-
side table. 'Like you said, if the fact you've got green
glitter in your hair and on the sheets is any indication, you could well have more complaints heading
your way should you decide to sell them.'

April stood in the middle of the bedroom, trying to get her breathing back under control. 'That
one was damaged in transit,' she said, tugging her
tee shirt down. 'All the others look fine.' She glared
at him, annoyed when he raised his eyebrows, as if
goading her to continue her diatribe. Needing breathing space, she shook her head, then hurried out of
the bedroom. 'I need a drink.'

In the kitchen, she pulled a bottle of wine from
the fridge. She was overreacting, she knew it. But
she was so sick of being tossed around like a leaf in
the wind by people who thought she wasn't capable
of sorting things out herself.

All her life she had allowed people to think they
knew what was best for her. She had gone along
with what her parents had wanted, had taken the
modelling assignments her agency had decided were

right for her, and then finally Richard. She'd given him carte blanche over her life at a time when she'd needed to focus on her father, expecting that he would act in her best interests.

It had only been after Richard had screwed her over, put the knife between her ribs and painfully twisted it, that she had taken a long, hard look at herself and vowed never to let anyone dominate her again. Never again to let anyone think they knew what was best for her, and in doing so imply that she didn't have the savvy to run things herself.

Logan sorting out her insurance without consulting her was like salt in her painful wound. For some reason it really mattered that Logan saw her as a strong and capable woman who didn't need rescuing every five minutes.

Okay, her current situation wasn't exactly helping her cause, and the evidence certainly didn't suggest she was competent and self-sufficient. So she didn't want to tell Logan about Richard—about how she had naively trusted him until he'd almost run her business into the ground financially, how he had manipulated her, betrayed her. For some reason she knew admitting that would make her feel even more wretched and incompetent.

Yet was there really any shame in what she had allowed to happen to her? Would Logan really judge her for being too busy caring for her sick father to keep her eye on what had been happening to her business? Would he blame her for allowing her ex-lover to embezzle funds from her business in order to finance his own new venture? For not recognising that he hadn't bothered to renew her insurance policy, nor fulfilled a huge amount of online orders, and had ignored final demands from her suppliers?

He'd taken her fledgling business to the brink of collapse.

After her father's death, and after she'd kicked Richard out on his backside, she'd returned to London, determined to rebuild her life *and* her business. No way would she allow anyone to take her for a fool again. She was running her own show now, keeping her finger very firmly on the pulse.

And if that meant making demands that people thought were unreasonable, they'd just have to suck it up.

CHAPTER SEVEN

LOGAN WATCHED HER from the kitchen doorway. While he'd hoped to coax her back to bed, the way she stood musing over two empty wine glasses, her back to him, signalled that a conversation was the only thing on the cards.

The woman was an enigma. One moment she was hot as hell, the next she was lambasting him about taking freaking liberties. What was he supposed to do? She hadn't been able to sort out insurance herself—and he couldn't help admiring the fact that she'd been so honest by admitting to the potential claim—so what was the harm in taking matters into his own hands and using his contacts to set up cover for her?

No big deal. It was the very least he could do.

He'd hoped it might make *him* feel better, too. Especially considering the conversation he'd had with Haydon last night.

'Yes, we're still in a relationship,' Haydon had confirmed when Logan had asked him to clarify the situation. 'And I'd consider it a favour if you'd represent Veronica in this matter, should she decide to go ahead with her claim.'

There was no damn way Logan would do that. He couldn't imagine acting against April, not when that worry he'd seen in her eyes pulled at him and made him want to be the one to lighten her load. 'You need to convince Veronica that she doesn't have a case,' Logan said. 'That if she goes ahead with this it could backfire on her big-time.'

'She's fiery,' Haydon said as if that explained everything. 'She's unlikely to back down. But if you were her lawyer you could perhaps steer her right.'

'I'm not prepared to do that. She has no real grounds to make a claim. There's no solid evidence, nobody else has come forward with similar complaints, it's basically hearsay.'

As Haydon sighed, Logan felt the ripple of guilt slide down his spine. Haydon rarely asked anything of him, had never once made Logan feel that he owed him, but it didn't stop Logan feeling that he did.

He owed Haydon much more than any favour the man could ask of him would ever repay. Without being taken under his mentor's wing as a teenager, given jobs with more and more responsibility, thereby developing his skills and aptitudes, Logan might never have gotten the opportunity to study law. Might never have been able to get his family back together and provide for them. Yet still he couldn't quite bring himself to agree to Haydon's request to represent Veronica.

'How about a compromise?' Logan said with considerable reluctance. 'I agree to pass Ms Sinclair over to a litigator I know will be a good fit for her. In the meantime, you try and convince Veronica that she's wasting her time.'

There was a long silence, during which Logan closed his eyes and let that guilt slide further down his spine.

Then, 'I'm not happy about this, son. I'm not happy at all.'

Logan felt the punch in his chest. 'I'm sorry you feel that way, but you taught me that a man has to be true to himself and his beliefs. That he should never compromise when either was at stake. You always said that integrity is the cornerstone of greatness.'

'Don't you go spouting my words back at me,' Haydon said, but there was humour and affection in his tone. 'Didn't I also teach you to respect your elders?'

'Which is exactly what I'm doing. I'm respecting you enough to tell it like it is.' Logan waited, hoping that they'd at least reached an amicable impasse. 'Why don't I call round at the end of the week? Bring a bottle of that single malt you like?'

'Bribery. I like it.' Haydon laughed. 'I certainly did teach you well.'

After he hung up, Logan had reluctantly gone ahead and sent April's details over to the litigator he'd mentioned to Haydon, then followed up with a call to explain the details of the potential claim she faced.

Now, as he stood watching April, Logan knew he had to man up and confess what he'd done. He had been trying to think of a way to tell her since he'd arrived, but then the whole insurance debacle had blown up. Briefly, he wondered why she was so hell-bent on micro-managing her affairs, but then maybe he couldn't blame her. He'd be mighty pissed off if someone tried to highjack *his* decisions. But, in his defence, he'd been attempting to help her out of a situation she hadn't been able to solve herself.

If he told her now that he'd arranged for someone else to take on her case, and that he had already been fully briefed, the woman would blow a damn gasket and likely throw him out of her apartment piece by tiny piece.

It wouldn't matter that he'd been acting in her best interests. All she would see was the fact that he had bypassed her and taken control of the matter himself. She wouldn't stop to consider that the guy he'd recommended was a really great litigator with a solid reputation. She'd focus on not having been granted the courtesy of being informed first.

He shuddered at the thought of the potential haranguing she'd subject him to, and wished he'd put on more than just the jeans he currently wore. In his defence, when he'd still been hoping to tempt her back to bed he'd figured the less clothing involved the better.

His gaze slid down to where her tee barely covered her soft round ass and his cock twitched in response. Sex between them had been inevitable from that very first encounter. Any fool would have sensed the sexual tension burning between them—mutual, highly charged, consenting. Yet because of the way she guarded herself around him he'd planned to take it easy. Take it slow.

She obviously had a need to protect herself. A need that went beyond basic human instinct and slipped into a desire to erect barriers and walls. He wasn't such a Neanderthal that he hadn't noticed she wanted sex on an equal footing, too. When he'd arrived he'd barely been able to kiss her, touch her, before she'd had her hand in his pants. Not that he was complaining. A man would be a fool to object to her very adept handling of his erection. Yet, despite that unexpected and much appreciated welcome, he worried that there was more to her taking control like that than simply a desire to get her hands on his cock.

It went deeper. Whatever it was had made her suspicious of his motives, of how things would be between them. Had some jerk hurt her in the past? Pushed a power base into the relationship that hadn't worked in her favour? Had she been subjected to a selfish, controlling man who'd taken care of his own needs while ignoring hers?

While he might have made decisions on her behalf, at least he was doing it with her interests at heart, to protect her. That surely didn't put him in the same realm as someone who tried to manipulate her for his own selfish ends. Did it?

Shit. He didn't like the idea of that. It made his gut clench and his hands ball into fists at his sides.

Despite her closing her eyes, to prove her trust when he was inside her, he had a feeling it had been an act—a deliberate attempt to take his attention from what he had seen in her gaze. Suspicion. Doubt. And, yes, maybe a smidgen of fear.

The tightness in his gut shot into his chest. If some guy had hurt her he'd make it his mission to seek the bastard out and get him to pick on someone his own size.

April chose that moment to turn and look over her shoulder at him, blinking a couple of times as if she was surprised by what she saw.

Considering the way he felt, thinking about some jerk hurting her, and the fury that shot through him like a frigging freight train, he wondered if his feelings were evident on his face. Had she glimpsed his dark mood and thought it was aimed at her and her outburst regarding the whole insurance thing?

With that in mind, he walked up behind her and slid his arms around her waist. 'You're taking a while with those drinks.'

It pleased him when she turned in his arms, although she only placed her hands on his forearms, as if she was still tentative following their altercation.

'It'll have to be wine. I don't keep strong spirits.'

'Fine with me.' He dropped a light kiss to her mouth. 'Sorry I upset you.'

He could feel her shiver, feel her relax a little against him.

'I'm not upset—not exactly. It just…pushed some buttons. I still feel like an idiot about not renewing the insurance and getting myself into this whole mess.'

What were those buttons? he wondered. Suddenly he had a desperate need to know.

'There's no need for you to feel that way. It could happen to anyone. If it wasn't for my PA dealing with such matters I'd undoubtedly forget to renew my *car* insurance, let alone anything relating to the practice.'

She caught her bottom lip between her teeth, sucked in a breath, then sighed. 'Well, I have insurance cover now—and thank you for that. Really.'

'You're welcome.'

He felt a loosening around his ribcage. The storm had passed. Although there was still the matter of handing her across to the new lawyer to broach.

'But as comforting as it is to have the business covered now, it doesn't really help me with Veronica. Since I don't have any real capital at this point, if she sues I could lose my business. She'd force me into bankruptcy.'

'Not if you counter-sue.'

'What?'

He slid his hands over her waist even as the warning rang loud in his head. *Back off now*, he told himself. *Don't slide in too deep, and definitely not into territory that's the responsibility of her new lawyer.*

He should keep his mouth shut, coax her back to the bedroom, where the ground wasn't quite so boggy and deep.

'Can I do that? Counter-sue?'

Seeing the hopeful light in her eyes made him feel like an asshole. What was he supposed to say now?

Yeah, you can counter-sue...or rather your new legal counsel can. You see, I'm dumping you onto someone else, because I don't have the balls to stand up to a man who is like a father to me. The man who gave me my first job, who saw something in me and made sure I got the opportunity to go to law school. The man who made it possible for me to care for and protect my siblings.

'It's a possibility,' Logan said with a shrug. 'But not always a recommended course of action. Anyway, it's jumping the gun. Veronica hasn't taken any action yet, and maybe she won't.'

Although from what Haydon had said it seemed Veronica had the bit between her teeth and had scented blood. There didn't seem any likelihood of her backing down any time soon.

'If counter-suing is a possibility, I think I'd like to explore it,' April said. 'That way I can be ready if the shit hits the fan.'

He should have known she wouldn't back down. That she'd be like a dog with a bone, wanting to chew off every bit of available meat.

'Counter-suing doesn't always work in favour of the client. It can open a whole new can of worms. If you counter-sued but lose, you'll have the original compensation claim to cover, plus additional expenses.'

April slid her hands up his arms, linking her fingers around his neck. Since there was a contemplative look in her eyes, as if she was still considering the points he'd just made, he sensed it was an unconscious action. Even so, he liked the feel of her hands on his skin, her fingers flicking idly through the ends of his hair.

'I thought you said there was wine?'

That brought her back from wherever she'd gone.

'Yes. Sorry.'

He reached around her and picked up the wine bottle. 'Why don't you grab the glasses and I'll open this?'

Absently, she nodded, and he sensed she had slipped into thinking mode again.

'I can't lose my business, Logan.'

He took a breath, knowing that sex was so far from her mind right then that any attempt on his part to instigate it would be insensitive at the very least.

'You don't want to be thinking along those lines.'

He moved to the small table at the end of the kitchen and opened the wine, then sat and poured it into the glasses she'd placed on the table.

'It's hard not to.' She sat opposite him. 'If this goes belly-up, I'm not sure what I'll do.'

'You can always go back to modelling,' he said, pushing a glass across to her. 'Looking the way you do, I'll bet you'd be welcomed back to the fold with open arms.'

She picked up her wine, sipped, then frowned. 'Modelling was never my choice. I don't even think I was very good at it. My heart wasn't in it.'

'Then why did you do it?'

She took a longer sip, then stared down into the liquid. 'It was my mother's dream. Following in her footsteps, so to speak. She was a successful catwalk model and she wanted me to be successful, too. I hated it—every minute.'

He hadn't expected such a revelation, but sat back and let her speak.

'I don't much like the limelight. Of course, my mother couldn't understand that, and she thought I was just being obstinate. She told me there wasn't much else open to me—that I should use my looks to get ahead because my brains wouldn't take me very far.'

Logan sipped his own wine, swallowing the bile that gathered in his throat. 'What the hell did she mean by that? As far as I can tell, you've got both in abundance.'

She smiled, but it was far too sad for his liking.

'I was never very good at school. Any time I tried to do well…up my grades, get better marks on assignments…it seemed to backfire. As hard as I worked, I just couldn't get ahead. So I stopped setting my sights too high and let Mum steer me into modelling.'

She tapped her fingers against the side of her glass.

'I never told them, but I took a computer class in my spare time, and the tutor noticed that I was struggling with certain things. After a few tests I found out I had a form of dyslexia.'

Logan had experience with that—his sister Colleen had been diagnosed with the same disorder. She had struggled at school and, as much as Logan had tried to help with her reading and spelling, had grown more and more frustrated, while Logan had become angry and increasingly impotent that he couldn't fix things for his young sister. It hadn't been until diagnostic tests had revealed the problem, and he'd been able to get her the help she needed, that he'd seen how much it had affected her confidence as well as her school work.

'That's tough. Did you get help?'

She nodded. 'I couldn't believe how much better everything was just by changing the colour of the screen and the font styles and sizes. I sometimes use coloured acetates when I read even now, and it's a revelation.'

'So much so that you left modelling and set up your own company?'

'I'm not sure I'd have done that if my father hadn't become ill. He lived in Manchester, and flatly refused to go into care, so I went to live with him to make sure he was okay.' She became thoughtful for several moments, then sighed. 'Long story short: I decided to set up an online business, mostly so I could work from home and be there for my dad. I absolutely loved it. Loved setting it up, deciding what items to offer, the excitement of receiving my first orders, the thrill of getting lovely letters and online comments from customers. I wanted it to be a safe place for women to experiment and enjoy themselves—which is one of the reasons I really love offering the party-plan.'

Logan hadn't realised he was smiling, but her infectious pleasure gave him a warm feeling in his chest. 'You don't mind being the centre of attention when you're doing those parties?'

She raised her eyebrows. 'Do you know, that's something I've never thought of before? But, no, I don't mind at all. In fact, it's fun and incredibly life-affirming, watching women enjoy and experiment with their sexuality.'

Before they'd had this particular conversation Logan hadn't fully realised just how much April stood to lose. It wasn't just about her business, it was about her sense of achievement at having battled a learning difficulty and not only knocked it on the head but stomped it to the ground.

He admired her more than he could say. And a spark of something fired deep in his gut, radiating outwards to swamp the rest of him. No way was he going to stand by and let someone like Veronica

Lebeck destroy what April had worked so damned hard to achieve.

'Maybe it's time to get proactive,' Logan said. 'We should start gathering evidence together, so that if Lebeck does decide to come at you we won't be caught with our pants around our knees.'

Her eyes went wide, her shoulders rolled back. 'We? Does that mean…?'

Logan shrugged, and reached for his glass to take a healthy swig. *What the fuck was he doing?* Damned if he knew. All he did know was that he wasn't about to hand her over to someone who wouldn't fight tooth and nail to make sure she kept her business. Who would never understand just what it meant to her.

'Makes sense for me to take on the case,' he said, as if it didn't matter that he was risking his relationship with Haydon by having to tell his mentor that he'd decided to represent April after all. 'Like you said, you don't want to have to go over everything again with someone else.'

'I… I don't know what to say. Are you sure you have the capacity? I mean, I know you have the New York case at the forefront right now…'

'I can handle it.'

He considered telling her about Haydon, about how his representing her could be considered a conflict of interest, but he didn't want to dull the light that came into her eyes or diminish the relief that left her on a long sigh.

He stood, topped up their wine, then picked up

the two glasses by their stems and gripped them in one hand. He held out his other hand to her.

'And now that's settled, why don't we go and handle each other?'

She took his hand, but remained seated. 'Shouldn't we make some ground rules about our working relationship first?'

'I'm thinking we've done enough talking for now.'

And look where it had got him. Up to his ass in complications. At least in the bedroom he knew where he stood.

'We should take a break.'

She laughed—a throaty sound that shot straight to his groin.

'You're a lawyer. You talk for a living.'

'Which makes it even more imperative that right now you should be concerned for my physical wellbeing.'

She tilted her head, looking up at him as her fingers tightened around his. He wanted to yank her out of the chair, drag her into the bedroom and devour her soft curves and warm flesh. Considering that his cock was now pressing against the seam of his pants with relentless optimism, he congratulated himself on his stoic restraint.

'First things first, Logan. We separate the personal from the professional—and because of that I want to be invoiced for your services. I don't want any freebies. I also need you to keep me informed of what steps you take in respect of my business.'

At heart, Logan had no issue with what she'd said—especially the part about keeping sex separate from their professional relationship. But what did she expect him to do? Check in with her every time he took a piss?

'You're saying you want me to run everything past you first? Even when I need to act fast in your best interests? That's not entirely how it works. But what I *will* do is keep you advised of what I intend to do if I think it could work against your interests in some way.'

She kept him waiting for a response, then took in a breath. 'Fair enough.'

'So we have a deal?'

She grinned and glanced down at the bulge in his pants. 'From the look of things, maybe we should seal the deal with something less formal and altogether more pleasurable than a handshake.'

Halle-friggin-luiah.

'I'm up for that—and that's not just a figure of speech.'

He returned her grin as he tugged her from the chair and led her to the bedroom. Placing the glasses down, he tipped his head towards the side table.

'Why don't you reach over and grab my new purchase. Let's take it for a spin.'

April did as he asked, affording him a tasty flash of plump, ripe ass as she leaned across. His cock jerked.

'Batteries,' she said waving the vibrator at him.
'I'll just go and grab some.'

Too bloody late. He was aching to grab something else entirely.

He took the toy from her and placed it on the bed.
'On second thoughts, we'll save that for later. Right now I want to be inside you, Ms Sinclair.'

April scrambled onto the bed, knelt, and stripped off her tee. 'Works for me, Mr Lawyer.'

CHAPTER EIGHT

APRIL WOKE IN the early hours. Her first thought was that she wasn't alone in the bed. Her second was that she hadn't planned on letting Logan stay the night. It made things different, somehow. Gave what they'd shared greater importance. But it was hard to be regretful when she was snuggled up to his warm masculinity, having been thoroughly pleasured through the night.

She'd never met a man like Logan. He was a generous and considerate lover, and *very* attentive to her needs. She wriggled some more, needing to get closer. When had she turned into a snuggler? Certainly not with Richard—and, since she'd never spent the whole night with a man before Richard, this was a new experience.

It was hard to deny that she liked it. Liked the feel of Logan pressing against her, his chest rising and falling with each slumberous breath, as she drew in the heady scent of pleasured, satisfied and still very horny male.

Feeling bold, she wrapped her fingers lightly

around his length. She hadn't meant to squeeze so hard that she woke him, but she couldn't help her grin when his eyes opened lazily and looked straight into hers.

'You're bloody insatiable.'

His gruff, throaty tone rippled right through her body and sent shockwaves from her nipples to her core.

'Are you saying you can't keep up with my pace?'

His hand covered hers. 'You didn't let me finish, I was about to say that I'm just the man to handle you.'

She tightened her fingers a fraction. 'Looks like I'm the one doing the handling...'

'Funny.'

It was extremely pleasant, lying next to Logan in the early hours, with only a measly slice of light coming through the slatted blinds. It was even better feeling his hands slide over her, making her shiver and moan.

When he pushed her onto her back she kept hold of his erection, rubbing him gently as his hands travelled down the front of her body. He cupped her breast, flicked his thumb over the hardening peak, then moved down slowly to explore the skin around her navel—hell, who knew that area was *quite* so sensitive?—before sliding his hand between her legs.

He set up an easy rhythm, and since she was already wet it wasn't long before she was breathing heavily into the silence of the room. Logan matched her, probably because she was working him in the same easy way. Oh, but it was lovely to slide into the day like this.

Logan withdrew his hand, summoning a complaint from April. He gave a low, sexy laugh as he eased her fingers from around his cock, then turned to grab the glittering green vibrator. Late last night April had inserted its batteries, but it still sat unused on the bedside table. They hadn't seemed able to keep their hands off each other long enough to actually try out the toy.

Now April's stomach somersaulted as Logan turned back to her with a feral look on his face. Encouraging her legs wider, he touched the toy lightly to her knee, and the cool slide of the plastic against her sensitive flesh made her shiver a little. He drew the toy up along her inner thigh, across her abdomen, before taking it slowly down her other thigh.

Every one of her feminine muscles clenched, awareness moving up to her breasts as Logan circled the tip of the vibrator around her areolae, making her nipples tighten into sharp buds.

'Aren't you going to switch it on?' April asked, her voice breathy. 'After all the trouble I took to get those batteries inserted.'

He gave her that cocky half-smile that she found even more of a turn-on than the thought of the toy in full vibrate mode.

'Someone's impatient this morning.'

She couldn't deny it—especially when he slid his finger towards the 'on' button. She grabbed a breath, held it as she waited, then gave a disgruntled huff when he moved his finger away from the switch.

There was no time to give a more verbal objection, because Logan had moved the toy down her body and touched the tip of it to the place where her heat raged. While she was no stranger to self-pleasuring with a vibrator, she'd never enjoyed it with a man at the controls. And when that man was Logan, the enjoyment factor rocketed off the scale.

He took it slow, torturing her with tiny flicks and controlled dips along her sensitive folds. She touched his wrist, instinctively wanting to take control, but then eased her grip. She'd waited a long time to enjoy adventurous sex. She wasn't going to back down now.

How many times had she asked Richard to try out some of her stock? How many times had he refused? So many that she'd started to think there was something wrong with her wanting to use them. More than once he'd alluded to that very thing. Said that maybe she was oversexed. That her job had turned her into some kind of nymphomaniac who couldn't get enough.

The truth was, after being with Logan, she didn't actually care. And she cared even less when Logan slipped the vibrator inside her. Just a couple of inches, but she loved the way he looked at her while he glided it slowly into her, before drawing back, only to do it all again.

April clamped her muscles around the plastic, trying to encourage Logan to increase the pressure. Instead he flicked the switch and a green glow filled the room. Another flick and it started to slowly vibrate.

Bloody hell.

April tried to steady her breathing, but it was just so damned erotic. Especially when he hovered the tip of it at her clit and slid it slowly around.

Knees bent, she pressed the soles of her feet into the mattress, lifting her hips to encourage him to slide it deeper. 'Will you please…just…?'

In the sultry glow of green, while the vibrator continued to whir softly, Logan's gaze held hers.

'You need to…just use the bloody thing and…'

His low laugh rippled down her spine, building on the electrifying heat that shot through her entire body. His chest rose and fell and he looked as if he were engaged in hard manual labour instead of simply working a vibrator, as his erection pressed against her side, thick and hard.

'You want me to satisfy you with this?'

April arched as he pushed the toy a little deeper. 'Yes!'

He pulled it back. 'You wouldn't prefer the real thing?'

In a shivering haze, she remembered how he'd boasted that his women usually preferred the real thing to a piece of plastic, and she realised that he hadn't been boasting. As good as it felt to play with the toy, what she really wanted was Logan inside her. Hard, deep and resolute.

'The…the real thing…'

He tossed the vibrator aside and was over her and between her legs before the toy had hit the floor and ricocheted over the carpet.

'Logan…condom…' she managed as he prodded her entrance.

'Fuck.'

Braced on his hands, Logan squeezed his eyes shut, chest heaving. Then he opened his eyes, reached for a condom from the side table, dressed himself and lay back over her.

For long moments he stared at her. She was about to ask him if anything was wrong when he pushed inside her with one determined shove. The rhythm he set was in direct contrast to the way he'd played with the vibrator. He drove her hard, pumped fast and deep, stealing her breath so that she snatched air in sharp, rasping gasps.

She tightened around him greedily, crying out when he positioned himself in such a way that sensation tore through her in savage and glorious intensity. Her G-spot, she thought dizzily. And then she couldn't think anything as he drove her upwards into a state of pure and excruciating pleasure.

She wanted to wait for him, for them both to climax together, but the press of his thumb against her clit made that impossible, and she couldn't have waited for him to join her if her life had depended on it.

She came, and seconds later Logan did too.

It was a long time before either of them moved. Then Logan lowered his head and kissed her, soft and slow. The air seemed fraught with the crackle of potent energy as he touched his forehead to hers.

April waited, aware that something had happened. That something had shifted. She couldn't name what it was, but it seemed to shiver through her and leave her feeling...different.

Saying nothing, Logan rolled onto his back, and they lay together staring up at the ceiling. Minutes passed until he reached out and found her hand, wrapping his fingers tight around hers. Did he feel the same? Had whatever this was between them shifted and changed things for him too?

April tried to make sense of it, wondering if she should try for casual conversation or simply pretend that nothing untoward had happened. But then Logan got off the bed, and April knew he was headed for the bathroom.

'Shit.'

April scrambled to her elbows. 'What?'

A whirring sound came from the floor near where Logan stood. He reached down and snatched up the still vibrating green giant. Holding it out, he turned to look at April.

'Reckon it's complaining about being made re-dundant?'

April laughed and dropped onto her back again, pleased to have the unsettling silence broken. 'It'll have to get used to it. I'm starting to prefer the real thing.'

He grinned, turned the toy off, and tossed it onto a nearby chair before leaving the bedroom.

April was battling with a choice—although it seemed a petty and pointless one, seeing as Logan had stayed the night and fucked her senseless for most of it.

Should she ask him to stay for breakfast?

He was currently in the shower—April having pilfered some of Miles's toiletries from Lizzie's room for him to use. It was just after seven, and Logan had a meeting at eight-thirty in central London, so April knew he wouldn't have time to grab breakfast anywhere else.

But what did it matter in the scheme of things? It didn't have any more implications than their spending the night together in a horizontal position did.

Once more she was overthinking things.

Although, it might be best if she just gave him coffee when he came out of the shower and let him go on his way. No doubt his PA would arrange some breakfast for him before his meeting.

Again overthinking.

He strolled out of the bathroom, looking fresh and so bloody gorgeous she wanted to jump him. He wore the same clothes he'd arrived in yesterday, but considering those clothes had spent the night in disarray on her bedroom floor they managed to look fine.

April tightened the belt of her dressing gown,

wishing she owned a silk robe rather than the old pink towelling one she'd had for years. But the heated glance Logan shot her as he came towards her indicated he didn't give a flying fig about the tatty old robe.

'Will you have time to get home and change?' April asked, knowing the answer was probably in the negative, seeing as he lived in Chelsea and would be pushed for time as it was without going to the other side of London first.

As expected, he shook his head before taking the coffee she held out. 'No need. I keep a couple of shirts and a suit at the office, just in case.'

In case of nights like last night? April didn't especially like the sound of that. Did he make a habit of one-nighters? Was that what this was? They hadn't discussed it being anything more than a quick scratch of an itch.

'Can I get you some breakfast? Eggs? Toast?'

He took a swig of coffee, then shook his head again. He had yet to roll down his shirtsleeves, and his forearms were on tantalising display. The sight of all that rippled muscle and sinew shot heat between her legs and made her stomach tremble.

'I'll grab something later.'

April swallowed, feeling a little deflated—which was stupid after all that deliberating on whether or not to offer him breakfast in the first place.

She leaned back against the kitchen counter, watching as he mirrored her and sipped his coffee.

April hated all this stupid deliberating she was doing.
Should she or shouldn't she offer him breakfast? Did
he or didn't he regularly engage in one-night stands?
It was insane. At what point did worrying about his
culinary needs or sexual proclivities take preference
over the real issue she was facing in her life right
now?

She would do well to remember what was really
important.

'Now that I'm your client, what happens next?'

There—see? Back to business. To the point. Black
and white.

'We can sit back and wait—which at this point is
my preferred option…' He took a swig of his coffee,
watching her over the rim of his cup in a way that
made her feel uneasy. 'Or we can get proactive. Ask
for proof of damage, confirmation that she used the
equipment as specified on the instructions. We ask
for timing, duration, doctor's report, photographs.'

'Photographs?'

'How else can she prove her case?'

April shivered. 'Bloody hell, I can't imagine anyone would… But then she'd always liked being out-
rageous.'

It made April's blood run cold in her veins. If
there were photographs—if the vibrator really had
malfunctioned and caused injury—the implications
could be astronomical.

'Is there any other reason she might be coming
after you?'

April glanced up into Logan's questioning gaze. Since he was now her lawyer, he needed to know the history between the two women.

'Richard, my ex, was my manager. Veronica hoped he'd take her on, and she blamed me when he didn't. It could be that she's holding a grudge about that.'

April shrugged, hoping that would be enough information. She really didn't want to get into the ins and outs of her relationship with Richard, and she especially didn't want Logan to know how stupid and naïve she'd been, letting him run her business into the ground while her father had been sick.

'Why did you split?'

Panic bubbled up. What should she say?

'We weren't really compatible. We both grew bored and it was just time to move on. What's the point of staying with someone when the relationship has served its time and purpose?'

Logan rolled his shoulders back and his expression grew guarded. Did he know she was lying to him? Did he somehow know what had really happened?

She had a wobbly moment, wondering if she'd maybe talked in her sleep.

He continued to look at her for long unsettling moments, then drew in a breath and checked his watch. 'I need to go. Can you meet me for a working lunch? Twelve-thirty?'

Since there was a definite frost in the air, April

once again wondered if Logan knew more about her past than he let on.

'Yes, sure. Where?'

'Dubois,' he said, rolling down his shirtsleeves and buttoning the cuffs. 'Pixaby Street. Know it?'

'I'll find it.'

He nodded, then crossed to her and gave her a chaste peck on the cheek, before slipping on his jacket and letting himself out of her apartment.

April stared after him, more than a little irritated by his suddenly stand-offish manner.

Perhaps she should have told him the truth about Richard. Okay, she'd made a mistake, letting her ex take her for a ride, but when push came to shove nobody was immune to being duped, were they?

Just accept the fact that you weren't born with brains, darling. You don't really need them anyway, since the way you look is a gift. Be thankful for that.

Her mother's voice echoed through her head, and memories of her taunts still had the ability to push every single one of April's buttons.

She couldn't remember a time when her parents had been pleased with any of her academic efforts, despite her many attempts to prove them wrong about her abilities. Deep down she'd always felt that there was more to her than the ability to put an outfit together, or to choose exactly the right shade of lip gloss to go with a certain colour dress, the absolutely right hairdo to complement that dress. Yet those were the only abilities her parents had seemed to think she had.

When she'd met Richard he'd taken over where her parents had left off. Overseeing the management of her career so that, in his words, she could concentrate on doing what she did best. Looking good.

When she'd moved to Manchester to care for her father Richard had offered to get her assignments in the area, but she'd been determined to take the opportunity to move away from modelling and find something that would fulfil the parts of her that had been hidden beneath a cloak of self-disbelief.

It had been pure chance that she'd fallen on the idea of running her own online business, and she'd loved it.

Until Richard had single-handedly tried to destroy it.

And now Veronica Lebeck planned to do the same.

If she failed to save her business this time, it would only prove that her parents and Richard had been right. She *wasn't* capable of anything other than modelling and looking good.

Which was a crock. She'd come through too much, learned too many valuable lessons, to allow other people to dictate what she was and wasn't capable of.

To hell with that.

And to hell with Logan if he was going to be pissed with her because she hadn't been entirely upfront with him about Richard. She certainly had plenty to be irritated about herself in that respect. Hadn't he kept things from her until they were a fait accompli?

Yeah. To hell with that.

CHAPTER NINE

LOGAN SLAMMED DOWN his phone just as Haydon entered his office. He'd been in an edgy mood most of the morning, since leaving April's place, after hearing her admit that she'd dumped her last lover when he'd served his purpose. His mood hadn't improved one bit on hearing that Haydon was headed over to see him.

Logan sat back, hooking his ankle over his opposite knee, his casual pose in direct contrast to the discomfort in his chest. His current disposition was made worse by the fact he felt like shit for having gone against the wishes of his mentor in representing April.

'I assume you got my message,' Logan said as Haydon took a seat on the opposite side of his desk.

'I've been doing a little research,' Haydon said, his gaze steady on Logan. 'This April Sinclair. Big doe eyes? Damsel in distress? She's like your wet dream, son.'

Logan's chest tightened but he said nothing.

'No way can you step back from this one, right?'

Haydon continued. 'Not when you've got the chance to do what you do best. Save the world. Or in this case a pretty blonde with a vibrator problem.'

Logan aimed a narrow-eyed stare across the desk.

'I understand how a man is led by his hormones,' Haydon continued. 'But maybe you should look at the bigger picture here. Clients won't want their lawyer associated with a sex toy case.'

'Then they can find a new lawyer.'

'Look, get this April to offer Veronica some freebies, maybe an apology, a bottle or two of bubbly, and then they can get drunk together and be friends again.'

Mortified, Logan realised that was exactly what he'd suggested when he'd first met April. 'We both know it's not that simple. This is basically turning into a witch hunt. She doesn't deserve that.'

It was Haydon's turn to narrow his gaze. 'Ah. You're sleeping with her.'

'That's nobody's business but mine. It doesn't impact my decision to represent her.'

'Come on, son. We both know how this works. How a woman can turn a man inside out before he even knows what's happening.'

Logan pushed back his chair and resisted the urge to place his feet on the desk. For some reason he needed his feet on *terra firma* while he discussed April. The truth was, she *had* turned him inside out, had unsettled him—which was why he'd been in this foul mood since he'd left her apartment that morning.

Something had happened last night, and again this morning. He'd found himself wanting more than just a casual hook-up, thinking that maybe they could do what they were doing for a while longer. See how things went.

That was until she'd dropped the bombshell that she'd got bored with her ex. That she'd tossed the sucker aside the moment he no longer suited her purpose. That it had been time to move on.

It shouldn't have hit him like it had—especially considering his track record with women. And it certainly shouldn't have come as that much of a surprise. In his experience people did what suited them the most, and to hell with the consequences. When the going got tough, they walked.

Before he could slide into bitter but long since dealt with memories of his parents, Haydon leaned forward.

'Since when do you get involved with clients?'

'Never,' Logan said. But this was different. When they'd started getting naked she hadn't technically been his client.

'I shouldn't have to tell you that you need to back the hell away from this.'

'Nobody tells me who I can represent,' Logan said, rapidly losing what was left of the shreds of his patience. 'Not even you.'

'Maybe not, but you need to use your damn head. The one on your shoulders, not the one in your pants. And while I'm not one to pass up an opportunity for great sex, there are limits.' He cast a shrewd eye at Logan. 'You just keep your wits about you.'

Sensing an easing of the tension between them, Logan grinned. 'Don't I always?'

Haydon stood and headed to the door. 'I'll keep working on Veronica. Like I said, that woman is stubborn as hell. Part of the attraction, I suppose. I never could resist a woman who digs her heels in until she gets what she wants.' He turned to Logan, who had followed him to the door. 'You find a way to work this out. That shouldn't be hard, seeing as you've been fixing things for others for most of your life.' He squeezed Logan's shoulder. 'Responsibility sits heavy on your shoulders, son, but they're broad enough to take it.'

After they said their goodbyes, Logan walked back to his desk pondering on Haydon's words. He'd never really considered that his responsibilities were especially heavy. As the oldest, it fell on him to protect and shield his siblings during their father's drunken rages and their mother's inability to cope. When both parents had eventually deserted their children, Logan had been determined his family would not be split up. He'd looked after his siblings then, and he looked after them now. So yeah, he had a responsibility to them. He had a responsibility to Haydon. He had a responsibility to his clients. And that now included April.

Nobody was going to make him renege on his word or his duty. All he had to do was make sure they were all protected, all taken care of. That meant getting all his ducks in a row. And in the meantime there was absolutely no reason why he and April couldn't continue to enjoy a little extra-curricular activity. Chances were she wouldn't be his client much longer, and it made perfect sense that when the matter was settled they'd both go their own ways.

He really didn't know why her earlier revelation had concerned him to the extent that it had. He was more than happy to enjoy a casual no-strings affair, and it seemed April was, too. He was acting like a bloody idiot, letting her get under his skin when he'd known from the start they were just enjoying a fling. Casual, no-commitment sex, which at any other time would have filled him with glee.

Hadn't he always balked at the idea of a *relationship*?

Hadn't he kicked into touch any woman who wanted *more*?

So why did it matter to him that April felt the same way? That she'd dumped this Richard guy when he had no longer been any use to her.

Instead of concerning himself with that he should be celebrating his luck, planning to make their time together a satisfying and mind-blowing experience.

For both of them.

April arrived at the restaurant early, having detoured to the premises of one of her wholesalers to collect some sample goods she'd ordered.

During the morning she'd thought about her conversation with Logan immediately prior to his change in attitude, and all she'd been able to come up with was that somehow he knew about what happened between her and Richard. That he knew she was covering for her ex in the hope she could keep Logan from thinking she was an idiot for not doing everything to protect her business.

When Logan walked into the restaurant she actually felt her breath catch. He tucked his sunglasses into the jacket pocket of a sharp, no doubt designer three-piece suit, with a crisp white shirt beneath. He spotted her, his intense gaze making her breath hitch again. Unlike the first time she'd seen him, he looked every inch the epitome of a top-class lawyer, making heads turn as he headed over to where April sat at the corner table he'd reserved. Yet beneath his commanding presence there was a dangerous edge to him that no amount of civilised clothing could camouflage.

He leaned across and kissed her cheek. A slightly less chaste peck than the one he'd given her earlier, but it still irritated her beyond belief—especially considering what they'd done to each other last night and again early this morning before the chill had set in. But she supposed it was appropriate, considering this was a business meeting.

Even knowing that didn't stop the jolt to her nerve-endings or the rush of heat through her blood as she watched him peruse the menu. It was impossible not to remember how much pleasure he could incite with those adept fingers, those skilful hands.

'How was your morning?' Logan asked, after they'd ordered and the waiter had moved away.

'Good. I managed to pick up some sample stock I ordered for a party on Friday night.'

He nodded, but April didn't miss the gleam in his eye. It made her relax a little. Maybe she'd imagined his frosty attitude that morning.

'What kind of stock?'

The gleam intensified and April raised her chin, accepting his challenge and pleased that they seemed to be sliding back to the place where they'd been before.

'Some lingerie, a remote-controlled vibrator, a belt…'

Logan nodded, his outward expression giving nothing away as to the nature of their conversation. To all intents and purposes they could be discussing the stock market, or even the weather. It was only the devilish heat in his eyes that said otherwise.

The waiter arrived to offer Logan a taste of the wine he'd ordered. After he'd filled their glasses and left, Logan leaned forward.

'I'd like to know more about that new stock…but, since this is probably not the best place to be when I've got the start of a raging hard-on, we should talk about something else.' He picked up his wine. 'Tell me something to get my mind off sex.'

April didn't want to do that. In fact, she didn't

want to talk at all. She wanted to get Logan somewhere private and show him exactly what was in her holdall.

She looked across at him, watching as he sipped his wine. She loved seeing a slightly flustered Logan almost as much as she loved seeing a highly aroused Logan. She knew the signs now. The way his jaw went tight, probably because he was clenching his teeth. The way his chest rose and fell beneath that crisp white shirt and dark waistcoat. The way his dark eyes promised such amazingly good times between the sheets.

'What do you want, April?'

The question jolted her from her sexy reverie and she blinked several times. Then she lowered her chin and looked up at him from beneath her lashes. 'I can't really answer that, because you told me we should talk about something else. That I should get your mind off sex.'

His mouth kicked up at one corner. 'And where exactly is *your* mind right now?'

'On sex.'

His nostrils flared slightly and he brought the glass to his lips again and sipped, all the while watching her with a tormenting gleam in his eyes. 'Specifically?'

She licked her lips, then picked up her own wine. Her intimate muscles clenched and she barely resisted the urge to squirm as her panties grew damp. 'Not sure I should tell you that. We *are* in a public place.'

She batted her lashes, earning a deep laugh from Logan. The sound was thick and carnal, and it sent shockwaves of lust straight between April's legs.

'You might as well tell me, since the damage is already done. I'm not about to leave this table any time soon without embarrassing myself.'

April glanced down in the direction of his lap and bit her lower lip. 'Poor you. Perhaps I should take pity and change the conversation after all—or perhaps I should tell you that I have some very sexy new underwear in my holdall.'

She almost laughed when Logan took a huge swig of wine.

'Of course, I say "underwear", but really it's only scraps of lacy material. It wouldn't cover much of anything.'

Now she did laugh at his muttered, 'Fuck… Are you trying to make me blow right here?'

Again, she batted her lashes. 'Just because I'm describing crotchless panties in navy see-through lace?' She made a play of reaching down for the holdall. 'Would you like to see?'

He sucked in a breath, his chest expanding beneath the tailored jacket and waistcoat. 'April…'

On a roll now, and loving that she had him on the back foot, she kept her expression innocent. 'The lingerie is very classy, and the other items are in discreet packaging. I'm sure nobody would notice if you wanted to take a peek.'

She slid the tote across the carpeted floor towards

him. His gaze remained fixed on her, his fingers drumming against the almost empty wine glass.

'What if I wanted more than a peek? What if I wanted a private viewing?'

'That could be arranged.'

'When?'

'As soon as you like.'

'What if I said we should skip lunch?'

'I'd say, your place or mine?'

Logan was already reaching into his jacket pocket to retrieve his wallet. 'My office is closest.'

'I don't think your PA would approve of us having a private party on work time.'

'We can lock the door.'

Hell, her brain was starting to scramble and it seemed as if the room had grown too hot for rational thought.

'Why don't we head to your place?'

He was already reaching for her hand, and the holdall.

'Let's go.'

CHAPTER TEN

BY THE TIME they arrived at his house on Chelsea Harbour, April was ready to drag Logan out of the cab.

He beat her to it.

He paid the cab, grabbed the tote, and then grabbed her.

She laughed as he hurried them up the steps to his front door, where he fumbled for the key. Seconds later they were inside the hall and he'd dropped the tote and pushed her up against the wall.

'Someone's in a hurry,' she said breathlessly, pulling at his tie and snapping open the buttons at his shirt collar. 'And that would be me.'

Logan gave a half-laugh, half-groan, and pushed her jacket off her shoulders.

While they yanked at each other's clothing, Logan kissed her. Urgent, raw kisses that made her head spin. But she managed to get his suit jacket off, then unsnapped the buttons of his waistcoat.

'I like a man who wears a waistcoat,' she said as she pulled if off and tossed it on a nearby chair. 'It's really sexy.'

'I'll be sure to remember that.'

Logan's own breathing was ragged, and he made short work of April's blouse, tugging it from the waistband of her skirt. Then he reached around, unzipped the skirt and pushed it down over her hips.

'How come you always get my clothes off before I get you naked?' she asked.

He had her down to her bra and panties, and while she had his shirt undone, displaying his muscular chest, she still hadn't unsnapped the fastening of his trousers thanks to being distracted by the raw desire she saw in his eyes.

He pulled her into his arms so that she had to wrap her legs around his waist, and he carried her through the house and up to the bedroom.

April had a second or two to take in a huge room, which looked out over the River Thames, before Logan plonked her down on the big bed with its burgundy duvet.

He unfastened her bra and feasted on her breasts, tormenting her nipples until she was arching up off the bed. Then he pulled off her panties and knelt between her legs.

'You're a fucking feast, April.'

There was something incredibly erotic and provocative about daytime sex—especially when it was kind of illicit. April wondered briefly if Logan had appointments that afternoon, and a strange thrill rippled through her that he might be foregoing them because he wanted her so much.

Then she couldn't string two thoughts together as her orgasm built, courtesy of his relentless mouth.

She came, and everything floated around her as her body gave in to the sensation.

Logan withdrew and came up over her. 'Yeah, a fucking feast...'

She ran her hands down his arms, but he got off the bed and went into the adjoining bathroom, coming back seconds later with a pack of condoms which, after selecting one, he tossed onto the bed-side table.

'Don't you have meetings?' April teased as he moved between her legs.

'Yeah. But looks like I'm playing hooky.'

He flashed her a fevered grin and positioned him-self at her entrance, stealing her breath as he pushed deep. The rhythm he set was fast and furious, wild and free. And April loved it. Using her intimate mus-cles, she gripped him hard, extracting from him a deep moan that was almost a roar. As the movement he set pushed her further up the bed with each thrust, April reached out and grabbed his shoulders, need-ing purchase even as she wanted to fly.

Her breath came in such gulping pants that for one heady moment she thought she might actually hy-perventilate, but she didn't have the chance to think further along those lines as she climaxed again.

Logan shoved harder, deeper, his hips like a pis-ton, relentless and desperate. He came hard, his head thrown back, teeth clenched, his breath hissing. And in that moment he looked so damned sexy that April felt her heart turn over.

It took for ever to get her breathing back under control—or maybe it just seemed that way. When Logan rolled onto his back beside her, she stretched in contentment. 'I really like playing hooky.'

He gave a lazy laugh, as if the effort of doing so was enormous. 'I'm developing a taste for it myself. Maybe I'll do it more often.'

April felt a twang of something beneath her ribcage. Did he mean generally? With other women? Or did he mean with her?

Not that she was about to ask. This was only meant to be fun, a fling. A way for her to enjoy great, scintillating sex. No commitments. No promises. There was no way she intended this thing with Logan to go beyond casual. Anything more and things got complicated. He might think he could start making demands that took them way past enjoyable sex and into the realms of control and manipulation.

She'd had more than enough of both for one lifetime.

She kept staring at the ceiling, her heartbeat slowly settling, and became aware of Logan turning to look at her.

'I can hear you thinking,' he said.

She huffed, for form, but it unsettled her a little—that uncanny ability he seemed to have that allowed him to tune in to her.

'Well, seeing as I'm not meditating right this moment, it's not really a long shot to acknowledge that thoughts might actually be going through my head.'

He shifted, settling onto his side, elbow bent, as he looked down at her. How annoying it was that he always seemed to get his equilibrium back before she did.

'Why don't you tell me what they are?'

'Why would I do that? A woman likes to keep an air of mystery about her.'

He ran his free hand over her abdomen, making her muscles tremble, then flattened his palm over her belly button. 'You certainly do that.'

Guilt trickled through her. About the things she'd kept to herself. The things that she didn't want to tell him. That she didn't want to admit and have him think her an idiot.

'The only thing you need to know about me at the moment is that I'm starving for food. You didn't get to feed me.'

His smile could have kept her satiated for weeks. 'You're complaining?'

'No, not for a moment. But a girl needs to eat. Do you have anything in your fridge?'

'No idea. Why don't you go and look?'

'You're expecting me to make my own lunch? Aren't I your guest? You invited me, remember?'

'I'll call for takeout. There are some menus in the kitchen drawer by the dishwasher. Go and decide what you want.'

With which, he swung off the bed and padded to the bathroom.

April sat up and looked around, but the only items of clothing she had available here in the bedroom were her bra and panties. Everything else was in Logan's downstairs hall.

Biting her lower lip, she eyed his shirt. Okay, it was clichéd, but she shrugged it on. His scent enveloped her. What *was* it about the man that could turn her to jelly even just after they'd had hot and glorious sex?

She went downstairs and found the menus he'd mentioned. As she perused them, he came into the kitchen.

'I've got a taste for pizza. You?' She glanced over her shoulder, her breath hitching as she saw him coming towards her stark naked. 'Don't catch your death,' she said with a grin, but it was only for something to say, seeing as he'd basically fried her brain cells with his raw, masculine deliciousness.

'You stole my shirt,' he said, grinning back. 'No doubt there'll be something in here that'll warm me up.'

It was only then she saw that he carried her hold-all.

'There's not much in there that will keep you *warm*,' she said, raising her eyebrows and thinking of the skimpy women's lingerie.

He pursed his lips and tilted his head to the side. 'Oh, I don't know. Why don't we take it upstairs and see what you've got?'

April swallowed, then covered her heated anticipation with a half-hearted wave of the menu. 'Food…
remember?'

'I'll order your pizza and ask them to deliver in
thirty minutes. That should give us time for a little
exploration.'

She went damp. How was it that he could whip
her satiated hormones back into a frenzy so bloody
fast?

He walked across to her as she deliberated, hiking the bag onto the counter beside her before pulling her into his arms. He unhooked the two buttons
she'd fastened on his shirt and slid his hands inside,
cupping her ass. Then he drew her in for a long,
lingering kiss that drove the thought of pizza clear
from her mind.

She sank into the kiss, sliding her hands around
his neck. His erection pressed hard against her core,
making her intimate muscles pulse with anticipation.

He drew away to press kisses against her neck, her
throat, before coming greedily back to her mouth. 'I
can't get enough of you.'

Still kissing her, he used the hand not holding her
tight against him to pull the holdall down from the
counter. Without releasing her he manoeuvred them
towards the central island, where he deposited the
bag. He spun her around so that she faced the island,
with her back to him. Then he reached around her
and undid the holdall.

'Let's see what we've got here…'

April watched, fascinated, as with his arms still around her he pulled out the items of lingerie and tossed them aside. All the while his hard length pressed against her ass, and she barely resisted grinding her hips back against him.

She wanted him. Again. She always seemed to want him.

He gave a low rumble of interest as he pulled out the box containing the doggie-style belt she'd ordered. Without removing the contents, he tilted the box and read the blurb.

"'Allows for improved thrusting and targets G-spot stimulation…'"

Oh, hell. His voice sounded like gravel, grating deep in his throat.

"'The non-slip belt provides extra comfort for the woman, while the man can provide deep and extended penetration without the danger of lower back strain.'" He pressed a kiss to her neck. 'Who cares about a little lower back strain?' He turned back to the box. 'But I digress…'

April's chest was squeezed so tight, the apex of her legs so wet and aching, that she placed her palms flat on the island counter to stop herself from crumpling to the floor as her knees lost the plot. Not that she could have gone far, since Logan was pressed tight against her, his cock leaving her in no doubt he was as turned on as she was.

"'Why not try the belt at different angles and in a variety of positions? Doggie-style is especially recommended, since this position allows for faster, harder sex.'''

April swallowed. 'Well, there's nothing wrong with your reading ability—I'll give you that.'

He laughed as, one-handed, he opened the lid of the box and shook out the contents. Seconds later, he had the wide navy strap around her waist. 'Why don't we test it out?'

She widened her legs, her core muscles throbbing. 'Why don't we…?'

His breathing rasped against her ear as he slid the strap further down her hips and pulled gently, tilting her pelvis. Her ass was pushed hard up against his erection in this position, and she sucked in a breath as he pressed down against her opening.

'Fuck, yeah…' he grated, and pulled on the strap again.

April steadied herself against the counter as he drew her body back even more.

'I can drive into you *hard* in this position. Is that what you want?'

Since she couldn't seem to form words, she nodded.

'You'd feel me deep inside you,' he said in a raw tone. 'And I know you'd grip me so damn tight.'

'Do it,' she ordered. 'Please, Logan…just do it.'

She closed her eyes, expecting his determined thrust, but instead he slid his length slowly along her wetness, over and over. He felt so big, and she was so hot, so wet. All she needed was for him to just…*push.*

Since he held her steady, the belt firm around her pelvis, she couldn't move very much, but she tried to push herself back against him. When she couldn't, she widened her legs even more.

Still he only stroked along her length.

She swallowed, threw her head back. 'For pity's sake, Logan. You read the damned instructions…'

'Don't have a freaking condom,' he said. *'Shit.'*

April couldn't believe she'd virtually instructed him to take her without thought of protection. So bloody desperate was she to have him inside her.

'In the bag,' she grated, already reaching for the holdall. 'I ordered some flavoured ones.'

'Holy shit,' he said. 'I love an organised woman.'

They both scrambled around in the bag until April located the box at the bottom of the hold-all and pulled it out. Her fingers felt clunky as she undid the lid and then tipped the condoms onto the counter.

'Hold the strap,' he ordered, and she placed her palms over the fabric, keeping it in place around her hips while Logan pounced on the closest packet, tore it open and slid the rubber over his erection.

Seconds later he'd taken the strap again, plac-ing one hand on her lower back, encouraging her forward.

April dropped her hands on the counter again, her body jerking forward as Logan tightened the softly padded strap. He nudged her entrance, and this time he didn't stop but pushed inside her. It felt amazing, the pull of the belt seeming to squeeze her intimate muscles and provide a tighter sensation.

When Logan pulled up on the belt again it pushed her ass so snugly against him that he managed to get even deeper. Unable to move, April could only take what he gave her, and she clenched around him as he continued to pump. He filled her completely, length and breadth, and there didn't seem to be a whisper of space between them.

She wanted it to last, but there was no way it would because she was already on the edge of orgasm.

Their joint breathing—thick and heavy—echoed through the air, accompanied by Logan's groan each time he shoved inside her.

April tried hard to hold back, to prolong this amazing sensation, but the experience proved too much. She squeezed her eyes shut and beneath her closed lids colours flashed and shapes exploded. She was hurtling upwards, flying around in some kaleidoscope of exquisite turmoil, and then all too soon she floated down again.

Still Logan thrust, his pull on the belt unrelenting, his hips driving forward, and with each push April found it harder to stay on her feet as he edged her towards the counter.

Then he gave a guttural shout and exploded inside her.

April kept her eyes closed as he came, loving the sensation of him pulsing inside her, the heady moment of intense connection as he filled her so thoroughly.

His hold on the belt lessened and she felt his muscles relax in the same way hers had. She leaned forward, half collapsing over the counter, and his body was a heavy weight as he relaxed over her. His chest rose and fell against her back as he pulled in air, and the chill of the marble countertop pressed against her nipples.

Logan kissed her neck. 'Okay?'

Oh, how she loved that raspy, sexy deep voice of his in the aftermath of orgasm. 'Mmm… Yes. You?'

'I don't think I have the words.'

She gave a breathy laugh as he lifted his body from hers, dropped the belt to the floor and pushed his hands up under the opened shirt to slide them over her back. She shivered a little, wondering if there'd ever come a time when she didn't respond so easily to him.

The thought made her a little sad. They weren't in this for the long haul, which meant she'd never have the chance to find out.

Thankfully, Logan stopped her from heading further down that particular road of thought. Grabbing her arms, he encouraged her to stand up and turned her to face him.

'You look too damn sexy in my shirt,' he said, glancing down to where her breasts were on full display. 'But, then again, you look even better out of it.'

He slid it from her shoulders and it slipped to the

floor next to the discarded belt. Before she knew what he'd planned, he'd placed his hands around her hips and popped her up on the counter-top. He stepped between her legs and placed his hands on either side of her face.

'That was bloody amazing.'

She could only agree—especially when he was looking at her as if he meant it.

'I think I might put those on special promotion,' she said, glancing down to the belt on the floor. 'And for once I can give a personal recommendation as to their effectiveness.'

Still holding her face, he dropped a kiss to her mouth. 'For once?'

Damn. She hadn't meant to say that. But something told her the time for keeping her secrets close to her chest had run its course—at least perhaps for some of them.

'My ex,' she explained, touching her hands to his waist. 'No way would he have tried that out.'

'Really?'

It might have been her imagination, but she was almost certain he looked smug right then.

'He wasn't the adventurous type. He preferred straight missionary—although, I think we did doggie once, in the dark.'

'Are you fucking kidding me? Was the guy all there?'

April laughed. 'He was a workaholic. Sex didn't seem to be a priority for him.'

Logan looked genuinely shocked. 'He must have needed his brain tested. How the hell did he manage to keep his hands off you?'

April shrugged, as if it hadn't mattered. But it had. And for a long time she'd thought it must have been her inability to turn Richard on. Her inability to turn any man on. But then, after Richard had done the dirty, she'd slowly reasoned that his mind had been on other more lucrative goals than having sex with her.

If sex with Logan was any indication, she certainly didn't seem to be lacking in the ability-to-turn-a-man-on stakes. He'd proved it over and over. Hadn't he said he couldn't seem to get enough of her? She had no doubt he meant it, at least temporarily, until they burned themselves out and decided it was time to call it a day.

Although there didn't seem to be much sign of that at the moment.

'I think we were both too focused on building our businesses,' she explained, while Logan watched her with that expression of disbelief on his face. 'The lack of focus on sex suited us both.'

'That's bullshit,' he said, and dropped his hands to her shoulders. 'You light up like wildfire whenever I touch you. I can't believe you were prepared to stuff that part of yourself down just to accommodate some dickhead who didn't have a freaking cock, by the sound of it.'

He sounded so fierce that she squeezed his waist.

'Some people have a stronger sex drive than others. Richard's was low.' She grinned, probably because he still looked so fierce. 'I'm glad yours isn't.'

'Fucking right.'

He stroked down her arms, then pulled her close and kissed her, deep and long. When he released her, he hiked her up into his arms and strode with her out of the kitchen.

'And right now I'm taking you back to bed, so I can prove it some more.'

CHAPTER ELEVEN

THEY FINALLY GOT around to ordering pizza just as the light faded over the harbour. From Logan's bed they had a stunning view of the reflected light from houses, apartments and moored boats.

'You can finish the last of it,' April said, sitting cross-legged next to Logan, who was leaning back against the headboard. 'I'm stuffed.'

Never one to pass up the opportunity for more good pizza, especially when he considered his energy levels could do with a boost after a particularly energetic afternoon, Logan grabbed the slice, grinned, and then bit down on it.

April laughed. 'I don't know where you manage to put it. You must have a cast-iron stomach.'

'A short while ago I seem to recall you telling me I had a six-pack and that you loved running your hands over it. Of course, I *was* giving you one of the many orgasms you've enjoyed this afternoon at the time.'

He watched her spare a glance at the diminishing supply of condoms he'd brought from the kitchen.

'I've given you almost as many. Or have they slipped your mind?'

He licked his fingers. 'That'd be hard. Especially since you're sitting there naked, with everything you have to offer on display, and I'm wondering when you might be ready to add to my tally.'

April glanced down at his own impressive offering. 'Please… Already?'

He tossed the last of the pizza into the cardboard tray and brushed off his hands. 'Like I told you,' he said, reaching out to grab her and pull her across his lap. 'Can't seem to get enough of you.'

And as Logan kissed her he knew they weren't just words meant to tease or persuade. He meant them. No matter how many times they were together, it wasn't long before he wanted her again. Wanted to run his hands over every part of her, to feel her soft and supple skin warm beneath his fingers. He wanted to kiss her, taste her. He wanted to be inside her.

No doubt the attraction would fade soon enough, but until then he planned to have April every way possible. And she certainly seemed to be thinking along the same lines. She was up for pretty much anything, and he gloried in her adventurous nature and her infectious desire to try whatever was on offer.

Earlier, when they'd taken a closer look at the new stock in her holdall, and at his prompting she'd told him about some of the other items she had for sale on her website, he'd teased her that he intended to place an order for one of everything.

She hadn't so much as batted an eyelid at his suggestion that they try out every one of his purchases. In fact, she'd tilted that sexy chin, given him a butt-wiggle, and told him to make sure to leave a website review after each erotic sampling.

She was something else.

Which made him wonder about the dickless idiot who'd basically ignored April's sensual side. What kind of man could have a relationship with her and not want to explore that essential part of her nature?

Only a bloody idiot.

No wonder she'd admitted to getting bored with the guy. What red-blooded woman wouldn't?

As for him? He couldn't remember a time when he'd enjoyed being with a woman quite so much—and not just for the sex, although that was exceptional and plentiful. He liked the layers of her. The way she could switch between caution and adventure. Between strength and vulnerability. The way she questioned him and challenged him.

Complementing her incredible body was a sharp brain and a quick wit. It was quite a combination, and one he found himself admiring more with each moment they spent together.

From the bureau across the room came the sound of his phone ringing. Enjoying the taste of April's mouth too much to end the kiss, he decided to ignore it. When it persisted, April broke the kiss and drew away from him.

'You should get that. I feel guilty about keeping you away from the office today, and it might be important.'

Logan couldn't think about anything as important to him right then as getting April back in his arms, but since she was scrambling away from him he knew that wasn't about to happen until he'd answered the call.

As he padded across the room he cursed whoever was on the phone—until he picked it up to hear his sister's voice. Then all his instincts went on full alert and his brain switched into gear.

April stretched contentedly as she watched Logan's splendid back view from across the bedroom. While what she'd told him was true, and she *did* feel guilty about keeping him from his work, she really loved being with him. The sex was amazing—that went without saying—and she had certainly been given first-hand confirmation that she'd been missing out for all these years. But, more than that, she loved the way they talked. The way he made her feel her own value, made her feel as if she had something to contribute with her opinions. That he was as interested in what she had to offer between her ears as well as between her legs.

Though he'd teased her about the items she sold on her website, and told her how he planned to try them all out with her, they'd also talked about the financial and operational aspects of her business. She'd told him about profit margins, loss leaders, and various other facts relating to the running of her business.

Of course, it could have been because he needed the information in order to represent her, but April thought it was more than that. He was genuinely interested, and seemed impressed by her knowledge, and also by her determination to take the business to the top. He made her feel valued more than anyone else ever had, and while his admiration was subtle, and could be easily missed, she never missed it.

Logan made her feel she was worth something.

Both in and out of bed.

'You need to do what I just told you, Colleen. I'll sort it. It'll be okay.'

April hadn't realised she'd drifted into a kind of reverie, thinking about her relationship with Logan, until she heard that last statement before he ended the call.

'My sister,' he explained, coming back to the bed. 'She's booked a holiday for the end of the semester next week and she can't find her passport.'

Although there was a hint of exasperation on his face, his expression was mostly indulgent. April remembered when she'd first met him how he'd spoken of his siblings with such warmth and tenderness. And how much she'd always wished for that kind of loving connection.

'What will she do? She won't be able to get a duplicate that quickly, will she?

'I told her I'll sort it,' he said, lying down and pulling April beside him. 'I know someone who'll help.'

April cuddled close, loving the heat that came from his muscular body, the scent of him that seemed to penetrate every part of her. 'I should have known,' she said with a smile.

'Should have known what?' Logan's arm tightened around her, drawing her closer to his side.

'That you'd know someone. That you'd sort it.' She tilted her head to look up at him. 'You take such pleasure in that. Being in control.'

'I've done it so long maybe it's second nature. Is that a problem?'

She waited for the tightness in her chest, that feeling of panic that knocked against her ribcage when old memories came calling.

All she felt was a softening, a warmth.

The unfamiliarity of that response caught her by surprise, but she didn't want to explore it right then. She was enjoying being with Logan too much.

'What about your parents?' she asked, wanting to know more about his family.

'Like yours, they're no longer on the scene. They died a while ago.'

April sensed he didn't want to talk about them. He looked so bleak right then. His eyes had gone flat and expressionless.

It made her push. 'Do you miss them?'

Logan huffed out a humourless laugh. 'Like a fucking hole in the head.'

She stroked her hand lightly across his taut stomach. She didn't want to make him miserable by asking him to talk about it, but she really did want to know more about him. More about his past.

'I'm sorry, Logan.'

She sensed a relaxing of his muscles and shifted closer to wrap her arm around his waist, offering support. She was rewarded with a hand over hers, a gentle kiss to her forehead.

'The old man was a waster. Eventually drank himself to an early death.'

For some reason that didn't come as a shock to April, although she hurt for Logan having had to experience it. 'And your mother?'

'Every time my father took off—which was often— she became more and more unstable. Couldn't have been easy for her...not with five young kids to feed and clothe. But then she left, too.'

Now April was shocked. She hiked herself up to look at him. 'Where did she go?'

'Went to look for my father, apparently. Not sure what happened. My mother eventually came back. But by then the authorities had placed us all in foster homes and that's where we stayed. The three little ones were kept together, but it was hard on Connor. He was sent to live with a couple who were experienced in dealing with "problem children".'

Logan's eyes had lost their bleakness, and it had been replaced by red-hot anger.

'What about you?' April asked softly. 'Where did you go?'

His shoulder jerked up in a careless shrug. 'I was fifteen. I looked after myself.'

'How?'

He was silent for a while, as if he was lost back in that time. Then he took a deep inhalation, let it out on a ragged sigh. 'Got lucky.' Another deep breath. 'And when I was old enough, and I had the means to look after them, I went to get them back.'

She had a vision of a young, cocky Logan, marching up to some official and demanding to have his younger siblings. Something warm and incredibly tender washed through her. She had some insight now into why he always needed to take control, to sort things, to make things right for everyone. It was because it was what he'd always done. What he'd been forced to do by circumstances.

She bent forward and kissed him, soft and slow, hoping to ease some of the pain she knew simmered beneath the surface as he relived those painful memories. Then she tucked herself tight into his side, dropped her head against his chest and listened as his heart beat steadily against her.

The light had faded, plunging the room into semi-darkness, cocooning them in this momentary haven. His arms drew tight around her, holding her to him, and he tugged up the cover to wrap it around her shoulders.

He pressed a kiss to her temple. 'Stay the night.'

She didn't know if wild horses could have dragged her away from him right then, so her answer came swift and steady.

'Yes.'

The sound of gulls screeching overhead and the early-morning light filtering through the gauzy drapes woke Logan from a deep and dreamless sleep. Surprising, considering the nature of their conversation last night.

He hadn't thought directly about his parents for God knew how long—certainly hadn't given any mind to reliving that painful part of his life. Yet being with April had somehow drawn those memories from the depths of his being, as if he needed a final cleansing of the past in order to step into the future.

Before he could dwell further on that April moved against him, her low and contented purr filling the space. Her skin felt warm, pliant, and she smelled so good that he breathed her in. She felt good against him, too, her plump breasts squashed into his side, her leg flung carelessly across his body and her warm centre pressed against his hip.

Pushing his nose into her hair, he breathed her in again. He really couldn't get enough...

It hit him full-on that he was in trouble.

It wasn't often that he asked women to stay the night, but now he couldn't imagine wanting to wake up without the warmth of April pressed against him. Nor could he imagine letting her go any time soon. Certainly not so that she could fall into the arms of another man.

The thought of her doing all the things they'd done with anyone else sent his pulse thumping, his chest banging, and his blood storming through his veins like a tsunami. He didn't think he would be responsible for his actions if he found out that another man had touched her the same way he had done.

He thought back to when she'd told him she wasn't interested in finding herself a man, that her total focus was on saving and building her business. She wanted to put her business first, and he couldn't blame her for that. He felt the same.

Or he had done.

Now he couldn't imagine not having both.

His business and April.

And there was no rule he knew of that said they couldn't both focus on their business and enjoy each other on the side.

'You're all warm and shaggable,' April mumbled against his chest.

He had already been at full-mast, but her sleepy, sexy voice gave him the final push to send all those unexpected thoughts packing and get back to what he really wanted to do.

'What are you planning to do about that?' he

asked, rubbing his hand up and down her hip before cupping her tight ass.

'Depends…'

'On what?'

'Whether you make good morning coffee.'

'I've got a great coffee machine.'

She stretched lazily, and then, before he knew what she'd planned, she rolled over to straddle him.

'That'll work.'

She looked all rumpled and sexy, her eyes alight with wicked intent.

'And just *what* do you think you're doing?' Logan asked, in mock censure.

She wriggled against him, her knees on either side of his hips, his erection sliding against her wet centre.

'You're an intelligent man. Work it out.'

When he grinned, she flicked her hair back over one shoulder, then placed her palms on his chest. There was a quality in her eyes that unsettled him for an instant. Thoughtful and serious. Disconcerted, he tried to shift their positions.

But she leaned down, her hands pressing harder against his chest. 'You're not going to be the one in control this time, Logan.'

Still her gaze unnerved him, making him feel as if her words meant more than a simple shift in sexual power.

He waggled his eyebrows and gripped his fingers around her hips. 'Well, since I don't like to disappoint a hot woman with early-morning sex on the brain, I say go for it.'

She watched him, and then she leaned down and ran the tip of her tongue from the notch of his collar-bone all the way to his navel. His stomach muscles jerked, his cock joining in the fun.

She flattened both palms to his chest again, then rose up over him, all that soft, warm, pliable flesh just begging for his possession. He thought to try and get her on her back again, but she shook her head slowly, as if she knew.

Keeping one hand on his chest, she reached across for a condom, then sat back and brought the packet to her mouth. With her eyes on his, she used her teeth to tear it open. Taking the condom out, she smiled.

'Tequila flavour.'

He was hard and throbbing, which was not helped by the feel of her curvy ass pressing against his thighs and her slick heat mere inches from where he wanted it.

'Just put the damn thing on.'

She snatched her hand back as he reached for it, holding the condom out of reach. 'Have a little patience. Maybe I want to play first.'

'Screw first,' he growled. 'Play after.'

'*My* rules apply this morning. You're not the one in control, remember?'

She slid the condom on slowly, rocking her hips in subtle movements as she worked.

Logan was damn near set to blow. 'For fuck's sake, April. Just get me covered so I can have you.'

He was now covered, so she rocked back and looked at him. 'You don't seem to get it, Logan. This time I'm having *you*.'

She said it with such determination, her eyes fierce arrows of steel, that he didn't even consider contradicting her. Besides, she was rising up onto her knees, her hands sliding down his torso to cup his erection. Then slowly, achingly bloody slowly, she lowered herself down. She felt amazing. Hot, wet, tight. He wasn't sure he'd last too long—especially with her rocking over him as if he were some kind of erotic mount.

He kept his eyes on hers, his breath tight in his lungs as she tilted her pelvis for one final push of her hips. Then she rode him, her body swaying loose and limber, her hair flowing over her shoulders, her breasts full, those rosy nipples hard.

He reached for her, cupping her breasts in his palms and squeezing them in time to the slow rhythm she set. Her hands covered his and she threw her head back, her throat a slim column of silky flesh just aching for his mouth.

Logan found it hard to breathe as she brought her gaze back to his. She was taunting him, daring him, driving him out of his bloody mind. In that moment he knew he'd never wanted a woman as much, never ached for a woman as much. And, damn it to hell, he'd never *needed* a woman as much.

A sense of power rushed to his chest, and a fullness swamped him. April squeezed him tight, her intimate muscles clenching around him as she lifted her body from his before plunging back down and taking the entire length of him inside her.

Still she rocked, holding his hands tight to her breasts. Her nipples pushed hard against his palms, her breasts warm and full. With one needy cry she threw her head back and rocked…faster, faster…

Logan climaxed, his shout of release melding with hers as they flew together.

Spent, he tightened his fingers around her hips, not wanting her to withdraw from him just yet. As if she knew, she waited until their breathing settled, then collapsed over him, her legs sagging, her hands landing on his shoulders. Unable to resist he reached up and took one nipple into his mouth, before transferring his attention to the other.

She leaned down, offering him her mouth. He took it, then folded her in his arms and eased her over his chest until she lay diagonally across him, her warm breasts crushed to his chest.

He stroked her hair. 'Thanks.'

'You're welcome.'

He felt a wave of tenderness move through him as he continued to stroke the silky strands of her hair. 'You're so damned beautiful, April.'

For a moment he felt her tense, and thought she was about to shift away from him. 'Beauty isn't everything.'

Her tone was flat, devoid of emotion. Had he said the wrong thing? About her being beautiful?

Then he remembered what her mother had said to her. That her brains wouldn't get her very far. That she'd be wise to rely on her looks.

A knot burned in his chest, the heat flaring down to his stomach. It was a callous thing to say to anyone, but to someone like April—who was not only beautiful but also smart, funny, strong and capable—it was not just cruel but a freaking lie.

He wanted to press the issue, to make her see how wrong her mother's comment had been, but since he sensed she'd pulled away from him and showed no desire to discuss it he kept his mouth shut.

Wanting to bring the mood back to where it had been before, Logan squeezed her ass. 'Want that coffee?'

She didn't reply immediately. Then, 'Absolutely.'

'And breakfast?'

'Are we sending out again?'

Logan grinned. 'There's an ace bakery around the corner. I'm a friend of the owner.'

'I bet you are.'

She turned, facing him, her expression amused. It settled something inside him after the whole 'you're beautiful' thing.

'There'd better be *pain au chocolat* or I'm going to mutiny.'

Logan laughed as he got off the bed, pleased that things between them were back on an even keel.

CHAPTER TWELVE

APRIL KNEW SHE had overreacted to Logan's comment, and it annoyed her that she was unable to accept a compliment without getting all hot and bothered by it. Probably because it had hit a raw nerve, reminding her that she'd lived her whole life being told that the only thing she had going for her was her looks, and that the only possible way she could earn a good living was by using those looks. The subtext being that she didn't have brains. That she was a vacuous creature who didn't have the intelligence for anything other than looking good.

Logan had told her she was hot, sexy and passionate, but he'd never told her outright that she was beautiful. Maybe it was the tender way he'd said it, or the admiration in his eyes, but it had highlighted her hang-up about being celebrated for her looks and not much else.

However, she'd determined to deal with it privately—she certainly didn't want it interfering with this amazing time with Logan. And in the weeks that followed, it had become less of an issue as they spent more time together and enjoyed many lively and heated discussions about a variety of topics that invariably led them to the bedroom, where they always called a truce.

April had felt more relaxed than she had in ages. It might be because there'd been no sign of impending litigation, or maybe it was due to the adventurous and plentiful sex she'd been enjoying, but she knew it was more than that. It was Logan.

As she loaded items into a small wheelie suitcase, to take to the party-plan gathering she had that evening, she tried not to think of Logan. That was impossible, of course. Especially considering they'd tried out pretty much everything she was packing.

Catching her bottom lip between her teeth, she stroked her fingers fondly along the softly padded doggie-style strap—one of Logan's particular favourites. She remembered how it felt around her hips. How Logan's hands would tighten around the strap, pulling her pelvis up hard against his body so that he could drive deep inside her...

He'd purchased one the day after they'd first tried it, and they'd certainly made good use of it since. During parties April struggled not to blush as she described the strap and how to use it, but her explanation was obviously spot-on, because the strap was fast becoming one of her bestsellers.

While April was happy to use samples of each toy they tested, Logan insisted on purchasing items from her stock. Which reminded her—she'd had a delivery that morning which included his latest purchase: a light bondage set, featuring a blindfold and hand-cuffs. April grinned as she retrieved the set from the delivery box, fantasising about when and how they would use it.

The 'how' didn't take much thought, but as for 'when'…well, that would likely be tomorrow, after they'd had dinner at a new by-invitation-only West End restaurant.

Feeling naughty, April popped the box into the front pocket of the case, along with details of the party-plan event. Since the gathering was in a five-star hotel close to Logan's office, if she left a little earlier than planned she could stop by and present him with it before the party. She wanted to see his expression. Wanted to see his eyes gleam with wicked intent. Maybe they could even sneak a heated kiss to keep her going until tomorrow.

As luck would have it, Logan's PA was in the foyer when April arrived. She gave April a smile and came over to greet her.

'Logan's finishing off a meeting,' she explained, ushering April towards the waiting area. 'But I don't think he'll be much longer. Can I store that for you while you're here?' she asked, indicating the small wheelie suitcase.

'That'd be great. Thanks.'

With her usual brisk efficiency the woman stored the suitcase behind her desk and then went off to get April a cup of tea. While she waited, April picked

up a magazine and thumbed absently through it—
but the sound of a woman's raised voice came from
Logan's office and hooked her attention.

The familiar high-pitched tone sent an icy chill
down April's spine. Placing the magazine down,
April leaned forward. She knew the owner of that
voice. She'd suffered its strident tone too many times
over the years not to know it, most usually when its
owner wasn't getting her way.

Veronica Lebeck.

As if on auto-pilot, April went to the door of Logan's office and pressed her ear to it.

'If you think I'm going to back off, you're very
much mistaken.' Veronica stated. 'That vibrator
caused me considerable emotional distress, not to
mention physical damage.'

'Come off it. I've had the toy tested. There's no
indication of any potential malfunction.'

That was news to April. Logan hadn't mentioned
having tests carried out on the vibrator.

'Because it's a different toy!' Veronica shouted. 'Not
the actual one that caused me pain and humiliation.'

'Which you conveniently seem to have mis-
placed.'

In contrast to the higher pitch of Veronica's voice,
Logan's only went lower, calmer.

'I wasn't going to keep the damn thing, was I?
Not after what it did to me.'

'Why the hell don't you just accept my offer and
move on?'

Offer?

The buzzing in April's ears cut off the rest of what Logan said. All she could focus on was that he'd offered Veronica compensation. When the hell had that happened? And why hadn't he thought to tell her?

'I want all this over with,' Logan said.

His voice remained low, but April could hear the suppressed annoyance in his tone. It matched the anger currently ripping at her chest.

'I'm up to my ears in more important things, and I don't have time to waste on this ridiculous debacle. Just accept the damn offer and we can all move on.'

He didn't have time to waste on this *'ridiculous debacle'*? Was that how he really saw it? Saw her? He just wanted it over with?

April's instinct was to get out of the building, to escape from the cloying atmosphere. But she was damned if she'd let him get away with his flippant dismissal of her and her problem. As if it meant nothing. As if she hadn't been worried out of her skull about her business imploding, about her growing reputation being ruined, about her need to prove to herself and everyone else that she really did have the skill and ability to run a successful business.

Before she could question her actions, she grabbed the handle and flung open the door to Logan's office.

Logan stood behind his desk, his eyes meeting April's as she glared across the room at him. Long moments passed during which righteous anger thumped in her chest, but Logan's expression gave nothing away.

'What's going on?'

'Logan's trying to fob me off—that's what's going on,' Veronica hissed.

As always, the woman looked stunning. Polished and groomed to within an inch of her life.

'But I'll tell you what I told him. No way am I accepting what he's offering. I want a decent financial reward for what I've been through.'

Logan was already moving towards April. 'Let me finish off here,' he said taking her arm and turning her towards the door without breaking stride. 'I'll call you later.'

He squeezed her arm, as if in warning, but April was having none of it. She shrugged out of his hold. There was no way she was going to be brushed aside.

'I'm not going anywhere. This involves me, and I'm staying put. I want to know exactly what's going on.'

'Does Haydon know about this?' Veronica asked, whirling on Logan.

Haydon?

While April looked from Veronica to Logan and back again, Veronica raised her perfectly groomed eyebrows. 'He doesn't know, does he? So not only did you refuse to drop her and represent me, now you're trying to dupe me into accepting your ludicrous offer.'

Logan had refused to represent Veronica? *For*

what? And how come he'd never told her that he knew Veronica? And who the hell was Haydon?

God. Her head was starting to spin.

'Just a minute,' April said, holding up her hands. 'Who is Haydon? And what does he have to do with any of this?'

'Nothing,' Logan said, and grabbed her arm again.

But before he could lead her, protesting, to the door, Veronica piped up.

'Haydon's my lover. And he won't take kindly to this latest attempt by Logan to go against his wishes.'

A knot was forming in April's stomach, accompanying the one tightening in her chest. 'What exactly *are* his wishes?'

'To get me fair compensation for what you've put me through. *Fair compensation*—not the travesty I've just been offered.'

'You've said enough,' Logan warned, leaving April's side to move towards Veronica. 'This meeting is terminated.'

'Oh, don't worry, I'm going. And there's no way I'm dropping this. In fact, I'm going to let everyone know about her dodgy little business, and about how she sells sub-standard products.' She stabbed a threatening finger at April. 'I'm going to sue the pants off you.'

She waltzed out through the door, leaving a deafening silence in her wake.

April stared at the door as Logan closed it. He came to stand in front of her, raised his hands as if he was about to reach out, but shoved them into his pockets instead.

'I didn't want you to hear all that.'

'Evidently. Why would you? Considering there's obviously things going on behind the scenes that concern me and yet I'm not a party to.'

'Sit down. Let me explain.'

'You didn't tell me you knew Veronica,' April said, ignoring his request. 'And you certainly didn't tell me that you were offering her any compensation. How was that supposed to work, anyway?'

With the way her heart was banging, April couldn't believe how flat her voice was. How reasonable she sounded.

'There was no reason to tell you that I knew her. I wasn't planning on representing you, and even when I did decide to do that my knowing her had no bearing on the manner in which I'd act on your behalf.'

April shook her head. 'How much compensation did you offer her?'

'That's not the issue right now.'

April was surprised she could actually find it in her to laugh right then, but the man really was an impossible bastard.

'It's not the issue?' she repeated as nausea began to churn in her stomach. 'I'll have to remember that when I file for bankruptcy.'

God, she had to move, make her frozen legs work. She walked to his desk, then back to the door, no-

ticing how he seemed to stand guard there, as if he
intended to stop her if she tried to leave.

Well, he could bloody well try. With the mood
she was in, the fury that ran through her veins, she
doubted anyone could currently stop her doing anything she wanted.

'How long have you been considering offering
her compensation? And who the hell is this Haydon
guy who hired you to do his bidding?'

'He didn't hire me. It's not—'

'How was it supposed to work? You pretend to
offer me advice, throw me some soothing messages
about Veronica not really having a case, tell me that
there's no real evidence, how it will all blow over
with some freebies and an apology? Did this Haydon then up the ante?'

April had hardly got the last words out before
Logan shot across the room, grabbed up a visitor's
chair, and placed it behind where April stood seeth-
ing.

'For God's sake, just sit.'

She was a shamble of feelings right then. It
seemed every emotion she'd ever experienced battled
for supremacy. The anger had abated a little, leaving in its wake a hollow feeling that spread through
her torso and down her legs. She really wanted to
hear the excuses he was about to offer, so she sank
into the chair, but kept her spine straight and her
shoulders back.

Logan brought another chair from the visitors'

area and placed it opposite her, then sat. He leaned forward, clasping his hands between his thighs.

'Haydon and I go back a long way. He knew you'd come to me for advice, and he asked me to pass you over to someone else so that I could represent Veronica instead. When I refused, and actually took you on as my client, he wanted me to make sure that Veronica was appeased in some way...offered compensation.'

Anger shimmered around the edges of the hurt, and April was glad of it. She'd rather feel fury than wretchedness. 'Her receiving compensation would mean acknowledging I was at fault.'

Logan raised his eyebrows. 'Not necessarily.'

April glared across the space separating them. 'Are you serious? Why did you even agree to help me in the first place? If you knew it would cause problems, a conflict of interest, why didn't you just send me on my way? You wouldn't have been the first lawyer to do that.'

'I owed a favour to someone and he called it in. Asked me to see if I could help you.'

Miles. Lizzie's other half.

'Until you mentioned Veronica's name I had no idea she was involved. I knew she was Haydon's current lover, but I didn't know if it was serious or even if he was still in a relationship with her.'

April tried to think back to that first meeting, although it was difficult to sift through her harried thoughts and feelings. 'When you did know, you didn't think to tell me?'

'Yeah, I did think to tell you, but there was no point worrying you over something that I wasn't going to let be an issue.'

Because he'd thought he could pull the wool over her eyes, April thought, as old wounds seared open. He'd thought she was too stupid to join all the dots and know she was being taken for a ride. Well, she knew now, and the bastard was going to face her wrath.

'You've been playing me from day one. Going behind my back. Making deals with the lover of the woman who has made my life a living hell.'

'I've made no deals with Haydon.'

'Oh, please. You make bloody deals in your sleep. Unfortunately, none of them seem to have been in my favour. And exactly how much money did you offer Veronica in compensation? I have a right to know, considering I'm the one who'll need to file for bankruptcy in order to pay it.'

His shoulders went back. 'That's never going to happen.'

'Because she turned you down? No doubt she'll be coming back for more. And when she does you can tell her to go to hell. I'm your client. You're my lawyer. There has to be some rule that says you have to act in my best interests.'

'Name one time I've not acted in your best interests.'

April gave an exasperated laugh. 'That's the point. I don't know. You go off and act as you see fit, without even telling me. How *can* I know, or trust that you've done the best for me?'

He kept his gaze squarely on hers. 'Because I say so.'

'You thought I was gullible,' April said, ignoring him. 'You thought I was stupidly naïve and easily manipulated.' She had to take a breath as all her old fears came flooding to the surface. 'Well, here's the thing, Logan. Maybe I was—and, believe me, I could kick myself for it. But if you think I don't see through you now, then maybe you're the one who is gullible and naïve.'

Something raw shot into his eyes. 'I'd never do anything to hurt you, April.'

Her throat tightened and she had to swallow. Over and over. Only when she knew her voice wouldn't betray her did she respond. 'Don't you think you already have? After I told you I had issues with decisions being made without my knowledge, you still went behind my back—like I'm not capable of making my own decisions. And now you're making it worse by trying to insinuate I've got the wrong end of the stick, that I've misunderstood your motives.'

'I had no intention of agreeing to Haydon's demands.'

Maybe not at first, but that had obviously changed. After all the time they'd spent together, after all they'd done, he still didn't think her smart enough for them to sit down together and agree to a plan to deal with Veronica.

Her head felt as if it would explode as everything crowded in on her. She knew she needed space— somewhere she could think all this through without the overpowering presence of Logan around.

She shot out of the chair and headed to the door. 'Well, it's over now, Logan. We both know where we stand. Let's just say it's past time for both of us to move on.'

'For fuck's sake, April. Will you just wait a god- damn minute?'

She turned, not surprised to find Logan up close and personal. She couldn't stand it. Couldn't deal with any more right then.

'In the interests of full disclosure, and to make sure it's crystal-clear, it's only fair to inform you that I'm no longer in need of your services. Not only do I intend on fighting this case against me with every- thing I have, I'll also take the opportunity to throw the bloody book at *you*.'

She marched out through the door before he could respond, heading to where his PA sat at her desk, looking uncomfortable. The woman gave a nervous smile as she handed April's case to her. April wasn't aware of much else as she hurried to the elevator and out of Logan's life.

Logan stared at the closed door. Everything inside him screamed to go after her, but his legs wouldn't work. She'd shaken him to the core. She'd ended it. Was walking out of his life. Just like that.

He couldn't blame her for ripping into him. Maybe he should have told her from the start, but he'd thought he could handle it without worrying her more than she was already.

April had been determined not to listen, not even to try and understand his position. He'd worked the situation as best he could and tried to be fair to all parties. Keep everyone happy. Look where it had got him. He'd upset the one person he'd never want to hurt in a million years. He was a bloody fool.

The meeting with Veronica had been his latest attempt to get her to drop the case. An earlier call from Haydon had alerted Logan to the fact that upon realising there was no real evidence with which to pursue her complaint, Veronica was planning to contact the tabloids and offer them a nice juicy story.

Haydon had tried to placate her, and Logan sensed his mentor was growing tired of the woman's continued vendetta as much as he was. Not wanting the unwelcome spotlight placed on his own connection with Veronica, Haydon had warned his lover to drop the whole thing and had given Logan his blessing to carry out his plan.

But, despite the incentive Logan had offered, he'd soon realised that Veronica had no intention of letting things drop.

At first there'd been a flare of interest in her eyes—until she'd found flaws in his offer. Frustrated, Logan had been tempted to offer her more—maybe money out of his own pocket—just to make the witch go away. April needed closure, so she could move on without the threat of litigation hanging over her.

She'd been right, of course. Financial compensation *would* be an admission of guilt on her part, and she didn't deserve that. She'd done nothing wrong.

He'd grown so aggravated by Veronica's flat-out refusal to see sense that he'd told her he was growing bored with the whole thing, that he had better things to do than be subjected to her games and he wanted it over with. Done.

He'd never anticipated that April would overhear him saying all that.

Shit. He'd royally cocked everything up. And he had a freaking ache in his chest and a giant-sized knot in his gut to show for it.

But why the fuck should he care?

She'd left without even giving him a chance to explain. Hadn't hung around long enough to try and work things out. At the first sign of a serious issue between them she'd just walked away.

He went to the cabinet in the corner of his office and poured himself a generous slug of whisky. He downed it in one. Poured another.

He should think himself lucky, being let off the hook this way. He didn't need all this angst.

She'd told him his services were no longer required.

Well, that's great sweetheart. Now we can all move on.

So why was he considering marching over to April's place and demanding to be heard?

She'd likely tell him to go to hell.

The thing was, without April in his life, hell was likely the place he'd be going anyway...

CHAPTER THIRTEEN

APRIL HAD THOUGHT walking away from Logan just over a week ago was the worst tear to her heart, but coming a close second was the tabloid headline she'd just seen outside the tube station.

Reality star victim of malfunctioning sex toy!

April snatched up a copy of the paper, assuring herself it was a bizarre coincidence, but a glance at the accompanying photo of Veronica shattered her hopes that everything seemed to have died down on that front.

Leaning against the wall, she read down past the jumble of words to the part that said Veronica Lebeck had suffered 'immense emotional distress'. That the faulty toy had compromised her love life and ruined her relationship with Haydon Peterson.

But it was the next part that hit April like a bullet.

Pursuing a claim against the company's owner, Lebeck is being represented by Logan

*Fitzpatrick, a high-profile lawyer with a stellar
success rate both nationally and internationally.*

She couldn't seem to breathe. Air locked inside
her chest, squeezing against her ribcage so painfully
she thought she might actually pass out. She struggled to remember her yoga breathing—in through
the nose, long, slow breaths out through the mouth.

Steadier, she read the rest of the article.

Apparently, Veronica was grateful for the support of her lawyer.

Well, they bloody well deserved each other, April
thought, refusing to deal with her feelings right then.
She had to focus on the implications of the article.

When she'd read it again, one thing stood out by
its omission. Nowhere had it actually named April
or her company.

That knowledge allowed her to take her first full
breath since seeing the newspaper, although she was
still outraged by the injustice of it all. Logan had
barely allowed the dust to settle before he'd agreed
to do Veronica's bidding. Before he'd been happy to
swap sides. What was he planning to do now? Screw
April for all she was worth? Destroy her business?
Drive her to bankruptcy?

While she might be bloody well down, there was
no way she was out. Damned if she'd allow Logan
bloody Fitzpatrick to destroy her.

He'd broken her heart, but that would mend.
Please, God, let it mend. No way would she allow

him to break her belief in herself, her belief in her business. She'd channel the hurt she felt into fighting. There was no way she was going to make it easy for him.

April shoved the paper into her bag and resumed her journey to meet a potential party-plan client. On the train, she took out her tablet and, instead of reading her notes about the forthcoming meeting, jotted down notes about her situation and came up with two solid points.

There was no concrete evidence to support Veronica's claim.

There was no indication of any malfunction in the toy.

Surely those facts alone quashed any potential claim? Logan had basically said so himself. So, while he was representing Veronica, that didn't necessarily mean he planned to make anything official. This was a volley, an attempt to get April to cave. That was all.

Her head spun with all the conflicting thoughts.

She was sick of this. Of lawyers. Of people trying to manipulate and control her. Surely there was some way out of this ridiculous mess without having to rely on other people for a resolution?

After everything that had happened, couldn't she and Veronica agree to solve this problem without the need of a third party sticking their oar in? They'd never actually sat down and had an in-depth, woman-to-woman discussion about it. Surely it was worth one last-ditch attempt to at least try for a solution?

* * *

Three hours later April waited in a busy wine bar near Marble Arch, her eyes never straying far from the entrance. Eventually Veronica swept through the door, her cat-like eyes zeroing in on her. While her nemesis made her way to the booth, April poured them both a large glass of wine from the bottle she'd ordered on arrival.

'I trust this is still your favourite tipple?'

Veronica slid onto the bench, shrugging out of her jacket. She gave the wine a cursory and derogatory glance. 'My tastes run more to vintage champagne these days.' Despite her dismissal of the wine, she reached out and took a large gulp before training those peepers on April. 'What's this about?'

April shrugged, as if the future of her business *didn't* rely on the successful outcome of this meeting. 'I was thinking that since we're both probably sick to death of this whole thing we might come to some mutually beneficial arrangement.'

Veronica sipped more wine, but there was interest in her gaze. 'Running scared, are we?'

'Not at all,' April said, holding the woman's gaze. 'There was nothing wrong with that vibrator, and we both know it. Look, all I want to do is build my business, get back on my feet after...'

April hadn't planned to spill her personal business to Veronica, but since this was potentially her only hope of solving the problem without involving more lawyers, she took a deep breath.

'Richard basically screwed me over. At a time when I needed support the most, Richard made my life hell.'

Veronica sipped her wine. 'Forgive me if I don't get my hanky out. We've all been screwed over by a guy.'

Beneath the swagger, Veronica looked sad and dejected, and April decided to reach out. 'I saw the newspaper article. I'm really sorry about you and Haydon.'

Veronica's eyes narrowed, then she shrugged and reached for the bottle. 'I'll get over it,' she said topping up her wine. 'Fucking men.'

'Yeah. You've got that right.'

'Not sure what *you've* got to gripe about,' Veronica said pouring more wine into April's glass. 'Logan-fucking-Fitzpatrick threatened me because of you. Not only did he demand I not give that newspaper interview, but he also said he'd hit me with a defamation claim if I named you or your business. Bloody cheek. I demanded Haydon do something, but he told me to do what Logan had said. The two of them are tight, but I never expected Haydon to take Logan's side against *me*. Haydon was furious with me when I did the interview. Can you believe it?'

April wasn't sure what to believe right then. Logan had tried to protect her? Had warned Veronica not to mention the name of April's business? But why? Wouldn't he relish the publicity for his new client?

'Isn't Logan representing you?'

'Huh. As if. He's still trying to fob me off by dangling that carrot.'

April shook her head and then, since her head was swimming anyway, swigged down some wine. 'What carrot?'

'He said he'd ask some New York TV mogul whose divorce case he's handling to give me a screen test for his latest blockbuster series. All I had to do was drop my case against you. Since he couldn't guarantee I'd get the part, I told him to stick it.'

Logan had offered to get Veronica a *screen test*? 'He didn't offer you money?'

'You're bloody joking. The man wouldn't budge an inch. Kept insisting you were in no way at fault. That there was no case to answer. That he wasn't going to let you accept liability when you'd done absolutely nothing wrong.'

April's heart thumped hard in her chest. He'd been protecting her, and all she'd done was lambast him with accusations.

'He's demanded the paper print a retraction about his representing me. I never actually said that, but I didn't correct them when they assumed he was.' She slugged more wine. 'Shit—what a bloody mess.'

Even as her heart was doing a happy dance, April actually felt sorry for Veronica. Okay, her methods were dubious, but since April had now sensed a crack in her armour, maybe they could make progress. Veronica was desperate for the limelight, and had demonstrated that she'd do anything to help her career. And, from the sad look in her eyes when she'd mentioned Haydon, it seemed the woman had a solid dose of heartache to go along with everything else.

April knew the feeling.

She shrugged off thoughts of Logan for now, and concentrated on her pitch.

'Why don't I get us another bottle?' April said, reaching for her purse. 'There's something I'd like to run by you. Maybe we can both end up winners in all this.'

'Well, it's better than nothing, I suppose.'

Logan looked across the veranda as his brother commented on the retraction the paper had made about his representing Veronica, saying how they were sincerely sorry for any inconvenience caused.

'Did you speak with Haydon?'

'Yeah,' Logan admitted, nursing a beer. 'I think he misses her more than he's letting on.'

Logan knew the feeling only too well. He missed April so much that some days he found it hard to concentrate. It was an alien concept to him. Usually his focus was impeccable. Especially where work was concerned. But lately…

'If you ask me, he had a lucky escape,' Connor said stretching his legs out along the deck, his gaze slanted sideways at his brother. 'Nobody needs a woman who gives them nothing but grief.'

Tipping down his sunglasses, Logan eyed his

brother. He caught the implication and decided to ignore it.

'Speaking of which,' Connor said grinning. 'Any more news on the sex toy lady?'

The punch of Connor's words hit Logan hard in his solar plexus, and he battled both irritation at his brother's flippant reference and something else he couldn't quite define.

To cover his discomfort he pushed the sunglasses back to the bridge of his nose and took a swig from his beer. 'Not since her email confirming she didn't want me to act for her any more and demanding I return the documents that belong to her.'

Logan had lost count of the calls he'd made to her. He'd gone to her apartment several times, only to be told by her friend Lizzie that she was staying with a friend in North London. Yeah... Most likely to avoid *him*.

He ached to see her. He needed her to understand his motives, why he'd acted the way he had. Somehow he had to make her realise that he'd done everything with her interests at the centre of it all. He wasn't ready to let her go. He wasn't entirely sure he ever would be.

'So why are you sitting on her documents, bro?'

Although they were shadowed by his sunglasses, Logan narrowed his eyes at his brother's knowing grin. 'You keep pushing it and I'll shove said documents straight up your ass, bro.'

Connor laughed and reached for his beer. 'And yet you didn't answer my question.'

'Because I'm still her best bet to deal with any fallout from this. She didn't give me a chance to explain anything. Just kept accusing me of doing my own thing, of not keeping her informed, of going behind her back.'

Connor touched the lip of the beer bottle to his mouth. 'You did go behind her back,' he pointed out helpfully. 'Your problem is that you want to fix things for her the same way you want to fix things for the rest of us. One day you'll have to realise that sometimes we all need to fix things for ourselves.'

'I'm her lawyer,' Logan said defensively. 'It's my job to fix things.'

Despite his protestations, Logan knew his brother had a point. Maybe he had pushed things too hard in his dealings with April. She'd said he hadn't listened when she'd voiced her need to understand what he was doing on her behalf. Maybe he hadn't. Maybe he'd kept her in the dark when he should have been more upfront.

The reasons hovered beneath the surface of his thoughts. It was because he wanted to be her white frigging knight. Wanted to look into those dazzling eyes of hers and know that he'd made everything all right for her. That he was the one responsible for creating her happiness. *Shit*. He wanted to be the one making her life run smooth and easy.

Deep in thought, Logan sipped his beer. Was his brother right? Was he too much of a fixer?

April didn't want that. Hadn't she told him that she'd basically lived her whole life having someone else make decisions for her? Her parents had decided what she was and wasn't capable of. Her mother had driven her into a career that had denied April the chance to do what she wanted.

He should have taken all that to heart. Should have understood that she needed him to be upfront and totally honest with her. He should have kept her informed about every single step he took, told her his plans for her, talked them out with her to make sure it was what she wanted. What she needed. April had had every right to be part of those decisions.

'Guess you're missing the sex, too.' Connor grinned as he brought his beer to his lips. 'That woman certainly put a smile on your face, or maybe that was more to do with her introducing you to the tools of her trade. Bet she knew her way around them.'

When Connor gave a low growl, Logan's chest burned. 'You need to watch your mouth, brother.'

'No offence.' Connor held up his hands. 'Just saying.'

Any other man and Logan would have shoved him from here to eternity for a remark like that, but Logan knew his brother's wounds went deep and forced him to make light of his own relationships with women. He had every right to do that after what he'd been through. Taking a fall for a woman who had set him up from the start. A woman who had used him, then run off, leaving him to pick up the pieces.

Logan often wondered what scars from their past his siblings carried, but they rarely spoke of what had happened to them, each of them getting on with their lives. But Logan knew it wasn't always that easy.

Being honest about things that went deep never was.

When Connor went inside to get two more beers from the refrigerator, Logan reached out to the side table and picked up his phone. It was time to end this stalemate with April. It was time to get this sorted. It was time to tell her everything about the revelations he'd just had.

And it was about time she answered his fucking calls.

His temper hiked as it went to voicemail. He tried again. Voicemail. And again.

This time he sucked in a breath. 'Answer my calls, April. If you want those documents back, give me the courtesy of five minutes of your valuable time.'

He stabbed the 'end call' button, his lungs pumping, blood boiling. But beneath his anger lay a bone-deep frustration and a terrifying fear that she might never forgive him. She might never give him the time of day so that he could apologise.

Where the hell was she? What was she doing? Who was she with?

It was driving him slowly insane.

Tomorrow he'd call at her place again. Persuade her friend to give him the address of where she was staying. He'd camp outside the door if he had to, but one way or the other he was going to see her, talk to her.

Two hours later Logan said goodbye to his brother, stashed the empty beer bottles in the recycling box, and went into his study. He felt fatigue deep in his bones, but he knew he was in for another night of broken sleep. He might as well do something constructive and get some work done.

The knock at his front door stopped him in his tracks.

CHAPTER FOURTEEN

Logan hadn't had time to prepare for the sight of April standing on the threshold of his home. Of all the scenarios he'd imagined, strangely, that hadn't been one of them. He'd never expected her to come and see him of her own free will—especially not considering the way he'd been virtually stalking her.

But, despite she'd damn near stopped his heart, she wasn't giving any indication that her visit was meant to be particularly amiable.

'Are you alone?'

Logan raised his eyebrows. What the hell was she insinuating? That he'd jumped into bed with another woman before it was even cold after her presence there?

He wasn't going to justify that question with an answer, so he simply stepped aside for her to enter.

She shoved past him. 'Good, then we can talk.'

He followed as she headed straight through to the living room, his gaze eating her up like a man denied sustenance for far too long.

She turned to face him with a haughty tilt to her

chin, her shoulders back and displaying breasts that he knew fitted his palms to perfection. Her expression gave nothing away, and incongruously he imagined she'd make one hell of a poker player. But because he couldn't get a steer on what she was thinking, or her reasons for being there, it pissed him off.

'So you want to talk now, do you?' Logan said, barely banking his temper as he made himself stroll into the room.

All he really wanted was to grab her, kiss that bloody scornful look off her mouth, and make her remember how damn good it was between them.

'Well, that's rich, considering I've been calling you half a dozen times a day since you did your disappearing act.'

'I didn't disappear,' April said. 'I went to stay with a friend. To get my head straight.'

He crossed to the balcony doors, hoping the view of sparkling lights from the harbour would go some way to easing his temper…along with the idiotic ache dead centre of his chest.

'Considering most of the rubbish that was in your head the last time we met, I guess that explains why it took so long.'

'Considering that what was in my head the last time we met was down to *your* underhand ways, it really should have taken longer.'

He kept staring out at the harbour, but since he needed something to do with his hands he shoved them in his pockets.

'You're making me sound like the spawn of the devil.'

He waited for her response, tension moving deep between his shoulder blades as he felt her glare straight at him. After long moments, she sighed.

'You don't make it easy, Logan. You go off doing your own thing, not bothering to tell me you're even thinking about offering any kind of deal. As far as I knew, Veronica didn't have much of a leg to stand on—then I overhear you offering her compensation in return for her dropping the case. What was I supposed to do?'

His answer to that was instant. 'You should have trusted me. You should have stayed around long enough to let me explain.'

The fact that she hadn't had cut him to shreds. He still felt the raw pain of desertion deep at the core of his being. He hadn't thought he'd ever hurt that way again, but even his parents' walking out hadn't ripped at his heart in the same way April's walking away from him had.

Again, there was a thundering silence, during which he willed her to tell him that he was mistaken. That she did trust him. That she had wanted to stay. But her response wasn't what he'd hoped for.

'You made it hard for me to do that, Logan.'

Briefly, he closed his eyes. Only when he knew the look in them wouldn't betray his tumble of feelings did he open them and turn around. Every time he looked at her his heart damn near thumped out

of his chest, in acute and imminent danger of landing at her feet.

'At the very least you could have given me the
benefit of the doubt. Asked me straight out about
the deal you heard me making without flying off the
handle and making assumptions.'

'Maybe you're right. I should have asked you
and not jumped to conclusions. But, as we'd already
had a conversation about keeping me in the loop, I
shouldn't have had to remind you. I was supposed to
be your client. You could have run it by me, got my
take on it. But, no, you went off with all guns blazing
and took matters into your own hands. Trying to sort
everything without letting anyone else get a look-in.'

Because she had a point, and because he was painfully reminded of the conversation he'd had with his
brother, Logan made himself breathe. Not an easy
thing to do—especially when he was pitted not only
against the tirade of her accusation but also the fact
that she was little more than an arm's length away
from him right then, and he could reach out and
touch her.

When had she stepped closer? Had he? He could
smell her sweet fragrance, feel her energy wrapping
around him, look into those magnificent eyes… She
had the power to steal the breath clean out of his
lungs.

'That's the second time today I've been accused
of trying to sort everyone's problems. Of going behind people's backs so I can fix things without even

consulting them. The thing is… Shit, I don't know what the thing is.'

'The thing is,' April said, with the ghost of a smile, 'you've been doing it for so long, you can't see how to do it any other way. It's just the way you are.'

Her words had a resigned air to them, as if she accepted the situation and knew there was no working through her issue with him.

He could tell her he'd changed. That he would try and be more upfront with her. That in future he'd run everything past his clients before he acted—that he'd run everything past *her*.

Yeah, he could say all that—except he wasn't sure he believed it himself, so he had little chance of convincing April.

She saw right through him.

Which meant he needed to get this over with as fast as he could. He couldn't bear having her in the same room, within touching distance, and not being able to sweep her into his arms and kiss the living shit out of her. Even more, he couldn't bear her spelling it out that it was over. That while she acknowledged he was the way he was she could never accept it.

'I'll get you those documents you asked for.'

He brushed past her, striding to his study on heavy legs. Once there, he opened a drawer to his desk and pulled out the folder.

He hadn't expected her to follow him, so he stayed behind his desk, needing the distance, because he didn't want to embarrass himself by grabbing her and begging her to give him a freaking chance. She'd made it clear that it was too late. He'd damn well ruined what they'd shared by being an intractable jerk.

Keeping his expression blank, he offered her the folder containing the business-related papers she'd asked to have returned.

'Thanks,' she said, taking them after a moment's hesitation. 'When I asked for these back, I wasn't sure of my next steps.'

Part of him just wanted her to leave. He didn't need to hear about her newly appointed legal representatives and how they were a far better fit for her, supporting her, giving her their advice, while checking and double-checking that she was happy with what they planned to do to represent her.

To hell with that. *He* was the only one who could represent her. The only one who, despite her accusations to the contrary, had her best interests at heart. And, while he might be dogmatic and controlling, nobody would have her back like he would. *Nobody.*

Angry with both himself and April, he sat and reached for the cigar sitting in his ashtray. When it was apparent she wasn't about to speak again, he stuck the unlit cigar in his mouth and pushed back in his chair.

'Was there something else?'

Her eyes lit, all that warm brown turning fiery with what looked like annoyance. She pulled over an easy chair, placed it in front of his desk, and sat.

'Tell me something. Why do you keep a bloody cigar on your desk? You've got one here, one in your London office, yet I never see you light up. What's the deal?'

Knowing she was as riled as he was by their encounter gave him a kind of satisfaction.

Taking the cigar from his mouth, he rolled it between his thumb and forefinger, studying it. 'I like having it in my mouth. It takes the edge off.'

Her expression turned circumspect. 'The edge off what?'

He shrugged. 'Whatever's on my mind at the time. Helps me concentrate.'

'So you buy yourself cigars to help you concentrate?' she said, as if mesmerised by the movement of his hands. 'Wouldn't you be better off with a pencil, or a pen, or something?'

He was pretty mesmerised himself right then. Mostly by the way she licked her lips, the tip of her tongue just visible, but sending a shock of reaction to his groin.

'They were to celebrate my first big win,' he said, before he'd even realised he was about to speak. 'A box of Cuban cigars.'

Her gaze shot to his. 'You bought yourself cigars to celebrate winning your first case? Most men would have gone for a luxury car.'

'I already had a luxury car,' he said. 'Besides, I didn't buy them. But you didn't come here to talk about cigars—Cuban or otherwise.'

'No.' She seemed to shake off whatever had put that huffy look on her face. 'Anyway, as I said, I wasn't sure of my next steps when I asked for the documents back, but now there's no real urgency because there's no longer any dispute.'

He sat back in surprise. It was the first he'd heard of this. But then, why would he? Haydon had ditched Veronica, so there'd be no news coming from that corner. And since April wasn't his client any more…

Did that mean her new lawyers had sold her out? Convinced her to accept some kind of liability? He'd have the fuckers struck off…

'Veronica dropped the case.'

Logan froze. That was the very last thing he'd expected to hear, and certainly not what he'd anticipated.

'How the hell did that happen?'

'We came to an understanding. I offered her work.'

Logan shook his head, wondering if he'd heard right. 'You offered her work? Veronica Lebeck? Doing what, exactly?'

April smiled. 'Don't look so cynical, Logan. Most people can be reasonable when the incentive is right—even Veronica. And it's not always about money. Not even for her.'

'That's news to me.'

Hadn't the woman screamed at him that afternoon in his office that there was absolutely no way she'd accept anything less than a figure with several zeroes behind it?

'Things change, Logan. Some people do, too.'

The implication wasn't lost on him. *Some* people. But not him.

'I asked her if she'd meet me,' April went on. 'I read that article in the paper and I knew that she'd been dumped by your friend.'

'I never agreed to represent her,' Logan felt compelled to point out. He'd been incensed by that—mostly because he hadn't wanted April to see it and assume it was true. 'I tried to call you to tell you it was a fabrication.'

April had the grace to look a little shamefaced. 'I wasn't in the mood to talk to you at the time. Besides, I saw they printed a retraction. Anyway,' she said before he could say anything else, 'I got the feeling she might be open to talking, to trying to reach some kind of arrangement which would benefit us both.'

She shifted in her chair, hiking her bag higher on her lap and drawing it close like a kind of shield.

'There's something I never told you about my past relationship with Veronica. When we were modelling we were both searching for a new manager after ours took early retirement due to ill health. Richard was considered one of the best and, although I didn't know it at the time, he was close to taking Veronica onto his books. I think the contracts had actually been drawn up, but then she tried to get him to re-negotiate the terms of their arrangement in her favour, and he dumped her and took me on instead.'

While his dealings with Veronica had ensured Logan could believe the woman would do something like that, he couldn't understand why April hadn't told him.

'Knowing that would have made it easier to try and negotiate with her. Why didn't you tell me that going in?'

She took a huge breath, let it out on a sigh. 'Honestly? I was embarrassed. Not because of the whole grabbing-Richard-as-a-manager thing, but because of what happened as a consequence. It's a long story, but basically my relationship with Richard became personal as well as professional. He didn't want me to give up modelling when my father became ill. He hated losing control over me, I suppose. Hated even more that I was determined to start a new career with my online business.'

She took another breath. Logan wanted to ask if she needed water, or a stronger drink, but he didn't want to stop her talking. He didn't want to stop her telling him everything.

'Eventually I thought he'd come around. As my father grew weaker I had to spend more time with him, and Richard offered to run things for me. It wasn't until after my father passed away that I found out he'd basically destroyed my business.'

'Fucker.'

Logan wanted to hit something. Preferably the bastard who'd hurt April. But instead of ranting, as he really wanted to, he knew he had to support April while she told him. So he remained quiet and let her continue.

'First off, I thought he'd done it to lure me back into modelling. He never made a secret of the fact he didn't think I was capable of being an entrepreneur, any more than my parents did. But then I found out he'd been embezzling funds from the business to pay off his creditors. He left me with huge debts, but I was determined he wasn't going to break me, and I was equally determined I would prove him wrong. I was going to prove *everyone* wrong.'

'And you did.'

She smiled, and it filled his heart to bursting.

'I did. Which leads me back to Veronica. When I told her what Richard had done, and she realised it hadn't all been roses for me, we were eventually able to come to an understanding.'

'What kind of understanding?'

'I've been approached by a well-known magazine to do a story on my business, to coincide with an international entrepreneurial women's event. They want the article to focus on women celebrating and enjoying their sexuality. I want to highlight a new range of underwear I'm selling, by a designer I met at a trade show. He's doing some pretty amazing things with lingerie. Anyway, we've both agreed to the magazine article on the proviso that we can use our own model.'

Logan's eyebrows came together in a disbelieving frown. 'You're telling me she agreed to drop the case for a photo shoot? I offered her a screen test with a New York producer. She said no.'

April smiled. 'It's not just a photo shoot. The designer has asked Veronica to be the face of his new range. He's just won an industry award, so Veronica thinks it will really help her to cement a new image. She wants a fresh start—especially since Haydon's ended their relationship. I think she really cared for him.'

'One thing,' Logan said, wanting to voice a niggle that wouldn't seem to go away. 'Why didn't you tell me? About your bastard ex and what he did?'

'It's not something to boast about, is it? Putting blind trust in someone and having them let you down quite so spectacularly. I played into his hands, didn't I? He wanted to convince me I wasn't capable of running a business and I went ahead and proved him right. I almost let him ruin me.'

'From what you've just told me, and from the great guns your business is going right now, I'd say you proved him wrong. Spectacularly.'

Her smile was full of pride. 'Thanks. I appreciate that. I'm sorry I didn't tell you from the start. I just didn't want you to think I was an idiot for giving someone such control over myself and my life.'

'I would never for one minute think that.'

What she'd told him shone some light on why she hadn't given him the chance to explain about the deal he'd tried to make with Veronica. Why she hadn't given him the benefit of the doubt. She'd been terrified of being duped again. Of being made a fool of.

And in his efforts to protect her, he'd played right into those fears.

It felt so good to get it all off her chest. To know that despite it all Logan seemed to be on her side.

She'd rehearsed what she would say while on her way to Logan's house. But as soon as he'd opened the door every thought had disappeared clean from her head, and her mind had turned stubbornly blank.

Would she ever be able to look at him and not feel that dizzying punch of reaction deep in her stomach? Would she ever not want to take every available opportunity to launch herself into his arms?

April had tried hard not to be distracted by how sexy he looked, how composed, when she had been growing more nervous and distracted by the minute.

Now, as he told her that he had never thought her an idiot, she knew it was the truth. Despite his infuriating and controlling ways, he'd never thought badly of her.

'I fought against you because I needed to keep control,' she said, wanting to make it clear that was why she had been so adamant about knowing what he was doing on her behalf. 'I needed to know what was happening at every single turn just to make sure you never hoodwinked me.'

'I get that,' Logan said. 'And it's understandable, considering what you've just told me.'

'I shouldn't have done that. Not with you. You've done nothing but try to help me. But I kept hold of my suspicion and… You were right when you said I should have given you the benefit of the doubt.'

Logan's shrug was full of tension. 'And you were right when you said I should have talked to you first—should have given you the chance to say what you thought of using the promise of a screen test to get her to back away from you.'

'She told me she thought she'd probably cut off her nose by refusing that. Said that Haydon might never have dumped her had she taken your deal.'

'Yeah, that's what he told me.'

'Is everything okay between the two of you now? I'd hate it if all this has ruined your friendship.'

'We're fine.' He hesitated, then leaned forward and stood. 'I need to tell you something, too. How about we have a drink while I spill?'

April waited until he came around the desk, then stood and hooked her bag over her shoulder. She couldn't imagine what he had to tell her, but there was one thing she did know. This time she would listen to what he had to say before flying off the deep end and jumping to conclusions.

She could trust him, she thought as he stepped back to let her through the open doorway. Deep down, perhaps she'd always known the truth of that. It was just her own prejudices and hang-ups that had stopped her accepting and believing it.

While he went to the liquor cabinet April dropped

her bag on a nearby chair and, as he'd done when she'd arrived, went to the terrace doors to look out over the harbour. She loved how the lights twinkled beyond, reminding her of how many times she'd enjoyed watching them from Logan's bedroom on those nights when they'd lain in bed together after making love.

And that was exactly what it had been—for her, anyway. Making love. She'd fallen in love with Logan, but had been too stubborn to admit it even to herself.

She turned, watching him as he poured brandy into two glasses. He had amazing hands. Big, capable, and very treacherous. She thought about how he'd rolled that cigar between his thumb and forefinger back in his study, and how she hadn't been able to stop the memory of how it felt when he manipulated her nipples in the same way. Of how it was when those adept hands trailed over her body, slowly and, oh, so dangerously, before sliding between her legs and sending her into a kind of insane and frenzied bliss.

Her hands shook as she took the glass from Logan.

'Want to sit?' he asked.

She didn't know what she wanted right then, apart from him to tell her that he still wanted her. That they could pick up where they'd left off before she'd gone and jumped to those conclusions.

She nodded and sat on the sofa, her heart dipping as he took the seat opposite her on the matching one. He sat forward, clasping the glass between his knees.

'Haydon is not just a friend—he was my mentor.'

'Your mentor? But he's not a lawyer. That news-paper said Haydon's in property development.'

Logan shook his head. 'No, he's not a lawyer. But, like I told you, we go back a long way.' He looked down at his drink, turning the glass this way and that. 'When my parents bailed, and we were split up and sent to different homes, I swore that I'd get us kids back together again. When I was fifteen I found work at a fish market in East London. I got paid in cash, so the authorities didn't ask questions. It was long hours, crap pay—but I didn't give a shit.'

April had a vision of this Haydon, mentoring a child of fifteen and making him work long hours for a measly wage. What kind of friend was that? But before she could voice her opinion she remembered her promise to herself to hear Logan out before jumping to conclusions. So she kept quiet.

'By chance I met Haydon. He was visiting some premises next door to the market with a view to pur-chasing them for development. He asked me to mind his car while he was inside—the area wasn't exactly respectable at the time—and he rewarded me with what was basically a week's pay. Being a pushy little shit, I asked Haydon if he had any work available. I was basically his gofer but a quick learner, and I soaked up every scrap of knowledge about how busi-ness worked. I worked my ass off for him.'

April caught her bottom lip between her teeth,

thankful she hadn't said anything before. She was warming to Haydon.

'Anyway, he saw potential in me and gave me more and more responsibility. I got to do research for him, run checks on competitors, sit in on meetings. By then I'd told him about my brothers and my sister, what had happened to them. He knew I was determined to get us all back together, and understood how, as the eldest, I felt it was my responsibility to care for my siblings. He helped me—not only financially, but with the authorities, too.'

No wonder they shared a bond. No wonder Logan thought he owed Haydon. April now had some idea of how incredibly difficult it must have been for Logan to go against what his mentor had asked him to do when she came on the scene.

'When I told him I'd always dreamed of being a lawyer, he made that possible, too. Helped me through college, law school.' Logan smiled and took a swig of brandy. 'He tried to steer me into choosing property law, but he understood my need to go into family law. I wanted to help families through tough times, to make sure kids got a fair deal when bloody adults tried to screw up their lives.'

Because of his own past. His own experiences.

April wanted badly to go to him. To tell him she understood. Instead she sipped her own brandy. 'Your relationship with Haydon sounds like an amazing one.'

'He was the closest thing to a father I ever had.

Supported me when I needed it, gave me grief when I screwed up.' He held out his arm. 'Tore me off big time when I got this just after my sixteenth birthday.'

'Your tattoo?'

'Yeah. He's not a fan of ink. I thought I was honouring him by having his company logo tattooed on my arm, but he thought I was a stupid little shit. His words. Said if I was planning on being a big shot lawyer, I'd better keep it covered with all those Armani shirts I'd be able to afford.'

'Was it Haydon who bought you the cigars?' April asked. 'To celebrate winning your first case?'

Logan's smile was a little wistful. 'Yeah. He promised me those cigars on my first day of law school.'

April was starting to like Haydon more with each passing moment. 'I'm so sorry you were put in a position where you had to go against him. That must have been impossibly difficult for you.'

He shrugged, but his eyes shone across to her. 'What was impossible for me was not helping you.'

April's heart kicked. 'What?'

'I owe Haydon a lot, but not everything. And before long you became everything.'

She swallowed as her kicking heart pushed into her throat.

'There was no way I'd do Haydon's bidding when it could hurt you, set you up for a fall. Although Veronica didn't have much of a case, an unscrupulous lawyer could have done some damage to you. Knowing that, I wasn't going to step away and leave you to the mercy of anyone else.'

April's eyes filled. 'I didn't want to be represented by anyone else. Just you.'

Logan was across the room and hunkering down in front of her before she could even track his movements. He took her glass and reached for her trembling hands.

'I've been a fucking idiot. I should have talked to you, given you the chance to decide what was best for you. It would have spared me going in like a freaking bull in a china shop, since you managed to sort things out for yourself.'

He squeezed her fingers beneath his.

'You've given me a salutary lesson, proved to me that my arrogance and conceit can sometimes work against the very people I love and want to protect.'

April squeezed his hands right back. 'I like your arrogance and conceit. It makes you who you are. But, given the opportunity, maybe I'd like it even more if you could perhaps tone it down just a bit.'

His lips flickered in a tentative smile. 'If I agree to do that, would you give us another chance?

April's breath caught, shimmering through her lungs on a burst of happiness. 'I'd give us another chance even if you didn't agree to it.'

He stood, drawing her up against him, his arms coming around her and holding tight. 'I love you, April Sinclair.'

Her heart simply turned over in her chest. 'I love you, too, Logan Fitzpatrick.'

With a quick and sexy grin, Logan slid them both into a deep and passionate kiss that held the promise of chances taken and a future bright with possibilities.

As the kiss turned erotic, April drew back a little. 'Would you like to see what I have in my bag? It actually belongs to you, anyway.'

The gleam in Logan's dark eyes was her answer, as was his sexy grin.

'It does?'

'Uh-huh. You bought it from my website, remember?'

Logan drew her closer again and started walking her backwards towards the hallway. 'Does it include a blindfold and fluffy handcuffs?'

April grinned. 'It might.'

'How many reviews does it have so far?'

'Five stars all the way.'

When Logan hiked her up into his arms she wrapped her legs around his waist and clung. He kissed her as he took the stairs two at a time, with her in his arms.

'Then let's go and make sure we add our own five stars to the tally.'

* * * * *

COMING SOON!

We really hope you enjoyed reading this book. If you're looking for more romance, be sure to head to the shops when new books are available on

Thursday 20th March

To see which titles are coming soon, please visit

millsandboon.co.uk/nextmonth

MILLS & BOON

THE HEART OF ROMANCE

A ROMANCE FOR EVERY KIND OF READER

MODERN

Prepare to be swept off your feet by sophisticated, sexy and seductive heroes, in some of the world's most glamourous and romantic locations, where power and passion collide.
8 stories per month.

HISTORICAL

Escape with historical heroes from time gone by. Whether your passion is for wicked Regency Rakes, muscled Vikings or rugged Highlanders, awaken the romance of the past.
6 stories per month.

MEDICAL

Set your pulse racing with dedicated, delectable doctors in the high-pressure world of medicine, where emotions run high and passion, comfort and love are the best medicine.
6 stories per month.

Celebrate true love with tender stories of heartfelt romance, from the rush of falling in love to the joy a new baby can bring, and a focus on the emotional heart of a relationship.
8 stories per month.

Indulge in secrets and scandal, intense drama and plenty of sizzling hot action with powerful and passionate heroes who have it all: wealth, status, good looks…everything but the right woman.
6 stories per month.

HEROES

Experience all the excitement of a gripping thriller, with an intense romance at its heart. Resourceful, true-to-life women and strong, fearless men face danger and desire - a killer combination!
8 stories per month.

DARE

Sensual love stories featuring smart, sassy heroines you'd want as a best friend, and compelling intense heroes who are worthy of them.
4 stories per month.

To see which titles are coming soon, please visit

millsandboon.co.uk/nextmonth

JOIN US ON SOCIAL MEDIA!

Stay up to date with our latest releases, author news and gossip, special offers and discounts, and all the behind-the-scenes action
from Mills & Boon...

 millsandboon

 millsandboonuk

 millsandboon

It might just be true love...

LET'S TALK
Romance

For exclusive extracts, competitions and special offers, find us online:

 facebook.com/millsandboon

@MillsandBoon

@MillsandBoonUK

Get in touch on 01413 063232

For all the latest titles coming soon, visit
millsandboon.co.uk/nextmonth